MW00723396

CHANDOR CHASMA

MELAS CHASMA

COPRATES
CHASMA

REVELATIONS

REVELATIONS

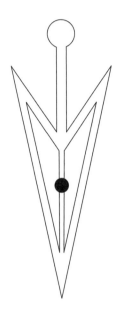

A NOVEL BY

M. SCOTT BYRNES

Blue Stripe Books

© 2006 M. Scott Byrnes.
Printed and bound in the United States of America.
All rights reserved under international and Pan-American copyright
conventions. No part of this book may be reproduced or transmitted in any
form or by any means, electronic or mechanical, including photocopying,
recording, or by an information storage and retrieval system—except by a
reviewer who may quote brief passages in a review to be printed in a
magazine, newspaper, or on the Web—without permission in writing
from the publisher. For information, please contact
Blue Stripe Books, 1015 31st Street NW, Suite 350,
Washington, DC 20007; ph (202) 250-8050.
www.bluestripebooks.com

This book is a work of fiction. Names, characters, places and
events are products of the author's imagination or are used fictitiously.
Any resemblance to actual events, locations or persons, living or deceased,
is purely coincidental. We assume no responsibility for errors,
inaccuracies, omissions, or any inconsistency herein.

First printing 2006

Library of Congress Cataloging-in-Publication Data

Byrnes, M. Scott.
Revelations : a novel / by M. Scott Byrnes.
p. cm.
Summary: "Mankind makes a discovery on Mars that alters our understanding
of God as we know it and introduces the likelihood that Armageddon is
quickly approaching. A brilliant young scientist must solve a cosmic riddle as
old as time itself to prevent our destruction"—Provided by publisher.
ISBN 0-9772674-0-7
1. Mars (Planet)—Fiction. 2. Armageddon—Fiction. 3. Scientists—Fiction. I.
Title.

PS3602.Y767R48 2005
813'.6—dc22
2005025165

To my wife, Jennifer

ACKNOWLEDGMENTS

Special thanks to my wife, Jennifer, for her unflagging support and encouragement. I simply could not have done it without you. To Jeff Stanish, who believed in this project from the beginning, and who offered invaluable encouragement, insights, and assistance. To my mother for her support and encouragement. Thanks to my wonderful editors Nancy Johanson and Deborah Rephan, for some very heavy lifting and skillful polishing. To the CCHH crew and all who took the time to read the earliest versions of the book. Your insights were extremely helpful to me as a first time novelist. To General Jefferson "Beak" Howell III, Director of the Johnson Space Center, NASA, for his time and insights. To Donald Herzog at the U.S. Geological Survey for his expertise. To Mr. Yaw Dei at the Ghana Embassy in Washington, D.C. To Greg Smith for taking the time to read the book and for his kind words of encouragement. To Lori Terling for her tremendous creativity and skill in designing the cover and endpaper. And to the literally hundreds of other people who touched this project in one way or another. I can only hope the end product is worthy of your efforts.

"Science and Religion…are two sides of the same glass through which we see darkly, until these two, focusing together, reveal the truth."

PEARL S. BUCK

PROLOGUE

Five Roman legionnaires watched in awe as flashes of heat lightning irradiated the dark clouds on the pre-dawn horizon.

A single spark from deep within a remote section of the thunderheads set off a chain reaction, until the entire cluster was popping with light and sound.

Among the legionnaires, Elucious sat upon his immense horse and inhaled slowly, savoring the moisture. Rain was all too rare in this part of the world, where it was even hotter and drier than his beloved Rome. Not that it mattered to him now. His task would be complete soon enough. Following the Nazarene's crucifixion, Augustus would, no doubt, summon him back to Rome. And, if the Emperor had any gratitude for a job deftly executed, Elucious would be returning to an estate far more expansive than the one he had left. The thought was a welcome tonic to the throbbing between his ears. The cheap red wine of the previous evening, and the even cheaper whores, had failed to quench his appetite—two more reasons to relish his return to Rome, where even the dregs of his amphorae were sweeter than the finest vintage here, and the opulent women far more appealing to his discerning palate.

The Roman officer reached up and pressed the brow band of his helmet. The plumes of a Legatus didn't come without a price. The additional three pounds were particularly burdensome today, in light of his headache. No seal or symbol had ever been more feared or respected in the history of the world, however, and Elucious had found that power intoxicating. He had also found it extremely useful.

Two months was all it had taken for him to build a case against the Nazarene known as Jesus, far less time than even the Emperor had hoped. Politicians had been intimidated, a populace stirred into frenzy, and a confidante pushed to betrayal. Pain and fear—two very simple ingredients, when mixed in the right proportion—could drive men to do almost anything. With any luck, Jesus himself would become a living example of that fact, renouncing his own god before the day was through.

Elucious couldn't suppress a grin as he gazed to his right. Beyond the massive frame of Symian, his young Tribunus, he could see hundreds of peasants gathered along the muddy road. More were arriving by the minute. All the better, he thought. The prophet's crucifixion would remind them of Rome's absolute sovereignty.

Elucious caught Symian's eye, and was rewarded with his second's assessment of the situation. "I would just as soon slaughter them all," Symian uttered with disdain. The huge man fidgeted in his saddle, his sweaty fists wrapped tightly around the reins. Leather cried out in protest as his hands flexed and relaxed, flexed and relaxed.

Symian reminded Elucious of a whippet before its first hunt, chasing its white-crested tail and pissing down its own leg, unable to control its excitement. Although he would have preferred a more refined understudy, Elucious reminded himself that Symian's ruthlessness had proven very useful of late. As a small reward, the senior officer decided to humor his charge. He turned to address the five legionnaires standing behind them. "What do you think, centurions? Must you earn your pay today?"

The armor-clad giants all smiled gamely, but none uttered a sound. Simple men of few words, they preferred to let their weapons do their talking.

Elucious turned back to Symian. "Well, the lions look hungry, should the need arise."

Suddenly, Elucious felt a strange vibration in his loins that jolted him from his wine-induced haze. Instinctively, he grasped his reins more tightly and surveyed the horizon. Was it an earthquake? He had experienced two before, years earlier, during his post in the Aegean. This felt different, though, and the peasants before him confirmed his assessment. They continued on with their muted conversations, completely undisturbed.

Something was very wrong though, and Elucious knew it. As he gazed down, he suddenly realized what it was. The steed was shaking uncontrollably. It was the source of the tremor. The hairs of its mane were standing straight up, as stiff as the plumes of his helmet!

It whinnied loudly and reared up, nearly throwing Elucious to the ground. Quickly, the Roman snapped the reins down sharply and dug his knees into the torso of the mighty beast. The well-trained animal responded immediately to the show of strength, while Elucious spun his head from side to side, searching for the source of its terror.

"Have you come to buy the Nazarene's freedom, old man?" Elucious heard Symian berate someone to his right. He turned quickly to see a cloaked figure emerge from Symian's long shadow. The old man must have come up from behind the legionnaires unnoticed, until Symian saw him heading for the crowd. He was covered from head to toe in a shabby wool cloak, not an appendage visible. A long stick protruded from the sleeve of his dark garment, serving as a cane. It sunk into the mud with each step, as the old man hobbled toward the throng of spectators gathered along the road.

"I'm afraid the sand on your feet won't be an ample price!" Symian bellowed. The legionnaires all broke out in laughter, as did Elucious. The old man, however, continued to walk, unfazed.

Enraged by the old man's indifference, Symian spat at him from atop his horse. "You stop and bow when addressed by the Emperor's guard, you pathetic Jew!"

To the shock of all five legionnaires, the old man neither stopped nor bowed, but rather slipped into the crowd. The blood rushed to Symian's face, and he snatched a spear from the hand of one of his soldiers. "Insolent barbarian!" he muttered, kicking his horse into a trot. "Maybe a shaft through the heart will teach you a little respect!"

As Symian converged upon the back row of the spectators, they turned from the road, wide-eyed. The enraged Roman officer towered above them, spear raised, ready to strike. The peasants scrambled out of his path, as did the others in front of them, in a ripple effect. Symian scanned the faces of the rabble eagerly, searching for the old man. Suddenly, a loud roar erupted from the crowd, causing him to look up, slightly startled.

Two chain-clad criminals had just come into view. They were being prodded by another legionnaire holding a whip. A grimy adolescent stood among the crowd staring at the criminals, engrossed by their death march. He didn't notice Symian bearing down on him from behind. The Roman was forced to tack slightly to avoid him, and as he passed, he kicked the peasant squarely in the head. The wooden stirrup caught the boy's ear under the lobe and ripped it forward. A rubbery piece of flesh hung limply from the side of the boy's blood-soaked head.

"Get out of my way, you waif!" Symian screamed.

Another cheer rose up from the crowd, this one louder than the last. Symian turned to his left to see Jesus dragging a heavy cross along the road. The crowd began to shower insults upon the false prophet. Symian turned back toward the peasants to resume his search. He forged his way further into the crowd, scanning terrified faces. The old man was nowhere to be seen.

Clearly frustrated, Symian yanked the reins across his horse's neck, and headed back to rejoin Elucious and the legionnaires.

Hours later, Jesus hung limply on the cross, head slumped toward his chest. Beads of sweat trickled down the sides of his face and mingled with the thin streams of blood from the barbed wreath. Each faint breath seemed like the last to the few remaining onlookers.

Unexpectedly, with a Herculean effort, Jesus raised his head. The muscles in his thin neck bulged from the exertion. His bloodshot eyes flickered open, and he focused on the horizon. In the distance, a cloaked figure ascended a rocky mountainside. Its strides were very long, and the figure seemed to glide effortlessly up the steep slope.

A mask of pain raked Jesus' face. He raised his head higher in defiance, eyes beseeching the skies above. "Why have you forsaken me?"

Jesus peered back out at the cloaked figure, still ascending the mountainside in the distance. He then looked down at the weeping people below him. "Why have you forsaken *them*?" he whispered.

Just as the final word labored from his lips, his eyes closed and his chin fell limply to his chest.

#   #   #

From the peak of the rocky mountain, Elucious peered out across the dry plain. Way off in the distance, upon a smaller hill, he could see Jesus upon his cross. His chin dropped decisively to his chest; it appeared that he had finally succumbed. It almost looked like the Nazarene had looked directly at him, seconds before dying. From almost a thousand paces, however, he couldn't be sure. It would have taken the sharp eyes of a younger man to be completely certain. The kind of vision that Symian apparently possessed.

Elucious gazed to his right to assess his young lieutenant. It had taken keen vision indeed to spot the cloaked figure on the horizon an hour earlier. The old man had almost made a clean escape, slipping off into the distance while the Romans enjoyed the crucifixion. But, alas, Symian had spotted him. And, the second he had pointed the old man out, Elucious knew there was no denying his agitated subordinate. Therefore, he and Symian had taken chase, the five legionnaires following them on foot. They had made such good time that Elucious decided to circle around the foothill, and ascend its far side in order to take the old man by surprise. Upon the plateau they now sat, waiting patiently for the old man to appear before them.

Suddenly, a black hood poked up over the ridge, followed quickly by the old man's torso and concealed legs. Elucious tried to make out a face beneath the hood, but he could only see shadows. The figure kept advancing on its original line, directly toward the soldiers.

Elucious' eyes narrowed, and a faint warning pulsed from deep within his mind. Something was out of place. It was the same old man from the morning, he was sure; the same cane, the same hooded cloak. But where was the slow hobble? Although still crouched, the old man's gait was anything but unsteady. In fact, he seemed to be gliding smoothly over the ground, devouring huge chunks of terrain with deceptive efficiency.

To Elucious' left, the five legionnaires glanced up from their fire, and saw the cloaked figure advancing toward them. They all retrieved their weapons and took station next to the two mounted officers.

The old man continued walking, head down, as if he hadn't even noticed the lethal welcoming committee directly in his path. Only when he was ten feet shy of the Romans did he stop. A strange wheezing filtered from beneath his hood.

"We have some unfinished business, old man," Symian called out from atop his horse. "Now, are you going to bow when I address you, or shall we add to the day's death toll?"

The hooded figure stood there silently, stooped over his cane, just as he had by the roadside. Unfortunately, this posture was not sufficiently obsequious for Symian. The Roman smiled. He stood erect in his stirrups, and slowly raised his cuirass.

"I present this offering of gold to your impotent god." Symian let the words roll off his tongue like sweet honey, as the stream of urine showered the ground. When he was finished, he sat down on his saddle with a satisfied grin.

"Remove his head," he commanded with a nonchalant wave of the hand.

The largest of the swordsmen withdrew his gladius. The hard, cold iron rang out as it slid from its sheath. He stepped smartly toward the old man, sword raised.

With lightning quickness, the cloaked figure sprang to a height of seven feet, and a vicious growl erupted from beneath its hood. The Roman soldier screamed in horror as a jet-black arm darted out toward him. A razor-sharp claw pierced the soldier's armored breastplate and tore clean through the legionnaire's back, spewing bits of blood, flesh and bones at feet of the other soldiers.

An iron-tipped spear whistled through the air toward the wraith's torso. In a fluid blinding motion, the black being caught the spear mid-staff with its left claw, and snapped it in half with its right. It then hurled the sharp end into the chest of the other spearman, and brought the blunt end crashing over the head of a charging swordsman. The Roman's helmet folded like tin into the center of his crushed skull.

The final swordsman charged, weapon raised valiantly above his head. The black figure converged upon him in one impossibly long stride. Before the sword had a chance to exact any damage, it was flying into the air, severed cleanly from the legionnaire's arm at the wrist. A midnight claw snatched the sword from the air at its apex. Long, bony fingers wrapped effortlessly around its hilt. The blade swept through the air laterally, and bisected the screaming soldier's head at his ears.

The spearman who had launched the first volley turned and began to run for his life. The wraith hurled the twenty-pound sword like a dagger, end-over-end. It whistled through the air before skewering the Roman between the shoulder blades. Only the ball-shaped pommel protruded from his back as he tumbled forward into the dirt.

The black being then turned sharply to face Elucious and Symian, both of whom were frozen with shock. Blazing red eyes locked them in a predatory stare.

Elucious reared his horse and bolted off toward the far side of the hill, while Symian drew his sword from its sheath. "Yahhh!" he screamed and dug his heals into his horse's ribs. The steed charged the cloaked figure immediately. Seconds before being trampled, the wraith stepped into the collision, thrusting its black arm forward like a ramrod. It shattered the horse's thick breastplate on impact and bore deep into its chest. Using the horse's head as a fulcrum, the creature lifted the dead animal's hindquarters clean over top, in a display of awesome strength. Symian's scream was quickly silenced, as the full weight of his horse came crashing down upon him.

The wraith stood erect and scanned the horizon. In five enormous bounds, it covered the forty yards to the far end of the hill, where Elucious had retreated earlier. It gazed out at the dust rising up from the valley floor below—the fleeting signature of a speedy horse.

It was well into twilight, and the sun had dipped beneath the hill, casting a soft purple hue onto the silhouette that was Elucious and his horse.

Elucious whipped his horse wildly, demanding more speed. Sweat dripped down from his brow and into his horror-stricken eyes. He felt the pounding of his heart inside his chest. The raucous thumping moved up into his neck, keeping almost perfect time with the hammering of his horse's hoofs. Slowly, another sound made its way to his ears. At first it was barely audible, an eerie echo. Elucious held his breath, trying to place it. Suddenly, the hairs on the back of his neck stood on end as he realized what it was—a scream.

Reluctantly, Elucious turned his head toward the source of the noise and saw something that made his blood run cold. A shadow, perhaps a hundred paces to his right, barely discernible in the dark, was running parallel to him. What could only be the tail of a long cloak snapped crisply behind it, like a flag in a stiff wind.

Suddenly, the figure veered left and began to accelerate. Elucious followed the line of the being's new vector, saw where their paths would intersect. With startling clarity, he recalled the sharp cracking of armor upon the hilltop, as the being's hand had pierced his legionnaire's breastplate. In his mind, Elucious heard that sound again, imagined it amplified. His body seized up.

Whoosh! His horse bolted left, nearly throwing Elucious to the ground. Fast reactions and awesome leg strength were the only things saving his mount. The near miss of what would have surely been a fatal tumble, jumpstarted his motor skills.

"Yahhh!" Elucious screamed, trying to squeeze even more speed from his horse. The Roman general held his breath again, listening for any indication of the black creature: the guttural scream, the pounding of its feet, the snapping of its burlap cloak in the wind. There was nothing. Only the heavy panting of his own horse, and the pounding of its hoofs on the dry lakebed.

Just as he began to draw in a breath, Elucious felt something wrap around his neck. His hands shot up immediately and he felt the cold, hard fingers of the creature tightening around his throat. He was then plucked from the saddle like a toy in the hands of a brute. Instinctively, he braced for impact, but before he hit the ground, he felt the searing pain of a razor sharp claw sweep across his windpipe.

The Roman's carcass hit the ground with a thud, tumbling literally head over heals for twenty yards before coming to a rest. The black being also skipped across the dry lakebed, but much more elegantly, in a controlled roll. It finally came to rest in a cloud of dust. It stood up quickly and scanned the horizon. Apparently satisfied that all was clear, the being pulled back its cloak and shoved its long spindly fingers into a pocket. It withdrew a bouquet of purple flowers and shook them firmly above the ground. Thousands of tiny seeds tumbled to the earth. A black hoof emerged from beneath the cloak, and crushed them into the dry soil.

#   #   #

Simultaneously, a mile away, a tall man peered up at Jesus' lifeless body, still nailed to the cross. He stared long and hard at the prophet's bloody face before whispering a parting word.

"*I* haven't forsaken them."

CHAPTER 1

Jonathan Moyeur, captain of the Santa Maria, twisted the frequency knob on the communications console. "Is that any better? Over," he practically yelled into the microphone in front of him.

"Ge_ _ ing b _ _ _ er." The broken response was barely audible.

Moyeur felt like kicking the instrument panel, but seeing as how the Graycore unit was custom-designed for this mission at a cost of nearly a hundred million dollars, he thought better of it. The engineering team had expected the equipment to function best at a frequency of 270 kHz, given the planet's environmental influences, but, as with many things he'd already experienced, there was a subtle albeit distinct difference between anticipated and actual results. Such was the price of being first to the planet. He was more than happy to pay it.

Moyeur adjusted the frequency again, and leaned closer to the microphone. "All right, how we doing now? Over."

"Much better," Kathy Palmer's voice rang out loud and clear over the bridge's speakers.

Moyeur typed a few notes into his hand-held PDA, which was synced in real-time with the ship's main log. "Okay," he said. "I've got a frequency of 210 kHz here. I want everyone to adjust their headsets tonight after the briefing." The captain made another note. "How about an E.T.A., Kathy?" he continued. His voice was calm and steady, but the lines of tension across his forehead told another story.

"We're about a half a click out. Should be there in two minutes."

"Roger. Hail me when you get there." Moyeur leaned back in his chair and wiped the perspiration from his brow.

#   #   #

Kathy Palmer stared out the thick windshield of the Grumman surface vehicle, dubbed "the R4" by the crew. Its powerful spotlights cut through the black night only to illuminate a blanket of thick dust being kicked up by gale force winds. Next to Kathy, Warren Trainer sat erect, with his gloved hands wrapped tightly around the steering wheel. His eyes were focused straight ahead, the picture of concentration. Suddenly, a thick sheet of sand enveloped the windshield, causing both Trainer and Palmer to duck instinctively. A second later the dirt blew free, and driver and passenger exchanged a nervous smile.

Kathy peered at the lower corner of the heads-up display. The red digital numbers of the odometer continued to tick off the distance to their target:

0000.17 km
0000.11 km
0000.07 km
0000.02 km.

Kathy held her breath as Trainer slowly brought the vehicle to a stop. She sat stoically for several seconds, listening to the wind howl and contemplating the significance of the moment. Small pebbles pinged off the vehicle's titanium hull. *Plink. Plink. Plink.* Occasionally, a larger rock would make contact—*crack! Plink. Crack! Plink. Plink. Crack!* The sound was unnerving. "Let's get this show on the road!" she said, thumbing the COM button on the panel in front of her. "Santa Maria, this is Palmer. Over."

Moyeur responded instantly. "I read you. What's your status? Over."

"We've reached the site. I'm ready to disembark."

"How are the winds?"

"Sustained at thirty miles per hour, with gusts of fifty." She could almost hear the gears turning in Moyeur's head. The wind speeds were just inside tolerance levels for a surface walk. While she awaited his response, Kathy focused on the H.U.D. again.

AIR TEMPERATURE: -85° F

At least the dust storm was good for something, she thought. At their current latitude and with clear skies, the temperature would be more like -175° Fahrenheit.

"Okay," Moyeur said. "You're a go, Kathy. But I don't want you out there any longer than twenty minutes."

"Roger."

"Forget about the surface samples," Moyeur continued. "Just run the geophysical diagnostics, series one and two. We can do the rest later. And I want you hooked up to a grappling line. I don't want you blowing away like some kind of baseball cap out there!"

Kathy saw Trainer grimace at the tactless comment. She simply shrugged and rolled her eyes. "Roger," she said. "Palmer out." Kathy flipped the COM switch off, before Moyeur could change his mind.

"Piece of cake, Kathy," Trainer said, motioning toward the windshield.

The gale had died down somewhat. Between gusts, Kathy could actually see the Martian surface in front of them, illuminated by the rack of floodlights on the R4's grille. She scooted out of her seat and into the narrow aisle that ran the length of the vehicle, placing her hand on Trainer's shoulder for balance. Between them, their Extravehicular Mobility Units (a.k.a., spacesuits) accounted for twenty-eight distinct layers of Mylar, Gore-Tex, Kevlar, Nomex and other materials. Not exactly the "human touch," but it was close enough to steady her nerves a little. "Kill the lights, will you, Warren?" she said. "I can't get a good read on the seismo with the shadows."

Trainer reached up and threw two switches. The ambient light filtering through the windshield died out instantly. "Go get 'em, tiger." He smiled and winked at her.

Kathy shuffled down the aisle, crouching to avoid the low ceiling.

"Hey you," Tillman Porter called from behind the B.R.A.I.L. guidance system's console. He flashed a Cheshire grin, and reached over the console with his left hand. His thumb encircled Kathy's, and his right hand came up to cement the union in a firm shake.

"Eureka!" he said.

Kathy's mouth was too dry to provide an audible response, so she gave him the thumbs-up signal instead. She proceeded to the back of the R4, and typed a three-digit code into the control panel next to the exit. The double doors opened slowly, and she stepped out into the small airlock. The interior doors then closed behind her. As a red light flashed above her head, Kathy reached for the keypad to open the exterior hatch. She froze. Her fingers trembled above the panel as the memory of her late grandmother came to mind. She could almost hear the old woman berating her from the grave: *Be careful what you ask for Kathy, you just might get it.*

Buzz off, Claire, Kathy whispered to herself.

By sheer force of will, she typed in the access code and held her breath. The doors slid open slowly, and before she had a chance to balk, Kathy stepped out into the darkness.

It felt like she was falling. The complete absence of light gave her no point of reference to gain a bearing. Her only sensory input was the sound of accelerated breathing, which echoed inside of her domed helmet. She'd been warned about this sensation early in her training, but nothing could have prepared her for the vast expanse of darkness. She began to hyperventilate.

Was she even standing? For all she knew, she was lying unconscious on the planet's surface. Hell, for all she knew, she was dead! Where were the goddamn lights? Through pure reflex, she reached up and pushed a button on the side of her helmet, activating her spotlight. The powerful beam washed over a trailer parked five feet in front of her.

Kathy steadied herself and turned back toward the R4. Unbidden, Moyeur's last words came to mind, and she pictured herself blowing across the Martian landscape. She reached around quickly and groped for the karabiner that was attached to the back of her belt. She couldn't find it! Where was it? Her palm brushed across the rubber-coated alloy, only to lose it again. She fumbled to pin it down, like a fisherman juggling a wet trout. When she finally had the hook firmly in her grasp, she gave it a tug. The grappling wire rolled out smoothly from the coil box. Before a gust of wind could send her hurtling into oblivion, she flung her hand out toward the R4 and snapped the karabiner onto the vehicle's railing. As she pulled on the line, she felt the tension and breathed a sigh.

At that very moment, however, she realized there was no need for concern after all. The wind had completely died. The sky was still thick with dust, but it was falling straight down like fine snowflakes on a calm winter's night. Her spotlight illuminated the particles as they tumbled from the strata. She could now see the planet's surface, out to a distance of about thirty feet. She lifted her left wrist to see the red digits of her watch. She'd already burned three of her allotted twenty minutes!

Wasting no more time, she worked her way over to the seismometer mounted on the R4's trailer, and unlatched the protective outer doors. They swung open smoothly. The powerful geophysical supercomputer cycled to life automatically, and ran through a series of self-diagnostics. The results were illuminated on the screen in a mass of text and graphics. Satisfied that the fifty million dollar piece of equipment had survived the ride with no ill-effects, Kathy pressed a button on the side of the machine. The large transducer descended slowly and stopped an inch short of the planet's surface.

A full-scale hurricane raged in Kathy's stomach. Her hands trembled above the keyboard. For a fleeting moment, she imagined herself as an Oscar nominee fidgeting in her seat before the envelope was opened. The contents of this envelope, however, would not just change the life of one person, but potentially alter the course of human history. Kathy almost didn't want to initiate the run. As long as she didn't know for sure, hope was still alive. After speculation became fact, there was no going back.

She had invested far too much to turn back now, though, so with gloved fingers crossed, she pressed down on the keyboard.

Instantly, P-waves shot from the transducer and bore down into the ground. They bounced back with altered amplitudes, based upon the various minerals encountered. The supercomputer calculated the refraction coefficients and assembled the results into an intelligible format. The unit processed for a full six minutes and then stopped. Slowly, one pixel at a time, an image formed on the screen. Kathy reached up and turned off her spotlight. From left to right, top to bottom, the image constructed itself. One line. Two lines. Three lines. Four lines. As the top half of the image came into focus, a tingling sensation began to form in Kathy's lower back.

"Yes!" she screamed. "I *knew* it!"

The young geologist threw her arms above her head and basked in the glory of a lifetime achievement. Tears streamed down her face.

Dominating the image and flanked on either side by muted shades of red and brown, she saw a wide band of neon. There was no mistaking it. *Barrettazine*. Below her now was as much of the element in a ten square foot deposit as existed on the entire planet Earth.

The course of human history had just been altered. Energy would now be as plentiful as oxygen, and as cheap as dirt.

As Kathy lowered her hands to initiate the shutdown sequence, she glanced up at the image one last time.

Zip!

A jolt of electricity rifled through her body.

What the hell is that? Kathy brought her face as close to the screen as her helmet would allow. She squinted, trying to figure out what, besides Barrettazine, was buried beneath her. As the possibilities narrowed, she felt her heart rise up into her throat. Her fingers sang across the keyboard, initiating a trace-shift to maximize the coherency of the image. Slowly, the pixels sharpened.

A chill rippled down her spine and the blood drained from her face.

"Oh, my God!"

Chapter 2

"**N**o. No. Nooo!"

Tim Redmond bolted upright from the cot in his tent, struggling to catch his breath. He wiped his face onto an already soaked T-shirt and ran his fingers through his thick blond hair. Despite being in a deep sleep only seconds before, his senses were now razor sharp from adrenaline. He fought to recall the gist of the nightmare, but the more he grappled with the memory, the more elusive it became. Finally, he flopped back down onto the makeshift bed and closed his eyes. Almost immediately, the strong, cold fingers of a deep slumber pulled him under. Just as he lost consciousness, he heard a voice beckon him from the farthest recesses of his mind.

They found it, Tim.

Hours later, Tim stepped from the shadows of his tent into the blinding sunlight. The intense heat enveloped him immediately, and he pulled up quickly to adjust. He dropped the heavy nylon bag from his shoulder and hunched forward, placing his hands on his knees for support. As the hot air singed his lungs, Tim wondered if he would ever grow accustomed to the blistering summers of western Africa. Somehow, he doubted it. The laws of nature weren't broken easily. A man of Nordic descent did not belong here. Not wanting to substantiate that fact further in front of the locals, Tim stood up straight, slung the knapsack back over his shoulder, and forged his way into the throng of emaciated refugees scattered before him.

The villagers huddled together in small groups, eyeing him curiously. The smoke from their huts hung thick in the air, as did the pall of death in their hushed conversations. The horror of the rebel raid three days earlier was still fresh in their minds, as were the savage wounds on many of their bodies. Ethnic cleansing was not a new phenomenon in Africa. Intimidation and fear were the standard tools of the trade, innocent civilians the victims.

Tim stepped carefully through the maze of bodies, handing out bottles of water. Grateful eyes thanked him. No words were exchanged. None were needed. Halfway across the scorched field, Tim spotted a small boy, sitting silently by himself. His knees were pulled to chest, his left arm wrapped tightly around his shins. The long-healed stump that used to be his right arm hung awkwardly from his shoulder, struggling to complete the embrace. The boy's chin rested on his knees, while his upper body rocked back and forth, slowly. The motion appeared cathartic.

Tim made his way over to the child and sat down next to him. He extended a bottle of water, fully expecting him to snatch it up. To his surprise, however, the offer went unacknowledged. The boy continued to stare vacantly into space. Dehydrated himself, Tim unscrewed the top of the bottle and pressed it to his own lips. He took a long draw, gulping loudly as the precious fluid slid down his throat. When done, Tim screwed the cap back on and gazed out at the grasslands in the distance. A small group of curious impala had gathered beyond the northern perimeter of the camp. Their nervous tails twitched as they grazed on patches of buffelgrass. A flight of white-crowned shrike darted over the west end of the field and circled. In unison, they dipped down sharply and landed on a barren patch. They burst into a chorus of busy chatter and burrowed into the dirt, performing their daily cleaning ritual.

A full ten minutes passed without so much as a word from the boy. Finally, Tim reached into his bag and removed a spiral notebook and pencil. He flipped to a blank page, and began to sketch. After a few minutes, he noticed the boy's head turn toward him slightly. He continued to draw, darkening the outlines of the buildings with broad strokes. After several more minutes, he put the pad and pencil down and retrieved the bottle of water from his sack. He unscrewed the cap and took another swig. As the liquid splashed down his chin, a pang of guilt washed over him. Such wanton waste was an outrage in this environment, but he was hopeful that the ends would justify his means. Re-securing the lid, Tim extended the bottle toward a clearing in the distance. Water jostled in the clear plastic container. "Eha ye Baabia se wobo ball a Ebeye fepaa!" he said excitedly, in perfect Akan.

.The boy's head snapped left and he looked Tim squarely in the eyes. The connection lasted only a moment, before the youngster refocused on the ground again. Tim set the bottle down next to the boy, retrieved his notepad and started to sketch a soccer field. The net between the goalposts was just taking shape when Tim heard the sound of gulping to his right.

# # #

Simon Fuller chose to meet the potential benefactor on the northern end of the refugee camp, as far from the stench of the temporary latrines as possible. His white linen shirt and khaki shorts were both neatly pressed—an impossibly clean look for the bushveld of Ghana. Despite spending ninety percent of his time in the field, he went to great lengths to support the Red Cross' fundraising efforts. Lugging a hermetically sealed outfit across half of Africa was just one of many small sacrifices.

Simon watched as the beat up old Land Rover—referred to affectionately by the camp staff as "the Wench"—rolled to a stop just short of the solitary baobab tree. Its massive trunk dwarfed the vehicle, but the sparse foliage from its branches afforded only a modicum of shade.

A short, pudgy woman opened the passenger door and slid down the side of the seat, a maneuver necessitated by the vehicle's high clearance. Upon meeting the ground, her boot caught a tuft of buffelgrass and turned over. She nearly stumbled back into the Wench, before regaining her balance. "Oh, dear," she said, bending over to retrieve some of the many papers that had flown from her portfolio during the tightrope act.

Simon was at her side at once. "Mrs. Filmore, are you all right?" he asked in his crisp upper-class English accent. He offered the woman his arm for support and motioned for the driver to gather up the rest of her papers.

"You must be Simon!" the woman beamed. Her puffy red cheeks and sparkling blue eyes had all the energy of a three-year-old high on Cocoa Puffs.

"Yes, Madam. Are you sure you are all right?"

"Of course I am, son," she said, still smiling. There was a southern twang to her American accent. She stepped back to get a better look at her guide. "Oh my! Since when did they start making Englishmen tall, dark and handsome?"

Simon stood there, dumbstruck. He was at a complete loss for words.

"I'm joshing with you, son! I'm a happily married Christian woman," Mrs. Filmore said. She swatted his arm playfully with her portfolio. "Now, let's go see this camp of yours!" She marched off toward a sea of tents, with Simon close behind.

Simon sat across from the energetic woman, watching her devour her lunch. The three-hour tour had gone very well, he thought. She'd come at him with some excellent questions, all of which he had answered easily enough. He was almost disappointed not to be challenged. As if reading his mind, Mrs. Filmore looked up from her plate. "I was hoping to meet Tim Redmond before I left," she said. "I'll be ostracized by the women in my church group if I don't come back with a picture of him and me together!"

Simon nearly choked on a dry biscuit, but he recovered quickly. "I'm sorry, Mrs. Filmore, but I believe he's still in Benin erecting a community center."

The woman slumped down in her chair, clearly disappointed.

"The chap's hard to keep track of, as I'm sure you can imagine." Simon dipped a plastic spoon into a small cup of applesauce and scooped up the last speck. He gazed out the tent's open flap and saw Tim playing football with a group of children in the distance. He wondered if his friend's proximity would scuttle the hasty fabrication. "He's not officially affiliated with the Red Cross, you know."

"Is that right?" the benefactor gaped. "That woman from *People* magazine sure seemed to think he was."

"Spotty bit of reporting, that," Simon replied. He was more than familiar with the two-paragraph blurb that had appeared in the magazine's "Where Are They Now?" section.

"Actually, Redmond runs his own outfit," Simon continued. "It's called The Spirit of a Child Foundation. The group builds community centers, provides instruction and coaching, organizes sports leagues…all focused on improving the quality of life for children in Africa."

Mrs. Filmore looked confused. "But…but I thought…" she stammered, "I thought he provided medical attention to the refugees."

Simon had to fight off the urge to laugh. Now, that was a new one. Most people came right out and used the words "miracles" or "healing"! *Medical attention* was certainly a more refined way of describing it. Although Simon had heard the rumors about Tim's childhood, he had never seen him perform any miracles while in Africa. "No, I'm afraid not," he said, apologetically. He watched the woman slump even further into her chair. Her left hand rose up and grasped the crucifix around her neck. "At least not in the traditional sense," Simon added quickly.

The woman perked up immediately.

"I mean, I've seen him pull children back from the brink of death before, without so much as an ounce of medicine."

Mrs. Filmore's cheeks flushed, and she inched forward. "Really?"

"Oh, yes. Pretty amazing stuff, actually," Simon confirmed. It was true. He had seen Tim resurrect children from a state of mental oblivion. So what if the woman was reading more into it? Far be it from him to dash her hopes. Before she pressed him further, however, Simon glanced down at his watch. "My goodness! I've been having such a splendid time speaking with you that I've completely overshot my one o'clock meeting!" He rose up from his chair.

"Are you sure Tim Redmond isn't here?" the woman persisted.

"I am truly sorry, Mrs. Filmore. If Mr. Redmond were here, I would be the first to know. Technically, he must have my approval to establish any operations within the boundaries of this camp." Simon motioned toward the tent's exit. "I hope your tour was beneficial. I'll see that Michael takes you back to your hotel now. If you have any additional questions, please feel free to drop me a note!"

As the woman passed before him, Simon gazed past her at the clearing in the distance. He saw Redmond kick a ball to a one-armed lad who ran onto it with a huge smile on his face. Several other children gave chase, causing a cloud of dust to swirl around them.

Simon peered over at a clock-like thermometer nailed to the post of the tent. The staff hated to be reminded of the heat, but the ubiquitous dials gave them a gauge for recommended water intake. It was inching over 107 degrees Fahrenheit. He shook his head and chuckled.

CHAPTER 3

Simon saw the trail of dust kicking up off the road in the distance long before he could identify the vehicle. The Wench was parked next to the baobab tree, so it couldn't have been any of the staff members. All requisitions arrived first thing in the morning, so it wasn't a supply truck either. It had to be Chissani. He followed the truck as it turned onto the access road. Its outline stood out clearly against the setting sun. An orange hue blanketed the endless plain and highlighted a group of zebras feeding in the distance. Three large hyenas prowled nearby. Their tails twitched anxiously as they eyed the youngest of the striped equids.

The white Ford Expedition finally pulled abreast of the Wench. A tall, olive-skinned man emerged from the driver's side. He wore khaki pants and a navy blue linen shirt with long sleeves, which were wrinkled from his long journey. His brown eyes drooped slightly and were red around the edges from exhaustion. His cheeks were shadowed with dark stubble, and his thick black hair was dusty and windblown from the open window. Nevertheless, his haggard appearance only reinforced his raw good looks.

It was nearly dark and Chissani headed toward the tent to his left, oblivious to the fact that Simon was leaning against the baobab. The Englishman chuckled to himself and called out, "Armando!"

Chissani swung around defensively. Upon recognizing Simon, his demeanor changed immediately. The lines of tension disappeared from his face and his shoulders relaxed. "Simon!" He ran over and hugged him. "It has been too long, my friend!"

His soft Italian accent was barely discernible. Both men laughed and slapped each other on the back.

"We've been busy," Simon said.

"Yes we have."

After separating from the embrace, the two men stood silently, face to face, assessing the physical changes they'd undergone since seeing each other last. Both in their early thirties, tall, strong featured, dark skinned, they could have been brothers.

"You haven't changed a bit, my friend," Chissani reveled.

"You haven't either, Armando."

The haggard man looked down at the ground, embarrassed. "You are too kind," he said, without looking up. "I'm tired, Simon. I don't know what's happening to me."

Simon threw his arm around Chissani's shoulder. "That's why you're here."

#   #   #

Tim sat at the makeshift desk—a large wooden plank from a medical supply pallet and a couple of saw horses used in the construction of the rations depot. The bold printed numbers on the corner of the forms he was reading came in and out of focus. He glanced at the kerosene lamp and confirmed his suspicion: it had less than an hour's worth of fuel. He'd be forced to retire soon.

Line 34a of subpart 3 on the form called for a present value calculation spread out over five years, at a 6.2% annualized rate of return. Ten years ago, he could have computed the answer in his head in mere seconds. Now, he struggled to solve it with a calculator. As he grappled with the equation, he had the sensation that he was being watched. He looked up quickly.

Three feet inside his tent stood the figure of a man who appeared more haggard than himself. Simon's soft brown eyes smiled back at him.

Tim leaned back in the dusty director's chair. "You know, if you keep sneaking up on people like that, you're going to be mistaken for a lion and shot, one of these days."

"And if you don't start using sunscreen, you're going to be mistaken for a crustacean and boiled!" Simon said, crossing the dirt floor of the tent. He stopped at the far wall and examined the dozens of photographs and letters hung from the dirty canvas by safety pins. Happy young faces beamed back at him, coming to life through the laminate paper and chemicals. "Judging strictly from these photographs, someone might get the impression that you actually love these children." Simon shook his head. "They'd be wrong though. I mean anyone who had any concern at all for their welfare wouldn't initiate a football match under the blistering heat of the midday sun!"

Tim cringed. He had no defense and he knew it. "Please forgive me, your starch-shirted magnificence," he said, executing his best seated curtsy.

Simon dragged himself to the director's chair across from Tim, and laid his burden down. "The humble servant is forthrightly and duly forgiven," he said with a wave of his hand.

"It won't happen again, Simon, I promise."

"You said that five years ago in Warri. Come to think of it, you also said it in Kumbo, Magaria, Bamba and Mali!"

Tim shrugged. He saw an opportunity to change the subject, and took it.

"Fundraising day?" he asked.

"Yes, unfortunately. A necessary evil, I'm afraid." Simon dug into one of the unbuttoned pockets of his shorts and withdrew a handful of pistachios. He carefully picked out some of the larger pieces of lint, before reaching across the table and depositing half in front of Tim. "An evil in which I've noticed you don't often indulge." He popped a nut into his mouth. The shell cracked sharply between his molars.

"What do you think I was doing before you came in here and began to harass me?" Tim pointed at the papers in front of him.

Simon leaned forward and tilted his head in order to see the documents. "Government grants?" He nearly choked on a shell. "Oh, *do* come around! That money is allocated before the budgets even get approved!"

Tim remained stoic.

"Why won't you let me introduce you to some of my benefactors? One inquired about you just today, in fact."

"Didn't we have this discussion a month ago?"

"Yes, we did. And two months before that."

"So, why do you keep coming back to it?"

"Because your funding is running out, Tim, and I, for one, would hate to see your program come to a grinding halt."

"Simon, I appreciate your concern. I really do. But I'm more than capable of looking after my own foundation."

"*Your* foundation? I thought it was for the children."

"It is for the children!" Tim snapped.

"Then why won't you get out of your comfort zone long enough to make it as good as it can be…for the children?"

"Simon, just let it go already, will you?"

"How can I let it go, Tim? How can I stand by and watch you squander your talents?"

"You don't understand, Simon." Tim could barely get the words out.

"You're right, I don't understand." Simon shook his head. "Whenever we have this discussion, I always hesitate, wondering if I should go any further. Despite my better judgement, I'm going to proceed this time. Tim, I respect you more than you will probably ever know…for what you are doing for these children and for the kind-hearted person you are. But there's something about you that's extremely selfish. The truth is, you don't want anything to do with this world. If you could, you would go through the rest of your life without speaking to another adult, ever. You'd be perfectly happy attending to the children. A very noble cause, make no mistake. But, believe it or not, there are bigger problems in the world. Problems that are responsible for more widespread suffering than what you see before your eyes in west Africa!"

Tim retreated into his shell, hoping Simon would give up. Unfortunately, the Englishman continued. "I think this attitude comes from something that happened to you in your past, Tim. Mind you, there's no way for me to know that for sure. In the five years we've been friends, you haven't said two words to me about your past, and I've respected that. Until now. It's perfectly clear to me now that whatever happened to you as a child is stopping you from sharing your God-given talents with the rest of the world!"

Tim looked Simon squarely in the eyes and maintained his cool reserve. Deep inside, however, his conflicting emotions were tearing him apart. He put himself in his friend's shoes. From Simon's perspective, he was being selfish. If he had allowed his mind to continue developing at the pace it was, there was no telling what good he could have done. Solve world hunger? No problem. Discover the cure for cancer? A piece of cake. Develop a limitless source of energy? Certainly within reason.

But Simon didn't know the whole story. Hell, even *he* didn't know the whole story. He didn't need to. Didn't want to. He'd learned enough. Maybe if Simon knew what he knew about himself, he would change his tune. He'd have to, wouldn't he? Unfortunately, he couldn't know. Not now. Not ever. And that fact was about to cost Tim the best friend he'd ever had. It was enough to make him break the promise he'd made to himself— to never speak about his secret with anyone. How good it would feel to share his secret with someone else, though. Just *one* person!

But at least one other person already did know, didn't he? If there was no one on Earth who had any complicity in the matter, then Simon was right, and Tim was wrong, terribly wrong. His talents would, indeed, be gifts from God, and he'd be a fool for squandering them. But, God wasn't the source of his talents, was He? The uncertainty was enough to drive him *mad...raving mad!* The thought shot through him like a blast of cold air. Tim shuddered and tried to push it from his mind.

Irrespective of where his childhood genius had come from, one thing was clear. Simon's resentment toward him had obviously been building. And why not? He was a man who had dedicated his entire life to the service of those in need, at his own personal expense...financially, physically, and emotionally. Simon could have been anything in life he wanted to be, of that Tim was sure—a high-powered financier, a doctor, an attorney, a television personality. He could have had the beautiful wife, the perfect children, the flat in London, and the cottage in Brighton. He might even have been happier, too. But no, Simon had chosen to help people, giving every ounce of himself in the process. Without a full explanation, Tim knew that Simon would never understand why he, too, didn't fully embrace the talents he'd been given for the benefit of the less fortunate.

Tim stared at Simon, knowing this was the moment of truth. Tell him! He wanted to so badly, but he knew he couldn't. Once he opened the door there was no telling what would storm back through it.

Tim watched helplessly as Simon rose from his chair and sulked to the tent's exit. Two feet outside, he glanced back. The lamp illuminated his tall figure and cast a long shadow onto the dirt. Tim's heart sank as Simon shook his head and walked off into the night.

"God didn't give me these talents," Tim whispered. A tear rolled down his cheek.

CHAPTER 4

Tim lay on his cot, staring up at the pictures pinned to the side of his tent. It was well past midnight, but the glow of the quarter moon illuminated them through the tent's open flap. For the past two hours, he had been rehashing his earlier conversation with Simon. No less than three times he had risen from his cot and started to make his way toward Simon's tent. But each time something had stopped him—a fear far greater than losing his best friend, as devastating as that would be. Each time horrifying memories had stormed back, until finally there could be no further debate. He would rather be alone than face the horror again.

In an effort to distract himself, Tim called upon a skill he'd developed as an adolescent. He closed his eyes and focused on his auditory assets. *Pfisss. Pfisss.* Two Scarab beetles hissed just outside his tent. *Criee.* A hawk screeched overhead. *Whoiee. Whoiee.* A Callithrix monkey whooped from a treetop in the distance.

As the monkey's cries faded, he heard a noise he couldn't place. It was very faint, but uniform—almost mechanical. He held his breath while struggling to identify it. What could it be? The soft rhythmic thumping reminded him of tribal drums. But that wasn't quite it. He focused even harder, pushing out all other stimuli. *What is it?*

Boom! A blast echoed through the camp, followed by a scream.

Tim leaped off his cot and ran out of his tent. He was sprinting, but to where he had no idea.

Boom! Another shot resounded in the darkness.

Tim's head spun toward the source—the southern corner of the camp. He saw torches flickering in the distance and the headlights of several vehicles. Another high-pitched scream rose into the night, and he bolted toward the fracas. Halfway there he saw a flash spew from the muzzle of a shotgun and heard the concussion reverberate into the night. A crowd of refugees stood behind two trucks, pleading with armed men in the flatbeds. The vehicles idled, their pistons thumping like distant drums. Taillights cast a hellish red glow onto the prone bodies of several refugees. Ropes bound the four men's hands and encircled their necks. The far ends were secured to the trucks' bumpers. The captives' eyes were wide with terror. Sweat glistened off their naked bodies.

Between the trucks and the crowd lay the lifeless bodies of those who had apparently come too close. Women and children wept over their husbands and fathers. The other refugees stood at a safer distance, pleading with the men standing in the flatbeds. The largest of the rebels held his shotgun in one hand, pointing it out at the crowd, like a deviant adolescent taunting a roped dog. He was yelling at them, no doubt giving his version of a political speech.

Tim had almost reached the scene when he saw Simon push his way through the crowd. The Englishman burst out into the dead zone, where three of the refugees had already met their end. "You are on the grounds of an International Red Cross relief effort!" he shouted. He was clearly winded. "Untie these people at once!"

A hush fell over the crowd. Refugees and rebels alike were caught off guard by the white man's courage. The gun-toting rebels stood mute. Slowly, they turned to their leader for guidance. The man's eyes became huge and he lowered his shotgun at Simon's chest. "Wo nnse ha!" he yelled.

Simon put his hands in the air, more to placate the rebel leader than to signal surrender. "Saa nipa yi won mmu oman yibe," he said, nodding at the men tied to the bumpers. "Faa nipa yi pese wo tena won wiase asomdwemu!"

The attention swung back to the rebel leader. He kept the gun trained on Simon's chest. "You think because you speak my language, you are smart? So smart you come to my country…tell me what to do?" he snarled.

"I'm not trying to tell you what to do. You are obviously in control here," Simon said.

"Yes, I am!" The man squeezed the trigger. One hundred fifty steel pellets leapt from the mouth of the gun at 1,100 feet per second. The tight pattern blew a hole into the soft dirt at Simon's feet.

"Stop!" Tim shouted. Three of the gunmen immediately trained their weapons on him. He threw his arms in the air. "Please don't hurt anyone! What do you want?"

The leader scanned the horizon nervously. He waited for a moment, looking and listening for signs of any organized force. Satisfied that there was none, he continued. "I am here to teach a lesson to these people!" He waved the gun over the heads of the refugees below him. "Do not oppose me, unless you are willing to die!"

He pumped the slide action of the Franchi riot gun. A red plastic shell ejected from the chamber and was replaced with a new one. He pulled the stock to his shoulder and peered down the barrel at Simon.

"No!" Tim screamed.

Crack! Something whistled by Tim's head. The sheer velocity of the projectile sent him to the ground. As he fell, Tim saw the rebel leader's forehead explode at the exact instant his muzzle flashed. The ground around Tim began to erupt from the fire of the other rebels.

"No!" A voice rang out from behind Tim, and he looked up just in time to see a speeding shadow leap over his prone body. The man ran headlong into the salvo of rebel fire, while issuing a thunderous return from his own pistol. Tim watched in awe as the two remaining gunmen fell lifeless, next to their leader.

The rear wheels of the truck spun to life as the driver gunned the ignition. Gravel pelted the heads of the refugees tied to the bumper. The ropes pulled taut around their necks and instantly cut off the supply of oxygen to their lungs. The refugees were dragged ten feet before the rear window of the cab shattered. The remains of the driver's head splattered across the dashboard and windshield. The truck's inertia dragged the refugees another five feet before rolling slowly to a stop.

The four rebels in the other vehicle remained in the flatbed, firing wildly in the direction of the deadly shadow. The fleet-footed marksman promptly altered his course. Instead of taking a direct line to the truck, he broke off parallel to it, and disappeared into the thick brush. The rebels continued to fire wildly into the darkness. One of them reached down and yanked up the heavy tailgate. All four hunkered down behind it, with weapons raised.

"Mma yen ko!" Tim heard the order and saw one of the rebels jump from the flatbed, next to the driver's side door.

Crack! Before his feet touched the ground, a 9mm slug eviscerated his left eye. His two-hundred-pound carcass hit the ground with a thud. The other three rebels opened fire again.

Tim followed the line of their barrels until his eyes met with the speeding shadow, forty yards out, and closing fast. The man's shoulders were square to his target, perfectly balanced. His right arm was raised. Fire spat from his pistol. His legs pumped, driving his feet quickly through the brush. Two of the rebels' heads snapped back into the flatbed. Suddenly, a fine spray of blood erupted from the runner's shoulder. He was knocked sideways, but maintained his balance and kept coming. His pistol never wavered from its target.

Crack! The remaining rebel fell over the side of the truck with a thud. His left shoulder incapacitated, he scooped up the gun with his right hand and scurried into the shadows beyond the truck. He only made it a few feet before he was downed by a final shot.

Tim jumped to his feet and scrambled toward his friend. As he drew closer, his heart sank. Simon lay rolled up into a ball. The back of his shirt was bright red at the torso. Gut shot.

"Simon!" Tim fell to the ground and carefully rolled him over. "I have to see the wound, Simon!" He grabbed hold of his shirt and ripped it open. Tim nearly fainted. Simon's intestines were a pulpy mangle. It was amazing he was still alive.

"What can I do? Tell me!" The deft marksman arrived at the scene. He threw his pistol to the ground and thrust out his hands, splaying his strong fingers before Tim like instruments on a surgeon's table. His eyes beseeched Tim to use them as he would.

Tears streamed down Tim's face. He could only look back at the man and shake his head.

"No!" The marksman's head dropped into his open hands. Fingers coursed through his dark hair. "No!" He jumped to his feet and screamed into the night. "What have they done?"

Tim felt a weak tug on his T-shirt and he looked down to see Simon staring at him through glassy eyes. "They are gifts, Tim," he said, struggling to get the words out, through a raspy gurgle of blood. "Despite what you might think." The whites of his eyes grew larger and he grappled for Tim's hand. "Use them..." he whispered. He squeezed Tim's hand and pulled it toward him.

"Okay, Simon." Tears rushed from Tim's eyes and fell onto Simon's cheeks. The Englishman lifted his hand, as if to catch them in his palm, but halfway to his face, it fell limp. Something inside of Tim broke, like a floodwall after decades of wear. It was his own life was pouring from him, and he had no will to stop it. Why would anyone want to live in a world where something so tragic and senseless could happen?

A montage of events flashed through Tim's mind. He remembered his first encounter with Simon, when he had overlooked Red Cross guidelines and allowed Tim to help the children in Warri. He remembered when Simon gifted him his old Jeep. Most of all, he remembered Simon's efforts to get him to open up to him, and his own refusal to do so.

Suddenly, Tim was shaken back to the horrible present.

"Save him!" The dark haired man stood over Tim. Every muscle in his lean frame was taut.

Tim looked up, helpless. "I can't," he whispered.

The man ran over to his pistol and picked it up off the ground. He stormed back and pointed it at Tim's head.

"Bring him back!" he screamed. "I know you can do it!"

"I can't!" Tim yelled back at him. "You don't think I would if I could? I *can't!*"

The marksman threw his gun to the ground and dropped to his knees.

CHAPTER 5

Tim stood outside Simon's tent, wishing he could breeze in and find his friend devouring a fistful of pistachios. What he would give to be chastised once more for carousing with the children or for not applying sunscreen. He had applied sunscreen today, though. The open-air funeral had taken place that morning, in a field near the camp. In accordance with Simon's written wishes, he had been buried next to the relief area he had been supporting at the time of his death. It was so fitting.

Tim felt hollow and undeserving of such a selfless friend. His high regard for the man wasn't exclusive. Simon's funeral had been very well attended. In only three days, word had traveled to most of the villages he had served during his tenure with the Red Cross. The African contingent numbered well over a thousand, including the five hundred refugees in the current camp and those who had walked, driven or bussed from the surrounding areas.

Simon had no relatives, but dozens of his colleagues had arrived from posts throughout Africa. The road to the camp looked like a used car lot that morning, with old Land Cruisers, Land Rovers and Range Rovers lining both sides for a quarter mile. Even several senior-level Red Cross executives had flown in to pay their last respects.

And it was this amazing man's friendship Tim had rebuffed only days earlier. The same man who had, in his written wishes, requested that Tim be given right of first refusal to any of his belongings. Riddled with guilt, he sighed and pushed open the tent's flap. He took one step inside before stopping cold. His heart skipped a beat. Sitting behind the desk, wearing his starched white shirt and khaki shorts, was Simon. Tim tried to speak, but nothing came out of his mouth. A second later, he noticed the sling that cradled the man's left arm, and he realized his error. It wasn't Simon, but rather the marksman who had tried to save him.

He had disappeared shortly after Simon's death, only to reemerge at his funeral. He hadn't said two words to Tim since holding him at gunpoint. He stared at him now and shifted awkwardly in his chair.

"You are probably wondering who I am," he said, with a faint Italian accent.

Tim nodded.

"My name is Armando Chissani. Simon was a close friend." He gestured toward the photographs on the desk in front of him. "I was just taking a look at some of these. I hope that's okay."

Tim nodded again.

Chissani chuckled. "Simon said you were quiet."

"Simon told you about me?"

"Yes, he did. A few things anyway."

"What did he say?"

"He said you were what we should all strive to be."

Tim swallowed hard. Another wave of guilt washed over him. "Where did you come from, if you don't mind me asking."

"From Italy." Chissani shrugged. "I arrived the night it happened." He pressed his face with a restless hand, as if trying to rub away the memory of an egregious error. "Had I unpacked before falling asleep, Simon would be still be alive."

It took Tim a moment to understand that Chissani was referring to his gun. He wanted to ask him why he had one in the first place, but that would have been a case of looking a gift horse in the mouth. "Did you come to see Simon?" he asked.

"In a way." Chissani rose from his chair and placed a few photos into a bag that was resting on the table. "He asked me to come. He wanted me to talk with *you*. He thought you could help me." He pulled on the drawstring of the canvas knapsack and slung it over his good shoulder. "But that seems inconsequential now." He walked past Tim and out of the tent.

Tim followed him into the blinding sunlight. He had to run to catch up with Chissani. The man's long strides carried him toward the roundabout. "How could I possibly help you?" Tim asked.

"Simon seemed to think you'd already gone through what I'm going through now."

Chissani reached the Ford and threw his sack onto the back seat.

"And what, exactly, is that?"

"It's not important now. I already know what I need to do." Chissani opened the driver's side door and hopped in.

"Come on, Armando!" Tim held the door open and stepped closer to the vehicle. "If Simon told you I could help, at least let me know how!"

Chissani inserted the key into the ignition, but stopped short of turning it. He peered at Tim through dark brown eyes. "Have you ever had solutions to very complex problems, concerning subject matter to which you've never been exposed, simply pop into your head? Have you ever overheard a conversation and understood every word, only to realize later that the language being spoken was one you've never studied? Have you ever had visions, Tim? Visions of events in the past that don't appear among the pages of any history books? Visions of events in the present that may be happening thousands of miles away, but appear in your mind's eye as clear as if they were happening right in front of you? Visions of future events? Events that haunt you to the point you can't sleep?"

Tim felt the blood drain from his face, and he took a step back. Chissani grabbed the door and pulled it shut. "I didn't think so," he said and turned the key in the ignition. The Ford's engine roared to life. "Be good, Tim."

Chissani gunned the engine, and the SUV whipped around the circle like a sports car. Once it reached the access road, it accelerated and disappeared into the distance.

CHAPTER 6

"Here you are, sir. A half package of Sweet 'n Low and two teaspoons of that powdered milk crap." Grinning, the young man pushed a cup of coffee through the opening of the horseshoe counter and waited for his superior to take it from his hand.

Norman Cox let the lad stand there for a few more seconds than he had to. Finally, he reached over and grabbed it. "Just the way I like it," he said, referring to the fact that the kid hadn't placed it down on the instrument panel this time. "Thank you." As he took his first sip, he gazed at the Helix security system above him. Twenty video monitors gave him a clear view of every potential entry point to the United Nations General Assembly building, as well as the interior of each room and hallway. He was currently following the progress of a tour making its way down the long hallway from the Dag Hammarskjöld library.

Cox took another sip of the coffee. Not bad. The kid might work out after all. He'd let him have it pretty good after yesterday's fuck-up, but the newbee had taken it like a man. He'd recovered pretty damn quick, too, and even managed to stay a little cocky. Yeah, he just might make it after all.

Crack! Crack! Crack! The sound of small weapons fire broke the silence. "What the hell!" Cox yelled. The ex-Marine jumped to his feet, oblivious to the scalding coffee that drenched his right hand. He snatched his headset off the console and placed it over his ears.

Prrrt. Prrrt. Prrrt. Automatic weapons fire issued over his headset. Cox looked up quickly at the three monitors labeled SECURITY COUNCIL. He was relieved to see that the room was vacant. He then turned his attention to the three monitors labeled GENERAL ASSEMBLY. He saw a black-clad figure emerge from a hole that had been blown out of the wall. As soon as the man was in the room, he fired short bursts from his machine gun into the air. The UN delegates screamed.

Cox slammed his hand on the general alarm. Immediately, sirens blared over the eighteen-acre compound and mechanized steel barriers shot up from the ground to block both the First Avenue and Forty-Sixth Street entrances. Members of the Bravo Security Detail grabbed their VIPs and rushed them to the nearest pre-defined secure zones of each of the four buildings within the complex.

"Commander, they're in the assembly hall! They're in the goddamn assembly hall!" The voice of Nicholas Draden blared over Cox's headset. His words were drowned out by more automatic fire.

"How many are there?" Cox yelled back. He waited a few seconds for a response. "Draden, come in! Where are you?" When he received no reply, he flipped a switch on the console labeled COM-8. "This is Commander Cox. We have a breach in A2! Element One, secure building entries! Bravo Detail, stay with your VIPs in the secure zones. All other elements, proceed to the assembly hall *now!*"

Cox flipped another switch on the console. "Draden, this is Commander Cox. Come in!" While he waited for a response, he counted no less than ten black-clad figures in the general assembly hall. A handful of them were herding the five-hundred plus delegates toward the seats in the center of the massive auditorium. Several more worked feverishly to wire what appeared to be backpacks to the doors. He could only assume they were explosives.

Crack! One of the monitors suddenly went blank. Then, like dominos falling, the other monitors went dark, following single, well-placed shots. The only image remaining was that of the speaker's lectern at center stage.

Cox flipped yet another switch. "This is Commander Cox calling out to anyone in the A2 security detail. Talk to me!" He waited anxiously. Just as he was about to try again, he heard a reply.

"Commander, this is Price!"

"Price, I read you! Where are you?"

"I'm standing at the door to the southeast entrance, sir. I'm going to..."

"*Wait!* Don't do anything until I instruct you!" Just then, on the only functioning monitor above his head, Cox saw a tall man stride confidently to the lectern. He was dressed in black, like the other members of the incursion team, except the mesh stocking had been removed from his head, revealing an attractive olive-skinned face. The man's left arm was in a sling. He tapped the microphone and proceeded to address the delegates seated before him.

"Your attention, please. We do not want to harm you, but you must pay attention!" the man said. "My name is Armando Chissani. I am a member of the Volenta. Two weeks ago, a chance discovery was made on Mars. A discovery that may signal the end of life on Earth as we know it. I am here to ask for the collective help of the world, to prevent this event from happening!"

"Oh my God," Cox muttered to himself. He buried his face in his hands. "A nut-job!"

CHAPTER 7

Tim gazed out the tinted window of the black Lincoln at the city streets that supposedly never slept. Whoever coined the phrase had never driven through Manhattan at one o'clock on a rainy Tuesday morning in November. The streets were devoid of people and, since passing over the Queensboro bridge, he had seen only a handful of taxicabs. That was it. Not the kind of homecoming he pictured.

He leaned back and closed his eyes. His head had been pounding nonstop ever since armed men in fatigues had corralled him from his tent at gunpoint five hours earlier. Without a word of explanation, they'd shoved him into a sleek, black helicopter and whisked him away to a remote airstrip. On the tarmac, Tim had finally received the semblance of an explanation, although it was woefully short on details. Apparently, Armando Chissani had taken hostages somewhere in the U.S. and he was demanding to see him. It was clearly a serious matter.

Following his ten-second conversation with the intelligence officer, he had been accosted by a team of airmen who had squeezed him into a pressurized flight suit and marched him into a huge hanger housing a hypersonic Aurora spy plane. He had thrown up three times during the two-hour transatlantic flight—twice in the plane and once on the tarmac at La Guardia. The two men sitting in front of him now had simply asked if he were finished, before shoving him into the Lincoln and heading off toward the Grand Central Parkway.

Tim pressed his forehead against the cold window, trying to shake the memory of the flight. His ears were still ringing, as the car turned left onto 43rd Street. As soon as they rounded the corner, he saw a fleet of news vans. Their rooftop satellite antennae were fully deployed and beaming signals to relay stations, which then transmitted all over the world. Hundreds of reporters milled about in front of the high gates of what he finally realized was their destination. Chissani had taken hostages at the United Nations building! A million questions rushed into his head at once. What was he trying to accomplish? How did he beat their security? Why had he asked to see him, of all people…a man he'd met only weeks earlier and then just briefly? None of it made any sense!

As Tim pondered the absurdity of it all, something outside caught his eye. A cameraman was running straight for the car. A stampede ensued, as others rushed after him. They converged on the Lincoln like a horde of vultures. He heard them shout questions and saw their bodies crush up against the windows. Bright lights poured into the back seat, causing him to shield his eyes. The two men in front remained perfectly calm, indifferent.

Finally, a group of police arrived and cleared a path to the main gate. As soon as it opened, the driver hit the gas. The Lincoln roared into the compound, passed the main circle, and descended a service road. When they reached the underground entrance, the driver brought the vehicle to a screeching halt. The man in the passenger seat turned around and threw a black raincoat into Tim's lap. "Drape this over your head until we're inside the building!" he commanded. Someone helped him from the car and led him toward the building. Once inside, the coat was removed.

Tim followed the couriers past a pair of armed guards and into a room. He realized they were in the crisis control center. It had a u-shaped console in the middle and a series of television monitors hanging from the ceiling. A group of military personnel huddled over electrical engineering schematics and structural blueprints, while others reviewed a videotape on one of the monitors. A two-star air force general pressed a button on the remote and the image froze. "See those wires just past the last seats in the front row?" he said. "They go from the doors on either side, up into the middle of the delegates."

"It's not going to matter, Gray," an army general replied. "We're not going to be coming through the doors anyway." Tim caught a glimpse of the patch on the man's arm—a blue background with three horizontal gold lightning bolts piercing a gold sword.

"Sir?" Courier One interrupted.

The air force general's head dipped slightly. He turned to identify the source of the disruption. Tim felt the hairs on the back of his neck stand on end. Chilling was the only way to describe the man's eyes. Set far back into his large skull, they were cold, intelligent and controlled. He had to be at least six-feet-four. His broad shoulders tapered down to his narrow torso, forming a v. He didn't say a word to the courier. He didn't have to; the cold stare was more than enough. He turned back to his cross-branch team and pressed another button on the remote, advancing the image. After a few seconds, he paused it. On the monitor, Tim saw Chissani. The general clicked the laser pointer and a beam of light illuminated the Italian's hand. He was holding something that Tim couldn't identify.

"It's not going to matter where we enter the auditorium, Dick, as long as he's holding that." He placed the remote down on the console in front of him. "We've got two options. We either figure out how to get a clean first shot, or we separate him from that switch." He nodded to his team and then made his way toward Tim. "Follow me, son!"

Tim did as he was asked.

The two walked past a group of military attachés on the way to the exit. Every one of them stopped talking and looked either into the bottom of their coffee cups or down at the floor. The general marched out of the crisis control center and down a long corridor. He opened the first door on his left and directed Tim inside. There were no windows in the room and only a few abstract paintings adorned the plain beige walls. The general pointed to one of the utilitarian chairs surrounding the small oval table. "Have a seat," he instructed, as he closed the door behind him. He strode directly to the table and placed his hands on the back of a chair in front of it. He leaned forward and appraised his charge.

Tim couldn't bring himself to look the man in the eye. He found the general's name badge instead—BAUER.

"I apologize in advance for not having more time, Mr. Redmond," Bauer began. "I promise to give you all the attention you deserve, in due course. That is, if you are still alive." Bauer's face remained deadpan. His eyes bore down on Tim. "But, for now, let's just get to know each other, shall we? Ask the simple questions that new acquaintances typically do."

Bauer took a seat and ran his hand across the table, wiping away some crumbs left behind by an earlier meeting. He crossed his legs and offered a false, congenial smile.

"What is your affiliation with Armando Chissani?"

# # #

Tim walked alone down the empty hallway toward the northern entrance of the General Assembly room. Bauer's instructions had been quite clear—keep his mouth shut and listen. Don't try to convince Chissani to do anything. It was clear that the general viewed Tim's presence as nothing more than a filibuster, a mechanism to buy his team more time.

As he continued down the hallway, he heard the soft humming of the fluorescent lights, the tapping of his shoes on the marble floor, and the rustling of the pine branches in the courtyard beyond the windows. He heard these subtle sounds, but failed to notice the stunning sculptures that lined the walls. He'd been in his own little world since Simon's death. A world where nameless military assets snatched him out of his tent with the detached efficiency of couriers retrieving an urgent package. A world where hypersonic spy planes ferried said package across the Atlantic under the cover of darkness, and war-mongering generals prosecuted its contents like so many customs agents searching for contraband.

Through all of this, Tim had struggled against an unseen force, one that had begun knocking on the door of his consciousness since Simon's last words. It had started as a polite tap, a single knuckle thudding dully on the window of the foyer. After being corralled from his tent by armed men in fatigues, however, it had escalated to a firm rap from the brass knocker. Following his encounter with General Bauer, the force began pounding the door to his mind with a battering ram. Even under normal circumstances, it would have been difficult to fight off, but under the stress of his current situation, it was nearly impossible.

As he continued down the hallway, Tim returned his attention to the matters at hand. He was about to come face-to-face with a man who was threatening to execute the entire U.N. General Assembly if his demands weren't met, demands that included a meeting with the heads of state of the five permanent Security Council countries, unquestionably the five most powerful men on earth. What was Chissani's motivation? What was his ultimate goal? Surely he wasn't prepared to execute innocent people, was he? During their encounter in Africa, Tim thought Chissani was confused, spooked, and maybe even a little unbalanced. He didn't seem like a cold-blooded killer, though. Bauer had even admitted—although reluctantly—that Chissani's men had inflicted no casualties during their raid, despite incurring the loss of four men themselves. How could anyone storm the General Assembly and take all its members hostage, without inflicting a single casualty? Tim surmised that Chissani must have taken extra risks with his own men to pull that off. He doesn't want to execute the General Assembly members! That's not his goal at all. But what, exactly, was his ultimate goal?

Tim realized he wouldn't have to wait much longer to find out. He came upon an enormous pendulum, swinging from the ceiling to his right. It was exactly as Bauer had described it. He then turned to his left and made his way to a set of double doors. He wiped the sweat from his forehead and listened for voices on the other side of the doors. It was as quiet as a sarcophagus. He reached out and rapped three times, as instructed. Several seconds passed, before he heard a rustling sound. Unexpectedly, a black snake shot out from beneath the door. Tim jumped backward, but his eyes never left the head of the serpent. After closer examination, he realized it wasn't a snake after all, but an exploratory mini-cam. As suddenly as it had appeared, the device vanished beneath the door.

Next, Tim heard whispering and the sound of wires being unraveled. The throbbing in his head intensified, as the unseen force rocked the door to his consciousness with renewed urgency. Tim massaged his temples with his fingers. Suddenly, the double doors burst open and Tim was literally yanked off his feet. As soon as he was inside, a man dressed in black pulled them shut and re-wired the explosives.

"Tim, I knew you would come!" Chissani yelled. As the Italian made his way across the room, Tim glanced to his left and scanned the terrified faces of the seated delegates. Chissani caught the glimpse and shrunk visibly. The haggard man stopped a few feet short of his guest. The bags under his eyes were now even more pronounced than during their brief encounter in Simon's tent. Lines of stress etched his unshaven face. His posture was reminiscent of the night Tim had first seen him—a loaded spring. Chissani gestured toward the U.N. delegates. "Ridiculous, isn't it?" he shrugged. "I'm sorry it has come to this."

Tim was incredulous. "Come to what, Armando? What are you trying to accomplish?"

Chissani glanced at the sole functioning video camera, mounted to the ceiling. He grabbed Tim's arm and led him across the floor to a discreet corner. "I'm trying to wake everyone up, Tim!" he whispered. There was an intensity in his voice that conveyed his fears far greater than words. "They've found it! On the red planet. They've found it!"

"Found what?" Tim put his hand on Chissani's shoulder, in an effort calm him.

"I tried to warn everyone, Tim, in responsible, rational ways. But no one would listen! I finally had to do something drastic…to get the world's attention!"

"Calm down, Armando. It's okay. Everyone is listening now."

"Yes, but no one is *hearing*, Tim! Even they don't understand!" Chissani motioned toward the U.N. delegates. "They don't believe me, not one of them. I can feel it! It's going to destroy us, if we don't stop it!"

Tim fought to curb his frustration. Chissani was obviously cracking, unable to focus on the root cause of his fears. He put both of his hands on Chissani's shoulders and peered directly into his eyes. "Armando, I will believe you. You were right to ask for me! I'm here now. Everything is going to be all right."

Instantly, the tension disappeared from Chissani's face and he smiled. "I know, Tim. Forgive me for babbling like an idiot."

Tim couldn't believe how suddenly Chissani had changed. In the snap of a finger, he was once again the calm, articulate man he'd met in Simon's tent. Tim decided to forge ahead quickly before the man's hysteria returned. "I only want you to answer two questions for me, Armando. And then we'll walk out of here together, okay?"

"Yes, of course," Armando said, completely relaxed and lucid.

"First, who found what on the red planet? And second, why is it going to destroy us?" Tim crossed his fingers, hoping to get some clear answers.

Chissani took a slow, deep breath and opened his mouth to respond.

Boom! Shards of glass showered down from the aperture in the ceiling's dome, and screams rose up from the U.N. delegates. A second later, the lights went out and a staccato of automatic fire erupted.

Boom! A concussion grenade rocked the assembly room. It blew Tim off his feet. Dazed, he looked up just in time to see fire spitting from the guns of rappelling soldiers. The deadly scene unfolded before him, the climax of his surreal nightmare. The muzzle flashes were the only source of light. He felt like he was inside of a techno dance club, with strobe lights spinning and flashing to the beat of deafening music. From total darkness, a flash revealed a flailing arm, clenched teeth, a writhing body.

Prrrt. Prrrt. Prrrt. Papers flew up from the desk, which one of Chissani's men had overturned for cover. A hail of bullets cut clean through the thick mahogany and shredded him. Another man ran for the door, but he, too, was mowed down. Tim looked up and saw a soldier free-falling from the hole in the ceiling, his arms and legs twirling like the blades of a windmill. The macabre scene came to him between muzzle flashes—a glimpse at sixty feet, again at forty feet, and then at twenty feet. It was like watching a movie, with every other frame painted black. His ears rang from the concussion grenades and blaring gunfire. His eyes filled with horrific images, and his nostrils rebelled against the acrid smell of gunpowder. The firefight raged on. Hot projectiles whistled past his head, and he realized how exposed he was on the floor. He crawled in the direction he'd last seen the auditorium seats. Halfway to the shelter of the chairs, he bumped into something. A fire flash revealed Chissani, splayed out on the floor before him. Tim grabbed his arm and dragged him to shelter.

Slowly, the gunfire subsided. Seconds of silence were followed by a single shot here and there. In the darkness, Tim felt a tug on his arm. He saw Chissani's mouth move, but he couldn't hear him through the ringing in his head. He leaned closer and placed his ear an inch from Chissani's lips.

"I now understand…why Simon wanted me to talk to you," Chissani said, coughing. Tim felt a warm splatter of blood on his cheek. "He thought you could stop it."

Suddenly, the lights flickered on. Tim saw dozens of soldiers filing into the auditorium. He felt another tug on his arm. "Be careful! He'll use you. He *needs* you!"

"Who needs me?" As Tim asked the question, he caught a black blur out of the corner of his eye. He looked up to see Chissani's last holdout bolting for the door. The man was halfway there, when a barrage of bullets cut him down. At that very moment, Tim felt a rush of warmth on his arm. Certain he'd been winged by stray fire, he looked down to assess the damage. He quickly realized that it was Chissani's blood. The man's head hung back at a severe angle, neck limp. Blood spewed from a hole directly between his eyes.

Gently, Tim laid Chissani's head down on the floor. He felt something cold against the back of his hand, and noticed that it was a thick black electrical cord. It wound up toward the middle of the assembly hall, where the U.N. delegates had been corralled.

Tim pulled on the wire. It came to him easily, free of any weight to stop it.

"Stop!" a soldier in fatigues commanded, when he saw what Tim was doing.

The order only hastened Tim's resolve. With the soldier bearing down on him, he pulled faster, and the rubber-coated wire piled up at his feet. Just as the two-hundred-pound killing machine lunged for his hand, he reached the end of the cord. Not only was it not attached to anything, it had never been spliced! It was a dummy wire…irrefutable evidence that Chissani had never intended to harm anyone.

CHAPTER 8

"And then what did he say?" The interrogator flipped to a blank page in his notepad.

"I've already told you!" Tim yelled. "And the three others who were in here before you!"

The man remained perfectly calm. He almost seemed bored.

"Why don't you tell me again," he muttered, through a half yawn.

"He said something was going to destroy us."

"Us, meaning mankind?"

"I can only assume that's what he meant."

"What makes you jump to that conclusion?"

"I didn't jump to that conclusion. You did! I was agreeing with you."

"I see." The man wrote a few notes in his pad.

"Look, you've had me in here for two hours. I've told you everything I know."

"Then why don't we cover some new ground," the man said. "Before today, had you ever heard of an organization called the Volenta?"

"No."

"You had never spoken to any members of that organization? Never attended any of its meetings?"

"No."

The man shook his head. "You see, you're contradicting yourself, Mr. Redmond. You already admitted to speaking with Armando Chissani in Africa last week. Why are you lying to us?"

"I'm not lying! I did speak with Chissani last week, following a friend's funeral."

"Exactly! But you said you've never spoken with a member of the Volenta. Armando Chissani was a member."

Tim forced a smile. It was a game. This guy was trying to frustrate him, while the others had tried to intimidate, flatter, and empathize with him. "Look," Tim said. "I know what you're trying to do, and I can appreciate your position. Believe me, I would like to help more. Unfortunately, I don't know any more than you do."

"Did Chissani ever mention the names of any of his associates or friends?"

"No."

"He never mentioned a man named Peter?"

The door to the interrogation room swung open and a man in his mid-fifties entered. His gray hair was slightly longer than military restrictions would allow, but neatly combed. It had receded at the temples, but was otherwise very thick. Lines of experience etched his tanned forehead and a deep cleft marked his chin. His eyes were the pale blue of glacier water, but despite their icy color, they were warm and personable. The man nodded at the interrogator who rose from his chair and exited the room. "Mr. Redmond, my name is Victor Stentz," he said, extending his hand.

As Tim shook it, he realized it was the first courtesy he'd been offered since being roused from his tent in Ghana.

"I run the Martian expedition team," Stentz continued, as he took a seat. "At least the operational side of it. The security and intelligence side is run by General Grayson Bauer, whom I believe you've already met." The man cocked his head toward the window-sized mirror to his left and flashed a conspiratorial smile.

Tim found it hard not to like the man. He reserved the right to change his mind, however, offering Stentz only a polite nod of the head.

"Bauer's not a bad guy, really. He's just a little too intense for his own good. Unfortunately, the arrival of Mr. Chissani has caused some unexpected stress. We're all on edge. The knowledge that someone else has learned about…our discovery is rather disconcerting. But I'm getting ahead of myself." Stentz sat back in the chair and folded his arms. "Let me cut to the chase, Mr. Redmond. Most of the people involved with our project believe you have some sort of complicity in the U.N. hostage crisis, whether directly or indirectly. Why else would Chissani visit you in Africa only weeks before his assault, and why would he ask to see you, while holding the delegates hostage? The majority of my colleagues believe we should detain you for further investigation."

Tim remained silent.

"I'm not of the same mind," Stentz said, loosening his tie. "I think you got caught up in this thing unwillingly. If we hadn't forced you to come, my guess is you would have declined Chissani's request for an audience. But, forced you were and here you are. Unfortunately, we can't go back in time. We can only play the cards we've been dealt."

Stentz paused, waiting for some kind of reaction. Tim didn't offer any.

"Look, Tim," he said. "Despite what you may think, I'm not CIA, NSA, or any other flavor of alphabet soup. I'm a scientist. I've actually followed your work very closely. You may not recognize me, but I was at the Jet Propulsion Lab in Pasadena. Years ago, I extended you an invitation to join our team. I was sorry when you turned us down. That was a long time ago, though. We've all moved on to new discoveries…new challenges. That's why I'm here now. To see if you would be willing to help us respond to this most recent challenge."

"Challenge?" Tim said. "It looks like you've already played it out. Zero U.N. casualties and a bunch of dead terrorists. Who can argue with results like that?"

"No one welcomes that kind of carnage, Tim, no matter whose side it's on. But I wasn't referring to the U.N. crisis, and you know it. I was talking about our discovery on Mars." Victor raised his white eyebrows. "Don't tell me you're not a little curious."

Tim sat quietly, knowing full well that a hook was being dangled before him. He also knew that the time to extricate himself from this situation was now, before he swallowed the bait. "Dr. Stentz…" he began, certain that anyone who headed up a team at the Jet Propulsion Lab had his Ph.D.

"Please, call me Victor."

"In the past eighteen hours, I haven't had a minute to myself. I was flushed out of my tent in Ghana by two armed men in fatigues, flown by helicopter to Accra, and jammed into a sardine can that also moonlighted as an airplane. Then I was flown through the stratosphere at speeds exceeding Mach 8, rushed to the U.N. building by two more armed men, prosecuted by an overzealous general, thrown into a firefight for which I was unwittingly the main diversion, and then yanked back into an interrogation room for two more hours of grilling. During this time, I've had a grand total of two glasses of water and an apple. I have a headache the size of Manhattan, and it's all I can do to stay awake! With all due respect, *Victor*, I haven't the least bit of interest in what's going on sixty-two million miles from here. I'm sorry to disappoint you, but I'd rather take my leave and find some place to sleep, before catching a flight back to Africa!"

Stentz sat quietly and looked Tim in the eyes. Finally, he laid his hands on the table and leaned forward. "I apologize for your treatment so far, Tim. Unfortunately, you've been under the jurisdiction of the military arm of this project. Had you fallen under my purview, I can assure you, things would have been handled differently. Fortunately, things are about to change. The President has just given me the green light to take you under my wing, as it were. I plan to make the most of that opportunity." Tim tried to hide his shock. The *President*?

"I'd like to make you a proposition, Tim." Stentz looked at his watch. "It is now four in the morning. At this very moment, there is a car down in the garage, with an *unarmed* driver, waiting to take you to a nearby hotel. You can get a hot shower, a good meal, and some much-needed sleep, all on Uncle Sam. That same car and driver will pick you up at the hotel at six in the evening and take you to a non-military location, where I will tell you absolutely everything I know about our discovery on Mars. If, after that discussion, you still don't want to join my team, I will fully understand. I'll send you back to Ghana on the flight of your choice, first class. What do you say?"

Tim peered back at the smiling man. He really did like him. It would be a shame to burst his bubble. Although he had no intention of joining his team, there was no point in passing up the free food and lodging. A hot shower, a good meal, and twelve hours rest in a real bed would prepare him for his long journey back to Africa.

"You've got yourself a deal, Victor."

CHAPTER 9

T im sat in his suite at the Ritz Carlton, enjoying the view of Central Park. It was still dark outside, but he had seen several joggers enter the park under the glare of streetlights. Taxicabs rolled slowly down 59th Street, delivering early risers to their offices. Foot traffic was also picking up, as pedestrians emerged from the cloisters of their buildings and descended gated stairways to the subway.

Tim sliced off another small piece of steak and rolled it through the rich demi-glaze burgundy sauce, before placing it in his mouth. He savored every chew. He would have enjoyed the meal even more if he weren't fighting off the fatigue that threatened to overtake him at any moment. Now that his stomach was full, however, he was eager to get some sleep. Maybe some shut-eye would stop his headache. One more bite and he threw the linen napkin onto the table. He pulled the heavy drapes over the wall-length windows and headed for the bed. He was drawing back the spread when the phone rang. He cursed Stentz under his breath. No doubt the man had accelerated his timetable. He picked up the phone's receiver. "Hello."

He heard nothing but a dial tone. Confused, he scanned the phone's console to see if the single ring was designed to announce a message. The light was not illuminated. While the receiver was still in his hand, the sound repeated. He realized it was coming from the computer on the desk and headed over to investigate. He wriggled the mouse to activate the screen and an Instant Messenger dialogue box materialized. An entry was already visible.

Peter: Do you know what the name Peter stands
        for?

Tim glanced back at the window. He'd already forgotten that he had closed the shade only seconds earlier. He scanned the room, wondering if a hidden camera was focused on him. He sat at the desk, pulled the keyboard from its enclave, and began to type.

Guest: Who is this?

The response rolled onto the screen in real-time.

Peter: Peter.

Guest: Do I know you?

Peter: Small rock.

Guest: What?

Peter: Small rock. That's what the name Peter
        stands for.

Guest: Are you a member of the Volenta?

Peter: I am a disciple, yes.

Tim slumped in the chair and shook his head. No one knew he was staying at the Ritz, except Stentz. Unless, of course, he had told General Bauer. That would signal a trap. On the other hand, members of the Volenta had already managed to take the entire U.N. General Assembly hostage, which meant they were more than capable of finding him, wherever he went. Either way, nothing good could come from the dialogue. Therefore, with the mouse, he guided the arrow to the lower left-hand side of the screen and initiated the shut down sequence. The screen turned green and an hourglass spun in the center before it finally went black.

Sighing, he slid off the chair and dragged himself over to the bed where he collapsed. A minute later, he was almost asleep when another beep from the computer startled him. He pushed himself off the bed and shuffled to the desk, wondering how the computer could have turned itself back on. Another message greeted him.

Peter: If you help solve the Martian mystery, I will
help you solve your own.

Tim thought about turning the computer off again, this time using the power switch, but he was more than a little curious. He perched on the edge of the chair and typed a reply.

Guest: I didn't know I had a mystery.

The response rolled onto the screen so quickly, he wondered if the person on the other end were using a voice-activated system.

Peter: No time to be coy, Tim. This computer is
being monitored. Right now, they think you're
browsing UAL.com for return flights to Ghana.

Guest: Okay, why don't you tell me what my mystery
is, then.

Peter: The origin of your gifts, of course.

Tim jumped up and ran to the door of his hotel room. He flung it open and looked down the hallway. No one was in sight. He closed the door, secured the chain, and returned to the desk. He took a moment to think. There had to be a way to call the person out, without committing himself.

Guest: I could find that out myself.

Peter: You could begin to approach the clues of their
origin. You could never fully unravel the
mystery.

Tim paused to think of an appropriate response, but before he could come up with one, another message rolled across the screen.

Peter: Besides, it's not the how or the what that
interests you. It's the *why*.

Tim's emotions took over. He banged out a response without thinking strategy.

Guest: I don't want to know!

Peter: You were meant to know. Why do you think
you are having such terrible headaches? You

were meant to pursue the answers! Until you
do, the voice in your head will continue to
haunt you.

The walls of the room were closing in on him. His headache intensified. It was excruciating. He wanted it all to end. He wanted it to go away.

Guest: I don't care who you are, or what you know! I
have no intention of getting involved. Ever.
Leave me alone!

Tim waited for a response, hoping none would come. After thirty seconds, he breathed more easily. He leaned forward and reached behind the computer for the power cord. As he groped for it, his face nearly touched the screen. Just as he was about to yank the cord from the wall, he saw a flash of movement. Blue letters rolled across the screen. His mouth fell open as he read the words.

Peter: "Suppose I had found a watch on the ground.
The mechanism being observed, the
inference we think is inevitable that the watch
must have a maker."

Tim grabbed the keyboard and pulled it closer to him.

Guest: How did you know that?

He waited for the response, but none came. He banged on the keyboard again.

Guest: How did you know that?

This time the answer scrolled across the screen very slowly.

Peter: If you help solve the Martian mystery, I will
help you solve your own.

Seconds later, the dialogue box disappeared and the United Airlines Web site replaced it. Tim stared at the screen. Flight itineraries from New York to Ghana stared back at him.

CHAPTER 10

Tim stood at the back of the elevator, trying not to stare at the two women in front of him. They were both gorgeous and perfectly coifed. Traces of lavender and magnolia hung in the air, making him wonder if they'd just returned from the spa.

Finally, a bell rang and the elevator doors rolled open. The two women stepped out and turned left, their shopping bags swinging from their manicured hands. As the elevator doors closed, he wondered if the driver had made a mistake. This building wasn't for briefings; it was for living. Good living. Five-course meals, shiatsu massages and racquetball at the health club on the top floor, old boy!

The bell rang again, and the polished doors opened. Tim stepped out and took a right, as the full-service desk clerk had instructed. He walked down the hall to unit number 3305 and knocked. No sound emitted from behind the soundproof door, yet more evidence of the building's fine construction. After a few moments, Victor Stentz opened the door. "Come on in, Tim! Let me take your coat."

Tim scanned the living room, while his host hung his jacket. A dark leather sectional rested on plush white carpet. Flames flickered in the stone fireplace. The logs looked so real that he had to remind himself he was in a high-rise. Original oil paintings decorated the walls. Billie Holiday waxed over speakers. Across the room, through floor-to-ceiling windows, he could see the New York skyline. Most of the lights within the office buildings were still illuminated. "Is this your residence?" he asked as Stentz led him down the hallway.

Stentz nodded. "I got in early. The market was depressed." He gave Tim a warm smile.

"Nineteen thirty?"

Stentz feigned a hurt look. "Hey, I might be graying, but I'm not that old!"

As they entered the dining room, Tim saw that the table had already been prepared. Two settings of fine china were laid out and red wine was breathing in a crystal decanter. A marble countertop separated the dining room from the kitchen. Three serving platters rested on top of it. The rich aromas of garlic, black bean sauce, soy, shrimp, beef and chicken rose up from steaming piles of Chinese food. He was surprised at how hungry he felt. Since his early-morning Internet correspondence, the thought of food of any kind had repelled him. He'd lain awake in bed for hours, while adrenaline coursed through his veins. Although he was utterly exhausted, he had been unable to fall asleep.

"Tse Yang," Stentz said, gesturing toward the platters. "Best in Manhattan. Let's dig in before it gets cold!" He handed Tim a plate.

"Honestly, Victor," Tim said, swallowing a mouthful of Szechwan style lobster, "how does a scientist swing a place like this?"

Stentz took a sip of his wine. "I see we've progressed beyond the pro tem urbanity of new acquaintances," he said.

Tim felt himself blush.

"I like it, though. It means we're making some progress!" Stentz put the glass down. "I'm a silver-spoon baby, Tim. I've been riding on the coattails of my forefathers for quite some time."

Stentz's self-effacing honesty caught Tim off guard and made him feel guilty for asking the question. "I'm sure you're downplaying your contribution, Victor."

"I didn't mean to be overly modest, Tim. I've made good money doing what I do, but let's be honest, this is a different league." Stentz motioned toward the window with a view that would probably be assessed at a couple million dollars alone. "I used to have a hard time with the whole trust fund stigma, but one day I took a look at myself and said, 'Hey, I work pretty hard. I have a passion for what I do, and I'm a genuinely happy guy.' No need to apologize for that!"

Tim fidgeted uncomfortably. "I wasn't judging you, Victor."

"Of course you weren't, Tim. It was a fair question. One that I would have asked, too, if I were in your shoes. It's prudent to understand what drives someone before you commit to working with him. And since we're being perfectly honest, do you mind if I ask you a question?"

Tim bristled. He felt like a fool for walking right into it. But fair was fair. "Sure, Victor. Fire away."

"Why did you walk away from the research and the quest for new knowledge, like you did?"

Tim had half expected the question, but that didn't mean he was prepared with an answer. If fair were really fair, their two questions weren't exactly equitable. Comparing their relative weights, measured in degrees of privacy, his question would only require a foot-scale, while Stentz's needed a gravimeter. He sat quietly for a moment, deciding on how much he wanted to share. "Too much, too young," he finally said. "I guess that's the best way to describe it. I was only a kid and ill-equipped with the experience and wisdom that should accompany such intelligence."

Stentz remained pokerfaced as he digested Tim's answer. "Well said, Tim," he finally replied. "But your answer only addresses a challenge you faced, not your rationale for walking away."

Tim returned Stentz's gaze. His blue eyes shimmered, reflecting the light off their surface and rendering it impossible to discern any shapes that may have been lurking in their depths. "I didn't want to set something in motion simply because I could, without the foresight to determine its outcome. Or more directly, Victor, I didn't want to endanger anyone." Pleased with his answer, he relaxed a little. There were a few important omissions, of course, but ultimately, it had come down to that.

"I respect that," Stentz said. He turned and retrieved an envelope from the butler's pantry behind him. "What do you know about cold fusion, Tim?"

Tim pushed his plate back and searched his memory. "First announced by Pons and Fleischmann in 1989," he began. "Using a palladium rod in a transparent tube, they performed electrolysis. From boiling point to vapor, they supposedly achieved energy output four times that of the enthalpy input." He stopped speaking, assuming his answer was sufficient. When Stentz didn't offer a rebuttal, he continued. "Unless something has happened in the past few years, Victor, it's still hotly contested. No one has been able to definitively prove or debunk it."

"What was your initial reaction, when you first heard the announcement?" Stentz asked.

"From a humanitarian perspective, I was hopeful. I mean, a discovery like that, if valid, could ease a lot of suffering around the world. Financial resources used to explore, extract, develop, and pay for current sources of energy could be reallocated to more altruistic causes. Pollution would be all but eliminated. Political tensions would ease. You could go on and on."

"What was your initial reaction from a *scientific* perspective?"

"Like most people, I was skeptical. At first blush, it looked to me like the experimental conditions weren't tightly controlled. The test tube, for example, was open...ostensibly to allow the heat to escape and be measured. Unfortunately, though, any number of elements could have entered the tube by mistake, spiking the reaction."

"Yes, but in the decades that followed, don't you think someone could have reproduced it? God knows enough people have tried."

"Maybe we *can't* reproduce it," Tim said.

"So, you don't believe Pons and Fleischmann's results?"

"I didn't say that. Just because we can't reproduce it doesn't mean it didn't happen." Suddenly, Tim felt something he hadn't experienced in a long time: challenged. He was engaged in a scientific debate with Victor and he was sucking up the mental stimulation like a sponge. "Let me tell you a story, Victor," he said, his voice rising excitedly. "For several years, I've used sports as a tool to rehabilitate traumatized children in Africa. One day, while playing soccer in Sierra Leone, a boy kicked the ball at a goal we'd erected from an aluminum garment rack. The ball hit the upper corner of the piping and sailed over it. It then landed on the roof of my truck, rolled off, bounced once on the ground, and landed right on top of one of the cones. I swear! It came to rest right on top of the cone! Now, I'm confident that no amount of time, money, or sophisticated instrumentation could reproduce that event exactly as it occurred. Maybe a breeze impacted the trajectory of the ball ever so slightly. Maybe it hit the smallest pebble on the ground. Maybe it was a little more humid on that day than normal—"

"Good old chaos theory," Stentz said, interrupting him.

"Yes, in that example, chaos theory would play a big role. Obviously, in scientific research, conditions are controlled much more closely. But, as I already pointed out, the Pons and Fleischmann experiment didn't have the tightest of controls."

Stentz fondled the envelope in his hands. "What if I told you we were able to reproduce the cold fusion effect, predictably and consistently?"

Tim's pulse quickened and he felt his face grow warm. Stentz tossed the envelope onto the table and it skipped over to him on a cushion of trapped air. "You were right, Tim. A trace element did find its way into the test tube," Stentz said. "Take a look."

Tim tore open the envelope and pulled out a stack of papers. He began to pour over the test results on the first page. He felt giddy, like a paleontologist discovering the fossilized remains of a new dinosaur. "This is incredible!"

"It took us six years, but we finally figured it out."

Something in the statement raised a flag with Tim, but he was too preoccupied for it to fully register. "What's this?" he said, pointing to a graphic depicting the atomic structure of an element—balls connected by thin pipes.

"That's it. That's the trace element."

Tim studied it closely.

"Barrettazine," Stentz said. "Undiscovered until fifteen years ago, when our research team proved its existence. Michael Barrett out of Stanford was the lead scientist." Stentz's statement clarified

Tim's confusion with the graphic and brought back the earlier flag.

"Wait a minute. You solved this thing *fifteen years* ago?"

"That's right," Stentz replied.

"Why hasn't it been made public?" Tim gawked. He stared at the man whose intelligence he had obviously underestimated. Stentz merely smiled back at him. The wheels in Tim's head churned, as he tried to catch up. Suddenly, it hit him. "It's not commercially viable, is it? This new element is too rare, and you haven't been able to reproduce it synthetically!"

Stentz kept smiling.

"And your voyage to Mars isn't for pure exploration either, is it? No way you could have rallied that kind of congressional funding only to further our knowledge of the solar system. It's a mining junket, isn't it? We're up there for the express purpose of mining this new element!"

"Bravo, Mr. Redmond." Stentz clapped his hands and laughed. "You see. Aren't you glad you stuck around?"

A mixture of emotions swirled through Tim. On the one hand, he was glad he had stuck around. This revelation was almost worth the price of admission, which he had already paid in spades. On the other hand, he was still confused. "So…what's the problem, Victor?"

Stentz pointed toward the papers in Tim's hand. "There's more."

Tim leafed through the rest of the documents: more results from the cold fusion testing, relative power outputs, estimated volume of Barrettazine to be mined by the Santa Maria on Mars and designs of power plants. Then, he came upon a seismic survey graphic showing a layer of brown, followed by a shade of pink, and, finally, a band of neon—the target element Barrettazine. Below the green, within another layer of brown, an obscure image had been circled with a red pen. Tim brought it closer to his eyes, to get a better look at it. The realization of what it was crept up on him slowly and then pounced. "No *way!*" he blurted.

Stentz nodded. "Kind of ironic, isn't it? Using the simple advancement of human knowledge as a front for a more pragmatic purpose, only to come full circle."

Tim flipped the page. A larger, clearer version of the image stared back at him. He saw thin, delicate bones separated by joints—five digits and a palm. It was a hand, remarkably similar to that of a human being.

"We're doing our best to multi-task," Stentz said. "Obviously, we still need to mine the Barrettazine, but it's not every day that we stumble upon the buried remains of an alien civilization!"

Tim couldn't believe what he was hearing. Not just a single skeleton, but an entire civilization!

"We've already excavated parts of a city, and we're trying to gather as much information as possible." Stentz leaned forward. "But...here's the rub, Tim," he said in a low voice. "As best we can determine, they all perished at once. Every last one of them died where they stood. Walking along one minute and dead the next. Simultaneously. All of them! We haven't been able to link any impact craters to that period. There is no apparent damage to the buildings or skeletons, except for decay, of course. Dosimetry analysis shows no excessive radioactive deposits in the bones to suggest a massive solar burst. If it were a virus, the beings wouldn't have been outside, going about their daily lives. The majority would have been holed up inside. Plus, they wouldn't have all dropped dead at the exact same moment. We're at a complete loss!" Stentz threw up his hands.

A sharp pain shot through Tim's head, causing him to wince. Stentz was so caught up in the Martian mystery that he didn't seem to notice. He kept on talking.

"And then, only weeks following our discovery, this Armando Chissani breaks onto the scene, talking about Mars. He was ranting about how it's going to happen to us too soon!" Stentz's normally tanned face turned pale. "I'm not quite ready to shave my head and join Chissani's cult, Tim, but you have to admit it's a little spooky." He collected himself and leaned back in his chair. "So, there you have it. That's why I asked you to stick around.

I've assembled a small but competent think-tank to sort it all out and I'd like you to join us."

Tim fought to remain conscious. If he didn't know better, he would swear he was having an aneurysm. It was amazing that he'd heard any of Stentz's comments through the searing pain in his head. He suddenly remembered the Instant Messenger session from earlier that morning: *If you help solve the Martian mystery, I will help you solve yours.* Had it been Stentz on the other end of that exchange? He had known exactly where Tim was, right down to the room number. The man was also extremely intelligent, had considerable government resources at his disposal, and he was determined to have Tim join his team. But how had he known the rest? How had he found out about the quotation? *Suppose I found a watch on the ground. The mechanism being observed, the inference we think is inevitable that the watch must have a maker.*

It didn't matter. It was all beginning to synthesize. Tim had tried to push it away by burying his head in the sand. It was obvious to him now that remaining in the dark was an impossibility. The switch was going to be thrown, with or without his participation, and he would just as soon know what was lurking in the room before the lights came on. "I'm in," he said.

CHAPTER 11

Tim followed Stentz up the stairway to the east entrance of the Pentagon. When they reached the top, he turned to scan the scene behind them. His first reaction was one of relief—relief that a staff car had picked them up at the airport and dropped them off directly in front of the building. Had they driven themselves, they would have had a long walk ahead of them. The parking lot was massive.

Beyond the far edge of the parking lot, he saw a steady stream of cars on Route One. Out past the four-lane highway, the dark waters of the Potomac River divided the state of Virginia from the District of Columbia where the Lincoln Memorial rose up against the blue sky in the distance.

"Come on, Tim!" Stentz yelled back at him, like a father prodding his son. The two walked across a concrete sidewalk to the Pentagon's entrance. Just before reaching the door, Stentz pulled out a photo ID card and handed it to Tim. "You're going to need this," he said.

Tim looked at it, once again surprised by Stentz's efficiency. The photo was the same as the one on his passport, probably pulled from a government database somewhere. That still didn't account for the speed with which the ID had matriculated through the security clearance process. No doubt, Stentz had started that ball rolling as soon as he learned that Tim was being snatched from Africa.

Stentz inserted his card into a turnstile and waited for the light to turn green. When it did, he walked through, stopping to wait for Tim. Tim inserted his card, but the light stayed red. The guard standing at the end of the row of turnstiles began to take more interest. He quickly removed the card, flipped it over, and tried again. This time the light turned green. He joined Stentz and the two strode down a long, wide corridor. It was only 9:30 in the morning, but the halls were already bustling with young, fit bodies packaged neatly into pressed uniforms. They were serious, but courteous, and the assembly moved along fluidly. Those on the inside of the hall traveled one way, and those on the outside another. There were no rogue pedestrians weaving through traffic here. The young gave way to statesmen, and nodded respectfully as they passed.

Tim followed Stentz down several more walkways, until they came upon one that was devoid of any traffic. They stopped at a plain black door. Stentz slid his access card through the electronic keypad next to it and typed in a code. A lock clicked loudly and Stentz opened the door. "You have to be accompanied to get in here," he said. "Your badge won't work," Stentz said as he opened the door.

Tim stepped into a narrow passageway. A quick motion caught his attention and his head snapped left to identify it. Twenty feet inside the doorway, a guard in fatigues stood erect, his hand resting on the butt of his holstered pistol.

"It's all right sergeant!" Stentz said. "He's with me." He strode to the guard station and signed in. Then he pressed a button for the elevator. He glanced over at Tim and offered a one-word apology for the excessive security: "Bauer." The elevator doors opened and he waved Tim inside.

As they descended, Tim reviewed the information Stentz had given him in the staff car on the way over. He was getting to the party late, and he was expected to come up to speed quickly. A Martian city belonging to a civilization that thrived 300 million years ago had been discovered south of the Ius Chasma, where the canyons reached depths of over three miles. After ten thousand years of existence, all life within the city had ceased to exist in the course of a single day. The think-tank members were still completely baffled. The crew of the Santa Maria had unearthed a host of skeletons. The beings were short in stature, standing, on average, only three feet high. Their skulls suggested they had a brain comparable to the size of a human being's. They had two arms, two legs, and five digits on each hand and foot. These remarkable similarities had prompted a great deal of speculation among the think-tank members as to whether mankind had descended from this race. Unfortunately, the fossils were far too old to render any DNA samples, but the theory was being explored through other means.

As these facts bounced around in Tim's mind, he came to the realization that the elevator was still descending. He wondered how deep this particular facility was, and whether or not it was part of the Pentagon's original construction or added later. The thought of some advanced civilization stumbling upon the buried ruins of the Pentagon, 300 million years hence, popped into his head. Would they be impressed by its sheer size? Would they be able to determine its function? If so, what would they conclude about the present civilization, given the fact that the Pentagon was so large?

The elevator finally stopped and the doors opened. Tim stepped out and stood stunned. He was staring out at a huge mission control center. The entire far wall was comprised of a set of giant video screens. The center one was as large as an Imax movie screen. It showed a computer-generated image of Mars from orbit. A white star stood out clearly, just north of the equator. He thought it must represent the Santa Maria, which was currently on the sunny side of the planet. Curved yellow lines originated from both poles and met at the equator. To the right of the lines, negative numbers counted down in increments of one. He guessed they were the hours before sunset. The "zero line" straddled shade and light on the far left side of the planet.

"Tim!" Stentz called to him for the second time. Tim pulled himself away from the control center and followed him down a dark hallway. They passed a number of doors before Stentz finally stopped and inserted his access card. He opened it and waved Tim inside. "No more guards, I promise," he whispered. The room was dark, except for the light coming from an overhead projector. A man stood next to a screen, pointing to an image. Stentz grabbed Tim's arm and directed him to a chair at the near end of a long table.

"What was the radius again?" a voice with an Indian accent interrupted the presenter.

"Two point six miles," the man at the screen said.

Tim got a good look at the image for the first time. It was an aerial view of the Martian city, with the Santa Maria clearly visible in the lower left-hand corner of the screen. This confirmed that a satellite was, indeed, circling the planet. He saw a small black dot superimposed in the middle of the image. A thin black line wound around it, at a radius of two point six miles, he surmised. He could see what looked like excavated buildings at random locations within the circle.

"And nothing outside that radius...not even a single skeleton?" The woman's voice was clear and absent any accent, at least from an American's perspective.

"Correct. So far, we've found nothing outside that circle," the presenter said. "But remember, we haven't had a lot of time to excavate."

"Any signs of a wall?" a man asked. His accent could have been from any number of Eastern bloc countries.

"Sorry, no signs of a wall," the presenter said.

"How about soil samples inside the circle versus those outside it? Any differences to speak of, particularly in the form of radons?" Tim asked. Everyone in the room turned to stare at him, including Stentz.

The presenter stood mute. He glanced over at Stentz for guidance, and received a nod.

"No. No difference in the soil," the presenter said. "But a good question." He peered out at the rest of the think-tank members. "Any more questions?" When none came, he shrugged. "Okay then, that's the latest. You've got the briefing packets in front of you. If you have more questions later, you know where to find me. If not, I'll be updating you again in twenty-four hours." He pressed a button on the remote control device and the overhead lights came on. As he headed for the exit, the stocky man nodded politely at Stentz. Once he closed the door behind him, all eyes fell to Tim.

Stentz rose from his chair and placed his hand on Tim's shoulder. "I'd like to introduce the newest addition to our team...Tim Redmond." Four sets of eyes assessed him. Tim felt like the new kid in school again—a trying experience he had endured many times as he continued to skip grades.

Stentz pointed to his right. "Tim, this is Pranab Shah. Pranab received his M.D. from Johns Hopkins. He is our go-to guy with regard to the human body, particularly as it pertains to diseases. Pranab has spent the last ten years at the Centers for Disease Control, documenting new strains of viruses and researching their effects on the body. Since we obviously have no better information on the Martians, we're using the closest approximation we can find—which is us."

Shah nodded.

Tim had to suppress a smile. Actually hearing the word "Martians" reminded him of the old B-movies his father had enjoyed so much. It was surreal to hear the term being used seriously, by one of NASA's leading scientists. He'd have to get used to it. This was as real as it got.

Stentz moved down the line. "Next we have Doctor Edgar Kirovsky, the principal physicist for the MIR space station, back when the Russians were spending money on their space program. Five years ago, he had the foresight to come our way and take a lead role in the design of the Santa Maria. I'm happy to say I was the one who recruited him. In addition to knowing everything there is to know about the Santa Maria, Edgar has extensive knowledge of Mars, astrophysics, the origins of our solar system, and just about anything space related."

Like Shah, Kirovsky simply nodded.

Stentz continued. "Doctor Bonnie Hollingstead is our resident expert on paleontology and sociology. She is the director of the Smithsonian Institution's center for advanced primate studies. She's also written over a dozen books on social dynamics among both ancient and modern civilizations, and she sits on the board of a number of universities in that capacity."

"Hello, and welcome," Hollingstead said.

"Thank you," Tim responded, grateful for at least one warm reception. He wondered how old she was. Given her impressive resume, she had to be in her late thirties. Looking at her smooth, attractive face and fit body, however, he would have guessed late twenties.

"Finally, we have Doctor Martin Bleakney, our geologist and archeologist. Martin developed most of the seismic equipment we're using on Mars to locate the Barrettazine. He knows a hell of a lot about rocks and how to extrapolate clues from them. It's also our good fortune that one of Martin's other passions is archeology. He was one of the only foreign archeologists invited to work with the team in Greece excavating the find at Akritori on Santorini."

Bleakney offered Tim a nervous smile and a wave of his hand.

Tim surveyed the group. He was excited, terrified, and self-conscious all at the same time. He began to second-guess the wisdom of joining such a distinguished team. He felt entirely inadequate: what if his so-called "gifts" were gone for good? He'd be exposed immediately, and branded a simpleton by the geniuses surrounding him. Would that be the worst thing in the world, though? After making an ass of himself, Stentz would probably cut him loose. Tim could then return to Africa and write the whole thing off as a bad dream. He could throw himself back into his work with the children, embrace the things he could control, and seal out the things he couldn't. *Tick. Tock. The watch has a maker.* Tim shuddered.

"Tim?" Stentz repeated.

"What?" Tim shook free of the chilling introspection. He saw that Stentz was staring at him, a little miffed. He glanced around the table and saw that the other think-tank members were all staring at him, too.

"I asked if you had any questions," Stentz said.

"No. No I don't."

Stentz nodded and turned to address the rest of the group. "Okay, I'll see you all back here in three hours."

The other four team members rose up from their seats, grabbed the red-covered briefing booklets, and headed for the door. As they passed by Tim, he could feel their eyes stealing a final curious glance. He caught Bleakney staring at him quite openly, but the Englishman merely nodded and diverted his eyes. Kirovsky's gaze was more direct. The Russian did not divert his eyes, but rather locked him up in a cold stare. Tim didn't know whether to write it off as a lack of social graces, or as posturing for dominance. Either way, he didn't like it.

"Come on, Tim. I'll show you to your work area," Stentz said, heading for the door.

Tim followed him down the hallway, away from the mission control area. They passed several more doors before reaching one without a security access pad. Stentz turned the handle and headed inside. The room was small and utilitarian. A desk contained a computer hooked up to a printer. A phone rested next to the keyboard. Two dozen books and binders were wedged between aluminum bookends on a shelf above the computer. Several of the books had red covers. A cork-board occupied the far wall. Its surface was barely visible through the pictures and letters that used to adorn his tent in Africa. Beneath the cork-board was his old cot, flush with the wall. Stentz had thought of everything.

"You have a room at The Latham Hotel in Georgetown, just across the river," Stentz said. "I encourage you to stay there in the evenings. It helps to get out and blow off some steam…stimulates the brain. Sometimes, when things are really flowing, though, we stay here. We all have a bed in our office. We could get you one with a real box spring and mattress, if you'd like."

Tim shook his head. He'd hardly slept the past two nights at the Ritz in New York. He was actually looking forward to sleeping on the cot.

"That's what I thought," Stentz said. He pointed to the desk. "You've got access to NASA Operations Research on Mars—otherwise known as NORM—on the desktop. If you have any trouble navigating NORM, or querying data from its various databases, let me know. You also have access to the Internet. But Tim, if I haven't stressed this enough already, secrecy is paramount. I don't want you to feel like a prisoner, but no emails to anyone are allowed, and no calls either. That goes for outside these walls as well. You're more than free to socialize with anyone you want, but you can't discuss anything related to this project. If you find a source for important information on the Internet—like an expert within a certain field, for example—let me know. I'll do my best to find someone comparable within our network. If we don't have those kinds of skills in-house, which I highly doubt, I'll do my best to bring someone in from the outside. In those binders you'll find all the previous briefing packets, and a host of background information on the Mars expedition."

Tim nodded.

"Okay, I guess I'll leave you to it." Stentz headed for the door. He stopped short of it and turned around. "In case you missed it, the morning's question is…why are the Martian buildings restricted to a perfect circle. You've got three hours to mull it over. We'll meet back in the group room at one fifteen sharp." He pulled the door open and stepped out into the hallway.

"Victor," Tim said, prompting Stentz to turn around. "A question came to me in the conference room, but I didn't want to ask it in front of everyone else."

Stentz looked pleasantly surprised. "Ask away, by all means! I'm glad you were listening."

"How was the landing site selected?"

"What?" Stentz appeared to be caught off guard.

Tim asked more directly. "Out of the entire planet's surface area—roughly 31 million square miles—how was the Santa Maria's landing site selected? I mean, how is it possible that the ship just happened to land on the one spot that used to be inhabited?"

"Sounds like two questions to me, Tim." Stentz flashed another one of his infectious smiles. "The answer to your first question is easy to figure out. Just poke through NORM. I'm sure you'll find it," Stentz said, pointing to the computer on the desk. "As for your second question, I don't have a clue. But that's why you're here…to answer what I cannot."

CHAPTER 12

Tim reviewed the printed files from the database query. Stentz was right about a couple of things. NORM did contain a wealth of information. It had taken him some time to identify all the available databases and to determine the type of information contained within each, but after that, he'd made pretty quick work of it. In front of him now was a listing of all Mars missions, dating back to 1964, when the Mariner 4 became the first spacecraft to successfully orbit the planet. He quickly flipped past all missions pre-dating the discovery of Barrettazine in 1995.

The next mission he came to was the Mars Global Surveyor (MGS), which was launched on November 7, 1996—eighteen months following the discovery of Barrettazine on earth. MGS was the first successful mission to Mars in two decades, following the Viking 2, in September of 1975. MGS achieved orbit around Mars on September 12, 1997. Instruments aboard included a high-resolution camera, thermal emission spectrometer, laser altimeter, magnetometer/electron reflectometer, ultra-stable oscillator and radio relay station. MGS had orbited the planet, performing extensive mapping of its surface. Tim was sure it had also done some preliminary Barrettazine prospecting from orbit, although any reference to Barrettazine was nowhere to be found in the public documents touting the mission's success.

The Mars Pathfinder was launched on December 4, 1996, and it landed on Mars July 4 of 1997. Independence Day. How nice, Tim thought. Independence from Middle Eastern oil reserves? Pathfinder had two payloads: instrumentation aboard the Pathfinder itself, as well as on the Rover surface vehicle it was carrying. Pathfinder instrumentation included an imager, magnets for measuring the magnetic properties of the soil, wind socks, atmospheric structure instruments and a meteorology package. The Rover surface vehicle instrumentation included three cameras and an alpha proton x-ray spectrometer—perfect for analyzing deep sub-surface mineral deposits.

Tim continued to leaf through the printed pages until he came upon two of NASA's most embarrassing foibles: the Mars Climate Orbiter in 1998 and the Mars Polar Lander in 1999. Both were lost on arrival to Mars. He wondered what the failures had cost Stentz and his team in the form of political capital, lost data, and time. He turned the page. The next mission was the Mars Odyssey orbiter, launched on April 7 of 2001. It was another ambitious and costly endeavor soon after the two other failures. Usually, the brakes were put on NASA spending following costly failures, at least for a while. Not in this case, however. To the contrary, funding for Mars missions actually *increased*.

To an outsider at the time, the obvious question had to be, why in the world was Congress stepping up its financial backing for NASA? It had to be baffling. To an insider, however, it was all too obvious. While the American public had been shouting, "Let's find out if there's water on Mars," Congress had probably been shouting, "Let's find those Barrettazine deposits!"

He went on to review the instrument package for the Odyssey spacecraft: a thermal emission imaging system and a gamma ray spectrometer for a Mars radiation environment experiment. All of these instruments were perfectly suited for satellite-based mineralogical analysis. And that was the beauty of the project. It was the genius behind the "pure exploration" theme that Stentz had branded within NASA. All of the tests being conducted and all of the accompanying instrumentation on the spacecraft were exactly what would be expected of an exploratory mission. No one would have batted an eye. Analyzing a planet's basic mineralogical makeup—both crust and sub-surface layers—was one of the first steps in planetary exploration. Why shouldn't they send up a host of spectrometers and imagers? It was just that the frequency and cost of the missions were reminiscent of an age long gone, a time when two superpowers were battling on the field of not-so-friendly strife…space; an age when being second was tantamount to abject failure. Where was the lever now? Where was the pressure to fund such ambitious exploration, now that the space-race with Russia was over? The answer was that it had become a race for energy, of course. The growing political instability in the Middle East and the pressure to find an alternative energy source had forced the U.S. to invest in the Martian expeditions. Barrettazine was the solution to many of America's problems, and timetables for Mars exploration had been moved up. It was so obvious now, Tim thought, but then, things are so much clearer in retrospect, aren't they?

Tim turned the page. The next two missions involved the Mars Exploration Rovers Spirit and Opportunity, both in 2003. The hunt had intensified. Two spacecraft had been launched within weeks of each other, and Tim surmised that the construction of the Santa Maria was probably already underway. It wasn't a question of whether or not the Barrettazine existed on Mars in sufficient quantities, but rather, where were the most accessible deposits located. The instrument packages for the two craft included an energetic neutral atoms analyzer, a geochemical lander, a high/super resolution stereo color imager, a subsurface sounding radar/altimeter, an infrared mineralogical mapping spectrometer, a planetary Fourier spectrometer, a Mossbauer spectrometer, and an alpha particle x-ray spectrometer. By God, they were going to find the right place to dig, no two ways about it. And therein was the answer to the question he had asked Stentz. The landing spot for the Santa Maria had been thought out in excruciating detail. It wasn't some haphazard decision, and it wasn't based upon orbital windows or accessible, debris-free landing plains. It was all about the Barrettazine. They had landed at the site of the largest Barrettazine deposit they could find!

Tim leaned back in his chair and took a deep breath. He was glad he'd taken the time to understand the history of the missions…and the logic behind them. He had clearly set himself up to answer the bigger question of why the Martian civilization had been concentrated in such a tight and almost perfect circle.

Determined to solve that mystery before the think-tank met again, Tim squared himself to the keyboard and started to bang away.

"Okay, NORM. Where's your not-so-public information?" he said to the screen.

Thirty minutes later, Tim tucked a stack of printouts under his arm and headed for the conference room. He almost collided with Bleakney, who had just emerged from his own temporary domicile. "Sorry," Tim said.

"Cozy as a B&B isn't it?" Bleakney sputtered, gesturing toward his room. "Pool's down the hall and to the right." The Englishman gave a short, suppressed laugh, like a man who had learned to keep his quirky humor to himself.

"Across from the sniper range. Yeah, I saw it when I came in," Tim quipped.

Bleakney looked up from the ground, deadpan. "No, that's the chemical weapons workshop. The sniper range is dead ahead." The Brit's eyes twinkled.

The two men walked into the conference room laughing. The three other members were already seated. So was Stentz. Like a couple of drunk sailors stumbling into a court-martial hearing, both Tim and Bleakney sobered up and found their places at the table.

"Okay, I think we started with Dr. Shah last time." Stentz followed the seats around clockwise. "Which means it's Dr. Bleakney's turn to open the discussion."

Bleakney shuffled through his papers. After several seconds, he located the sheet he was looking for and began his dissertation.

"Well, I looked back at the elemental breakdown of the soil within the inhabited area, to see if there were—"

"Actually," Kirovsky said, cutting him off. "If we stick to the procedure and continue clockwise, it would be Mr. Redmond's turn to initiate the discussion."

Tim frowned. Obviously, Kirovsky didn't accept newcomers gracefully. It wasn't that he was unprepared to discuss his theory. It was simply that he was unaccustomed to having someone come at him so directly. Stentz sensed his unease and stepped in. "Given the fact that Mr. Redmond is joining us late, Edgar, I thought we'd let him experience a couple go-rounds first."

Kirovsky raised his hand as an apology. His lugubrious expression was over the top. Despite Kirovsky's body language, Tim knew he was enjoying every second of the conflict, especially the part where he had remained silent and allowed Stentz to rescue him.

"—any difference from the uninhabited area that we missed before." Bleakney finished the remainder of his opening sentence in an attempt to ease the tension in the room.

"Hold on a second, Martin," Tim said, before Bleakney could continue. "I'm sorry for interrupting. It's extremely rude of me." Tim wasn't brazen enough to look Kirovsky in the eye when he said it, but he thought the verbal insult had hit the mark. "Perhaps Dr. Kirovsky is right. You've been brainstorming with closed presentation, followed by open discussion. Correct?"

"Correct," Shah said.

"Timing on opening presentation?"

"Ten minutes!" Hollingstead said.

"Great," Tim said. He stood up and headed to the white board at the front of the room. He pointed to his watch. "Victor, do you mind?"

"My pleasure," Stentz said as he depressed the button on his tachometer.

"Question," Tim began. "Why would a civilization restrict itself to an almost perfect circular area measuring only five miles in diameter?" He drew a large circle on the white board. "But, before we even get to that question, I have a more interesting one. How does the first manned spacecraft to Mars happen to land on the only twenty-one square miles that used to be inhabited? I mean, what are the odds?" He brought his marker back up to the white board and drew two parallel lines across the circle, one a fifth of the way down from its northern pole, and the other a fifth of the way up from its southern pole. Then he turned to face the think-tank members.

"Let's just assume that, like Earth's northern and southern poles, the two Martian poles were not the most hospitable to life.

Given the planet's distance from the sun, its obliquity, and extremely elliptical orbit, my guess is its poles were ice-capped, even 300 million years ago." He blackened out the area of the circle above the northern line and below the southern one.

"So...excluding the poles, let's say that the middle three-fifths of the planet was inhabitable. How many square miles would that leave?"

Bleakney whipped out his calculator and began typing in some figures. Before he could complete the calculation, Tim sounded off again. "Roughly thirty-one million square miles. Thirty-one million square miles of inhabitable surface area, and the Santa Maria happens to land smack dab in the middle of the only city on the planet! What are the odds of that happening?"

Bleakney once again began to punch the numbers on his calculator, and once again Tim was too quick with the answer. "One-and-a-half million to one!" Tim boomed. He glanced over at Stentz, who remained the picture of equanimity. Tim caught Kirovsky out of the corner of his eye. The Russian was pointing an accusatory finger at his diagram and was about to speak. Tim cut him off. "Some of you might have questions about my assumptions." He took a peek at his watch. "But since I still have seven minutes left let me try to anticipate and answer those questions. In the process, I'll circle back and attempt to answer the original question of why the Martian civilization was restricted to such a tight area."

He paced in front of the white board. He felt good. His headache had been reduced to a dull throb in the back of his skull and was hardly noticeable; his mind was too occupied with the flurry of ideas popping into his head. "Assumption number one," he began. "This civilization was indigenous to Mars. It didn't arrive on the planet in some massive circular spacecraft and then continue to flourish for thousands of years. From what I've gathered from past briefing packets, excavations so far have revealed no evidence of any spacecraft. Besides, at the time of their demise, the Martian technology was comparable to mankind's in the tenth century."

He paused and waited for pushback from the others. He got none. "Assumption number two. The city that the crew of the Santa Maria discovered was the only one on the planet." Tim stood with hands outstretched, eyebrows raised, inviting protest. Despite the fact that everyone was respecting the mandatory quiet period, he could sense their unrest. He dropped his hands to his sides. "Okay, I don't buy that either. I think there were more cities...272 more, to be exact."

Kirovsky grunted. Bleakney chuckled.

Tim continued. "So, if the 272 other cities are all circular—and I believe they are—and they are all the same size—which I don't believe, but we'll assume for the sake of simplicity—that would make the odds of landing upon any city at random 5,500 to 1. Quite a long shot, I think you will all agree." Tim saw Stentz hold up two fingers, letting him know he had as many minutes to wrap up his opening.

"Assumption number three," he said. "No one on the mission control team knew that the planet had ever been inhabited. Meaning that stumbling upon the ruins of one of the cities was truly by chance." He glanced over at Stentz again. The man remained a closed book. "Like the second assumption, I simply don't believe it was by pure chance that the Santa Maria landed on the site of ruins." Tim surreptitiously glanced at Stentz again. This time he raised his eyebrows in surprise. "However, I also don't believe anyone on the mission control team knew about the ruins either."

No one in the room made a sound. Tim peered at each of the think-tank members and decided they were trying to make sense of the two opposing statements. How could the discovery of the ruins not be by chance if no one knew about them? Tim let them chew on the question for a while longer.

"There was actually a one-hundred percent chance that the Santa Maria crew would discover Martian ruins, regardless of the chosen landing site!" Kirovsky said, breaking the silence.

Tim looked down at his watch. He saw that his time had, indeed, expired. He looked back up at the Russian. "Very good, Doctor. And why is that?"

"The prospecting efforts conducted by the previous missions identified 273 deposits of Barrettazine on Mars. It was a guarantee that the Santa Maria was going to land on one them, for the purpose of mining the mineral. And, like us, the Martians had found some use for the Barrettazine, too. In fact, so important was this use that they restricted their cities to locations that contained large deposits of it."

Tim nodded at Kirovsky respectfully. Stentz began to jot down some notes into his portfolio.

"But what use did they have for the mineral, and why were the cities circular?" Hollingstead asked.

"My guess is they were using the Barrettazine for energy," Kirovsky said. "I think we'll find the makings of some kind of generator beneath the city. If they leveraged a single generator whose power output was restricted to a certain distance, then a circle would make perfect sense. The outer ring of the city would fall uniformly within the limit of that power output radius."

Stentz peered at Tim. "Your same conclusion?"

Tim nodded his head. Not in agreement with Kirovsky's theory, but rather to signify he was thinking about it. "It's a decent theory," he finally said. "Definitely worth investigating."

"But?" Stentz pressed for a more conclusive response.

Tim frowned. "Well," he said. "I just don't think the Martians knew the Barrettazine was there. Consequently, I don't think they were using it as some energy source, or even mining it for some other purpose."

"What are you talking about?" Kirovsky exploded. "You just spent ten minutes establishing your hypothesis that the Martians found some use for the Barrettazine and consequently migrated toward its deposits! Now you're saying they *didn't*?"

"*You* said the Martians had found some use for it," Tim said, correcting him. "I think it went beyond useful. I believe they needed it to *survive*."

"But...they had no idea it was there?" Stentz repeated Tim's earlier supposition.

"Correct," Tim said.

"Okay, I'll admit it. I'm confused," Hollingstead said.

"So am I," Tim said, grinning.

Kirovsky threw up his hands in disgust.

"What do you need, Tim?" Stentz asked.

"More time and access to more information."

"Fine," Stentz said. "After we're done here, let me know what you're not getting from NORM. In the meantime, we're going to investigate Dr. Kirovsky's theory about a subsurface energy source or mining network."

CHAPTER 13

Kathy finished the initialization sequence and pressed the ENTER key to begin another run. A low rumble rose up from the bottom of the unit like distant thunder, but soon settled into a constant hum. At the higher frequency, the hum of the seismometer was drowned out by the whining of the Dredge, the Santa Maria's mining vehicle. She looked up from the computer screen toward the location of the Dredge, about a quarter of a mile south of her current location. Although the machine was well beneath the surface, she envisioned the huge circular rotor ripping through the planet's crust en route to the Barrettazine shelf two hundred feet below. As vivid as the image appeared in her mind's eye, it didn't compare to the one available to her physical one. Against the flat, dull light of the horizon, a steady stream of rock and dirt was being ejected forty feet into the air by the Dredge's powerful exhaust vacuum. The droning of the rotor rose an octave. It probably encountered an iron deposit, Kathy guessed. Her suspicions were confirmed as the red plume of dirt suddenly turned dark charcoal. She watched as the ferrous material shot into the sky and came to rest on a growing mountain of soil. Judging from the size of the hill, Kathy guessed the Dredge was about a hundred feet below the surface well past the ruins. That would mean a number of Martian skeletons were probably already buried in the debris.

Kathy scanned the horizon. It looked like a black and white lithograph was taped to the inside of her visor, except the blacks were really more like reddish browns. The sunlight was harsh and made the rocks on the planet's surface stand out from the soil with disturbing clarity. Even the line marking the horizon was laser sharp against the flat, colorless sky.

Standing at what used to be the center of a large city, Kathy pictured it in all its glory. She imagined a blue sky, the product of a once oxygen rich atmosphere, and terra cotta-colored buildings jutting up from the flat plain three stories high. She pictured hundreds of the diminutive beings walking down narrow streets while shopping for food or clothing, and their children running and laughing. She pictured outdoor cafés, with the beings sitting at tables, enjoying a midday meal...the sun warming their faces, as they watched the children playing in the street...the sound of their laughter.

And then, suddenly, it all ended. Every single one of them died where they sat, where they walked, where they ran and played.

She shuddered. She was standing on the very spot where a cataclysmic event had occurred...a tragedy whose magnitude was only surpassed by its mystery. "What happened to you?" she whispered. Sixty feet beneath her, there was likely the skeleton of a young woman much like herself. Maybe she'd been a mother watching her child play in the street when the end had come. Had it been over in an instant? Had the woman the time to feel sad or wonder where her child was? Had she the time to run over and embrace him? To comfort him in his pain, even as she herself struggled through it?

She felt a wave of nausea. Without a child herself, she could only begin to imagine the maternal bond. She'd seen evidence of it, though, between her sister and nephew. Jane would sit in a rocker with Nicholas in her lap, stroking his sandy brown hair while reading him a story, until he fell asleep. She would lift his limp body, gently lay him in his crib, and kiss him on the forehead. As she gazed out across the dry plain, Kathy pictured Jane cradling Nicholas in her lap in the middle of a hard, cold street. She pictured Nicholas writhing in pain and crying out for his mother to help him. She pictured Jane sobbing and confused, unable to help her dying son in any way.

A shrill beep from the seismometer signaled the end of its run. Mercifully, it yanked Kathy from the horrific nightmare. She peered at the computer screen and was shocked to see that the image was blurry. She adjusted the settings, all the while praying it wasn't the beginning of a serious malfunction. The picture cleared up for a second, but became blurry again. Kathy blinked. Suddenly, she realized that her tears were the source of the problem. She shut her lids firmly to stop the flow; the few remaining drops fell to her cheeks. Once composed, she opened her eyes and focused on the colorful output from the monitor. She examined the soil signature ranging from a depth of 240 feet, which was slightly below the Barrettazine shelf, up to a depth of 200 feet, a little above the Barrettazine shelf. If there were a generator or mining tunnels, they would be visible within that area. She studied the graphic closely. Magnesium, silicon, iron and Barrettazine were all clearly visible, but she saw no sign of tunnels, and certainly no generator of any kind.

She shook her head in frustration. It had been a long day, with no positive results. Earlier that morning, she'd driven twenty miles to the south to do some seismographic work in the upper Solis Planum, at the site of another Barrettazine deposit. She'd found the Barrettazine all right, but that was it. For three hours she combed the site, taking readings from a variety of depths and locations. Not only had she failed to find any evidence of mining tunnels or a generator, she hadn't found a single skeleton or any evidence of ruins either. Now, after coming back to the original target area, she'd already completed four runs. She had started at the center of the city—or as close to it as they could determine—and spiraled outward, like the circular lines of an old fashioned lollipop. And despite the fact that the think-tank's hypothesis made sense, she had found no evidence of mining tunnels or a generator. She hoped that Vivicheck, who'd been sent fifty miles west to the site of yet another Barrettazine deposit, was having better luck.

She shrugged. They were playing a guessing game. Employing the scientific method, she corrected herself. Gather clues, interpret them, postulate a theory, test the theory, and interpret the results. If your first theory doesn't work out, start over again from step one, hopefully a little wiser, but back to step one nonetheless.

As she initiated the unit's shutdown sequence, she couldn't shake the horrific thought of her sister and nephew caught in the Martian cataclysm. *Sixty feet below you right now is the skeleton of a woman, just like you. Was she walking to work? Was she shopping? Was she a mother? Did she get a chance to hold her dying child one last time?* She shook it off, and focused on the shutdown sequence. She typed in another command. Like the name of a song on the tip of her tongue, the question hounded her. *Did she get a chance to hold her dying child one last time?* Kathy fought off the urge to run another scan at sixty feet, the depth of the ruins. She was in a profession that called for logic, not hunches. If she wanted to be in the business of chasing hunches, she might as well have remained a teacher's assistant, chasing dinosaur bones in Montana. This was worse than a hunch, though. A hunch was a feeling you followed to prove out a theory, or to find an elusive treasure. This had nothing to do with either. It was simple curiosity. Besides, what were the odds that there would be the skeleton of a mother cradling her child down there? And if there were, would it make her feel any better, or simply worse? *Did she get a chance to hold her dying child one last time?* "Screw it!" She depressed the control-pause buttons on the keyboard. As soon as she did, she felt like an idiot. The cursor on the screen sat flashing, waiting for a command. What the hell was she doing? She typed in a few commands and waited patiently for the unit to cycle back to ready status. Each second was a struggle against her pride of discipline, which prodded her to shut down and move on to the next site, as she'd been instructed. The voice in the back of her mind, however, was stronger.

Finally, a beep signaled that the unit was ready for another run. She adjusted the upper bounds of the search depth to fifty feet and pressed the ENTER key. The unit hummed and two minutes later, the run had been completed. The graphical image began to slowly paint the screen. The familiar color of magnesium oxide and silicon dioxide, which comprised over eighty percent of the planet's crust, dominated the screen. The image continued to build, layer by layer, fifty feet...fifty-two feet...fifty-five feet. As it reached sixty feet, Kathy's heart began to race. *Did she get a chance to hold her dying child one last time?* She leaned toward the monitor. Sharper, dark lines broke up the monochromatic image of the magnesium layer. She fingered a ball to the right of the keyboard and watched an arrow appear on the screen. While depressing the shift key, she dragged the arrow across the dark area on the left-hand side of the screen. A box framed by dashed lines appeared. She typed in a few more commands. The image enlarged. It was definitely a Martian skeleton. Kathy's heart rate accelerated.

Just beyond the skeleton's outstretched fingers, she saw something small and round. A child's skull? A line—its spine?—ran from the middle of the circle to outside the boundary of the image. She followed a wider line to the Martian's arm. It seemed to be connected to something around its wrist. Unable to decipher the object, she pressed a button on the keyboard to save the image for later printing, and then hit the ESCAPE key. The image on the monitor cycled back to the full-sized version of the run. It was now fully complete.

Kathy stared at the screen for a full minute. Once again, she wondered if her equipment were faulty. The color stopped roughly three-quarters of the way down the screen. The lower fourth was completely black. In the interest of time, she had only adjusted the upper boundary of the focus depth. She hadn't adjusted the lower range of the search from her earlier runs. The screen should be showing an image between the depths of fifty feet to ninety feet, yet there was no image below seventy-five feet. That was odd. There should have been an image. The only way the screen could be blank was if...

Excitedly, she adjusted the upper focus depth to 70 feet and stretched the lower boundary back down to 240 feet. The run was going to take a while, but it didn't matter. By following her hunch...no, giving into her curiosity...she may have made an important and unexpected breakthrough.

CHAPTER 14

Craig Anderson sat at his desk, staring out at the forest of oaks and poplars. Their leafless boughs reached up imposingly toward a clear blue morning sky. They looked like giant guardians standing watch over one of the most secure plots of land in the world. The fifteen-foot barbed wire fence that encircled the perimeter, the battery of surface-to-air missiles, the array of motion sensing devices, the hidden cameras, and a team of heavily armed guards helped, but it was more interesting to think of the trees standing sentry.

A phone chirped softly on the corner of the analyst's desk. He peered at the display and saw no name, number, or area code. He knew who the caller was, at least he knew his code name. The director told him to expect the call. The phone chirped again. Still, no information about the caller's origin showed up on his display. Anderson wondered how he did it, and he wanted to see how many rings it would take the tracking system to break through whatever countermeasures the man was using. After the fifth ring, he picked up the receiver. There was still no evidence of the caller's origin, but Anderson didn't want to piss him off.

"Yes?" Anderson said in a low voice. The door to his office was firmly closed. He'd checked to make sure less than five minutes ago. This was the type of call that demanded a little more discretion than usual.

"Is this all the information you have?" the voice on the other end asked.

"Yes, sir. That's the entire file."

"You mean to tell me that you lost him for five years?"

"Yes, sir. Following his father's death, he vanished." Anderson cringed and waited for the tongue-lashing he expected to come. It didn't. The silence was almost worse: each passing second was like torture.

"He was on the sensitive persons watch-list."

"Yes, sir. I know."

"That's why we have such a list…so certain people don't disappear one day, and show up in the wrong place the next."

The analyst thought about explaining the fact that the watch-list, originally created to ensure that brilliant minds around the free world didn't get snatched up by the communists, was no longer as tightly controlled as it once was. It wasn't like the CIA could spare a team of field agents to track people on the sensitive list twenty-four-seven, not anymore. They now had a different charter, one that called for those same field agents to track suspected terrorists. He hadn't risen up through the ranks by being an idiot, however, so he held his tongue. "Yes, sir. I know."

"What about Chissani? Do you have any more on him?"

"Sir, I believe we're very close to getting the list of names you requested. We should have them by the end of next week." Anderson was glad there was at least some good news to report.

"The end of next week?"

Although the voice was steady, Anderson could feel the fury pouring through the tiny holes in his ear piece. He began to panic. What had seemed to be simple requests, at first, had proven to be a hell of a lot trickier, once he'd peeled back the onion. "Sir, you're talking about getting private information from the Vatican. I'm sure I don't need to tell you how private—"

"Son, stop right there! If I wanted excuses, I would have spoken with the director personally."

Ouch! Anderson knew there was a very real chance the director was listening in on the call. He also thought the man on the other end of the line probably knew that. Yet he didn't care!

"I want those names by the end of *this* week. As for finding out where Redmond was from 2000 to 2005, I'll track that information down myself."

The line went dead in Anderson's ear as the caller hung up. Despite all the resources he'd marshaled, he had failed to fill in the blanks in Redmond's history. Perhaps more amazing to him, however, was that, somehow, the man with whom he'd just spoken would make good on his promise. He would find the information on his own, Anderson was sure of it. For his own part, he'd make damn sure he got the list of Volenta members by the end of the week! Staring at the phone, he realized that in his panic, he'd forgotten to look at his caller ID display during the call. He sat there debating whether or not to call in a favor. Did he even want to know? He didn't have to think about it for too long. *Hell yes, he wanted to know!* Anderson picked up the receiver and dialed an extension by heart.

"Don't tell me you've reconsidered," a voice said on the other end of the line.

"No, we're still on. Twenty bucks, and you're giving me three and a half."

"Yeah, right. And I'm singing at halftime. You're giving *me* three and a half points, Sherlock, and it's fifty bucks!"

"Oh, that's right. Sorry."

"Sorry, my ass. What's up?"

"I was hoping you could do me a favor. I just got off a call a minute ago, and I forgot to write down the inbound details."

"No problem." Anderson heard fingers tapping on a keyboard, followed by a moment of silence. "How long ago?"

"I hung up less than a minute ago. Call duration was about a minute and a half, I'd guess."

"From your desktop phone?"

"Yes."

"Not according to the switch. The last call you took on your desktop was internal, from…" There was a brief pause. "Holy shit! Anderson's moving up in the world, huh?" There was another brief pause. "The last *external* call you took was two hours ago. One Patrick Wallace at DOD on K Street."

"You're telling me there is no record of any call coming inbound to my phone after the director's?"

"That's what I'm telling you."

Anderson shook his head in amazement. *How the hell did he do that?*

Chapter 15

Sitting at a desk inside his junior suite at the Latham Hotel, Tim pored over the classified information on his computer. He almost wished he hadn't asked Stentz to access it. There was a lot of it, and it was very technical. In the last three hours, he had scrutinized the anatomical breakdown of different elements, including Barrettazine, and their interactions under certain conditions; radioactive isotopes on Mars and their concentration levels across different surface layers and locations; orbital eccentricities and planetary angles of obliquity phased over millions of years; and inner and outer core composition and evolution of Mars. In that time, he'd managed to get through a mere fifteen pages of data.

He sighed and pushed his chair back from the desk. He couldn't bring himself to fight through the jargon any longer. It was simply too technical, and his head was pounding again. He wondered how much longer he could stand the incessant pain before it drove him mad. He stretched and rose from the chair to close the blinds. He then strolled over to the bed, turned out the light, and collapsed onto the quilt. He was asleep in seconds.

Four hours later, Tim awoke with a start. The muscles in his neck and shoulders were tight, and he felt anxious. At first, he assumed another nightmare had awoken him, but his unease remained. If anything, it had increased upon waking. He had the unsettling feeling someone was watching him. Slowly, he curled his neck to peer past the foot of the bed. It was pitch dark in the room, and he couldn't see anything. He held his breath and listened. There was a noise by the window. It sounded a little like breathing, but more like wheezing. A chill shot up his spine. How could someone have sneaked into his room? The hotel was being watched, he was sure of it. He'd spotted at least two undercover agents, or whatever they were called, when he arrived at the hotel. He couldn't explain it, but his attention had been drawn to them instinctively. One had been standing at the back of the hotel bar, pretending to engage the bartender in conversation. The other had been sitting on a bench across the street from the hotel, reading a newspaper. Tim had seen him through his window earlier in the evening. How he'd known they were plants, he couldn't explain. Intuition, he guessed. But it made perfect sense— they were watching the front and back exits of the hotel. How, then, had the intruder managed to sneak in through the second-story window? It was the only possible entrance to his room. He remembered deadbolting the door to his suite and sliding the chain in place. As soundly as he may have been sleeping, he would have heard someone rattling the chain or cutting it free.

Without moving on the bed, he continued to listen to the wheezing. His mind raced through a series of scenarios. If the man meant to harm him, he probably would have done so by now. Inexplicably, a bizarre thought popped into his head: *How do you know it's a man? How do you know it's a* human?

As if the intruder had read his thoughts, the wheezing accelerated. It sounded as if it were approaching him. Tim sprang from the bed and scrambled for the wall switch at the room's entryway. Halfway there, something grabbed his ankle and sent him flying. As he tumbled to the ground, it crashed down next to him. He rolled away from the noise and leapt to his feet again, using his hand as a guide against the wall to find his way to the bathroom. He scrambled inside, slammed the door shut, and locked it. "Get out of my room!" Tim yelled as he flipped the bathroom light on. Hundred-proof adrenaline rushed through his veins, and he thought his heart would explode. He backed up against the far wall next to the commode and watched the door knob, waiting for it to turn.

BOOM! BOOM! A loud pounding startled him further.

"I said get out of my room! There's CIA crawling all over the place!" Tim yelled again.

"We *are* the CIA, you idiot!"

"Oh, shit," Tim muttered to himself. He took a deep breath and cautiously opened the bathroom door.

"Open the door, *now!*" a voice demanded from the hotel hallway.

Tim lifted the chain, turned the deadbolt, and swung the door open. Three men stood in the hallway, staring at him. He recognized one of them as the man at the bar. "What's up, fellas?" he asked sheepishly.

One of the men rushed past Tim and into the room, nearly tripping on the overturned lamp. "What the hell's going on?" he demanded while scanning the living area.

Tim was mulling over a more fascinating question, like what had compelled him to call three armed CIA agents fellas?

"Well?" the man insisted.

"I tripped over the lamp cord on my way to the bathroom," Tim said

"Why were you yelling?" another agent asked.

"I...I had a bad dream."

"Yeah...and did a number on this lamp!" the agent inside the living area said.

"Let me see." The eldest of the men marched further into the room from the hallway.

Tim turned to follow him, but he felt a firm tug on his elbow. He looked back to see the third agent glaring at him. "Stay right here, please," he said.

After another five minutes of poking through the room, both agents returned to the front door. The eldest man shook his head. "Be more careful, all right?"

"Yes, I certainly will," Tim said.

The three agents exited the room and Tim closed the door behind them. He turned to survey the damage he'd caused. He stepped over the shattered lamp in the hallway and plopped down on the edge of his bed. All was quiet, except for his laptop: the fan—grossly approximating wheezing—was working overtime, trying to cool a CPU that had been left running for the past eight hours.

Tim rubbed his eyes. He couldn't believe he'd mistaken the sound of a laptop fan for wheezing. He wanted to write it off to sleep deprivation, but he knew that fatigue wasn't a leading cause of paranoia. And if there was one thing he'd always been with himself, it was honest. "You're starting to lose it pal," he said to himself.

CHAPTER 16

The door swung open from the inside, and Tim stepped through.

"I heard you had a hell of a night," Stentz greeted him. He walked Tim to the elevator and signed them both in at the guard station.

"What do you want me to say?" Tim asked.

"How about 'sorry for making you look like an ass, Victor?'" Stentz said. He pressed the elevator call button, and when the door opened they stepped inside.

"You should have heard Bauer this morning! He's convinced you orchestrated the whole scene in order to call out his security personnel."

Tim felt like telling Stentz he'd known where two of the three were before they showed up at his door, but he didn't. He had a more fundamental bone to pick. "Since we're on the topic, why were those guys casing my room, anyway?"

"I already told you that security for this project doesn't fall under my purview, Tim. Besides, they weren't there to case your room. Every member of the think-tank is staying at that hotel. Those men are posted to the hotel, not to your room. They're there for your protection."

"Protection from whom?"

The elevator stopped, and the two waited for the doors to open.

"Not from little green men, I can tell you that much," Stentz said with a smirk. He stepped out of the elevator and headed down the hall.

Tim followed behind him, searching for an appropriate

comeback. "You know, those guys showed up awfully fast, which tells me my room is probably bugged."

Stentz stopped and turned. "Look, Tim. There are things I can control, and there are things I can't. Whenever I get upset about violations of my personal privacy—or my team's, for that matter—I remind myself that I have nothing to hide." He hesitated for a moment and peered down the barren hallway. "You don't have anything to hide, do you?"

"No, Victor. I don't have anything to hide. But I don't like people spying on me, either."

Stentz put his hand on Tim's shoulder and shepherded him down the hallway again.

"I know, Tim. None of us does. We just need to play this game for a while longer. In the meantime, try to think about the control we've been given in other matters. If we say jump, people ask how high. Not many scientists have that kind of support, Tim." He stopped at the door to the conference room. "I know this is all a hell of a whirlwind for you, I really do. I also know you haven't been sleeping well, which is probably compounding your stress. All I can say is that I believe what we're doing here is more important than any of us realizes. And, like it or not, there's no B-team waiting in the wings. If we don't figure it out, no one will. Understand?"

Tim nodded.

"Good!" Stentz patted him on the back. He pressed his ID badge to the access panel and held the door open.

Tim walked into the room feeling like his father had just given him a pep talk after the girl he asked to the junior prom turned him down. Except he had never asked anyone to the junior prom; nine-year-old high school prodigies weren't high on the popularity scale. He took his seat at the table, nodding at the rest of the think-tank members already assembled.

Stentz threw a stack of papers onto the table and rubbed his hands together excitedly. Energy radiated from his face. "Okay," he said. "I've got some good news and some bad news. Which would you like first?"

"How about a little good news," Hollingstead said. There were no objections. Everyone seemed to need a pick-me-up.

"All right, good news it is," Stentz said. "Looks like Dr. Kirovsky may be right. We found what appears to be a large underground chamber, directly beneath the center of the city. The seismographic images show a grid of massive, uniformly spaced columns, which don't extend all the way to the ceiling. Therefore, we know they're not designed for support. Since we only have seismographic images, however, we can't tell much. They could be rods to channel some sort of energy field, or mechanical pistons. Who knows? I'll just say that it looks promising." He distributed a stack of handouts to each member. "We're in the process of capturing more seismic images around the perimeter of the chamber. We're hoping there's an access tunnel of some sort," Stentz said.

"How high is the chamber?" Shah asked.

"About ninety feet high from floor to ceiling, and it's about two hundred feet long and a hundred feet wide."

As the conversation continued between Stentz and the other think-tank members, a strange feeling welled up inside of Tim. It didn't come on him all at once. He felt an impending sense of doom, like an arthritic sensing the coming of a storm in his joints. In his mind's eye, he saw a black horizon and a thick cloud of purple dust advancing from far off in the distance. He hadn't had one in over seven years, but there was no mistaking it: the visions were back. He heard Stentz say, "We believe it was sometime early in the civilization's history."

"So what about the bad news?" Kirovsky asked.

Pieces of the discussion came to Tim through the haze like distant echoes, but as hard as he tried to concentrate, he couldn't fight off the vision. It crashed back over him like a tsunami. He saw a flat plain with short, clay buildings—a city. Small beings walked along narrow streets blithely, oblivious to any danger. From the distance, the purple cloud accelerated, like an image from a time-lapsed weather camera. It billowed up and rolled forward, enveloping the small creatures. Suddenly, a cloaked figure appeared on the horizon where the clouds had originated.

It advanced toward Tim from the distance. The haze billowed up momentarily, concealing the figure, but when the clouds blew clear, the wraith was closer. Finally, it stopped directly in front of Tim, staring at him with enormous red eyes. Two sharp claws shot out from beneath the cloak, but before they could seize him, Tim took flight into the sky. He peered down onto the purple fog, knowing the black being was still down there, waiting for him. The haze began to swirl, like the steaming potion of a witch's cauldron. Within it, he saw something flopping around violently, in a fit of convulsions.

"Ieeieeeee!" A Martian's face popped up through the fog. Its scream was primal and tortuous. Its hand reached out for Tim, beseeching him for help.

"Auughh!" Tim jerked forward in his chair, as if waking from a dream-induced free-fall.

Stunned by Stentz's bad news—the fact that no other ruins had been found at the sites of three other significant Barrettazine deposits—the think-tank members hadn't even noticed Tim during his episode. They stared at him now, shocked.

Tim sat there vapid, staring back at his new colleagues. He felt sweat pouring down his forehead and cheeks. Without a word, he leaped from his chair, stumbled from the room, and dashed down the hallway to the bathroom. He barely made it to the sink before throwing up. After he was done, Tim turned the handle of the faucet and splashed cold water onto his face. Through the reflection in the mirror, he saw Stentz enter the bathroom.

"Tim, what's going on? Should I call a doctor?"

"No, I'm all right now. It must have been something I ate." Even as he spoke, another image flashed in his mind, a memory he had tried desperately to erase, of himself as a young man in a hospital bed, with leather straps securing his wrists to the mattress. He would have killed himself, if given the chance. He would have done anything to stop the maddening voice that had been raging inside of his head. The thought of going through that experience all over again made him lose the rest of his breakfast.

As Tim retched, Stentz laid a hand softly on his back. "Tim, it's okay. Your theory was a good one. So what if it didn't pan out exactly as you thought?"

Tim almost laughed. "It's not the theory, Victor," he said. He scrubbed his face with a hand towel. "Look, I'm really sorry. My participation on this team was a mistake from the beginning. I appreciate all you've tried to do for me, but it's not going to work out." He pushed past Stentz and into the hallway. He felt himself coming apart at the seams. He wanted to get out of the Pentagon and find a private place to collapse.

"You need some rest, Tim. That's all," Stentz said, following him down the hall. "I'll have a car take you back to the hotel. Get some sleep. Come back in a few days when you feel up to it."

Tim pressed the elevator call button. He looked back at Stentz. It was obvious the man didn't know when to throw in the towel. Tim was reeling, up against the ropes, gloves hanging limply by his sides, waiting for the knockout blow. Meanwhile, Stentz was shouting, "Just two minutes left in the round! Bob and weave, boy, bob and weave!" Tim didn't have the energy to argue with him.

"Good idea, Victor. Give me a couple days," he heard himself say, but he knew he'd never return to the project. When the elevator door opened, he jumped in and blocked Stentz's entry with a raised hand. "Go back to the group, Victor. I'll be fine."

As the elevator ascended, he felt his stomach clench. His headache had returned with a vengeance. He slid his back down the wall of the elevator until his butt hit the floor. He wrapped his arms around his knees and rocked back and forth. *Pull it together, Tim. Just get to the hotel.*

#   #   #

Tim had been face down on the bed for what seemed like hours. He was utterly drained, too exhausted to sleep. Half-baked ideas fired in his mind. Adrenaline coursed through his veins. There is no torture like losing your mind, he thought. Except it didn't come out that clearly. The idea had, instead, come out jumbled—

torture your mind. Tim saw himself standing next to a large clear cylinder, filled with formaldehyde. His brain floated in the liquid. The top half of his skull had been sawed off with some dull instrument, and the remaining bloody cavity was empty. Gangrene grew over the edges, like decorative ivy. He proceeded to stab at his brain with a butcher knife, while laughing hysterically, like a mad scientist. Suddenly, a hand grew out of the brain and started to fight off its attacker.

Tim fought free of the hallucination, rolled off the bed, and began to pace around the room like a drunkard trying to shake the spins. He picked out different objects and concentrated on them, hoping his focus would divert his mind from the maddening thoughts.

Bulgari clock, quartz movement, made in Italy, pewter finish. The time is 1:23 P.M., 83 minutes past noon, 4,980 seconds past midnight, 48,180 seconds into the day. He replaced it and moved to the desk. DELL computer, Microsoft Word, Microsoft PowerPoint, Microsoft Excel, Microsoft Explorer, AOL Instant Messenger...*a broken string. AOL...a broken string.* Like a free climber finding a handhold while sliding down a sheer cliff, he latched onto something. The fingers of his mind dug into the crevice, and held on tight. He noticed that his computer was up and running, though he was certain he'd turned it off following the wheezing-fan escapade the previous night. He also heard a very faint beeping. Tim looked down at the computer screen. An AOL Instant Messenger dialogue box occupied the upper left-hand corner of the screen. A string of red characters was already visible.

Peter: Close the blinds, Tim.

Tim peered out the window, hoping to spot the mysterious Peter, the same way he'd identified the CIA agents. He followed the canal to the side-street bridge. One of the CIA agents sat on the bench, sipping from a Styrofoam cup. He didn't see anyone else along the banks of the waterway, though. He scanned the windows of the office building across the canal, but they were tinted, preventing him from seeing inside. He pulled the drapes across the window and sat down at the desk. More words scrolled onto the screen in real-time.

> Peter: Be very quiet and follow my instructions. After last night, you know the room is bugged. The telephone and computer lines are also tapped. I need to get you off this line quickly. If you understand, press the number 1 key.

Tim didn't care if he were being baited. The diversion was quieting the storm in his head. He could feel his sanity fighting to push through the maddening maelstrom. He pressed the number one key and waited.

> Tim: 1

> Peter: Good. Now follow these instructions to the letter. Very quietly, walk to the door that allows entry to the adjoining suite. Slowly turn the knob and open it. The hinges have been greased liberally. They won't make a sound. The latch will, however, so be careful! Come over now.

As soon as Tim read the last word of the command, his computer powered down. He didn't hesitate. He rose up from the chair and quietly made his way to the door. He wrapped his fingers around the knob and slowly turned it clockwise. He felt a rush of anticipation. *Who is this guy? How did he know so much?* He pulled the door open slowly and peered inside. There was no one in it. The room was empty! *What the hell is going on?* Tim began to retreat back into his own room when he spotted a laptop computer on the desk next to the window. The shades were pulled tight. Even from the door, he could see an opened dialogue box on the computer's screen. He stepped into the room, carefully closed the door behind him, and strode over to the desk. He sat down in front of the computer and read the message that was already displayed.

> Peter: Nice work.

Tim typed a reply.

Tim: Who are you?

Peter: I'm the one with the answers.

Tim: Answers? You haven't given me any
answers!

Peter: They're all laid out in front of you, Tim. You
simply refuse to see them.

Tim: Cut the bullshit! I don't need riddles or vagaries
right now. I need facts, in plain English.

Tim felt his head spinning and his stomach clenched into a painful ball.

Peter: Okay. *Question:* Why are you falling apart,
Tim? *Answer:* You're like a race car. Your
brain is the car's engine, capable of incredible
speeds. But you are out of oil. You have the
pedal to the floor, but the pistons are grinding.
Your engine is overheating. *Solution:* In the
mini-fridge are a number of foods high in
vitamins B6, C and E. They also have a high
concentration of tryptophan. Eat them until
you are full. You will feel better very quickly.
You will also be able to sleep.

Tim: Why tryptophan?

Peter: You know why, Tim. Stop being lazy and *think!*

Tim snapped.

Tim: I can't think right now!!!!

Peter: In plain English, Tim, tryptophan is brain food.
It's an amino acid that stimulates the
production of serotonin. Serotonin is the key
neurotransmitter that allows your brain cells
to communicate. Because you have much
higher brain activity than the average human,
you need much higher levels of serotonin. Go
get some food.

Tim rose from the chair and strode over to the mini-fridge built into a wall cabinet. Instead of the soda, beer and packaged snacks that filled most hotel refrigerators, this one contained a number of clear Tupperware containers with labels affixed to them: Avocados, Turkey, Eggs, Walnuts, Salmon. He selected two of the containers and took them back to the desk. He popped the lid off the avocados. Once he got a whiff of the fruit, his instincts took over. He grabbed a green wedge and stuffed it into his mouth. After he had devoured the first bite, he couldn't get enough. He reached into the container with both hands, and began shoveling more into his mouth. When he had consumed most of the container, he saw a new message from Peter.

Peter: You could go faster, you know.

Tim grunted. He reached up, wiped his dirty hands on his shirt, and began to type.

Tim: If I eat any faster, I'll choke.

Tim pried the lid off the nuts. He reached in, pulled out a handful, and popped them into his mouth.

Peter: I was referring to your car. It was designed to go faster. MUCH faster.

It took Tim a second to remember Peter's earlier analogy— engine as brain. As he made the connection, more words scrolled across the screen.

Peter: The problem is, as soon as you start to pick up speed, you pull the emergency brake.

Tim: I thought we agreed on plain English.

Peter: You're fighting it, Tim. That's what's causing your headaches. You need to let go.

The comment roused Tim from the warm calm that was beginning to set in.

Tim: Easy for you to say! I bet you don't have someone or something locked in your subconscious, trying to break through!

Peter: You're right, I don't. What does it feel like?

Tim wondered if he were the subject of some type of experiment. Was Peter the research doctor? Was he trying to help

Tim or hurt him? Perhaps his only interest was the test subject's reaction to various stimuli. He appeared to be right about the food, though. Tim was feeling more relaxed…almost drowsy. He decided to give Peter the benefit of the doubt.

> Tim: It feels like someone is trying to break into my mind and take over.
>
> Peter: Therein lies your problem. You are viewing it as a hostile takeover, when you should be treating it like a friendly merger.

"Son-of-a-bitch!" Tim said out loud. If Peter knew so much about what was happening inside of his mind, chances were good he had something to do with it. He tried to type his response quickly, but fatigue was setting in. His motor skills had slowed considerably. After a few miscues, he finally got the words out.

> Tim: What is going on inside of my mind? Who is trying to break into my consciousness?

He waited anxiously. The response finally came.

> Peter: Ha Ha Ha.

Tim shuddered in his chair. A chill went down his spine.

> Peter: I'm sorry, Tim. I just think it's rude to laugh behind someone's back.

Despite his rage, Tim felt himself nodding off. He had to concentrate on every keystroke, and even then, his response came out jumbled.

> Tim: You think this fumny? Som king of joke/
>
> Peter: You will find out who's knocking in due course, Tim. I promise.

Tim fought to keep his eyes open.

> Peter: And, if you had any idea how long I've awaited your return, you'd know that I don't find the circumstances remotely amusing.

And, as if on command, Tim slumped over the laptop and fell asleep.

CHAPTER 17

K athy eyed the eighty-foot drilling rig, which rose up like a monolithic radio tower from what used to be the center of the Martian metropolis. Standing high above the flat plain, its top was the first object to catch the rising sun. What was normally flat light now appeared much more brilliant, intensified by the highly reflective aluminum scaffolding. It had taken most of the night to erect the tower, and Trainer was just now wheeling the two portable halogen lighting stations back to the R4's trailer.

"We're ready when you are, Kathy," Peter Vivicheck's voice rang in her helmet. She saw him waving at her from the base of the tower. Moyeur and Porter were standing next to him and Trainer was halfway there, too. As she made her way over to the tower, she couldn't help but be amazed they were actually going to use it. It was designed to drill deep into the planet's crust for the express purpose of taking mineral samples. In the event the seismic readings had been inconclusive, they would have been forced to use the rig to get physical samples of the Barrettazine. With her at the helm of the seismo, however, there was never any ambiguity. Something was either there, or it wasn't. Fortunately, the Barrettazine was exactly where they expected it to be.

But, alas, they had found the most improbable of uses for the tower. Since the massive rotor of the Dredge was far too clumsy to penetrate the access tunnel to the chamber without collapsing it, they had to use the drilling rig instead. It was their only option, but it didn't mean she had to like it.

"You up for this?" Moyeur asked, placing his hand on her shoulder.

Kathy nodded. She wanted to get it over with.

Trainer came over with the harness in his hands and bent down to make it easier for her to step into. Once her feet were through the loops, Trainer slid the straps up her legs, and tugged on the belt until it was tight around her waist. Then he reached behind her and pulled the shoulder straps over her arms. Once they were in place, he snapped the adjoining clip at her breastplate.

"Too tight?" he asked.

"It's fine, Warren," she said. She knew he had argued against sending her down, but even after using the largest drill bit, the hole was too narrow for everyone but her.

"Piece of cake, Kathy," he said. He glared at Moyeur and headed over to Porter, to help him secure the winch.

"Okay, Kathy. In and out," Moyeur said. "The camera is going to get it all, so you don't need to provide any commentary, unless you want to." He made an adjustment to the small camera attached to the top of her helmet. "Make your way down the center of the chamber. Get some close-up shots of the columns and the far wall, and head back along one of the side walls. Got it?"

"No problem."

"Good." Moyeur walked over to the base of the tower.

Trainer was waiting with the rappelling line in his hand. "Ready?" he asked.

"Let's do it," Kathy said. She waited for Trainer to snap the karabiner around the steel hoop of her harness at chest level. She wished he could have clipped it to the one around her waist—a much more comfortable ride—but they had all agreed she needed to dangle perfectly straight to make it down the hole. As soon as she heard the karabiner snap into place, she shuffled over to the tower and climbed up the railing to where the winch had been attached.

"Right through there, Kathy," Porter said, motioning to a gap in the scaffolding.

She nodded, squeezed her way through and sat on a pipe that spanned the opening. She sneaked a peek at the small black hole in the ground beneath her and sucked in a deep breath. She watched Porter turn a knob on the control panel and saw the slack from the rappelling line wind its way up into the huge reel above her head. When it was taut, he turned the knob back to neutral. The reel stopped. She edged her way off the scaffolding and dangled freely above the hole, wincing slightly as the nylon straps dug into her shoulder blades. The pressure made it hard to breathe, so she pulled herself upward and rolled her shoulders to adjust them. Then she let herself down again, until her full weight was supported by the line.

"Here we go, Kathy," Porter said. "If I'm going too fast or too slow let me know. My hand is going to be on this dial the whole time, okay?"

She nodded again, but felt like screaming, "Let's go already!" Instead, she gave him the thumbs up sign. Seconds later, the reel began to spin and she descended. She didn't need to look down to know when her feet and legs had dipped below the planet's surface. There was no way to detect a variation in temperature or wind through the suit, so it wasn't by any conventional sensory input that she knew she'd entered the hole. She just did. As soon as her head was in the hole, however, she was startled by the proximity of the dirt to her face. It was no more than seven inches from her nose. Her pulse shot up immediately, and she began to breathe quickly. She felt like she was being buried alive, lowered by somber pallbearers into her own grave. The walls of the tunnel seemed to narrow and she felt as if they were squeezing the air out of her lungs. She thought of getting stuck halfway down and running out of oxygen before they could dislodge her.

Her head snapped back as she tried to look up through the hole to find the sunlight above. The back of her helmet smacked the wall and pushed it forward, causing her visor to hit the wall in front of her. Like a Ping-Pong ball, her head snapped back and forth against the sides of the tunnel. Instinctively, her legs shot out to the side, bringing about her worst fear. She was stuck. Before she thought to yell for help, the rappelling line unraveled onto her head. Several feet of it coiled up in front of her face. Kathy now had no distance between her visor and an obstruction.

"Stop! *Stop!*" She yelled. She was hyperventilating. She tried to kick her legs, but her knees were pinned tightly against the side of the tunnel.

"What's wrong, Kathy?" Porter's question came through the speakers in her helmet.

"Just hold on a minute!" she gasped. She fought off the urge to thrash her arms and legs and focused all of her energy and attention on breathing. The idea of being packed tightly into a frozen tunnel of dirt, well beneath the surface, was not very calming. Instead, she tried to convince herself that she was somewhere else. She pictured a wide-open field, on her grandfather's farm in Indiana. The sky above her was blue, and endless. A few white clouds floated by, propelled by a soft breeze. Kathy inhaled slowly, imagining honeysuckle in the air. She saw herself running freely across the field, over the rolling hills, her arms and legs flailing giddily. She began to relax. She pictured soothing hands massaging her bare legs, kneading the taut muscles until the tension was gone. Like a clutch re-engaging its gearbox, Kathy felt herself regain control of her legs. Slowly, they fell free of the wall and she slid down a few feet until the slack from the line tightened. "Okay, Tillman, crank it back up."

"Roger," Porter said.

A second later, Kathy was descending again. She continued to focus on the image of her grandfather's farm. She pictured herself lying on the ground, looking up at the sky and picking out animal shapes within the clouds. As the time passed, she became more and more relaxed; she nearly fell asleep before Porter's voice startled her.

"You're about ten feet above the access tunnel, Kathy. Tell me when you reach the bottom."

"Okay." She opened her eyes and watched the dirt pass in front of her. Suddenly, the dirt ended and the spotlight on her helmet illuminated a tunnel. "Stop!" Kathy yelled. An instant later, she felt her boots touch solid ground. "I'm on the bottom."

"Roger," Porter said.

Kathy dangled from the taut line, testing the stability of her legs and the ground under her feet. Satisfied, she unlatched the karabiner from the harness and stood in the middle of the access tunnel to the chamber. It was roughly six feet high by four feet wide—plenty of moving room for the diminutive Martians. Compared to the tunnel from which she had just emerged, it looked like some grand hallway of a French chateau.

Kneeling, she pulled a rectangular attitude indicator from her utility belt and placed it on the ground. The device told her that the tunnel's decline angle was roughly twenty-two degrees. She stood up, snapped the attitude indicator back onto her belt, and began to descend. She examined the walls and discovered primitive drawings of dark shapes engaged in commerce. Suddenly, she came across an image that made her stop. "I sure hope the camera's getting this," she said for the benefit of the recorder. "It looks like a court hearing of some sort. Hey…that's what I saw on the seismo. It was a ball and chain around the skeleton's wrist! Amazing!"

The murals explained a great deal about the Martian's daily lives, including their commerce, their agrarian activities, their law, and their social structure. Unfortunately, nothing on them addressed the rationale for circular cities. Kathy figured that answer and others were waiting for her further down the tunnel, in the chamber itself. The thought of it quickened her pulse and prompted her to hasten her descent.

Finally, the tunnel leveled out and terminated at a crude doorway. The portal blocked her advance and stood as the last obstacle to the giant chamber. The image of a black hand had been etched onto its surface, fingers splayed wide. She didn't have to be a hierologist to figure out what it meant. *Stay out!* Although she had never been superstitious, an inexplicable sense of doom welled up inside of her. She felt cold. Whatever lay behind that door had remained undisturbed for 300 million years. Maybe it should stay that way. A vision of her grandmother came to her: *You can't always assume a door was meant for entry, Kathy. Sometimes doors are meant to keep things in…nasty things.*

Kathy moved toward the door and stopped inches short to listen. She could swear she heard a faint rumbling behind it. *What if this thing is booby-trapped?* She pressed her hand against the portal and was amazed to feel it give a little. She increased the pressure, and the massive door swung open, slowly and smoothly. It was a remarkable feat, an engineering marvel. The door had remained unused for 300 million years, and yet it opened without effort. Kathy took one step into the chamber and stopped cold. Little black beings were everywhere, dancing on the walls, shimmying up the columns, and covering the ceiling above her. The murals were more sharply defined than those in the access tunnel.

She felt a twinge of vertigo. The chamber was massive. The spotlight on her helmet couldn't even reach the far wall. It was another engineering marvel, carved out of solid rock. The giant columns, at least ten feet in diameter, rose up like carved chess pieces on a board. They were perfectly symmetrical and perfectly aligned.

"All right, the seismograph didn't lie," she spoke clearly into the microphone in her helmet. "Most of the columns don't extend all the way to the ceiling. Looks like they stop about twenty feet shy." As she walked around a column, admiring the detail of the murals, she ran her gloved hand across its smooth surface. "These beings were master craftsmen, there's no doubt about that. I mean—" Kathy's fingers slid across a tiny gap in the stone. "Wait a minute." She wiped away the dust, and her mouth fell open. There was a door on the face of the column, about eight inches square. In the middle of the door, where the dust had been wiped clear, was a hook to pull it open. Below the hook were dials with symbols on them. Three rows of dials, like the combination lock on a briefcase.

"The columns might be hollow. There's a door cut into this one, about two feet above the ground. It has some kind of combination lock on it, as bizarre as that sounds." She placed a finger on one of the dials and advanced it to another symbol. She heard something move within the column and she jumped back. She fought the urge to run. *Sometimes doors are meant to keep things in…nasty things.*

"There's something moving inside. It almost sounds mechanical." She brought her helmet closer to the column. "It definitely sounds mechanical!" She touched it again. "Feels like something is rolling around inside." As suddenly as it began, the noise stopped.

Kathy thought long and hard about her next move. She walked around the chamber and stopped in front of the door again. It was still closed. Should she pull the loop? *Sometimes doors are meant to keep things in…nasty things.* Kathy hesitated. Finally, she looped her forefinger over the hook and pulled. The door didn't budge. When she tried to pull her hand away from the door, she noticed her glove was stuck between the hook and the column. She pictured herself in a macabre Larson cartoon: *After surviving the 65 million-mile space journey, shimmying down a 70-foot hole of frozen tundra the width of a pumpkin, and evading the chamber's booby-trapped entrance, the astronaut died of starvation after getting her hand stuck in the Martian's cookie jar.*

The harder she pulled to free her hand, the less funny the situation became. She tugged as hard as she dared, not wanting to rip the suit, and the door sprung open without warning. She tumbled backward and her butt and helmet hit the ground with a thud. When she sat up, she found herself peering into the opening. Sitting on a thin, stone shelf, she saw something that looked like a vitamin capsule. A very large capsule to be sure, but a capsule nonetheless. Rising to her knees, she inched her way closer to the column. She reached into the hole and pulled out the capsule. Its surface was shiny and black. On the top of it, etched in white, were the same three symbols she had dialed up on the combination.

CHAPTER 18

"I didn't expect you back so soon," Stentz said, waving Tim through the door. All the way to the sign-in station, he stared at the younger man. There was something very different about him. Was this the same guy that had hastened a retreat just twenty-four hours earlier? The formerly vapid young man who had stumbled into the elevator with throw-up all over his shirt? He was now the picture of health. His skin had a lustrous glow to it. The bags under his eyes had completely disappeared. He was showered and nicely groomed. There was a bounce in his step that Stentz hadn't remembered seeing before. And there was something else, something beyond the physical. It was something in Tim's eyes. It was like the kid had just been given a 200cc injection of pure, undiluted confidence. "You know, when I said you should take a couple days off, I meant it," he said. "I was actually thinking more like three or four." The elevator doors opened and he waved Tim inside. "I mean, you look great. Don't get me wrong, Tim. You obviously got some sleep. I just want to be sure you're not coming back too soon."

"I'm ready, Victor," Tim said with a smile.

There was that look again, that look like Tim knew something that he didn't. Stentz was almost unnerved by it.

"Okay," Stentz said. What he felt like saying, but didn't, was that time would tell. After Tim's episode the previous day, Kirovsky had taken it upon himself to share Tim's history with the other think-tank members: that Tim had been a child prodigy; that he had been labeled the next Einstein by many in the scientific community. The supposition, Kirovsky concluded, was premature and entirely unfounded, as evidenced by Tim's abrupt departure from the scientific community at age seventeen—just when he was starting to be included in real research, conducted by proven scientists.

Stentz had done his best to defend Tim's honor, but following the young man's meltdown, it had been difficult. It was probably inconsequential anyway. Even Stentz didn't think Tim was going to return. He'd seen the look in the young man's eyes as he responded to the suggestion that he take a few days off. Tim's agreement had been nothing more than an empty promise, a gesture to placate Stentz long enough to get the hell out of the building. Yet here he stood again, announcing that he was ready. Stentz sure hoped he was right.

When the elevator doors opened, Stentz led Tim toward the conference room. "Arty was about to brief us on the chamber...the one we found under the city," he said. "Did I cover that before your departure yesterday?"

"Yes, I remember something about it—ninety feet high, two hundred feet long, a hundred feet wide."

Stentz was amazed. He shook his head and laughed. "Remind me to never second guess your attention span." He placed his access card on the panel and was about to open the door when Tim stopped him.

"I have a request, Victor. I never told you, but I have a medical condition. A digestive issue, really." He reached into his pocket, pulled out a piece of paper and handed it to Stentz. "I've never paid much attention to it, but with all the stress and lack of sleep, I think it finally caught up to me yesterday. I'd appreciate it if you stocked the small refrigerator in my individual work area with these foods."

"Of course," Stentz said. "You should have told me in the first place. I'll see that it gets taken care of today."

As Tim entered the darkened room, all heads turned. He could feel the nervous tension immediately. Everyone handled it differently, but it was obvious they were all uncomfortable. Bleakney's eyes darted in his general vicinity but never actually landed on his face. Hollingstead smiled. Shah glanced at him, but only briefly. And true to form, Kirovsky stared directly at him, with a condescending smirk. Tim stared right back at him and offered a confident smile. The effect was immediate, and almost comical. It was the last thing Kirovsky had expected. He redirected his attention to Van Damm who stood next to the projector screen.

"All right, let's get back to it," Stentz said.

"Right." Van Damm pointed to an enlarged image of a black capsule on the screen. "So, after scanning it, they cut it open." He pressed a button on the remote, advancing the image. "Inside the capsule was a scroll with writing on it."

Several of the team members shifted in their seats and leaned forward to get a better look at the symbols.

"As you can see," Van Damm continued, "horizontal lines of distinct words, each separated by a single space. Eighty-two unique characters are distinguishable on this page of script."

"The characters on the heading of the scroll are the same as those on the outside of the capsule," Shah pointed out.

"Yes, our best guess is that it's a date of some sort," Van Damm said.

"The date the scroll was created?" Shah ventured.

"Perhaps the chamber is their version of the National Archives, an account of their recorded history," Hollingstead offered.

"That idea had crossed our minds, yes," Van Damm said.

"A jackpot find if it is, aye?" Bleakney said excitedly. "Might save us a lot of time and effort. Would make our participation here inconsequential!" He laughed.

"You'll never be inconsequential, Martin!" Hollingstead patted his shoulder.

"Do any of the symbols match known text on earth?" Shah asked.

"It's too early to tell," Van Damm said. "We're just now pulling together a team of linguists and hierologists. As soon as they've had a chance to look at it, we'll let you know."

"You might want to call Assan Ismail, Chairman of the Near Eastern Studies Department at Hopkins," Hollingstead said.

"He's first on our list," Van Damm said.

"I'm sorry for coming in late. I've obviously missed something," Tim said. "Where was the capsule found?"

"There are four rows of columns inside the chamber," Van Damm said. "The black capsule was found in one of the columns. We believe the sole purpose of the columns is to store the capsules."

"And from which column was this capsule taken?" Tim asked, pointing to the image on the screen. "How far along into the chamber?"

"It was taken from one of the first columns Palmer encountered. The murals on the outside of the column suggest a period early in the civilization's history, if, indeed, it's an archive as Dr. Hollingstead has suggested. The further down the chamber, the more sophisticated the murals become."

"We should probably think about finding the most recent capsule," Tim said. "Might provide clues about the civilization's destruction."

"That's the plan," Van Damm said. "We're confident of the location of the last column, at least the last column which contains scrolls. Halfway down the chamber, the murals on the columns stop. The team's first objective is to pull and catalogue all the scrolls from the last column with murals. They'll begin working their way back in time from there."

"That might be overkill," Tim said. "I'd much rather see the last ten scrolls from the final column, and then a small sampling of capsules spread across the civilization's entire history."

Van Damm chewed on the suggestion for a moment. "You're probably right. What do you think, Victor?" Van Damm looked at Stentz for confirmation. When he received it, he continued. "I'll amend the crew's orders as soon as we wrap here."

"Is it safe for Palmer to continue to access the tunnel in the same way?" Hollingstead asked.

"We're having the Dredge create a larger access tunnel to the chamber. Now that we know it's been carved out of solid rock, there's very little chance it will collapse," Van Damm said.

"We'll give you updates about the text as soon as we get the linguistics team assembled. Shouldn't be any more than forty-eight hours. We'll also pass along the details of additional scrolls as we retrieve them. In your briefing packets are pictures of the murals we pulled from Kathy's helmet cam. You might want to concentrate on those until we make some headway on translating the scrolls." Van Damm excused himself and headed out the door.

As soon as the overhead lights came on, the alpha dog moved in for the kill. "Apparently, your theory about the circular cities didn't pan out, Mr. Redmond," Kirovsky said. "You really must learn to take yourself less seriously."

The tension-meter in the room redlined. Tim heard what he thought was humming coming from the chair to his left—one of Bleakney's nervous ticks. "No more sorry than I, Edgar, about your unsubstantiated theory," Tim said. "A historical archive does not a generator make, does it?"

"I guess that makes it even, then, huh?" Bleakney the peacemaker said.

"Not really, Martin. But in the interest of group harmony, I'm willing to leave the scales balanced," Tim said as he looked directly at Kirovsky.

Kirovsky's cheeks turned crimson, and his hand tightened into a fist. He brought himself back under control quickly. "We're all big boys and girls here, Tim. I'm more than willing to risk a little egg on my face, for the pleasure of hearing you prove out your theory."

Tim looked over at Stentz. "Do we have five minutes?"

Stentz shrugged. "Sure," he said.

Tim rose from his chair and walked over to the white board. "If you recall, Edgar, I theorized that the Martians needed the Barrettazine to survive and, consequently, they had concentrated their cities in areas that sat atop significant Barrettazine shelves. Is that how you remember it?"

"Yes, that's how I remember it," Kirovsky said. "I also recall you saying that, although they needed the Barrettazine to survive, they weren't aware of its existence." He smiled like a man revealing a fourth ace in a hand of five-card stud.

Tim nodded. "Yes, that's right." He picked up a marker and drew a circle on the board. "Let's consider our planet for a moment." He drew the letter N atop the circle and the letter S on the bottom. "Earth is effectively a big magnet, with a northern and a southern pole." He placed his marker on the North Pole and drew a semi-circle around the right side of the planet, connecting it to the South Pole. He then repeated the exercise on the left side of the circle. "The positive and negative poles of the magnet repel each other, creating a force field around the earth. It's this force field—or magnetosphere—that deflects the daily onslaught of particle radiation emitted by the sun. Without a magnetosphere, this particle radiation—or solar wind—would ravage the earth, making our planet uninhabitable."

"You missed your calling, Mr. Redmond," Kirovsky said. "You could have been a substitute science teacher at any junior high school in the country!"

Tim ignored the Russian and drew another circle on the board. He then sketched two poles and a magnetic field, just like the drawing next to it. "Like Earth, we believe that Mars accreted warm, and as such, developed multiple, distinct layers close to the time of its formation—4.5 billion years ago. Shortly thereafter, a dynamo effect between its iron-rich inner core and its liquid outer core created a healthy global magnetic field, just like the Earth's magnetosphere today." Tim paused and glanced at the rapt faces of the other scientists. "Unfortunately, at some point, the planet's liquid outer core cooled, causing Mars to lose its magnetism." Tim wiped the magnetic lines clean with the dry eraser.

Bleakney nodded and grinned.

"So that's what killed them?" Shah asked. "The magnetosphere failed?"

Tim smiled. "Hold that thought, Pranab." He drew another circle and stenciled an x outside of its perimeter, at the ten o'clock position. "On September 12, 1997, the Mars Global Surveyor achieved orbit around Mars, with the mission to analyze the planet's atmosphere and certain surface characteristics. One of the instruments aboard the MGS was a very powerful magnetometer. After extensive readings, this instrument confirmed that Mars no longer has a magnetosphere, at least none capable of supporting life. In fact, the planet's magnetic field is roughly $1/30,000^{th}$ the strength of Earth's. That much was expected."

Tim paced in front of the board, feeling more at ease than he'd felt in a long time. "What wasn't expected, however, was that the magnetic field wasn't generated globally from the planet's core, like it is on Earth. It's localized within the planet's crust. Numerous readings were taken from the Mars Global Surveyor, and there didn't seem to be any rhyme or reason for the variances in magnetism within the crust. At some locations, the magnetic field was very strong, and at others, it was nonexistent. The NASA team was, and still is, baffled."

Tim glanced at Stentz, who was perched on the edge of his seat, as were the rest of the think-tank members. "As we already know, the Barrettazine is found in shelves beneath the planet's surface, usually at a depth of fifty to five hundred feet. The thickness of the shelves varies from a few inches to twenty feet, and the area of the shelves varies from twenty-one square miles, at the site of the largest deposit, to just over one square mile at the site of the smallest deposit. Accordingly, the mass of these shelves also varies greatly, from just over sixty-four million metric tons to a few hundred thousand metric tons."

"I'm starting to get bored, Mr. Redmond," Kirovsky said. "Is your plan to bury us in details about the size and location of the Barrettazine deposits?"

Tim smiled. "Don't you see Edgar? That's the whole point!" he said. "The NASA team assembled reams of data about the size and location of the Barrettazine deposits, without giving a whole lot of thought to its characteristics. The research team had already proven that the element was capable of generating a cold fusion reaction. The NASA team's job was to find ample deposits. They poured all of their energies into finding the Barrettazine and less into understanding it. In all fairness to the research team, with only trace amounts of Barrettazine on Earth, it was impossible to test for certain characteristics anyway. It was impossible to understand some of its other properties."

Again, Tim glanced at Stentz. The expression on the man's face was one of wonder, a child walking down the steps on Christmas morning.

"Properties like magnetism!" Stentz boomed.

"Yes, Victor, like magnetism."

Bleakney raised his hand. "But the Barrettazine shelves are buried. How can they have a magnetic charge underground?"

"That's an excellent question, Martin," Tim said. "This is obviously a very unique element, one we are just now beginning to understand. For example, by my calculations, its magnetic field density is twenty times greater than neodymium iron boron—an intensity great enough to form a force field sufficient to repel the solar wind. A localized magnetosphere, if you will."

"So…that's why the cities are all located above the Barrettazine deposits," Hollingstead reasoned. "Without localized magnetospheres, the Martians would die of exposure to particle radiation!"

"That's right," Tim said.

"But the Martian field team recently surveyed three other sites rich in Barrettazine, Tim," Stentz said. "They failed to find any evidence of life above them."

"Yes, I know," Tim said. "The size of a force field is a function of the mass of the Barrettazine deposit and its depth beneath the surface. A deposit with insufficient mass will fail to produce a strong enough force field to repel the solar wind, while even a massive deposit with a strong force field will be useless, if its shield fails to extend above the surface. I logged onto NORM from the hotel this morning and reviewed yesterday's fieldwork. Two of the three sites the team surveyed had Barrettazine deposits of only a few inches thick. Despite being expansive deposits in terms of surface area, their mass would not be sufficient to produce a strong enough force field. The Barrettazine at the third site, although sufficient in mass, was simply too far down to project a force field above the planet's surface. Its magnetic field would have peaked below ground at the time of the Martian's existence."

"I'm sold, Tim!" Shah said. "But how does all of this explain the circular nature of the cities?"

Tim looked over at Bleakney, the geologist in the group. "Would you like to handle that question, Martin?" he asked.

"A bipolar magnetic field, created within a single piece of material, is always distributed uniformly. Regardless of the shape of the Barrettazine deposit, if magnetized, it would develop two distinct poles, one negative and one positive. The lines of force created from those two poles repelling each other would arch up to form a circular dome."

"And that's why the Martians formed circular cities, to fit under the protective shield of the magnetic force fields," Tim said. "They weren't advanced enough, technologically speaking, to understand geomagnetism. They had probably never even seen Barrettazine before, but they were smart enough to know that once they ventured outside the range of the circles for any extended period of time, they became sick and died."

Stentz collected his papers and stuffed them into his portfolio. Rising, he said, "I've got to share this with some people." He looked at Tim. "You just had a very big day!" He then addressed the entire group. "We're finally getting somewhere. We still need to figure out what, if not the loss of a magnetosphere, killed the Martians. Why don't you take what we've learned today and begin generating other extinction scenarios. Let's plan on meeting back here tomorrow morning at eight."

As Stentz reached the door, Kirovsky spoke up. "There's no need to reconvene tomorrow morning."

Stentz turned to face him. "What?"

"If Mr. Redmond's theory is true, we already know what destroyed the Martians," Kirovsky said. Everyone stared at the Russian, waiting. He savored the attention. "Isn't that right, Mr. Redmond? Irrespective of their localized magnetospheres, the Martians' fate was already sealed."

The attention turned back to Tim. "Yes, you're right, Edgar. I'm just not convinced about the timing."

"What are you two talking about?" Hollingstead pressed.

"Go ahead, Edgar," Tim said.

"The reason solar winds are deflected by the magnetosphere is because they are charged particles...mostly protons and electrons. Tiny magnets, if you will," Kirovsky explained. "When they encounter a planet's magnetosphere—another magnet, but infinitely more powerful—they are repelled. Ostensibly, the same way they would be repelled by the localized magnetic fields created by the Barrettazine shelves."

"So, what's your point, Edgar?" Shah asked.

Bleakney broke in. "Without a global magnetosphere, a planet's atmosphere becomes severely ionized and boils away." He rubbed his fingers together and made a fizzling sound. He could have been a grammar school kid playing smash up derby as easily as a world-renowned geologist.

"And, regardless of how much protection their localized magnetosphere afforded them against particle radiation," Kirovsky continued, "the Martians would have surely perished without an atmosphere to breathe."

"That's why there was no damage to the buildings or the skeletons?" Shah asked. "The Martians simply collapsed where they stood?"

The scientists considered everything they had learned so far. It all made sense. There had, in fact, been no damage to the buildings. There were no signs of a natural disaster, at least none beyond a magnetosphere shutdown. And the Martians had been caught completely by surprise.

"Well, it certainly sounds viable, given everything we know," Hollingstead said.

"Not exactly." Tim said. "Their fate was, indeed, sealed when the magnetosphere began to fade. The atmosphere would have slowly burned away, just as Martin has described."

"How slowly?" Stentz asked.

"It would depend on how quickly the planet's liquid outer core cooled. There's no way to know for sure. Could have been thousands of years…millions of years—"

"But not overnight," Stentz surmised.

Tim nodded. "Correct, Victor. It wouldn't have happened in a single instant, as everything else we've discovered on Mars seems to suggest. The loss of their magnetosphere would have eventually killed the Martians." Tim scanned the faces of his pro-tem colleagues. "Unfortunately, something else got to them first."

CHAPTER 19

Tim lounged in the comfortable winged-back chair in his suite, reviewing the briefing packet he'd been given that morning at the Pentagon. It was only nine in the evening, but he was already tired. It wasn't the kind of strung out fatigue that had haunted him since his arrival in New York several weeks ago, but rather the weighty exhaustion that came after a hard day's work. He felt like an entirely new man. The serotonin was doing exactly what Peter said it would. His critical thinking was razor sharp and his temperament had mellowed considerably. For as far back as he could remember, he'd never slept a fourteen-hour stint, as he had following his online discussion with Peter. Even hunched over a desk, with his face squarely planted on the keyboard of a laptop computer, he'd enjoyed the sleep of the dead. And it felt like tonight was going to be no different. He'd have to set his alarm before slipping into bed.

Tim reached behind him and set the briefing packet on the desk. He'd been staring at the pictures for over an hour and still hadn't been able to glean any new information from the murals. One thing he did know, however. Hollingstead was right about the chamber: it had to be a library of sorts. The scrolls had to be a record of the Martians' history, and stumbling upon them had been a stroke of good luck. If the writing could be translated, they'd provide a far more accurate account of the Martian civilization than clues from the murals. Unfortunately, that was a big if. With no link to any known text on Earth, he doubted the linguists would successfully translate the scrolls. Had there been writing on the walls to accompany the murals in the chamber, Tim would have given the linguists a better chance. At least then they could have associated certain words with pictures. Unfortunately, the team of the Santa Maria had failed to find anything on Mars with both writing and pictures.

As Tim rose to call it a night, he felt his subconscious prodding him again. The sensation wasn't nearly as intense as it had been before his exchange with Peter; instead of the banging of a battering ram against the door to his consciousness, it was more like the soft ringing of chimes. As he was unraveling the mystery of the Barrettazine's magnetism just fifteen hours earlier, the chimes in the back of his mind were providing him with clues. *Ring-ring, look over here. Ring-ring, you're getting warmer. Ring-ring, something isn't right with this picture.* Something had been wrong with one of the pictures he'd analyzed that morning. He just hadn't had the time to figure it out. After solving the magnetism mystery, he had set off for the Pentagon straight away, leaving the other question burning in his mind. Now, the chimes were prodding him to return to the mystery.

He decided to postpone his sleep for a few more minutes and headed back to the desk. He turned on his computer, and while waiting for it to boot up, he pulled the draperies aside and looked out the window. It was dark outside, but he could still see one of the CIA agents on the park bench, keeping watch over the hotel's back entrance. He looked further down the side street, but saw nothing. He was about to return to the computer, when his attention was drawn to the loading dock of the office building across from the canal. A white delivery truck was parked there. Out of curiosity, he watched the truck for a few minutes. Finally, he drew the draperies shut again and pulled up to his computer.

He logged onto NORM through the secure remote connection that Stentz had given him and made his way back to the magnetometer images from the Mars Global Surveyor. He pulled up the image that had prompted the warning from his subconscious that morning. He hadn't looked at it for more than a few seconds, before the bell in his subconscious began to ring again, telling him that something wasn't right. He brought his face close to the screen and scrutinized the entire area. He couldn't find anything wrong with the image. It was exactly what he would expect to see in an area with a strong magnetic field—closely spaced, wavy parallel lines, like the grooves of tilled soil. They were superimposed onto the image by the magnetometer. *Ring-ring, down here. Ring-ring, something queer.*

Tim put his finger on the mouse and brought the pointer to the directional scroll bar to the right of the image. He clicked on the down arrow. The image scrolled southward, revealing the central flatlands of the Sinai Planum. There were several dark lines, spaced farther apart, and curling away from the Barrettazine shelf above it. Again, it was exactly what he would expect to see in an area with very little magnetic force itself, reacting to the influence of the Barrettazine shelf to the north of it. *Ring-ring.* The bell in his head persisted. He enlarged the image and studied the magnetic flux lines closely. He brought his face even closer to the image. His nose was almost touching the screen. He focused on a single black flux line, at the point where it originated on the left-hand side of the screen. He followed the line to the right, inch by inch, as it traversed the planet's surface. When he reached the middle of the screen, he knew something was amiss, but he couldn't tell what. He backtracked and followed the line again. Suddenly, it hit him. *Son of a bitch!* He leaped from the chair.

Tim paced the room, wondering if he should go to Stentz with the discovery. No. He didn't have rock solid proof yet. Besides, what if Stentz were involved? Whoever doctored the image had to have access to it. Not just any access, but access early on, before anyone had a chance to raise questions. What kinds of questions? What was buried beneath the surface, in the middle of the Sinai Planum?

Tim stopped pacing and stood quietly in the middle of the room, thinking. He couldn't go to Stentz until he had more proof. Although he didn't think Stentz was involved, going to him with a flimsy argument would merely tip off whoever was at the heart of the deception. Returning to the computer, he scanned the image again. He followed several of the magnetic flux lines from the left side of the screen. In the middle of the Sinai Planum, the lines became slightly clearer than the original ones generated by the magnetosphere. To the naked eye, it was almost impossible to tell. There was a difference, though, and he knew it. Two of the magnetic flux lines, for a distance of an inch, had been created by a graphics application to hide something. *What the hell was out there?*

CHAPTER 20

Trainer placed his hand on the far right dial, rotated the wheel one position, and waited. A deep rumbling emanated from inside the column. It sounded like he was in a bowling alley, with urethane balls rolling through an underground feeder system. He wondered what type of mechanical system the Martians had employed, since either electric or fuel-driven motors were out of the question. It had to be an intricate pulley system, complete with weights and counter balances. He couldn't wait to find out for sure, if and when they were given the directive to dissect one of the columns. Right now, however, his orders were simply to retrieve a random sampling of capsules from a number of columns throughout the chamber.

As he peered into the square storage bin at his feet, he realized he only had room for one more capsule. He had already stacked fifty or so in the bin. When the rumbling in the column stopped, Trainer swung open the undersized door and reached his gloved hand inside. He pulled out the ancient tablet, flipped it over and stenciled the number 23 on the back to denote the column from which it had come. He carefully placed the capsule into the basket and stood up to stretch.

Further down the chamber, he could see the lights of Peter Vivicheck's helmet darting left and right. He chuckled to himself. From the moment they had discovered the ruins, Vivicheck had been looking over his shoulder every five minutes. "Relax, Peter," he said into his microphone. At their current depth beneath the surface, they couldn't communicate with anyone above ground, but their units worked perfectly well between them. "I've got a full bin here. I'm heading back up."

"My bin's almost full, too," Vivicheck said. "I'll be right behind you."

"Great, I'll see you up there." Trainer carried his bin toward the chamber's exit and stared at the columns in wonder. He still couldn't believe they had actually stumbled upon an ancient civilization. It was an astronaut's dream come true, although he could understand why Vivicheck was spooked. Walking the planet's surface at night was eerie, but standing in a massive black crypt, dwarfed by imposing columns with dark Martian shapes, was enough to scare anyone.

Trainer shook the chill from his bones and picked up his pace. He passed through the door to the chamber, which had been propped open with a heavy air compressor—Vivicheck's idea. As soon as he entered the access tunnel, he stooped to avoid hitting his head on the ceiling. It caused a strain on his back muscles, and he knew he'd suffer all night. Too bad there was no spa on the Santa Maria. A nice sauna and Swedish massage sounded like a piece of heaven.

A minute into the tunnel, he came upon a tiny circle of light on the floor. Just as he'd done on his way down, Trainer stopped to peer up the chute. He could barely see the sunlight through the pinhole opening seventy-five feet above him. For a second time, he shook his head. How Kathy had the guts to come down that rat hole, he had no idea. Just the thought of it gave him the willies. He shuddered and headed toward the newer tunnel excavated by the Dredge. It was at roughly the same incline angle as the Martian tunnel, but much larger. And for that, he was grateful. Suddenly, he heard a muffled scream. As he strained to listen, a deafening boom rocked the tunnel. He almost fell to the ground as pieces of rock fell from the ceiling all around him.

The walls of the tunnel shook back and forth. He gripped the bin tighter and fought to maintain his balance. Then, as abruptly as it had begun, the shuddering stopped. He stood in the tunnel, shocked and perplexed. Mars had no tectonic plates, so an earthquake was impossible.

"Peter!" he yelled into his microphone. "Are you alright?" He waited for an answer, but none came. Finally, he detected the faint sound of shouting, but it was impossible to understand through the static. It had to be Vivicheck, and he was getting closer. Trainer heard a single word repeated. It became more intelligible with each passing second. "...n...n...un...un...run!"

The tunnel shook violently again. More rocks began to fall around Trainer's feet. He took off on a sprint, hoping to reach the surface with his precious cargo. A wave of rage washed over him as he envisioned the likely cause of such a disaster. If he survived, he promised himself he'd kill Moyeur for authorizing seismic charges, or allowing the Dredge to mine the area, while he and Vivicheck were in the chamber.

Dodging the debris, he finally saw a beam of light from the tunnel's opening. Dirt poured down around it. He accelerated, but his legs felt like iron posts. Every step was an effort. His chest was burning and sweat poured down his face. He could hear Vivicheck's screams in his earpiece. The second he burst through the opening of the tunnel, he put the bin down and turned back for Vivicheck. He ran through the tunnel's opening with his hands over his head as a shield from the falling rocks.

"Help!" Vivicheck's cries were more desperate.

Trainer ran as fast as he could over the piles of rubble, while guarding against snapping an ankle or wrenching a knee. He was twenty feet down the tunnel before he saw the light of Vivicheck's helmet. He could barely make out his silhouette through the thick dust. "Peter!" he yelled. He sprinted toward the light and pulled out the steel wire from his utility belt. "Grab my grappling line!" Vivicheck grabbed it immediately.

Trainer turned and started to sprint up the tunnel. He heard a deep rumble, and a huge chunk of rock crashed down behind them. A cloud of thick dust rolled forward and blew them out of the tunnel with it. The entrance collapsed.

Trainer was yanked to the ground by his grappling wire, as Vivicheck collapsed. The two lay prone for several seconds, catching their breath.

"You all right, Peter?"

Vivicheck jumped to his feet and stared at the rubble, like he was waiting for something to emerge from it.

"Are you all right, Peter?" Trainer repeated.

Vivicheck pulled on Trainer's grappling line, yanking the larger man off the ground. "Get up!" he yelled. "*Get up!*" Without another word, he ran toward the R4, pulling Trainer behind him.

"Peter, what are you doing?" Trainer yelled from behind, trying to keep pace with him.

"Get away! Got to get away!"

# # #

"I was halfway across chamber when everything started to shake," Vivicheck said. "I fell to the ground and one of the columns came crashing down next to me. I got up as quickly as I could and made a beeline to the door."

"And left the bin sitting there on the ground?" Moyeur demanded. He stood at the small table within his private quarters, fingers splayed out across its surface, leaning in toward Vivicheck.

"Massive chunks of granite were falling from the ceiling, sir. I barely made it out of there alive. I wouldn't be sitting here now, if I'd lugged the bin with me!"

Moyeur turned to Trainer. "Did you get a good look at the wreckage?"

Trainer nodded. "Yes, sir. There's a massive surface depression. The entire thing must have imploded."

"Goddamn it!" Moyeur reared from the table and began to pace.

Trainer had never seen him more agitated, but he had good reason. Mission Control would be none too pleased to learn that the chamber was lost.

"It just started to shake for no reason? You didn't hear a click or shudder when you pulled the last scroll free?" Moyeur asked Vivicheck.

"No, sir," Vivicheck said. "I didn't hear anything when I pulled it out. Besides, if it were booby trapped, it would have happened immediately. I was halfway across the chamber when the place started to shake."

Moyeur bit down on his lower lip.

"So, you're sure there was no mining going on?" Trainer asked Moyeur again.

"Of course not! Nothing! No charges. No digging. We didn't even have another surface vehicle anywhere near the place!"

Trainer shook his head. "It must have been ready to go then. Maybe all the Dredge work we'd already done weakened the structure."

Moyeur turned his attention back to Vivicheck. "Okay, Pete. Do you have anything else for me before I link with Control?"

Vivicheck squirmed. He started to say something, but swallowed the words before they came out.

"Well?" Moyeur pressed.

Vivicheck stared at the tabletop. "I'm not sure. I...I thought I saw something along the side of the chamber...as I was walking out."

"Before the shaking began?" Moyeur asked.

"Yes, sir."

"Well, what the hell was it?" Moyeur marched back to the table again and stood directly across from Vivicheck.

"It was probably just one of the murals, sir," Vivicheck said. "But...I swear I saw something moving. Right along the far wall. It was like a flash. I only saw it for a fraction of a second."

Moyeur's raised an eyebrow. "What did it look like?"

"It was probably my lights catching one of the murals. But it looked like a large black shadow, streaking down the outside of the wall."

"A *shadow*? Like a shadow being cast by a Martian?" Moyeur said, clearly joking.

"No sir, not like a Martian," Vivicheck responded seriously. "At least not like any of the skeletons we've recovered. This thing was a hell of a lot bigger." The room fell silent for a long time, as the absurdity of the statement sunk in. Finally, Vivicheck retracted it.

"Like I said, it was probably only a shadow."

Moyeur nodded. "I'm glad you said that. You've saved me the trouble of giving you a psychological eval."

Chapter 21

Tim spun the business card on the surface of the glossy table. It slowed, and finally stopped. The contact information was upside down, but he could still read it: *Don Culver, Deputy Director of Satellite Imagery, U.S. Geological Survey.* If anyone could find the original magnetometer images from the Mars Global Surveyor, it had to be this guy, Tim thought. He was taking a big risk, though, showing up at the USGS unannounced and unbeknownst to Stentz and Bauer. He'd half expected to be detained at the front desk when he presented his Pentagon ID and stated the purpose of his visit. To his relief, however, the security guard didn't scan the badge. Instead, he picked up the phone and politely announced a visitor for Dr. Culver. Five minutes later, Tim found himself in the Deputy Director's office, shaking the man's hand. Five minutes after that, Culver left him alone at the table in his office to personally locate the images in question. As he awaited his return, Tim tried to think up a story to tell Stentz, in the event he was caught.

"Okay, here are all the magnetometer images we have from MGS," Culver said as he stepped back into his office. He dropped two massive binders on the table in front of Tim and turned to a page with a Post-it note attached to the top of it. "Here are the ones showing the Sinai Planum. Ten pages in all."

"That's great, Don!" Tim beamed. "How did you find them so quickly?"

"I was Bill Stark's second when the Global Surveyor was in orbit. This was my baby!"

"Well, I certainly came to the right guy then." Tim leafed through the pages. He came to the same image he had seen in the classified section of NORM. His heart leapt. He leaned over to get a better look at the flux lines. Much to his disappointment, he could tell they had been doctored, too.

"You want to tell me what you're looking for? I might be able to help," Culver said from over Tim's shoulder.

"Oh, pretty mundane stuff really. Nothing you'd probably give a flux about." Tim smiled.

Culver laughed as he headed back to his desk. "I get it. Classified. Just thought I'd ask."

Tim continued to leaf through the pictures, disappointed to see that no others featured the specific area in question. "Are these all the magnetometer readings from the Sinai Planum?"

Culver peered over the rim of his coffee cup. "Yep. That's it. Something missing?"

"Maybe," Tim said. "I could have sworn I saw an image at one time that I can't find here."

Culver leaned back in his chair and propped his feet on an open drawer. He nibbled on the corner of the Styrofoam cup, thinking. "Well, apart from the MGS, the Pathfinder would have been the only other craft to include a magnetometer as part of its package. Unfortunately, the Pathfinder didn't go anywhere near the Sinai Planum."

Tim shook his head. "I must have been mistaken then."

"I'm ninety-nine percent sure that all the images are there," Culver said. "But we could call the Jet Pro Lab or Goddard. They've got the same ones."

"I already went to them," Tim lied. "They didn't have it either." There was no way he could ask for copies of the images from another NASA site without calling attention to himself. It was dangerous enough to come to USGS headquarters. "Like I said, I must be mistaken." He closed the binder and stood up. "I appreciate your help though, Don. I should have come to you in the first place. Can I put these away for you?"

Culver waved his hand. "Nah, I'll re-file them before I head out."

Tim nodded respectfully. "Well, thanks again, Don. Have a good night." He was a foot into the hallway, when he heard Culver call to him.

"You know what you could do?"

Tim poked his head into the office again.

"You could go directly to Malin, the boys who actually built the magnetometer. They usually keep copies of the images, too." Culver rubbed his chin. "If they were the prime contractor for the mission, they would've received the images first, processed them, and then passed them along to NASA."

Tim felt his pulse quicken. "Great idea!" he said.

"I've got a buddy over there," Culver said, rising from his chair. "If you give me your mailing address, I'll have him FedEx you copies of the images."

"That would be a big help, Don."

"It's no problem at all."

Tim began to write the address of the Latham hotel on a notepad, before reconsidering. He ripped the note off the top and stuffed it in his pocket. "These guys have me staying in a different hotel every time I come out here," he said. "I get them confused half the time."

"Tell me about it. The OMB and their negotiated contracts!"

Tim remembered the name of the hotel down the street from the Latham, jotted it down, and handed it to Culver.

"It's the Monarch Hotel in Georgetown...on M street. Unfortunately, I can't remember the exact address."

"No problem. That's what the Internet's for, right?"

Tim shook Culver's hand. "I really can't thank you enough, Don."

As he strode down the hall, he made a mental note to call the Monarch Hotel from the USGS lobby. The concierge would need to know a package was arriving in his name.

CHAPTER 22

"*Collapsed?*" Kirovsky shouted. "You have to be kidding!" The think-tank members sat stunned by the news of the chamber's demise.

"I guess using the Dredge wasn't such a good idea after all," Shah said.

"Use of the Dredge did not cause the chamber to collapse!" Van Damm said defensively from the front of the room. "The worst case scenario was that the access tunnel would collapse, and then only at the point of contact. There is no way the Dredge caused the entire chamber to collapse!"

"How do you suppose it happened then?" Hollingstead asked.

Van Damm took a deep breath. "We don't know yet. There is the remote chance the thing was booby trapped, but we doubt that's the answer."

"I agree," Bleakney said. "Why would a civilization booby trap an archive it had worked so hard to preserve? From the way they designed the capsules, they clearly wanted them to endure for a long time."

"Did they get any scrolls out before it collapsed?" Tim asked.

"Yes. The sampling you asked for. About fifty capsules," Van Damm said.

"And there's no way to salvage the rest?"

Van Damm shook his head. "Over a hundred-thousand *tons* of rock fell onto an already fragile casing. I'm afraid the capsules and the scrolls were reduced to dust instantly."

The gravity of the news sank in further. Stentz broke the silence, before it became oppressive. "Okay, Arty, thanks for the update," he said. Van Damm seized the opportunity to make a quick exit.

Stentz gazed out at the think-tank members. "Is it a pretty big blow? Of course it is. I'd be lying if I said that I wasn't irate when I heard about it. But we have to focus on the positives. We got fifty capsules out, a sampling spread across most of the columns down there. They've already been cut open and photographed by the crew. You have copies in your briefing packets."

Tim flipped open the small binder in front of him and leafed through the digital images of the scrolls. The text was very small and compact, but he could still see the symbols clearly.

"The linguistics team has been assembled," Stentz said. "They're the best in the world, bar none, and they're pouring over the images as we speak. In the meantime, you've had plenty of time to digest the murals. What have you got for me?"

All eyes turned to Hollingstead. The paleontologist/sociologist flipped through her spiral notebook. "We may be lacking in quantity of pictographs, but the ones we have are pretty telling. They were meant to provide insights to their culture, just as the scrolls were, I'm sure. They illustrate distinct phases of evolution, socially, politically and technologically—"

As Hollingstead shared her thoughts with the group, Tim got lost in his own. He didn't believe the collapse of the chamber was a result of the astronaut's mining efforts. Before the Dredge had been used to create a new tunnel to link up with the ancient one, it hadn't been within a quarter mile of the chamber. There was no way it could have compromised the chamber's structural integrity. The vault had been carved out of solid rock. It would have been stable without any supporting columns, but ten had actually extended all the way to the ceiling. Consequently, it could have probably withstood a sizeable surface explosion. None had taken place, however, so why had it suddenly collapsed?

At face value, a booby trap sounded like the most reasonable explanation. Maybe the team had failed to flip some kind of safety lever when they entered the chamber. Maybe the removal of a scroll from the last column had set off a chain reaction. But, to

Bleakney's point, why? Why would the Martians go to all the trouble of carving the chamber out of solid stone, creating airtight capsules, and coating the scrolls with a material that preserved them for millions of years, if they didn't want them read? It didn't make sense.

His mind jumped to the altered magnetometer image. Who had doctored it? What were they trying to hide? Was something out in the Sinai Planum that shouldn't be there? Were the collapsed chamber and the doctored image linked? Had the chamber itself been doctored, too? Had it been sabotaged?

A chill raced down Tim's spine as he recalled Chissani's words at the U.N. *They've found it. On the red planet, they've found it! It's going to happen to us too if we don't stop it!* Had Chissani learned something he wasn't supposed to? Had he been killed because of it?

Tim was convinced it wasn't paranoia that had caused him to withhold the information about the magnetometer image. Someone out there was trying awfully hard to keep a secret. He had already doctored classified documents, planted a saboteur onboard a NASA spacecraft, and even killed Chissani. With that kind of reach, Tim was afraid to speculate who it might be, and to what ends the person would go to protect the secret. Surely a child prodigy turned humanitarian would be expendable, too.

CHAPTER 23

F rom halfway down the hall, Agent Anderson heard his phone ringing, and he ran to his office to retrieve it. He swung around the doorframe, took two long steps, and picked up the receiver mid-ring.

"Hello?"

No one responded. Anderson cringed and waited for a number to pop up in the phone's display window. He breathed a sigh of relief when one finally did. He didn't recognize it, but at least it was a number.

"Hello?" he said again.

"Who the fuck did you give the list to!" a man yelled.

Anderson used the full length of his phone cord to reach his office door. He kicked it shut with a well-placed foot. "Ramsey?" he whispered.

"Don't you *ever* say my name!" the man spat. "Who did you give the list to?"

"What's wrong?"

"Three of the people on it have been killed in the last thirty-six hours, that's what's wrong!"

Anderson fell into his chair and rubbed his eyes. He had known something terrible was going to come of this assignment. "I can't tell you that," he said flatly. There was another long pause on the other end of the line. Anderson used the time to think ahead.

"I'm afraid that answer is unacceptable, Colin. Do you know how we got that list?"

Anderson wanted to hang up, before he learned something he didn't want to know. He was already in too deep, though.

"We had to enlist a cabinet member, Colin, a longtime friend of Cardinal Rombard in Boston," Ramsey said. "Do I need to tell you how exposed we are now?"

Anderson sat quietly, trying desperately to figure a way out of the mess.

"I'm going to ask you again," Ramsey said. "Who did you give the list to?"

"I don't know," Anderson sputtered. It was the truth. He only knew the man's codename and reputation.

"You know who I am, Colin," Ramsey's voice was ice. "You know what I do. You know what I can do to you, with a snap of my finger. Don't make me ask again!"

Anderson's heart pounded. He knew Ramsey was quite serious about reaching out and touching him. The man was more than capable of orchestrating a nasty accident.

"I don't know his real name. I only know his codename," he whispered into the phone. He looked around his office nervously, as though someone were going to materialize from thin air and slit his throat before he could give up the goods. "It's *Gideon*."

"That doesn't help me, Colin," Ramsey said. "You do want to help me, don't you?"

"That's all I know, I swear! The Director himself gave me the assignment!" Anderson was practically pleading now. "He's the only one who knows who Gideon is." He waited for a response from Ramsey, but the line was dead. He rose from his chair and paced the office. He'd just sold out the Director. What the hell was he going to do now?

Chapter 24

Tim quietly closed the door of the adjoining suite and made his way to the laptop on the desk near the window. It was still running, and the Instant Messenger dialogue box was still open. The screen had been refreshed, however, erasing all evidence of his previous conversation with Peter, when he had informed him of the discovery of the chamber and scrolls. He placed his hands on the keyboard and tried to summon the mystery man.

> Tim: Are you there?

The response came almost instantly.

> Peter: I'm always here.

Tim shook his head. Who was this guy? Was he sitting in front of his computer twenty-four hours a day?

> Tim: Who are you?
> Peter: Events are unfolding more quickly now, Tim. You will find out soon enough. In the meantime, what do you have for me?

Tim shrugged. It was always like this. Peter wanted to know everything Tim knew first, before volunteering any insights himself.

> Tim: The chamber collapsed. It destroyed all the scrolls...all but fifty. They were able to get the random sampling out first.
> Peter: Have the capsules been opened?

    Tim: Yes. I have pictures of the scrolls. If you'd like
            to see them, I can meet you somewhere
            tonight.

   Peter: It's too early to meet, Tim. Please put them on
            the desk before you leave for the Pentagon
            tomorrow.

    Tim: Fine.

He thought briefly of laying in wait, but he knew Peter would sniff it out.

   Peter: So...the chamber just collapsed?

    Tim: That's what Mission Control is saying. They
            think it was either booby trapped or damaged
            by the mining work.

   Peter: What do you think?

    Tim: I think it was sabotaged.

   Peter: Really?

    Tim: Yes. There's something bigger going on here
            and I think you know what it is.

   Peter: Please continue.

Why did Peter insist on being so coy? If events were, indeed, unfolding more quickly, then why didn't he come clean? Why didn't he just tell him everything he knew...treat him as an equal? Instead, their relationship was more like Sensei and Deishi— master and student. Despite his frustration, however, Tim realized he was enjoying the game. He'd never met his peer intellectually, and although intellect was just one attribute of a worthy mentor, it was an important one. Was Peter his equal, or even his superior, when it came to intelligence? Or, did he just have access to more information? He decided to play by Peter's rules for a while longer.

    Tim: In the process of proving that the Barrettazine
            was generating localized magnetospheres for
            the Martians, I ran across a NASA image that
            had been doctored. There's something in the

Sinai Planum emitting its own magnetic field, and I don't think it's Barrettazine. Someone within NASA, or someone who has access to the images, is trying to hide it.

Peter: Go on.

Tim: I went to the US Geological Survey headquarters in Reston yesterday, to see their copy of the image. It had also been doctored. I'm having the original image from Malin Space Sciences delivered to me. Hopefully, nobody's gotten to that one.

Peter: What if the Malin image hasn't been doctored? What if it suggests the presence of something else out there? Where do you go from there?

Tim was stymied. He didn't have an answer to that question. He had planned to cross that bridge when he got there.

Tim: With everything else that's transpired, I'd say my options are pretty limited. I don't know whom to trust.

Peter: Everything else?

Tim: A saboteur onboard the Santa Maria for one. The collapse of the chamber seems to be evidence of that. And Chissani's execution for two. He was incapacitated in my lap when he took a bullet to the forehead!

Tim stopped typing, and waited. He was prepared to sit there for as long as it took. Finally, Peter's response came.

Peter: Welcome to the battle, Tim. I'm glad you finally decided to engage.

The dialogue stopped, and Tim threw up his hands. "Then why don't you give me the battle plan?" he whispered to the screen. "Better yet, why don't you tell me what we're fighting for?" He was preparing to type the question, when Peter beat him to the punch.

> Peter: Let me add something else, Tim. Ranking
>   members of the Volenta are being
>   assassinated. Three disciples have been
>   killed in the last thirty-six hours. If you include
>   Chissani and Fuller, that makes five in the
>   last two months.

Tim gasped. He'd suspected early on that his friend from Africa, Simon Fuller, had been involved, given his connection with Chissani. But, having it confirmed was a shock. As he thought about it now, it became even more obvious. Simon had encouraged him to use his "gifts." He said he had a much greater responsibility to mankind than simply helping children in Africa. What kind of responsibility did Simon have in mind, exactly? He wondered if Simon had been put in place to prime him for this very battle, as Peter had put it, before he was killed. Who exactly had killed Simon? Was it really a random rebel attack...or was there more to it?

> Tim: It seems like you already have all the
>   answers, Peter. Why do you need me? Why
>   do we need to play this game?
> Peter: Have I done wrong by you so far, Tim?
> Tim: No.
> Peter: Then please trust me on this. It's VERY
>   important that you figure this mystery out by
>   yourself. I can give you clues and I can
>   confirm suspicions, but I can't lead you down
>   the path. Do you understand?

Tim remembered Peter's original proposition: *You help me solve the Martian mystery, and I'll help you solve your own.* He decided if he had to play by Peter's rules, so should Peter.

> Tim: Okay, Peter, I'll play it your way. But, where is
>   your contribution? You promised to help me

solve my own mystery, if I helped you with the one on Mars. Where is the quid pro quo?

There was a long pause. Finally Peter's response came.

Peter: Fine. Clue number one: why do you suppose the Missing Link in man's evolutionary roadmap still remains at large?

Tim: That's all you're going to give me?

Peter: There's plenty there, Tim. You need to dig a little deeper.

Tim thought about pressing Peter for more on the subject, but he decided to pursue a more immediate question.

Tim: I'll do that. I want one straight answer from you, though, about something you said earlier this week.

Goosebumps popped up on Tim's arms and legs. His hands began to shake on top of the keyboard. *Do I really want to know? Am I ready to know?*

Tim: You said you've been awaiting my return for a long time.

Peter: Yes.

Tim's whole body began to shake. He tried to think of a way to arrive at the question slowly. A way to potentially reduce the shock of it all. As he formulated his first volley, he realized how shocking the endgame might be.

Tim: Have you been waiting longer than twenty-eight years?

Peter: Yes.

Tim shot up from the desk and paced the room. *Do I really want to know?* A torrent of emotions swept through him. What was the difference if Peter had confirmed it? Hadn't he suspected it all along? Was it maybe even better to walk the fence, suspecting but not knowing for sure? Finally, he returned to the desk and sat down in front of the computer. Suspecting wasn't good enough anymore. He had to know for sure. He brought his shaking hands to the keyboard.

> Tim: Longer than

Tim paused. He could hardly ask it.

> Tim: Longer than a thousand years?
> Peter: Yes.

A surge of adrenaline shot through Tim's body. It felt like his limbs had been wiped down with sponges and attached to car batteries. His head swam. Tears streamed down his face. He thought he might pass out. He could hardly steady his hands long enough to query the endgame.

> Tim: Have you been waiting for my return for more
>   than two thousand years, Peter?

As Tim waited for the answer, he couldn't breathe. He had always suspected he was very different. It wasn't just the intelligence, it was something deeper. Who was he? From his very first exchange with Peter, he had thought the man might be able to answer the question for him. How else could he have known Tim's father's dying words—words that had been whispered into Tim's ear in the confines of an empty hospital room? *Suppose I had found a watch on the ground. The mechanism being observed, the inference we think is inevitable that the watch must have a maker.*

The excerpt was from William Paley's book, *Natural Theology*. As soon as he heard it, he had known his father was sharing his deepest thoughts regarding his son's existence. His next words had not been pulled from any book, though. They had been his father's own. *But, what if, upon inspecting the inner workings more closely, the craftsmanship belies the emblem? Not a counterfeit, but a masterpiece, whose maker remains a mystery.* The memory of those words swirled through his mind as he waited for Peter's response. It finally came.

    Peter: That's the question I've been waiting for you
             to ask, Tim. But, you need to ask it more
             directly.

Tim found himself looking at the flesh of his fingers in a whole new light. He whispered the words as he typed them.

    Tim: Am I Jesus Christ returned?

It was the first time Tim had ever mouthed the words. He'd wondered it a thousand times, but had never been so bold as to verbalize the question. As Peter's response began to scroll across the screen, a surge of electricity poured through Tim's body.

    Peter: In response to your direct question, Tim, no,
             you are not Jesus Christ returned.

The air rushed from Tim's lungs. A wave of relief washed over him. The question had finally been answered. He no longer had to carry it around with him. He felt a tremendous burden of responsibility lifted from his shoulders.

    Peter: Think BIGGER.

The dialogue box vanished, and the computer screen went black.

CHAPTER 25

Tim strolled through the lobby of the Latham and headed up the stairwell to the second floor. It had been a completely unproductive day at the Pentagon. The linguistics team had been unable to translate the scrolls, and no new evidence had been uncovered regarding the destruction of the chamber. On his way back to the hotel, however, he had stopped at the Monarch to collect the FedEx package from Malin. He hoped it would contain some better news.

As soon as he entered his room, he removed his coat and ripped open the envelope. He pulled out a stack of pictures and flipped through them. He saw flux lines at Arsia Mons, Pavonis Mons and Ius Chasma. Finally, he reached the set of photos from the Sinai Planum and took the time to study them more closely. When he got to the second to last image, he stopped cold. There it was. The same magnetometer image he'd retrieved from NORM and seen at USGS headquarters, with one significant difference: instead of the straight lines he'd seen in the doctored images, these curved sharply away from each other.

Tim pumped his fist in triumph and proceeded quietly to the adjoining suite. He sat down at the computer and summoned Peter.

> Tim: Are you there?
>
> Peter: Yes.
>
> Tim: I received the magnetometer image from Malin. There is something strange out there in the Sinai Planum! The flux lines curve sharply away from each other at a specific point!
>
> Peter: So, what do you want to do about it?

Tim: I want to find out what it is, of course!

Peter: Are you going to announce it at your Pentagon staff meeting tomorrow morning? Ask Van Damm to pass it along to Moyeur?

Tim sat back, surprised. How did Peter know Van Damm and Moyeur by name? And how had he known Van Damm was the person who sent all Mission Control communiqués to the crew? Was Peter a member of the think-tank or Mission Control staff? Tim recalled all the online conversations he'd had with Peter and tried to narrow the possibilities. It didn't take him long to recognize the futility of the exercise. Peter could have been anyone. Regardless of his true identity, he had just made a very good point. Tim couldn't come out and announce the discovery. If there were a saboteur aboard the Santa Maria, he or she could destroy the object in the Sinai Planum as easily as they had collapsed the chamber.

Tim: You're right. I can't go public with it. The problem is, I don't know whom to trust.

Peter: Come on, Tim, *think*. You're smarter than this! What would you like to happen?

Tim: I'd like someone from the crew to go out and run a seismometer search on the object. Find out what's buried out there.

Peter: So, what's the problem?

Tim: I don't have access to the communications equipment. That's the problem!

Peter: If you did have access, what would you say?

Tim: I'd send an official communiqué from Van Damm to Moyeur, calling for a three-person team to run a seismometer search at the coordinates of the anomaly.

Peter: And what are those coordinates, Tim?

Tim bristled at the question. Why did Peter want the coordinates? What could he possibly do with them? As if Peter had sensed his unease, another message scrolled across the screen.

> Peter: Have I done you wrong so far, Tim?
>
> Tim: No, you haven't, Peter. But what could you possibly do with the coordinates?
>
> Peter: I thought you said you'd direct a seismometer search at the location of the anomaly.
>
> Tim: That's right, if I had access to the communications equipment. Do you have access to the communications equipment?
>
> Peter: No need for questions, Tim. Either you trust me or you don't.

Tim bit his lower lip and waited for the chime in his head to provide some direction. Myriad questions abounded: *What if Peter is the one directing the saboteur aboard the Santa Maria? If he were, then why was he interested in unraveling the mystery? Why would he have called for the destruction of the chamber? Was Peter on the inside, a member of the Mission Control team? He had to be, didn't he? How else could he hope to contact the crew?* Finally, one undeniable truth materialized. Without Peter's help, he would be curled up in a hospital bed right now, fighting off visions and an incessant migraine. Tim picked the magnetometer image off the desk and calculated the coordinates.

> Tim: 11.21.43 south latitude, 85.52.10 west longitude.
>
> Peter: Thank you.
>
> Tim: What are you planning to do?
>
> Peter: Oh ye of little faith.

Suddenly, Tim heard footsteps on the padded carpeting of the hallway outside the room. He listened more intently and realized his hearing had become much more acute. He detected the sound of a plastic key sliding into the electronic lock of a door at the far end of the hall. Returning his gaze to the screen, he saw another message from Peter.

> Peter: I have a present for you, Tim. Open the desk drawer and turn to page twenty-one in the briefing packet.

Tim pulled open the drawer and, under the Gideon Bible, found the scroll images he'd left for Peter earlier that morning. He pulled out the packet and flipped to page twenty-one. Early into the text, a single symbol had been circled in red.

> Tim: What's this?
>
> Peter: You tell me.

Tim stared at the symbol for a full minute, but he didn't recognize it.

> Tim: I have no idea. I've never seen it before.
>
> Peter: Are you sure?
>
> Tim: Yes, I'm sure.
>
> Peter: Remember what I said about letting go, Tim? Try again.

Tim took a mental picture of the symbol and closed his eyes. He tried to relax and allow his thoughts to flow freely. He saw a dark horizon and the same purple haze of his earlier vision. A black figure advanced toward him. Suddenly, the image in his mind began to rewind. The purple fog blew back against the horizon, and disappeared altogether. The sun came out. Tim saw the Martian city and the diminutive residents walking along its streets. Day quickly turned back to night. The images began to rewind more quickly: Day again, quickly followed by night. It accelerated. Tim could only catch glimpses. Before long, it was just a blur. Finally it stopped.

There was nothing but darkness, solitude and peace. Suddenly, as if it had been there the entire time, the answer popped into his head. Tim saw the symbol. He knew what it meant.

> Tim: It's the Martian symbol for Jesus Christ.
>
> Peter: Bravo!

CHAPTER 26

Kathy looked up from the seismometer's control panel and out across the flat horizon. In the distance, she saw dust rising into the thin atmosphere. It was perfectly calm outside, so the dust trail had to be coming from the excavator. She guessed that Vivicheck was still an hour away, although he had left the Santa Maria at the same time as she and Trainer. The custom-designed Komatsu wasn't built for speed, and it certainly wasn't designed to travel long distances. Its engineers would have a fit, if they knew about this unexpected trek. Forty-three point seven miles to be exact—the distance between the Santa Maria and the coordinates provided by Van Damm the previous night. At an average speed of just under twenty miles per hour, it hadn't been a particularly difficult journey for Trainer and her in the R4. Vivicheck's journey in the excavator, however, was much more difficult. It wasn't just the time required to drive it such a distance, but the risk. Why had Moyeur insisted that the Komatsu make the journey, too? Why not send out the R4 on a scouting mission first? Then, if she didn't find anything with the seismo, they needn't bother with the excavator. What if the vehicle broke down? It would be a logistical nightmare to ferry supplies back and forth from the Santa Maria to fix it. She didn't make the rules, however, and when Moyeur got a priority-one directive from Mission Control, she knew he was going to follow it to the letter.

The seismometer beeped, announcing the completion of its run. Kathy peered at the screen, eager to see what the hubbub was all about. If she hadn't already grown to expect the unexpected on this bizarre expedition, her first thought would be that something was wrong with her equipment. How many times had she thought that, though, only to be proven wrong?

She had a clear reading down to a depth of about forty feet, but then the image became fuzzy. She'd seen this type of interference before in theoretical lab work, but how could there be a transverse electromagnetic field cutting across her plumb line here? She supposed it could be due to a naturally occurring isotope, but it would have to be an awfully large deposit, the likes of which they had yet to see on Mars.

"...you think?"

Kathy only heard the last part of the question. She looked up from the seismometer mounted on the trailer, and down the length of the R4, finding Trainer's reflection in the side view mirror. "What did you say?" she asked.

"I just got off the repeater with Vivicheck. He wants to know if he should turn around."

Kathy glanced at the seismometer image again and shook her head. "Tell him to keep coming!"

"What's up?" Trainer asked.

"I don't know. Whatever it is, it's emitting some pretty strong electromagnetic waves. They're washing my image from the north, so I know I'm not directly above it."

"Can you pinpoint it?" Trainer asked.

"We might have to move around a little, but I'll find it. Problem is, even if I get directly over it, I doubt I'm going to get a very good image. Electromagnetic waves can act like a cloak to a seismometer."

"I'd better tell Moyeur."

"And what do you think he'll say?" Kathy asked quickly. There were several seconds of silence, while Trainer considered it.

"He'll probably want some guidance from Mission Control."

"Exactly. And how long do you think that will take?"

Trainer didn't respond so Kathy ventured her own guess. "They'll probably tell us to return to the ship...to give them time to assess the images."

"Okay, Kathy, we're on the same page. I don't want to make this trip again any more than you do, but I've got to tell him something."

Kathy gazed north and wondered how far out Vivicheck really was. "Why don't you tell him that we found something. Tell him we're waiting for the excavator to confirm it." It was the truth. There was no need to get into the electromagnetic waves.

Trainer was silent for several seconds. Finally, he nodded. "Fine. You'd better find something worthwhile, though."

Kathy felt the satisfaction of a small victory as she turned back to the seismometer. It looked like Van Damm or someone on his team knew what he was doing. Somehow he'd known that the seismometer wouldn't produce a crisp image. Why else would he have insisted on sending out the excavator on the first trip?

Vivicheck pulled back on the lever and the treads of the excavator dug into the soft ground. The massive vehicle lurched backward and crawled slowly up the ramp. Once it was on the flat-and-level, he pushed the lever forward again and guided the vehicle toward the growing pile of dirt a hundred yards to the south. Once there, he threw another lever and the front-scoop pitched forward. Forty-six tons of dirt rained down onto the planet's surface. A familiar red plume rose up from the ground like the dust cloud from a demolished building. Vivicheck reversed from the discard pile, and headed back toward the ramp. He stopped at the top and peered at Kathy, who stood at the precipice of the wall to his right. They both had a perfect view of the sheer cliff at the bottom of the ramp. "How much deeper?" he asked.

"That should be far enough. Start scraping away layers from the wall, until you hit it. Take it nice and slow."

He nodded and powered the vehicle down the ramp.

"Kathy, you're not going to believe this."

She turned toward the R4, where Trainer was staring at her through the windshield. "What is it now?" she asked.

"Moyeur's ordered us back."

"*What?* We're almost there!"

"He said the priority-one directive from Van Damm wasn't sent by Mission Control."

Kathy stood dumbfounded. "They sent it by mistake?" she asked.

"No. Van Damm said he never sent the directive at all."

Kathy was speechless. What the hell was going on? Was Mission Control saying they had a communications breach…a mole in the Pentagon? This expedition couldn't get any more bizarre! She wanted to ask Trainer what he thought was happening, off the record. He'd been a career NASA man. Surely this kind of stuff was way out of the ordinary.

"Whoever sent the message must have known something, Warren," she argued. "Moyeur doesn't really expect us to pack up and walk away before we find out, does he?"

"He left no room for misinterpretation, Kathy. We've been instructed to pull out immediately."

"Can't you just hold them off for a little while longer?"

"We could be in danger, Kathy!" There was sternness in his voice that she'd seldom heard. "Now I want you to—"

"I've got it!" Vivicheck yelled. *"Holy shit!"*

Kathy swung back toward the excavator and peered at the sheer-faced wall in front of it. She stood frozen in shock. She had never seen anything more beautiful in her life. She was completely overwhelmed.

Then it began to move. Her fascination turned to horror.

"Peter! Watch out!"

CHAPTER 27

"How could we not have anything on video? We've got cameras all over this goddamn place!" General Bauer roared.

The colonel in charge of system security, Larry Miller, didn't blink. "Sir, in my experience, electronic tracking is a much quicker and more effective way to identify a breach. Having said that, I'm very confident that the message didn't originate inside the Pentagon."

"It was included in the batch transmission! How the hell did it get in there, if it didn't originate in the Pentagon?"

"Sir, my team is looking into that as we speak."

"Well, I don't need someone to look into it, Larry. I need someone with answers!" Bauer shook his head and glanced over at Stentz and Van Damm. Both men remained silent.

The phone on Bauer's desk rang and he picked it up. "Bauer here." He nodded. "Fine. Send him in." Seconds later, a tentative tap rattled the glass window of his office door. "Come in!"

A young man with wire-rimmed glasses entered the room and stood just inside the doorway. He wore a white oxford, also known as *contractor garb* to the military personnel. Miller walked over quickly to have a word with the kid before he opened his mouth. After twenty seconds of whispering, Bauer had had enough. "What's going on?" he barked.

"Sir, we've gathered some interesting data that may shed some light on the situation," Colonel Miller said, "but I'd like to have some other people look into it before I brief you."

Bauer stared at the young contractor. "Is that what you think, son?"

"Sir?"

"Is that what *you* think? Do we need to have some other people look into it?"

"Sir, I'd be lying if I said I understood the mechanics of it, but I'm confident I know how it was done…in principle, anyway."

"Let's hear it."

"Yes, sir." The young man cleared his throat. "As you know, most of our communications with the crew are compressed and sent in a batch transmission each evening, usually around 1900 local time. The batch includes official directives from Director Stentz and Mr. Van Damm, notices from the National Oceanic and Atmospheric Administration about any irregular sunspot activity that might effect communications equipment on Mars, early warning data on dust storms sweeping across the Martian surface provided by STScI, approved emails from family members to the crew, and other data relative to systems monitoring onboard the Santa Maria." The tech whiz paused to make sure everyone was with him. "All of these individual messages are encrypted, compressed into a single data package, and then sent directly to one of six Tracking and Data Relay Satellites—TDRSS—orbiting earth. It's then sent via Ka-Band wavelength at 16-million words per second to the high rate receiver on the communication's satellite circling Mars. From there it's sent to the Santa Maria's communication system, where it's authenticated, decoded, unpacked and distributed to the crew members."

"Yes, we're well aware of how our communication system works," Bauer said impatiently. "Get to your point!"

"Yes, sir. We have no evidence whatsoever of a security breach at any of the points I just mentioned. Not at the Pentagon, not at either of the relay satellites, and not onboard the Santa Maria."

Bauer, Stentz and Van Damm exchanged confused glances. They then looked back at the whiz kid, rapt.

"The message wasn't in the compressed data package that left the Pentagon, and it wasn't in the package that was relayed by the TRDSS satellite circling earth either." The young man stepped forward. Dimples emerged on his cheeks as a smile stretched across his lips. "The first time the directive showed up was at the communication satellite circling Mars!" he said excitedly. "Don't you see? The message was hijacked in space, somewhere between Earth and Mars! How they did it, I have no idea. But there was no delay in the transit time between the two relay stations. That means the message was intercepted, decoded, uncompressed, modified, and resubmitted all on the fly, as it traveled through space!"

"Who has access to that kind of technology?" Bauer asked.

"General," Colonel Miller spoke up before his contractor had a chance, "even *we* don't have access to that kind of technology. It simply doesn't exist. That's why I wanted to get some other people to look into it."

Bauer shook his head in disbelief. He glanced over Stentz and Van Damm, both of whom stood incredulous.

The phone on Bauer's desk clamored, breaking the uncomfortable silence. He picked up the receiver and listened intently. "No, I'll get him myself."

#   #   #

When the door swung open, Tim was caught completely by surprise.

"Hello, Mr. Redmond," Bauer said. His massive frame filled the doorway, blocking Tim's entry. "Victor has his hands full this morning, so I told him I'd come up and get you myself." He gestured for Tim to join him in the hallway.

"Thank you," Tim said uncomfortably. It was the first time he'd seen the general since being grilled by him at the U.N. "Is everything all right?"

"Actually, it's been an interesting twelve hours, both here and abroad," Bauer said. "But I'll let Victor share those details with you." He stopped to sign them in at the security desk and then led Tim toward the elevator. The sergeant at post snapped Bauer a crisp salute as the two passed. The general returned it, and Tim couldn't help but notice how fluidly he moved for a man so big.

"So, how are your accommodations?" Bauer asked as he pressed the elevator call button.

Tim was surprised by the question. He didn't see the general as the chitchat type. Small talk was better than interrogation, however, so he was happy to oblige. "The room's small, but comfortable. My photos from Africa are a nice touch."

"Victor's idea," Bauer said. "And the hotel in Georgetown? Are you finding everything you need there?"

The chimes in Tim's head started to ring. He felt the muscles in his neck tense. *What a surreal conversation. Where was he going with this?* The elevator arrived and the doors opened. "No complaints about the hotel either," he said, as they both stepped in. "My room is spacious, and the service has been impeccable."

Bauer nodded approvingly. There was a long silence as the elevator descended. Finally, the general broke it.

"The Latham is known for its food, you know," he said.

Tim bristled. He could feel the man's eyes on him, but he didn't dare look over.

"Good nutrition is a must for peak performance," Bauer continued.

Tim stared straight ahead at the elevator doors. *Does he know? Is it him sending the messages? Was* he *Peter?*

"I hear the hotel's amenities are also fantastic," Bauer said. "I understand every room has its own high speed Internet connection."

Tim tried to control his reaction, but he could feel the blood rushing to his face. The game was up! Bauer obviously knew everything. *But why is he being so coy about it?* Tim made a connection. *Peter is coy too, isn't he? Could Bauer really be Peter? Is he dropping clues now, just waiting for me to acknowledge it?* Tim craned his neck slowly to the left and looked up at Bauer. The general was staring straight at him. "Pe…" he began to form the name Peter when the chimes in the back of his head went haywire. "Peaceful little canal in the back too." He finished the sentence without missing a beat.

The elevator stopped and the doors slid open.

"Yes, good location too." Bauer stepped out with Tim. "Victor said you've been an invaluable addition to the team, Mr. Redmond. I just wanted to let you know we *all* appreciate your help." Bauer veered off from the hallway and headed toward the mission control area.

Tim continued down the hallway toward the conference room. His heart was pounding. He placed his ID badge over the control panel and opened the door. Bleakney and Hollingstead were already seated at the conference table. He greeted them both and took a seat. As he opened his folder, the three remaining members of the team walked in. Stentz appeared angry as he made his way to the front of the room. He took a deep breath before jumping right in. "Yesterday evening, a message was sent to Moyeur calling for the reconnaissance of an area in the Sinai Planum," he said.

Butterflies swirled in Tim's stomach. He had to force himself not to react. Peter didn't mess around. When he said he was going to do something, he did it. But how?

"The communiqué wasn't sent by Mission Control," Stentz said. "It was a dupe."

A few gasps escaped from the mouths of the think-tank members. Bleakney raised his hand tentatively. "I'm sorry," he said. "My American slang may be failing me. When you say 'a dupe,' do you mean a duplicate or do you mean a counterfeit?"

"The latter."

"How is that possible, Victor?" Shah asked. "How does someone hack into the Pentagon?"

"We have no idea who did it, or how," Stentz said. "We're trying to figure that out. In the meantime, we're devising a message confirmation procedure, to ensure it doesn't happen again."

"Did the team find anything at the site, following the fake directive?" Hollingstead asked, voicing the question Tim was dying to ask, but didn't dare.

Stentz didn't say a word. Rather, he plugged the AV cord into the back of his computer. He grabbed the remote off the table, dimmed the lights, and turned the projector on. The image came up immediately.

Tim almost lost his breakfast. *Oh my God, what did I get them into?* It looked like a picture from a war zone. The excavator's front grille was flush with the ground, and its rear wheels were sticking straight up in the air. He followed the arm of the vehicle to where the cab was supposed to be. To his relief, there didn't appear to be any damage to the steel cage that enclosed the operator. No sign of forced entry, either. *No sign of forced entry? Why would I even wonder that?* Suddenly, Tim saw what must have been the source of the incident. There was an iridescent ball in the middle of the scoop. It was beautiful. All colors of the rainbow shimmered off its surface.

"As you can see," Stentz said, "when the dirt beneath it gave way, this sphere fell into the excavator's shovel and caused the vehicle to upend."

"Was anyone hurt?" Tim asked.

"Vivicheck managed to walk away with little more than a few bruises. He was lucky."

"How big is the sphere?" Kirovsky asked.

"Four feet in diameter," Stentz replied.

"And it caused that huge vehicle to tip over?" Hollingstead asked.

Stentz nodded. "We don't know its exact weight, but it would have to be over seventy-five tons to tip the vehicle like that."

Bleakney piped up immediately.

"That's impossible!" Bleakney said, shocking everyone with his fervor. He grabbed a calculator from his pocket and began to punch in some numbers. "At four feet in diameter, that's a volume of a little under thirty-four cubic feet. Divided into seventy-five tons, you'd have..." He stopped and shook his head. He ran the numbers again to make sure he hadn't made a mistake. "...four thousand four hundred eleven pounds per cubic foot. That's over three times the density of iridium! And that's assuming the sphere is solid!"

"Yes, I know, Martin," Stentz said. "Open your minds, people, because I'm just getting started."

"*Is* the sphere solid?" Tim asked.

"We don't know. A strong electromagnetic field is rendering the seismometer useless."

"Have they taken a sample of the alloy...run it through the mass spectrometer?" Bleakney was on the edge of his chair.

Stentz shook his head. "Already tried it. We can't get a sample. The material's too hard."

"All they need is a shaving," Bleakney said. "A glancing pass with the industrial laser should do the trick."

"They just found it eight hours ago!" Stentz snapped. "We're lucky to have as much data as we do. Until we understand why it's emitting electromagnetic waves, I'm not asking anyone to break out the industrial laser, glancing pass or otherwise!"

Bleakney shuffled his papers.

"I'm sorry, Martin. I didn't mean to snap at you like that," Stentz said.

Bleakney offered a semblance of a smile. "No apologies required. An inane suggestion by me. The safety of the crew needs to be considered first, of course."

There was a long, uncomfortable silence. Finally, Kirovsky spoke up. "Have they analyzed the soil around it yet? Do they know how long it's been there?"

Stentz stood quietly. He appeared to be lost in thought and oblivious to the question. The Russian was about ready to ask again when Stentz spoke up. "Three-hundred million years, Edgar," he said. "The sphere has been there for roughly *300 million years*."

The think-tank members exchanged glances, as they made the connection to roughly the same period the Martians perished.

Stentz reached down and unplugged his computer, before looking out at the group. "Amazing, isn't it? Like I said, we only discovered it eight hours ago, so we have very little data. What little data we have, however, is in these briefing packets." Stentz passed out the red folders and tucked his computer under his arm. "I'd like nothing more than to discuss it with you, but in light of the security breach last night, I'm needed at another meeting. I'll come back as soon as I can." He headed out the door.

The think-tank members sat quietly, leafing through their briefing packets. After two minutes of silence, Shah finally spoke up. "Is it me, or is the madness metastasizing?"

Several heads nodded. Shah couldn't have chosen a better word. In Tim's mind, he saw cancer cells spreading from organ to organ. It was the perfect analogy for the string of bizarre events: the collapse of the scroll chamber, a breach of Mission Control security, the discovery of a very dubious object in the Sinai Planum—an area absent of Barrettazine and, consequently, one in which the Martians would never venture.

Kirovsky peered at his cohorts with raised eyebrows. "Well, it's obvious to me that the sphere wasn't created by the Martians. In addition to its density, rigidity, and emission of alpha particles—" he thumped his finger on the briefing packet— "according to this, it's perfectly round, down to the tenth decimal place!"

"And what does that sound like?" Bleakney asked.

"The plutonium core of a nuclear bomb," Tim said.

Kirovsky nodded solemnly. "Perhaps we should consider the possibility of mass genocide."

"By whom, Edgar?" Hollingstead closed her briefing packet. "We've already concluded that the Martian's technology was comparable to tenth-century Europe. What threat could a civilization like that pose to one capable of developing a massive nuclear weapon?"

"You're right, Bonnie." Kirovsky leaned back in his chair. "I don't know what I was thinking. I forgot that over the course of human history, there has never been a case of one-sided genocide. The Crusaders never marched on Constantinople, the Conquistadors never rolled across South America, the British never slaughtered the Zulu, and your forefathers never massacred the American Indians!"

Hollingstead glared at Kirovsky, but after some reflection, her expression softened. "Point well taken, Edgar," she said. "Let me just ask you this, then: if the sphere were some type of nuclear bomb, how much damage would it cause, given a diameter of four feet?"

Kirovsky didn't need to think about it long. "I would think that a single warhead that size, given comparable yields to the weapons we have today, could easily destroy all life on the planet."

"Then where is the blast crater? And why is the sphere still intact, if it exploded?" Hollingstead asked.

"I wouldn't expect a blast crater on the surface of Mars," Kirovsky said. "The most devastating explosion from a weapon that size would be airborne, at an altitude of roughly thirty thousand feet, I should imagine."

Tim suddenly realized that the man sitting across from him hadn't always applied his knowledge of physics to the art of building spacecraft.

"It would blow the atmosphere completely off the planet," Kirovsky said. "To answer your second question, I can only assume this weapon was a dud. Perhaps it was set to explode at a certain altitude and never did. Instead, it fell to the surface of the planet, intact."

Hollingstead stared at Kirovsky, trying to find a hole in his theory.

"Let's get back to Bonnie's original question," Tim interjected. "I acknowledge your point about the history of genocide on Earth, Edgar, but, in most of those instances, the conquering force stood to gain something: the Conquistadors wanted gold, the British wanted diamonds, and the early American settlers wanted land. Under the scenario you've just described, what would the conquerors hope to gain?" Tim stopped to let everyone think about it for a moment, before continuing. "They would have to be extraterrestrial. If not, they would have committed mass suicide themselves by blowing the atmosphere off their own planet. Therefore, we can assume they weren't interested in the land at all, because the explosion would have rendered the planet uninhabitable! If the extraterrestrials wanted some of the planet's mineral deposits, why didn't they simply take them? The Martians probably wouldn't have noticed or cared. They lived on such a small fraction of the planet's surface area…" Tim trailed off as the obvious struck him at the same moment it did the others.

"The Barrettazine!" Bleakney said. "The extraterrestrials wanted the Barrettazine!"

"But they didn't get it!" Hollingstead said. "It's still there, undisturbed."

"Perhaps something happened to the extraterrestrials themselves, before they got a chance to take it," Kirovsky said.

As his colleagues continued to explore the possibilities, Tim got lost in his own thoughts. Something had been said earlier that still bothered him. He struggled to recall what it was. It was on the tip of his tongue. He had filed the statement away in the back of his mind, to consider it later. He cursed himself now for not addressing it immediately. Suddenly, it hit him. He put it off, because *he* had been the person doing the talking. He had said, "I acknowledge your point about the history of genocide on earth, Edgar, but in most of those instances, the conquering force stood to gain something: the Conquistadors wanted gold, the British wanted diamonds, and the early American settlers wanted land." What was it about the statement that had given him pause? He relaxed and allowed the voice within his subconscious speak.

You forgot about the Crusaders, Tim. What was their motivation?

CHAPTER 28

Tim knocked lightly on the doorframe to get Stentz's attention. "Come on in," Stentz said, waving his hand.

Tim walked into the office and took a seat.

"So, how did the discussion end up this morning?" Stentz asked.

"Some very interesting thoughts, as you might imagine."

Stentz waited for Tim to elaborate. "Do you mind sharing them with me?" he finally asked.

"For the first time, I think we all agree on one point," Tim said.

Stentz put down his pencil and gave Tim his full attention. "And what point would that be?"

"The sphere introduces the likelihood we're talking about two unique civilizations, not just one."

Stentz leaned back in his chair. "I'd have to agree with that," he said. "What else?"

"We'd like to have the crew take a more precise carbon dating measurement of the soil around the sphere. It would be nice to know how long it's been there relative to the age of the Martian skeletons."

"A logical request, and one that's already in the works. What else?"

"We're interested in getting some aerial spectrometry of the site. An impact crater would suggest the sphere smashed into the planet, head on. A trench would indicate that it came in at an angle and skipped across the surface until it stopped."

Stentz raised his eyebrows. "What if neither exists?"

"That would be the most interesting scenario of all, wouldn't it, Victor? It would mean the sphere was guided in for a soft landing."

"Or that it was manufactured on Mars," Stentz said.

Tim shrugged. "Of course, we have to consider that as a possibility, too."

"But you don't think it was."

"It's too early to say for sure, but no, I don't think so."

"Do you believe the sphere is the source of the Martian's destruction?" Stentz asked.

"Again, I think it's too early to come to that conclusion, but we did bat the idea around."

"If that were the case, what do you think motivated it?" Stentz asked.

Tim shifted in the chair and called upon the voice in his subconscious to answer the question. *Does Stentz already know the answer?* Following Peter's suggestion, he cleared his mind and tried to relax. He waited for as long as he thought reasonable, and when nothing came, he hedged. "I'm afraid that's too complex a question to answer through induction alone."

"I realize we're getting ahead of ourselves, Tim, but if there *were* two civilizations—as we both believe—and the non-indigenous civilization destroyed the Martians, do you think we'll ever find out why?"

Tim shook his head. "No, I don't. Not the way things stand right now."

Stentz looked surprised. "And how do things stand right now?"

Tim edged forward in his chair. "You and I both know that a team of *linguists* isn't going to crack the Martian text, Victor. Please tell me that someone else is working on translating the scrolls."

Stentz casually peered through the windows that lined his office. "I hope you can appreciate my position, Tim," he said. "For reasons you can't possibly know, I have to keep some things classified."

"Like how the message with the coordinates got to Moyeur?"

Stentz looked Tim squarely in the eyes. "Yes, that's one such example. We have a vague idea how it was done, but I promised Bauer I wouldn't disclose it."

Tim felt adrenaline pumping in his veins. He was getting closer to the truth. "What do you have to lose by telling me who's working on the scrolls?"

"What do I have to gain?"

Tim was confused. He didn't know which card to play next. There was such a fine balance between providing too much information, and not enough. He craned his head around slowly, to make sure no one was walking down the hall. Satisfied it was empty, he leaned forward a little further. "I might just have the crib," he whispered.

Stentz threw back his head and laughed. When he noticed Tim wasn't laughing with him, he stopped. "Come on, Tim. How could you possibly have the crib?"

"I think you know more about my history than you've admitted, Victor. I think you know that I used to have visions. Visions that some people loosely termed clairvoyant."

Stentz nodded. "Yes, Tim, I did hear that. But I honestly never believed it. I brought you here for your intelligence. And on that score, you've exceeded my expectations." He peered through the windows again. "Now, are you actually asking me to breach top secret security because you're having *visions*?"

Tim tried to read Stentz, but it was impossible. Should he explain his dialogue with Peter? Even if Stentz weren't Peter, he might still be willing to accept him as a reliable source of knowledge. But what if Stentz were behind the cover-up? Would Tim be placing Peter in danger by mentioning his name? But then again, Bauer already knew about Peter, didn't he? Tim's head was spinning as he tried to come up with the perfectly measured response.

"Yes," he heard himself say. "I'm asking you to breach top secret security because of my visions."

Thirty minutes later, Tim was walking up the steps to CIA headquarters with Stentz by his side.

"Remember, these guys don't know anything about the discovery on Mars," Stentz said. "They think the text is an experimental language coming out of DoD."

"Got it," Tim replied. He'd never seen Stentz more uncomfortable.

"It would have been a lot easier if you'd just given me the crib," Stentz said.

"Now, where's the fun in that, Victor?" Tim said, trying to bring some levity to the situation.

Stentz grunted and shook his head.

When they arrived at the security desk, the guard addressed them politely. "Do you have an appointment?"

"Yes," Stentz said. "We're here to see Michael Frowitz. My name is Victor Stentz."

The man behind the desk produced a pair of forms. "Fill these out, please," he said. "I also need some form of identification. A government ID or drivers license will do."

Stentz was prepared for the request and handed him their Pentagon security badges. The guard swiped the IDs through a magnetic reader next to his computer. Tim couldn't see the computer's screen, but he could only imagine what was now displayed. The guard stared at the monitor for a moment and then studied the pair more closely. He picked up a receiver, dialed an extension, and announced the visitors. He then nodded and hung up. "Mr. Frowitz will be right down."

"Thank you," Stentz replied.

Minutes later, Tim and Stentz gazed at the Martian text on a twenty-seven inch flat screen monitor. "How did you codify the characters?" Tim asked the CIA cryptographer, Seth Krall. The man was a necrophiliac's dream date. His face was sickly pale and he had dark bags under his eyes. Tim wondered how often he made it out of the building.

"We digitally scanned the photos you gave us and catalogued all the unique characters," Krall said. He placed his hand on a special keyboard to the left of a standard one. "We programmed this modified keyboard so that each character has its own position.

It has a hundred-character capacity, but the language you gave us uses only eighty-two of them."

Tim glanced at the keyboard and saw that decals of the Martian characters had been pasted onto the keys. He was genuinely fascinated. "What process do you go through to break the code?" he asked.

"Technically, in order to *decode* something, it must be *encoded*, so we really haven't broken any code, sir. With what you've given us, it's more of a translation process than anything. I have to hand it to you DoD guys, though. You're the last of the romantics... creating an entirely unique language before you encrypt it." Krall laughed. "If you asked me, I'd tell you it's a waste of time. I mean, it was a stroke of genius to use Navajo in World War Two, but it's all about technology now. The Germans knew that, even back then. With today's thousand-bit ciphers, it's still nearly impossible to break a code...without the key."

"So...what steps are you going through to *translate* the text?" Tim asked, correcting his terminology.

Krall began to demonstrate using the keyboard. "It's all done by supercomputer," he said. "The system works through the text and tries to identify common words. Determiners like 'the,' 'a,' 'this,' 'that,' and 'which' are the most commonly used, followed closely by prepositions and pronouns. Of the fifty most commonly used words in the English language, the three categories I just mentioned account for thirty. Prepositions are the easiest to identify, because they often start a sentence."

Tim was enjoying every minute of the discussion. To him, cryptography was the perfect hybrid between the analytical and the mysterious. He felt a nudge on his back and peered over his shoulder at Stentz. Stentz gave him a stern look that could only mean *let's get on with it*. Tim re-engaged the cryptographer. "Okay, so once those words are identified, what does the system look for next?"

"At first, the computer can only allocate probabilities for the common words. We need the context of a complete sentence to make a definitive identification."

"So, after coming up with probabilities for the common words, the system then tackles the sentence structure?"

"Exactly. And that's where it gets tough. Without nouns and verbs, a sentence doesn't have a lot of context. Unfortunately, verbs and adverbs only account for ten of the fifty most commonly used words. Nouns account for none. Using a set of complex algorithms, the system attempts to assign probabilities for common verbs and adverbs, based upon the placement of the determiners, prepositions and pronouns." Krall turned to see if his guests were following along.

Tim held up his hand as a signal to pause. He stared into space thoughtfully. The translation process made perfect sense to him. It was completely logical. Clearly, the supercomputers would be able to translate the text, with the right input—input in the form of information Bauer had probably refused to provide. The cryptographers needed context themselves. Was the text an assembly manual for a child's tricycle, or driving directions from the White House to Coit Tower in San Francisco? Was it a recipe for clam chowder? Without that context, Tim had serious doubts that even the supercomputers, with their complex algorithms, could translate it.

Another considerable challenge occurred to Tim. Given that the text was about Mars, and Martians, there were bound to be many nouns that didn't even exist in English: words for the food they ate, the tools they invented, and the jobs they worked. Many of these things would not have equivalents on Earth. Tim was afraid that even knowing the Martian symbol for Jesus Christ wouldn't help. What exactly did the Martian symbol for Jesus Christ mean anyway? Why had it popped into his head so specifically? Why hadn't it come to him as the symbol for a "prophet" or some form of religious figure? Tim redirected his attention to the cryptographer. "Okay," he said. "I understand everything so far, but it sounds to me like you've got a lot of holes to fill."

Krall blushed. With some color in his cheeks, Tim thought he appeared a lot healthier. The blood receded quickly, however, and the cryptographer returned to the ranks of the living dead.

"Well, you didn't give us a lot to go on, did you?" he said defensively. "With no context for the text, we've been consigned to crunching it by brute force."

"What exactly does crunching it by brute force entail?" Tim asked.

The analyst pointed to his right. Tim turned to observe several other analysts at similar workstations, plugging away. At the end of the room, behind a glass wall, he saw stacks of giant processors.

"Stored in those supercomputers are millions of volumes of text across a variety of fields," Krall said. "Novels, poems, treatises, instruction manuals, encyclopedias, religious doctrine, you name it. The text you've given us—including the common word probabilities already identified—is being compared, sentence by sentence, to the volumes in those supercomputers. Based upon sentence structure and length, frequency of common words, length of other words and many more factors, we're trying to determine its context. Compared to known works, does the text you gave us appear to be political in nature? Is it a war plan? Is it fiction? Is it a medical journal? Once we determine its context, we'll go from there."

Krall's comments confirmed Tim's belief that using brute force would get them nowhere.

"What if I gave you a clue?" Tim said.

Krall's face lit up. A smile spread across his lips and disappeared just as quickly. "I'm afraid that would be cheating," he said seriously. "You came to us to see if the language could be translated. It wouldn't be a fair test of its viability, if you gave me a clue, would it?"

"I'd only be revealing one symbol," Tim said.

The analyst glanced around the room to see if anyone was watching them. The other cryptographers were all heads-down. He shrugged. "It's not the key, is it?" he asked.

Tim shook his head.

"Sure, why not? I've got to tell you, though, giving me one symbol isn't going to make much of a difference."

Tim glanced at Stentz who was listening intently. "Go to page twenty-one of the text we gave you," Tim instructed.

The analyst pivoted in his chair and typed a few commands on the standard keyboard to his right. A page of Martian text came up on the screen. Tim reached out and placed his finger on the monitor. He could feel Stentz leaning around him to see exactly which symbol he was touching. "That's the symbol for Jesus Christ," he said.

Stentz stumbled forward and nearly fell to the ground. He grabbed the back of the cryptographer's chair just in time to save himself from a nasty tumble.

Tim turned to glare at him and wished he had a camera. He thought of an old MasterCard commercial: trip to Mars, $128 billion dollars; CIA encryption system, $43 million dollars; the expression on your boss's face when you disclose the Martian symbol for Jesus Christ, priceless.

"Okay," Krall said. He typed several commands using the standard keyboard and then reached over to the modified one. He scanned the keys and located the symbol Tim had pointed out. He pressed it and leaned back in his chair. "All right," he said. "The supercomputers are processing."

"Thank you," Tim said.

"How long will it take to process?" Stentz asked.

Krall laughed. "You guys are all the same! You want it yesterday," he said. "Unfortunately, this process doesn't work like that. My guess is it's going to take a couple of days. I limited the comparison to religious material, but even at that, it's going to take a long time. There's a lot of fuzzy logic going on in there."

Tim saw Stentz shrink. He decided to close out the discussion himself. "Well, again, thank you for your time," he said. "Please let us know if that gets you anywhere."

"No problem," Krall said, rising from his chair. He shook hands with his visitors and then waived to his boss.

Frowitz came over immediately. "Get everything you need?" he asked.

"Yes. For now anyway. Thanks for the update," Stentz said.

"No problem. Let me walk you back to the security desk."

As they passed a few tables on their way to the exit, Tim noticed that the screen of each analyst contained samples of the

Martian text. "How many guys do you have working on this project?" he asked Frowitz.

"Ten of my team are on it full time."

"That seems like a lot."

Frowitz nodded. "It is. But when priority-one instructions come down from on high, I like to follow them."

"Don't we all!" Stentz said quickly.

Tim wondered from how high within the CIA the instructions had come, as he followed Frowitz out of the room. The door had nearly closed behind him, when he heard shouting. Frowitz immediately reopened the door and poked his head inside. Tim peered over his shoulder.

Seth Krall was pumping his fists in the air and dancing down a row of desks. "Yeah, baby!"

Tim wondered if the guy were doing the samba or the rumba. Either way, he'd never seen it executed so poorly. The dance of the living dead!

CHAPTER 29

Tim watched Stentz walk into the briefing room carrying his computer and a stack of briefing packets. Victor didn't acknowledge the think-tank members, who were all present and seated, but proceeded to the front of the room and placed the computer and briefing packets on the table. Reaching into the breast pocket of his sport coat, he produced a piece of paper and read from it. "'You are from below; I am from above. You are of this world; I am not of this world. I told you that you would die in your sins; if you do not believe that I am the one I claim to be, you will indeed die in your sins.'"

The think-tank members sat mute.

Stentz continued. "'For I have come down from heaven not to do my will but to do the will of him who sent me. And you will know the truth, and the truth will set you free.'"

Hollingstead spoke up first. "Why are you reading passages from the Bible, Victor?"

"Good question. To be more specific, they're direct quotes from Jesus Christ."

"Then why are you reading quotes from Jesus Christ?" Kirovsky asked, irritated.

Stentz scanned the faces of the think-tank members. His silence was unsettling. Finally, when he was sure he had their full attention, he dropped the bomb. "The quotes that I just read are from the Martian scrolls, word for word."

Tim heard a scream. He turned to identify the person responsible, but he only saw confused faces. Everyone was still staring at Stentz, and although stunned by the news, they seemed oblivious to the shrill outburst. It was surreal. The outburst had been so clear. If it hadn't come from a member of the group, then where had it come from? Was it possible that he had imagined it? He shrunk in his chair, balking at the thought of his dementia returning.

Suddenly, with great relief and an equal dose of surprise, he realized that he had indeed detected a scream. To his amazement, however, he hadn't detected it audibly, but rather, chemically. He saw the entire process in his mind clearly, like a student absorbing a lesson. Stentz's statement had shocked the other members of the team, causing their hypothalamuses to become electrically stimulated, which in turn had activated their pituitary glands to release epinephrine and norepinephrine. He could hardly believe it, but he had actually detected the increase in electrical and biomagnetic impulses in the brains and spinal chords of the people around him! He had also sensed the increase in their muscle tension, brought on by hormones excreted from their adrenal glands. Even now, he could smell the biochemicals and perspiration effusing from their pores. It was amazing! And, if his ability to detect these responses weren't enough, his mind had translated the impulses into a format that would register instantaneously as a scream—the perfect auditory representation for the physiological stimulus.

Tim returned his attention to the think-tank members. No one had spoken a word in response to Stentz's assertion. They simply stared at him as if he'd lost his mind. "What's wrong? Cat got your tongues?" Stentz said, grinning. "I know it's hard to believe, but in their effort to translate the scrolls, the linguists kept running into the same symbol time and time again. Due to its pervasiveness and placement in the sentences, they believe the symbol represented a god of some sort, or at least an important religious figure."

Tim knew Stentz was lying. They had both agreed that it would be best not to reveal the true source of the revelation. The fact that Tim had identified the symbol through a vision probably wouldn't sit well with the academics in the room.

Stentz continued. "The linguists went on to hypothesize that much of the text following the ubiquitous symbol was quoted directly from the Martian religious figure. Since the Bible is the most readily available source of religious text in the western world, the linguists used supercomputers to compare the text in the scrolls with text in the Bible. More specifically, they compared the text from the Martian religious figure to quotes from Jesus Christ." Stentz paused. The group was still stunned. "In many cases, the same Martian symbols were showing up in the same order as words from Jesus Christ. It proved to be the key to translating the scrolls."

Another long period of silence passed before Kirovsky spoke. "So, just like that? By identifying one symbol in the Martian text, the linguists were able to translate the entire language? I'm sorry Victor, but I can't accept that."

"I purposefully oversimplified the process, Edgar. Would you like me to bore you with the technical details?" Stentz asked.

Before Kirovsky could respond to the question, Shah spoke for him. "I would," he said.

"Okay." Stentz nodded. "The linguists used supercomputers in the early stages of the translation process to compare the Martian text to characteristics of the English language. They drew parallels between the most commonly used words in English to the most common Martian symbols, and then compared the positioning of common words within sentences to the positioning of the Martian symbols. Using this method, the linguists were able to identify probable determiners, conjunctions, prepositions and pronouns. With that as a foundation, the supercomputers matched the quotes by the Martian prophet to those of Jesus Christ, starting by pairing sentences of similar length, and then identifying overlapping common words within those sentences. And even with that as a starting point, I understand your skepticism, Edgar. The translation shouldn't have come so easily. The one thing you haven't considered, however, is the fact that so many of the quotes between the Martian religious figure and Jesus Christ were almost identical. That's what allowed the linguists to translate it so quickly."

Tim could tell from their expressions that the think-tank members still weren't convinced, prompting Stentz to show his frustration.

"See for yourselves!" Stentz said, handing out the briefing packets.

A few minutes of silence passed as the think-tank members read through the packets.

"You're saying that this is the *exact* translation of the scrolls?" Kirovsky asked, holding up the briefing packet.

"Yes, it's the exact translation," Stentz said. "The first three pages in your packets are direct quotes from the Martian prophet, consolidated from the various scrolls. Starting at page four, the unabridged translation of the scrolls begins, in chronological order."

"How do you know they're *direct* quotes from the Martian prophet?" Hollingstead asked.

"The symbol for the Martian prophet bookends the text. It's their standard method for identifying the spoken word, just like we use quotation marks," Stentz replied.

"How can this be? I just don't understand what this means." Shah was starting to lose it and Tim thought he knew why: Shah wasn't Christian.

"Why are you all dancing around the truth?" Bleakney asked, wide-eyed. "Isn't it obvious? This proves the existence of God! It also proves that Christ was his son!"

Tim was amazed at how animated the normally shy Englishman had become. He detected the chemical reactions between Shah and Bleakney—intense hostility.

"Hold on, Martin!" Stentz said. "I think it's a little early to be drawing conclusions about God and Jesus Christ."

"How else can you explain it?" Bleakney said, digging his heels in. "God obviously sent his son to Mars, just as he sent him to Earth 300 million years later!"

"How can you possibly jump to that conclusion?" Shah yelled.

"How can you possibly *deny* it?" Bleakney continued. "It's Christ incarnate. His lessons are in the Martian scrolls, exactly as they are in the Bible!"

"And what Bible would that be, Martin?" Shah said, rising to his feet. "There have been countless translations of the Bible over the years, each subject to the whims of those doing the translating. And what about the language barrier? Translating Hebrew into English alone is responsible for major variations from the original text. You're now comparing quotes from a certain *version* of a Bible to quotes from scrolls that have been translated from *Martian* to English. You can multiply the error probability by ten!"

"Did you get to the last page of the packet, Pranab?" Bleakney held up the briefing packet for Shah to see. "It's the page that identifies the degrees of freedom and translation accuracy. Go down to the third line." Before Shah could get there, Bleakney read the line for him. "It gives a correlation coefficient of .942, with only two degrees of freedom. Your translation inaccuracy argument just went out the window!"

Shah took a step toward Bleakney, but Kirovsky grabbed his arm before he advanced further.

"Stop!" Stentz yelled.

The room fell silent and Shah reluctantly returned to his seat.

"Let's just take a few steps back, shall we?" Stentz said. "If I'm not mistaken, no one in this room is clergy...or Swami."

Tim was impressed that Stentz knew the term for a Hindu priest.

"Let's flesh this out without drawing any conclusions about religion here on earth, shall we?" Stentz glared at Bleakney.

The Englishman blushed and retreated into his shell. Tim thought Stentz's proposal was a good one in principle, although he had his doubts about its viability in practice.

"Why don't we pick a fictitious name for the Martian prophet." Stentz's gaze fell to his papers. "Mead," he said, holding up his portfolio and pointing to the brand name. "Is that acceptable to everyone?"

There were no objections.

"Now, I'm not saying that Mead was Jesus Christ incarnate, but it's difficult to deny the striking similarities between their teachings. For the sake of argument, however, let's say Mead's quotations matched Buddha's rather than Jesus Christ's. It still begs the same question: why would God send a prophet to both Mars and Earth?"

Immediately, Bleakney returned to his pulpit. "To teach us how to live, of course. To teach us right from wrong."

The room fell silent again.

"Perhaps a more pertinent question is, *how* would he send the prophets to each planet?" Tim said.

A look of incredulity swept across Bleakney's face. "Haven't any of you read the Bible or gone to Sunday school? He'd simply will it to be. You know, the Immaculate Conception."

"What if God were bound by the laws of physics like the rest of us? How would he send the prophet then?" Tim asked.

Bleakney shook his head in frustration. "What do you mean 'bound by the laws of physics'? He *created* the laws of physics!"

"Shut up, Martin," Kirovsky said.

Tim leaned forward. "Follow along with me here," he said. "What if the laws of physics, as we know them, applied to God, too? How would he send prophets to civilizations throughout the universe?"

"He might send them in a ship of some sort," Hollingstead muttered.

"Perhaps a sphere, four feet in diameter, made of an unknown substance, capable of withstanding tremendous impact, heat and cold," Kirovsky added.

Tim raised his eyebrows.

"How do you explain the Immaculate Conception then?" Bleakney asked. "How does the prophet make it from the *spaceship* to the womb of a chaste female?"

"Maybe the ship contains another being," Tim said. "Or an angel, if that suits you, Martin. The angel's sole task is to find an appropriate host."

"And then what?" Bleakney sputtered. "Does the angel have sex with the host? Is that what you're suggesting?"

"Not at all," Tim said evenly. "Perhaps the angel injects the host with an embryo while she's sleeping. The host wouldn't even have to know. The sanctity of the Immaculate Conception would remain intact," he said, realizing that they were quickly departing from Stentz's nondenominational scenario.

"Then how was Jesus Christ born of flesh and blood?" Shah asked. "How, if he was this God-like embryo, did he not possess any God-like physical characteristics?"

Tim thought about it for a second before responding. "To God, wouldn't the physical characteristics of the prophet be inconsequential? In fact, wouldn't God want the prophet to look like any other being on the planet? Without a God-like appearance the onus would be on the being's message, not the prophet's ability to influence people with his amazing beauty or physical strength."

"So, you're suggesting the embryo would morph to possess the same physical characteristics of a child born naturally of the female host?" Hollingstead asked.

Tim nodded.

"Except for it's mental characteristics, which would be God-like," Kirovsky concluded.

Tim nodded again.

"Where does the angel go, then, once he's found the host and injected the embryo?" Bleakney asked.

Tim thought he knew the answer, but something about the situation on Mars didn't support his theory. "I don't know," he said.

"If what you're saying is true, Tim," Shah said, "where's the sphere that brought Jesus' embryo to earth?"

"I'd be willing to bet it's buried somewhere in Israel."

Shah grunted. "Is that right?" he said. "How does a thousand dollars sound?"

Tim was shocked. He couldn't believe anyone could be so insensitive. If proven right, his theory would drive more political unrest in the world than any other discovery in history. And Shah wanted to place a wager on it?

"If it isn't too much trouble, I'd like in for a thousand as well," Bleakney said before Tim could respond to Shah.

How quickly the tables turn, Tim thought. Not five minutes ago Shah was ready to jump across the table and pummel

Bleakney. Now, they were a unified front. Tim turned to address Stentz. "Victor, at one time, you told me that this group had a great deal of influence. You said that if we said jump, people would ask how high."

Stentz nodded. "That's right."

"I'm assuming, then, if we wanted to re-task a Hyperion hyperspectral satellite, that wouldn't be a problem."

Stentz shifted in his chair. "If you're talking about sending it over Israel, that might take a little work." He rubbed the side of his face thoughtfully. "But in light of what you're talking about...yes, we can probably make that happen."

Tim pointed at Shah and Bleakney. "You've got yourselves a bet."

CHAPTER 30

Tim gazed at Hollingstead as the waiter held up the bottle of wine for her inspection. He still hadn't fully recovered from the shock of seeing her in a cocktail dress. The thin black material hugged her body in all the right places. Her hair was pulled up, exposing her high cheekbones and striking blue eyes. As soon as she'd walked into the restaurant, Tim's head, and every other man's in the place, had snapped to attention. He didn't need some voice in the back of his mind to announce her presence. Simple rules of attraction had managed just fine.

The waiter poured and left them alone.

"How is it that you know so much about almost everything, but nothing about wine?" she asked.

"Despite what you might think, I'm not a walking encyclopedia of knowledge," Tim laughed.

"Could have fooled me." Bonnie sipped the wine and eyed him over the rim of her glass.

Tim marveled at her. She was absolutely captivating: smart, beautiful, playful, and sexy—practically custom-made to his specifications. As he stared into her eyes, he realized how difficult it might be to keep her at arm's length. The last thing he wanted to do was compromise her safety. He realized he'd been staring too long and quickly answered her question. "Why am I ignorant about wine? Although South Africa boasts nearly three percent of the world's wine production, western Africa—my home for the past five years—produces almost none. Grapes don't grow in tropical zones. They need temperate to dry climates."

"See, there you go again. Genius!"

Tim felt himself blush. "And I invited you to dinner for this abuse?"

"Oh, come on, Tim. It's fun!" Bonnie laughed. "Honestly, name one topic, other than wine, that you don't know more about than I."

Bingo! She threw the fastball right over the middle of the plate and he didn't have to fish for it. "How about human evolution?" Tim said.

Hollingstead sank back into the soft leather booth. Tim had given the maitre d' a hundred dollar tip to lock down this particular location. In a corner, it afforded him a clear view of the entire restaurant. Shortly after being seated, he had watched two men in suits enter the restaurant and head for the bar. The chime in the back of his mind had told him they were CIA. They were following him wherever he went.

"Being a paleontologist, I might have a leg up on you there," Bonnie responded.

"See? I don't know everything about everything."

"You might be surprised. I'd be willing to bet that you know almost as much about evolution as I do." Bonnie sat up and placed her forearms on the table.

"How about a thousand dollars?" Tim said, deadpan.

She froze for a moment. When she realized he was making light of Shah and Bleakney, she burst out laughing. Bonnie reached over and touched Tim's arm. It was just a brief caress, but it prompted a warm tingle inside of him. He caught a hint of her perfume and sensed the sexual pheromones rising from her body.

"Seriously, Tim," she said, "even for specialists in the field of human evolution, there are a lot more questions than answers."

"Like the fabled missing link?"

"Exactly! I mean, with all the technology we have today, you would think we could prove categorically that man evolved from apes. But, alas, we haven't even been able to prove that yet."

"Why not?"

"Well, for one thing, we don't have a lot of fossils to work with. An esteemed colleague of mine once said that the grand total of transitionary period biped fossils could fit within a single coffin. And every time someone announces another breakthrough—Lucy, Piltdown man, Java man, the skull of Chad—they all fall through under further scrutiny. They are either later period bones of man mingled with much older bones of apes, or they fall squarely within one classification or another...either ape or man. Never the transitionary species that we've all been looking for."

"Can't DNA mapping help? I mean, with everything we're learning about the human genome, can't we determine once and for all that we've evolved from apes?"

"DNA doesn't last that long, Tim. It's proven to be an amazing tool for paleontologists focused on the Holocene period—ten thousand years ago to the present. But, when looking at the Pliocene period—five million years ago to two million years ago— it really can't help us. Besides, even if we could find some DNA that had been somehow frozen for millions of years, it would have to be pristine...perfectly preserved to delineate between species."

Tim tried not to fidget. He couldn't be getting better background information. He simply needed to keep Bonnie on track. "Are man and ape really that similar?" he asked.

She stared into her wineglass thoughtfully. "How much do you know about DNA and gene sequencing, Tim?"

"Only the basics," he said. "DNA contains the hereditary instructions that define the individual characteristics of every living thing. Each DNA strand is basically a backbone with numerous base chemicals attached to it...in pairs. The base chemicals are cytosine, adenine, guanine and thymine. How these base chemicals are paired and sequenced along the strand determines everything about you: your eye color, your height, your intelligence, your disposition, your susceptibility to certain diseases...everything."

Bonnie laughed. "Just the basics, huh? I think you owe me a thousand dollars!"

"Come on, Bonnie!"

The waiter arrived with a platter of calamari. They both watched him in silence as he laid out the small serving plates. As soon as he was out of earshot, Bonnie leaned forward to whisper, "Well, Mr. Smartypants, did you know that modern human DNA is ninety-eight percent identical to that of a chimpanzee?"

"I did not know that."

"And did you know that geneticists still have no idea what ninety-seven percent of the DNA in our bodies does? They call it junk DNA."

"I didn't know that either," Tim lied.

"And did you know that in modern day humans, only one in a thousand gene sequences are different? The other nine-hundred ninety-nine are exactly the same!"

"You got me again." Tim lied for the second time.

"Getting back to my point, it's the tiniest differences in gene sequencing that can make huge differences in the physical and mental characteristics of a species. That's why the DNA would have to be pristine in order to answer the missing link question." Tim shifted in his chair. The next question was a tricky one, but he desperately wanted an expert's opinion.

"So...according to all the available evidence, the jump from Australopithecus to Homo habilis—apes to man—can't be explained scientifically." It was a statement, not a question.

Bonnie started to cough, nearly choking on a piece of calamari. Tim was getting ready to administer the Heimlich maneuver when she waved him off. After taking a swig of water and catching her breath, she began to laugh. "Don't tell me you're a creationist, Tim!"

"I didn't say that I was a creationist, Bonnie. The question is simple. Strictly speaking, is there any scientific evidence that can explain such an evolutionary jump?"

"If you're not implying creationism, then what's your point?"

"Come on, Bonnie. Coming at it from a purely scientific approach, despite what your *intuition* tells you about evolution, what happened? How did apes make the jump to becoming man?"

Bonnie took a gulp of wine and furtively glanced around the restaurant, like the paleontologist police were poised to revoke her doctorate. "That's a pretty big caveat, Tim," she said. "But, if you're forcing me to come up with an alternative explanation, other than natural evolution..." Hollingstead leaned back and looked up at the ceiling. She took a few moments to ponder. "From the available evidence—which you'll remember fits inside of a single coffin—I'd have to say that apes were genetically tweaked by some unknown force. Not a huge tweak, mind you, but tweaked enough to set a new course...destination Homo Sapien."

Tim picked up his wine glass for the first time. *No further questions for the witness, your Honor.* As he looked over the top of his glass, he caught Bonnie's stare. Her eyes were so alive...so provocative.

"Here you have me supporting creationism," she said with a wry smile, "before the entrée has even arrived." Bonnie raised her own glass and took a sip, her eyes glued to his. She placed the wine down and leaned forward, offering him a spectacular view of her supple breasts. "Which makes me wonder what other compromising positions you'll have me in by the end of the evening."

Tim took another gulp of his wine, sensing the chemicals pouring from Bonnie's body. He could even feel his own rising up to meet hers, intermingling in the air between them. How was he supposed to resist this?

CHAPTER 31

S tentz threw the two-inch thick briefing packets on the table and peered out at the think-tank members. Their calm reserve was a study in self-control, as every single one of them was practically jumping out of their skin to see the results from the satellite. For the past two days, they'd been relegated to pontificating on the origins of Jesus Christ, without any hard data. Their discussion had turned into nothing more than an ideological debate, uncommon ground for people who had spent their entire lives in the study of science.

Stentz took his time plugging the A/V cord into the port of his laptop. Tim could tell he was enjoying the tense silence. Stentz liked being center stage, and that's exactly where he'd found himself since the discovery of Barrettazine. Tim wondered what Stentz would have done for a living had he not gone into physics. Perhaps the stage would have been the ideal place for him, he reasoned. The man certainly had an actor's presence.

After he had tightened the A/V cord, Stentz looked up to address the group. "As you've probably guessed by now, we finally received the satellite shots." He pressed the power button on the projector's remote, and the image from his computer illuminated the large screen behind him. Magnetic flux lines blanketed the relief map of northern Israel. It was a twenty-square-mile parcel of land, just north of the West Bank and east of the Mediterranean Sea. "The Argentines were good enough to re-task their SAC-C satellite for us," Stentz said. "But, given the fact that NASA supplied the bird's magnetometer, I thought it was only fair." He stood in front of the screen and waved a hand over the area. "Here we have a seven-mile swath of the far western section of Israel. As you can see from the absence of any significant flux lines, there's not a high intensity magnetic field, like the one generated by the sphere on Mars." He advanced the presentation to the next seven-mile swath.

Immediately, Tim sensed the energy in the room spike, as he had sensed several days ago. He peered at the image and saw why: three miles southeast of Nazareth, circled in red, the magnetic flux lines bowed at a point. Shah and Bleakney exchanged a horrified glance.

Stentz took a step to his right and placed his finger in the middle of the anomaly.

"A significant magnetic force is being generated here," he said. "It's even stronger than the one being generated by the sphere on Mars."

Bleakney's facial tick and nervous humming emerged. Shah remained stone-faced. Hollingstead and Kirovsky both shifted in their seats.

"After further investigation, however, we determined that it's a particle acceleration facility," Stentz said. He advanced the presentation to the final seven-mile swath.

Tim noticed several areas where the magnetic flux lines wavered slightly.

"There are some small anomalies here," Stentz said. "But nothing strong enough to be a sphere." He turned to the group. "Unfortunately, that's it for northern Israel."

Tim slumped into his chair, completely deflated.

"The reason we had to wait so long for the satellite results was that we broadened our search," Stentz said, advancing the presentation. Tim perked up again. "We made passes of the entire country, in seven-mile swaths, just as we did for northern Israel. The areas that you see circled in red are potential hits based upon magnetic intensity. And, as was the case in northern Israel, through investigation, we were able to discount every one. They're all man-made sources."

Tim was shocked. He had not only thought his theory was the only plausible explanation, but he had *felt* it was true. To discover he was wrong seriously shook his confidence. Where did he go from here if he couldn't trust the chimes in his head? He felt the eyes of his team members on him, but he couldn't bring himself to meet their gaze. At least Bleakney and Shah were gracious enough not to rub it in his face.

Stentz handed out the briefing packets. "The detailed data is all there," he said, looking at Tim. "I encourage you to review it if you have any questions or concerns."

Tim knew that *questions or concerns* translated to *doubts* where he was concerned. He did have doubts, though. So, as Stentz tried to spawn another discussion regarding the link to Christ in the scrolls, Tim poured over the briefing packet. He reached the third page before raising his hand. "Victor, may I ask you a question?"

"Sure, what's on your mind?"

"Why did you cut off the Sea of Galilee in your presentation?"

Stentz frowned. "Well, first of all, it didn't contain any anomalies, Tim," he said.

"Didn't contain any anomalies?"

"That's right," Stentz replied defensively.

"Here's one at two teslas." Tim held up the briefing packet and pointed to the occurrence about a mile into the sea, off the southwestern coast.

"Tim, that's not even one-twentieth the strength of the Martian sphere!" Stentz snapped. "Had we chased down every single occurrence at two teslas, we'd still be doing the groundwork! Do you have reason to believe the flux density of the sphere on Earth would be significantly less than the one on Mars?"

"No," Tim stated. "I don't. Except, you're comparing apples to oranges. How far beneath the surface was the sphere on Mars when its flux density was measured?"

"A little over fifty feet," Stentz said.

"How deep is the Sea of Galilee?" Tim asked.

"I don't know, Tim, but it's not deep enough to make up the difference."

Shah raised his hand. "Excuse me, but what are you two talking about?"

"Magnetic intensity decreases as it travels through different materials," Tim said. "If the sphere in the Sea of Galilee is deep enough, it could conceivably be the same flux density as the sphere on Mars, but not register as strongly on the magnetometer."

"That's a fresh water lake, isn't it?" Kirovsky asked. "It doesn't look very big on the map either…maybe five miles across? It couldn't be deep enough to make a difference of twenty times, could it?"

Stentz stepped back to his computer and plugged in the high speed Internet cable. He was clearly annoyed. "Tim, if you weren't already in the hole a few grand, I'd bet you another thousand that the lake is no more than two hundred feet deep!" He double clicked on his Internet Explorer icon.

"The sphere's at a depth of 142 feet, actually," Tim stated, like it was a well-known fact. The think-tank members all turned to stare at him. Victor's jaw flexed. He proceeded to Google and typed in his search criteria: SEA OF GALILEE DEPTH.

As the site processed the request, Hollingstead gawked at Tim, mystified. "How could you possibly know the sphere is at a depth of 142 feet, Tim?"

"It still wouldn't make up the difference in flux density, would it?" Shah opined.

Tim ignored the questions. He sat quietly while Stentz double clicked on a promising Web site and scrolled through the text.

"One hundred fifty seven feet!" Kirovsky found it first.

The group was visibly stunned. Tim's speculation about the depth of the sphere was simply too close to the maximum depth of the lake to be coincidental. After a few seconds, Hollingstead and Shah blurted out their questions again, almost in unison.

"How can you possibly know the exact depth of the sphere?"

"How could it make up the 20x delta?"

"Martin?" Tim gave the geologist the opportunity to explain.

"I'm afraid you've got me, too, Tim. I know all materials have different conductivity ratios, but I'm no expert in magnetism."

"Oh, come on!" Shah boomed. "Could water be that much different than soil?"

Tim glanced at Shah. He almost felt badly for having to break the news to him. "The conductivity ratios that Martin is referring to are called dielectric constants," he said. "Generally speaking, they represent the electromagnetic conductivity of any given material. A vacuum is the most conductive medium for magnetism, obviously. As such, the dielectric constant for a vacuum is the baseline measurement of one. Numbers are assigned to other materials based upon their conductivity relative to a vacuum. A material two times less conductive than a vacuum is assigned a two, a material three times less conductive is assigned a three, and so on. Dry soil, for example, has a dielectric constant of three, while granite has a constant of five, and limestone an eight. Any guesses what the dielectric constant is for water?" Tim peered at the team members. Shah wouldn't even return his gaze.

"Eighty!" Tim said. "Therefore, if you run a set of calculations, taking the flux density of the sphere on Mars at fifty feet, with an average dielectric constant of 4.5 for the iron-rich soil, and then you assume the same flux density of the sphere on Earth, conducting through water, with a dielectric constant of 80, you conclude that the sphere is 142 feet below the surface."

The think-tank members were speechless. Who knew about dielectric constants, anyway, let alone recite their values from memory? And who could run a mental calculation of such magnitude?

After several seconds of silence, Stentz spoke up. "Are you that confident, Tim?"

"Yes, Victor. I'm that confident."

"You know how tough this is going to be to verify, don't you?" Stentz asked.

"Yes, I know."

#   #   #

Tim sat quietly in Bauer's office while Stentz explained the most recent development to the general. He gazed at the walls of the office, trying to avoid direct eye contact with the man. Satellite pictures of Mars served as impromptu wallpaper, in the otherwise sparse room. At fifteen miles high, the peak of the Olympus Mons volcano jutted up through reddish dust clouds, blanketing its

420-mile base. The frosty hood of the northern ice cap glowed like a halo from sunlight poking over the horizon. The Valles Marineris gorge stretched for 3,000 miles along the planet's equator. As Tim stared at the image, the room around him began to swirl. He pictured himself standing on the edge of the gorge. A strong wind kicked up and swept him off his feet. He was in a free-fall, tumbling headfirst, treacherously close to the sheer wall of the cliff. The abyss grew darker and darker the farther he fell. Purple haze excreted from the sides of the cliffs, like steam rising up the walls of a shower. He tried to fight off the vision, but he was already too deep. He noticed the haze wasn't rising off the surface of the cliff, but rather spewing out from caves that littered its face. He peered downward and saw the ground rising up quickly to swallow him. He jolted himself free of the vision just as Stentz concluded his presentation.

"Are you out of your mind!" Bauer yelled. "Do you know how sensitive the Israelis are right now?"

"Yes, I know," Stentz replied.

Tim was all too aware of the stance the White House had taken on the most recent Palestinian-Israeli squabble. As a result, current U.S.-Israeli relations were at an all-time low. It was highly unlikely the Israelis would consent to a U.S.-led expedition on their soil— or in their lake, as the case may be. In fact, the more he thought about it, Bauer's team would have to conduct said expedition without any Israeli involvement anyway, to preserve the secrecy of the sphere—a concession that wouldn't have been granted at the height of friendly relations, let alone right now.

"You do realize we'd have to go in unannounced," Bauer said. "And if the team were caught…" he shook his head gravely.

"I don't think it's worth risking an international incident over this, gentlemen," Tim interjected.

"Aren't you the one insisting it's out there?" Bauer asked. "Now, when the heat's on, you're not that confident?"

"You're missing my point," Tim said.

Bauer's face reddened. "Why don't you explain it to me more clearly, then!"

"I don't think it's worth an international incident, because I believe it's a foregone conclusion. The sphere is there."

Bauer laughed. "You've got to love scientists, don't you, Victor? Always ready to confidently state their theories, and then never around when they're proven wrong in the field. I've got a new theorem for you, Mr. Redmond: the degree of providence applied to any situation should be directly proportional to the number of lives at stake. In other words, when you get out of the lab, check that cocky attitude at the door!"

"Wow, if that's not a lack of gratitude, I don't know what is!" Stentz charged. "Tim single-handedly cracked the Martian scrolls only days ago, and now you're rebuking him?"

"I'm glad you brought that up, Victor." Bauer's blue eyes narrowed. He peered across the desk at Tim. "How *did* you crack the scrolls anyway? How in the hell could you have possibly known the Martian symbol for Jesus Christ?"

Tim looked over at Stentz, who returned his stare confidently. He knew in an instant that Stentz hadn't sold him out. It had to be one of the CIA cryptographers. Could Bauer have been the one who issued the priority-one directive to translate the scrolls? Did a two-star general wield that much power? He didn't think so, but he couldn't be certain. Perhaps all two-star generals weren't created equal.

After getting no response from Tim, Bauer pressed again. "How could you know that, Tim? I'd really like to know. And don't try to sell me a load of bullshit about divine intervention!"

Tim had enough. "Look," he said rising from his chair. "You guys asked *me* for help on this project, remember? It wasn't the other way around. If you don't want my help anymore, say so. I'll be on the first plane back to Ghana before you can say *unsolved mystery!*"

Stentz opened his mouth to respond, but Bauer cut him off. "It's not that I don't want your help. It's that I'd like to know who else we got in the bargain. Who's feeding you information?"

Tim was about to leave when he felt Stentz's hand on his elbow. The man was standing next to him and leaning over Bauer's desk.

"General, I don't know who you're used to dealing with, but nobody talks to me or my people like that," Stentz said. "Now, if you don't want to be a team player on this one...if you don't want to investigate this site in Israel, let me know. Because, when push comes to shove, I bet I could get a team out there in less than seventy-two hours...without your help!"

Tim braced for Bauer's wrath, but before the general could respond, Stentz dragged him out of the office. As they passed through the doorway, he half expected a rearward assault. To say that he was impressed by Stentz's stand would have been a monumental understatement.

When they reached the conference room, Stentz stopped in front of the closed door. "Tim, why don't you tell the group to take the rest of the day off," he said. "I have a few fires to put out. I'll see you all in the conference room tomorrow morning at eight o'clock sharp." He turned and headed down the hallway toward his office.

"Victor," Tim called.

Stentz stopped and looked back.

"Thank you."

Stentz flashed his winning smile, winked, and took off down the hallway.

Tim was happy to have the afternoon free. He had a few of his own fires to put out.

CHAPTER 32

Tim opened the door to his room at the Latham slowly, half expecting to see the place sacked. It wasn't. Everything was the way he'd left it. He strode to the window and tossed a shopping bag onto the desktop fronting it. He pulled a roll of string from the bag, unwound about a foot-and-a-half, and cut it. Then, reaching into his pocket, he withdrew a small key bearing no other markings than the number 124 engraved on its side. He looped the string through the hole in the key, tied it around his neck, and stuffed it under his shirt. Next, he turned on his clock radio and proceeded to the adjoining suite.

The computer was still on the table next to the window, and he took a seat in front of it. For the past four days, he had tried to reach Peter, to no avail. The man who had normally responded within seconds of his first query was AWOL. Tim was concerned that whoever was killing the ranking members of the Volenta, may have also gotten to him.

> Tim: Are you there, Peter?
>
> Peter: Yes.
>
> Tim: Where have you been? I've been trying to reach you for the past four days!
>
> Peter: I know.
>
> Tim: So, why didn't you respond?
>
> Peter: You've been doing remarkably well on your own, Tim. You shouldn't use me as a crutch.

A flash of anger welled up inside of him. Didn't Peter think he deserved that explanation first, instead of making him sweat through four days of silence? Suddenly, he remembered what he wanted to say, what he should have said within the first seconds of Peter's response.

Tim: B

He had already typed the first letter of Bauer's name but something held him back. The chime in the back of his mind told him to be more vague, although he wondered why. After everything he'd shared with Peter, and after everything that Peter had shared with him, why would he feel skittish now? He changed the context of the sentence slightly.

Tim: Before you say anything else, you must know that someone is aware of our conversations. We're being monitored.

Peter: Of course someone knows.

Tim: That doesn't bother you?

Peter: There's a difference between someone being aware that conversations are occurring, and knowing the content of those conversations. His technology is very advanced. Obviously, he's aware that transmissions are being exchanged. My technology is equally advanced, however. The contents of the messages are secure.

Tim thought back to his encounter with Bauer in the elevator. He tried to recall everything the general had said. Suddenly, he remembered something important.

Tim: He knows about the special food that you told me to eat!

Peter: You think he learned that from our online conversations? What have you been eating at the Pentagon?

Tim remembered that he'd asked Stentz to stock his mini-fridge. Could Stentz have tipped Bauer off? Or had Bauer just searched his room at the Pentagon? Either way, it would explain Bauer's knowledge of the food. Perhaps the transmissions really were secure.

Peter: Relax and tell me what you learned in school today.

Tim: A great deal.

Peter: I figured as much. You're beginning to interact with your subconscious more effectively. It's improving not only your mental abilities, but your physical ones, too, isn't it?

Tim: I'm sensing things, Peter. I'm detecting emotions through electric impulses in people's brains and the chemicals rising from their bodies. I know if someone's lying or surprised or excited.

Peter: In time, you will discover other new talents.

Tim: Like what?

Peter: I'll let you figure that out. What have you learned about the situation on Mars?

Tim: The Martian scrolls have finally been translated. As I'm sure you already know, there's a stunning similarity between the teachings of Jesus Christ and the prophet on Mars. In some cases, the teachings are word for word.

Peter: Yes, interesting, isn't it? Coincidence, you think?

Tim: Far from it. I think the message is universal. I believe prophets are being sent to budding civilizations all over the universe. The same lessons are being taught over and over, sometimes word for word.

Peter: Prophets being *sent*? Sent from whom?

Tim shook his head. He knew Peter was toying with him, so he decided to throw him a curve ball.

Tim: From God, of course.

There was a pause. Tim pictured Peter trying to formulate a question that wouldn't be leading, but would at the same time elicit the truth.

Peter: And how is God sending forth these
prophets?

Tim smiled. It was a good question. Not exactly leading, but central to the truth.

Tim: Via metallic spheres, four feet in diameter,
made of an unknown alloy. Incredibly dense,
impossibly hard, impervious to heat or cold—
like the sphere found on Mars.

Peter: They found it, did they?

Tim: Yes. And the team responsible for mission
security wasn't pleased at all with your
message to Moyeur.

Peter: It wasn't *my* message, Tim. You found the
anomaly. You had the coordinates.

Tim: How did you get the message to Moyeur?

Peter: I already told you, Tim. My technology is
ample.

Tim chuckled. *Ample?*

Peter: Let's get back to the sphere, shall we? I think
you're playing with me, Tim. What does it tell
you?

Tim: It tells me that God is bound by the laws of
physics. It tells me that God is perhaps
different from the all-knowing, omnipotent
being we think he is.

Peter: Go on.

Tim: In fact, it tells me that God may actually be an
advanced civilization, not a single
consciousness.

Peter: If it's an advanced civilization, why would they
send prophets to all corners of the universe?

Tim: It's a question of semantics, Peter. Just
because God may not be a single being
doesn't mean that the advanced civilization,
in the collective sense, can't espouse the
same principles.

Peter: So, the charter of the advanced civilization might be the same as God's, or what most people think of as God?

Tim: Yes.

Peter: And what charter is that, Tim?

Tim: To teach us how to live. To help us grow and develop.

Peter: Let's get back to the *facts*. At least those you've managed to uncover so far. How is the prophet born a member of the indigenous civilization? How was he born a Martian, for example?

Tim: The advanced civilization

Tim continued to type, but the characters failed to populate the screen. Peter had broken his transmission mid-stream somehow.

Peter: Let's call them the Zaileen, for the sake of argument.

Tim shuddered. They weren't talking hypothetically anymore, were they? Peter knew the name of the omnipotent civilization!

Tim: How can you know that?

Peter: We're having a hypothetical discussion, Tim. Zaileen is easier to type than "omnipotent civilization."

As coy as ever, Tim thought.

Tim: Fine. Here are some hypothetical answers to your hypothetical questions. The *Zaileen* send a pod to Mars, which lands in the Sinai Planum...an area they know is uninhabited due to the Martian's need for the localized magnetospheres. There's no Barrettazine shelf in the Sinai Planum, ergo the sphere goes undetected. A Zaileen emerges from the sphere and proceeds to the Martian city, where he finds a suitable host. He injects the host with an embryo. The embryo contains the intellect—and soul if you will—of a Zaileen, but germinates inside the womb of a Martian to be born in the physical form of its host. Prophet is born. Prophet goes forth with lessons. The seeds of spiritual growth have been planted.

Peter: Interesting term…seeds have been planted.

Tim: Why do you say that?

Peter: We'll get to that later, much later. So, then what happens?

Tim: What do you mean, what happens?

Peter: Let's get away from the hypothetical for a moment, Tim, and return to the cold, hard reality. What happens if the civilization doesn't adhere to the teachings of the prophet?

Tim balked. He knew exactly where the conversation was heading, but he didn't want to go there. It was the truth. It was the cold, hard reality, but he didn't want to acknowledge it.

Peter: What happened to the Martians, Tim?

Tim knew the answer to that question. He'd known for several days now. He didn't want to admit it, though, not even to himself. Typing it would be even worse. Peter could obviously sense Tim's reluctance, and his self-denial.

Peter: What happened to the Martians, Tim?

Tim: They were destroyed.

Peter: They were EXTERMINATED.

Tim took a deep breath.

Peter: Why would the Zaileen do that, Tim?

Tim: Self-preservation.

Peter: You're batting a thousand, Tim. But I'm curious. How did you come to that conclusion so quickly?

Tim: The Martian prophet and Jesus Christ arrived at the same time in our respective evolutionary lifecycles. Our technological evolutionary lifecycles, that is.

Peter: *Technological* evolutionary lifecycle?

Tim: Throughout man's history, it's been proven that different cultures evolve at different paces. Even within cultures, there's a different pace of evolution technologically versus socially versus spiritually. Those cultures with an affinity for war tend to evolve technologically much more quickly than they do spiritually. Those cultures with a premium on the individual tend to evolve spiritually more quickly than they do technologically. The Martians were not technocrats. They had a very modern social structure for ten thousand years before their technology began to accelerate. Here on Earth, however, we only had a modern social structure for a few thousand years before our technology began to accelerate. Yet, the Zaileen sent the prophets at the same point in our respective *technological* development. If they were genuinely concerned about advancing a civilization spiritually, they would have sent the prophets at the same phase of our social development. By sending the prophets at the same phase of our technological development, the Zaileen must be looking to make a judgement about a civilization before it becomes too advanced technologically… advanced enough to challenge them…ergo, self-preservation.

The words had poured out in a rush, and now Tim sat back in his chair to read them. A knot formed in his stomach. He knew it was the truth. He felt it. What he had just typed was at the heart of everything Peter had wanted him to learn. He imagined Peter pouring over the text, word for word, noting areas where Tim had been wrong and where he had been right. Finally, Peter's response came.

Peter: You impress even me, Tim. You are right, of course. About everything. You didn't just get the facts right, but you fully understand the logic behind them. The Zaileen have been around for seven billion years. Four billion years ago, they were challenged by a civilization with an *affinity for war*, as you put it. They were almost wiped out. But they prevailed in the end. In the interest of self-preservation, they resolved to abandon isolationism and become more involved with the matters of the universe. Consequently, they came up with the idea of the prophets. Prophets to spread the ideals that they themselves had come to cherish. It was a beautiful plan, masterfully conceived and well intentioned. Unfortunately, over billions of years, it has mutated into something horrible. In the last billion years, do you know how many budding civilizations have been sent prophets?

The typing stopped. Peter obviously wanted to give his understudy time to speculate. Tim had no idea, but he couldn't wait to find out. How pervasive was intelligent life throughout the universe?

Peter: Over 2 million! That's *civilizations*, Tim, most with millions of inhabitants, and many with billions. Do you know how many of those civilizations have been allowed to continue?

Or, said differently, how many have not been exterminated?

Tim was afraid to even speculate. Seventy-five percent, maybe?

Peter: 0

Tim clutched his stomach; he wanted to throw up. In that instant he had felt the collective annihilation of trillions of lives. How was such mass genocide allowed to continue?

Peter: So, finally you see what's at stake, what we're fighting for.

Tim had suspected very early on that there was more to the Martian mystery than met the eye. But not in his wildest dreams had he imagined something like this. Peter was talking about God. Whether it was a single all-knowing consciousness or a civilization called the Zaileen, it all translated to the "Supreme Being." All the prophecies in the Book of Revelations were true. And it had already happened to millions of civilizations! How did Tim get involved in this? What possibly qualified him to challenge a civilization like the Zaileen?

Tim: What role can I possibly play in this?
Peter: You have been chosen.
Tim: Don't give me that bullshit. I'm just a man!
Peter: Are you unwilling to try?
Tim: Of course I'm willing to try! You're going to be terribly disappointed, though.
Peter: We'll see.

Tim jumped up and paced the floor. Sweat was already pouring down his face. It felt like the weight of the world had been placed back on his shoulders. Being Christ revisited would have been a relief now. At least that would only be carrying the weight of one world. Now, he somehow bore responsibility for the entire universe! He returned to the computer to see another question.

Peter: What else have you uncovered?

Tim: Screw what else I've uncovered! Please tell me I'm playing a small role in this insurgence! Please tell me there are others involved, others much more powerful I am!

There was a very long pause. Tim wondered if Peter had broken off the transmission. Finally, his response came.

Peter: *I'm* involved.

The answer hit Tim like a blow to the stomach, like the reprimand of a disappointed parent. He felt even more unworthy.

Peter: Now, let's move forward, Tim. Time is running out. What else have you uncovered?

Tim wondered if it was even worth telling Peter about his vision earlier in the day. Not because he was unsure about its significance. There was definitely something important in the caves along the sheer-faced cliffs of the Valles Marineris—more specifically, the Ius Chasma area of the gorge. The question was, how would any directive to investigate it bypass the new electronic security procedures put in place by Bauer? More importantly, was the risk to the crew worth it? Tim knew that the depth of the Valles Marineris was over four miles at points. From his vision earlier in the day Tim had no way of knowing how far down the caves were. Any more than a thousand feet would probably put them out of the reach of even the longest rappelling line available to the crew. He almost got dizzy himself thinking of someone hanging from a thousand feet of line, staring down another four miles to the bottom of a gorge. Add the further risk of a saboteur, or something more dangerous lurking within the caves, and the prospects became even less appealing.

Tim: There is something important in the Ius Chasma, in the caves along the cliffs.

Peter: What is it?

Tim: I don't know. I just know that there's something in those cliffs that shouldn't be there.

Peter: Fine. I will send another message to the crew. What else have you found?

Tim: There's a sphere in the Sea of Galilee.

Peter: Are you sure?

Tim: Yes, I'm sure. The rest of the team isn't, though. They're debating whether or not to investigate it.

Peter: Maybe they don't want you to know the truth.

Tim: Maybe so.

Peter: Is that all you found in Israel?

Tim shook his head. How could Peter know? He had just noticed it himself two hours ago, while waiting to have blood drawn at the clinic. He'd been pouring over the data from the SAC-C satellite, when he noticed an extremely faint magnetic occurrence outside the city of Jerusalem. The flux density was hardly enough to register. The chime in the back of his mind had sounded loudly, though.

Tim: There's something ten miles east of Jerusalem, in Qumran. I don't know what it is, but I think it's important.

Peter: It is important, Tim. And it's only for you.

Tim: What do you mean it's only for me?

Peter: You're going to have to find out for yourself. You can't tell anyone you're going, though. What you find there is only for you. No one else can know about it.

Tim: How am I going to get to Israel without anyone knowing? I can't go to a restaurant without the CIA following me!

Peter: You are you. You will find a way. Enjoy your trip.

Tim: Wait!

The screen remained blank for several seconds. Tim thought Peter had logged off before he was able to stop him. Finally, he was proved wrong.

Peter: Yes?

Tim decided to take a wild swing in the dark. From his evolutionary discussion with Hollingstead the prior night, he was convinced that mankind didn't evolve from apes naturally as most people suspected.

Tim: I dug into the missing link mystery like you
        suggested, and I have a question for you.

Peter: Yes?

Tim contemplated the query and considered how ludicrous it sounded. In light of what he'd just learned about the Zaileen, however, nothing seemed impossible.

Tim: Why did you create mankind?

The screen remained blank for a long time.

Tim: I'm asking you a direct question. Why did you
        create mankind?

After a beat, the response finally came.

Peter: I created mankind as subterfuge, Tim. As
        fodder in which to hide *you.*

The period at the end of the sentence blinked twice and then the screen went dark.

CHAPTER 33

"I can get a team into Israel," Tim said, from the open door of Bauer's office.

The general looked up from his desk, surprised. He tipped his head to the side to try to peer around his unexpected visitor.

"Victor isn't here. In fact, he doesn't even know about my proposal," Tim said.

Bauer looked even more surprised. "Why would you come to me first?"

Tim walked into the general's office and shut the door behind him. "You think I hide behind Victor, that I use him as some sort of shield. I'm here to let you know that isn't true."

Bauer remained silent.

"I also thought about what you said yesterday. About how prudence should rule outside the lab and about how, in the real world, people's lives are at stake. I wanted to let you know that I heard you and that I'm willing to step out of the lab, as it were."

"Are you telling me that in addition to coming up with a plan, you'd like to be involved in its *execution*?"

Tim nodded and took a seat across from Bauer.

"Field work isn't for cowboys, Tim. It takes a hell of a lot of planning and training."

"I'm aware of that," Tim said. "I'm also aware that the closer to reality, the more secure the cover. I didn't expect you to send in a team of Navy SEALs wearing black slickers and driving a Hummer."

"Okay, so let's hear the plan," Bauer said.

"I've got some personal contacts in Israel that might be helpful," Tim said.

Bauer's jaw flexed. "I have some personal contacts in Israel too, Tim. In the Mossad! Who do you know?"

"That's really the point, isn't it, General? The people I know run in circles far removed from the people you know. Academics typically don't draw as much attention as colonels in the Mossad, do they?"

"You'd be surprised."

"I might be. But my plan doesn't rely on the loyalty of my contacts or their discretion. They wouldn't even know what we were up to."

Bauer perked up visibly. "So give me the details."

"We go in under the auspices of an environmental research project," Tim said, "to study the impact of water pollution on children. The Sea of Galilee would just happen to be the water source we selected for our research."

Bauer stared back at Tim poker-faced. "I'm still listening," he said.

"Of course, we'd have to take multiple water and sediment samples of the lake. We'd have to use a submersible pump for the lake-bottom samples. While we were doing that, we could sneak a peak at the sphere."

"It wouldn't work," Bauer grunted. "The Israeli government is looking for opportunities to snub the United States right now, private and public sector alike. You ask their permission to conduct an experiment like this and they'll shoot it down in a heartbeat!"

"I wouldn't be asking for their permission. In fact, it wouldn't be a U.S.-led experiment at all. At least, not as far as the Israeli government is concerned. Permission and permits would be requested by several Israeli-based organizations."

"And those would be?"

"Ben Gurion University and the Andala Institute for Environmental Studies—AIES."

Bauer leaned forward and placed his forearms on the desk in front of him. "Who do you know?"

"I know the director of AIES. We share a common interest ...children. He's long championed new Israeli pollution control legislation, largely on the platform of children's health. For a month out of every year, he donates his time and expertise to the Red Cross in Africa. That's how I met him."

"And Ben Gurion?" Bauer asked.

"Well, it's been a while, but I used to work closely with several physics professors at Tel Aviv University; on a think-tank, of all things. We were focused on developing a high-energy neutron facility for commercial use. Again, interestingly enough, a field to be made obsolete by the discovery of Barrettazine."

"Physics professors? What would they have to do with an environmental study?"

"Nothing. But you have to understand the Israeli scientific community. They're a very tight-knit group. It was through the physics team that I met and befriended many other scientists, one being the department head of Environmental Hydrology and Microbiology at Ben Gurion University."

"How well do you know him?"

"It's a woman, actually," Tim said. "Again, it's been about ten years, but I've had dinner at her home several times and met her family, if that tells you anything."

"What kind of equipment do you think they could marshal?" Bauer picked up a pen and jotted a few notes on the pad in front of him.

"Well, I'm assuming we're not looking to completely excavate the sphere. I mean, it would be too heavy to haul out of there anyway."

"Of course not. We just need to be able to visually ID it. If it's been there for a couple thousand years, as you say, it's probably under a few feet of silt. Could your contacts come up with a big enough pump?"

"I'm sure they could," Tim said confidently.

"What makes you think they'll let us use their equipment without being involved in the project?"

"They won't," Tim responded. "We'd have to involve them."

Bauer raised his hands emphatically.

"At least in part of it," Tim amended. "But, hey, fair is fair. Their country, their equipment. We'll do the grunt work—

collecting lake-bottom samples. They get the glamorous work—collecting beach samples." A smile spread across his lips. "If there's one thing scientists love more than being cocky in the lab, General, it's being cocky on beaches. Beaches with babes."

"Touché, Mr. Redmond, touché."

CHAPTER 34

K athy stood at the far end of the empty dining hall, watching the double-door entryway. When the microwave bell sounded, she opened the door and removed a steaming cup of coffee.

"Good morning, sunshine!" Trainer said.

Kathy swung around to greet him and nearly spilled the scalding brew on his shoe.

"A little jumpy this morning?" he asked. "Maybe you should drink some of that to steady your nerves."

Kathy grabbed his arm and hauled him toward the door.

"What's going on?" he protested.

"I'm glad you got here first. I need to speak with you in private."

As they passed a counter on the way to the exit, Trainer reached over and grabbed a breakfast bar. The two headed down the dimly lit hallway and took a left into the supply bay. Kathy guided Trainer all the way to the back. "What's up?" he asked, peeling off the bar's bright wrapper and taking a healthy bite.

"Did you get any e-mail messages in the latest upload?"

"Yeah. I got one from Brian," Trainer said, referring to his teenaged son.

"Anything strange about it?"

"No. Just high school stuff. He won his first-round district wrestling match and asked some girl named Susan to the junior prom. You know, standard stuff. Those memories should be fresher in your mind than mine, Kathy."

Normally, Kathy would be eager to discuss Warren's family.

Now was not one of those times, however. "I got an e-mail, too," she said, "from my *grandmother!*"

Trainer's mouth fell open, revealing a swath of half-eaten blueberry jelly on his tongue. "I thought she was—"

"Dead." Kathy finished his statement. "For fifteen years! I have no idea how the message made it through the security screening process, but it did."

"What did it say?" Trainer whispered.

"It was a set of coordinates, followed by a single sentence: *seek and you shall find.*"

"Have you pinpointed the coordinates?"

Kathy nodded. "I was a little confused at first. It detailed a square grid, five feet by five feet. But it was perpendicular to level."

Trainer's eyes narrowed. "Underground?"

"My first guess, too. It had a negative disposition to plane, so I pictured a small Barrettazine shelf like a tabletop underground. But instead of being flat, this one would have been on its edge, sticking straight up like a plate in a dishwasher." Kathy stopped talking and held up her hand as a sign for quiet. When she was satisfied that the adjacent hallway was still clear, she continued. "Then, I located it on a map. It's not underground. Technically it is, I guess. It's along the Ius Chasma, Warren, on the face of the cliff, a few hundred feet down. It's got to be the mouth of a cave!"

Trainer shook his head in disbelief. "And you have no idea who the email is from?"

"None."

The two stared at each other. They both knew what the other was thinking.

"Kathy, you know as well as I do that we can't go investigate it. Vivicheck was almost killed the last time we followed a bogus directive!"

"That was an accident, Warren. The sphere wasn't dangerous. It just happened to fall loose of the dirt at the wrong time."

"You're forgetting about the chamber, Kathy. Despite the party line, that vault didn't implode because of mining or seismic work in the area."

"Wait a minute! You were the one selling the party line! You said the chamber was probably booby-trapped by the Martians!"

Trainer bit his lip, thinking.

"What's going on?" Kathy prodded. "Is there something I don't know?"

Trainer remained silent.

"Well?"

Trainer rubbed his chin thoughtfully, before finally giving in. "Vivicheck said he saw something down there, just before the tremor. He said it looked like some kind of black being, but a lot bigger than a Martian."

Kathy's eyes grew wide. "Was it aggressive? Did it attack him?"

"Actually, Vivicheck said it ran away as soon as it saw him."

"Oh, my God! This is unbelievable! Why don't the rest of us know about this?"

"Moyeur wanted us to keep a lid on it. It was dark down there, Kathy. Vivicheck wasn't even sure what he saw."

"Yeah, but what if there's a link between this being and the sphere? It could be a ship, for all we know! How are we supposed to figure any of this out, if we don't investigate?"

Trainer shook his head. Kathy could tell he was torn. He didn't like being kept in the dark any more than she did. "You realize what's going to happen if we go to Moyeur with the email," he said.

Kathy nodded. "I already have a plan. In two days, you and I are scheduled to return to the sphere, to gather more soil samples for carbon dating. I say we take a detour."

CHAPTER 35

Tim gazed across the Sea of Galilee—or Lake Kinneret, the name his hosts had used the previous evening. It was not yet eight in the morning, but Dugit Beach was already coming to life. An old Honda minivan pulled off Junction 92 and rolled to a stop in the parking lot. College-aged men and women emerged, but much to his disappointment, they weren't the team of eager biologists he'd been waiting for. He glanced at his watch again. His hosts had been adamant about starting no earlier than the time outlined on the permit, and it appeared they were going to be true to their word. He felt completely exposed without the team of locals as cover.

He hadn't been a bit nervous at dinner last night with Naomi and her graduate students. His own research team turned out to be a pleasant surprise. The two Navy SEALS had been extremely personable, and more importantly, credible. Granted they were officers, and ranking ones at that, but given the SEALs' reputation for men forged of steel, he hadn't expected much in the way of social graces or intellect. To his amazement, however, the two men were not only extremely knowledgeable of marine biology, but they were as smooth as statesmen. It was a good thing, too, being brought in as professors Hinkle and Roundtree from Stanford and Berkeley.

He watched the "professors" as they donned their diving gear beside the open door of the minivan. Their slicks were worn and tattered—B-grade rental gear they wouldn't have touched had it not been for the need to project a certain image. Unfortunately, the image of two professors quickly disintegrated when they removed their shirts—both men were ripped. Their pecs were pronounced and rock hard, their stomachs inverted ice trays, and the veins in their arms bulged out from cantaloupe-sized biceps. He just hoped they would be in their gear before the Israeli scientists arrived. His discomfort must have been obvious.

"Take it easy, sir. We're just out for a little swim," the salt-and-pepper haired SEAL said with a grin. "Right, Professor?"

The other SEAL looked up from his respirator. "Right you are, my good man," he said in a highbrow British accent.

Tim couldn't believe how calm they were. Then it hit him: compared to most of their other missions, this must have been like collecting holiday pay. Maybe it was gratitude, then, that had prompted them to call him "sir," even after his protests. He had no idea what their real names were, or even what rank they held, except that they were both officers. Based upon their ages, he guessed they were commanders, or even captains. It was absurd that they call him "sir." "Remember to bury it again after you ID it," Tim said nervously.

Both men nodded.

All three turned when they heard the crush of gravel. Two Ford pickup trucks with trailers rolled into the parking lot. One of the trailers held a hydraulic submersible pump with *Heidra 250* stenciled across its burnt orange frame. An orange buoy rested next to it, half of its diameter concealed by the cables that encircled it. An aluminum-hulled fishing boat rested in the trailer of the second truck.

"Looks like our vessel, Professor," Hinkle said. "And you thought you'd never get a command!"

The other man slapped a pair of diving fins across his colleague's chest. They clapped loudly in the morning air, like a wet towel snapped bullwhip style. "Just for that, you're driving and I'm diving!"

Tim stood on the shore and cupped his hands over the top of his sunglasses, to fight off the glare of the water. He saw the orange buoy bobbing up and down on the small waves. The fishing boat floated stationary, while its sole occupant stared toward Mount Tabor to the distant west. Tim guessed the boat was close to a mile from the shore, and to his satisfaction, there wasn't another vessel close to it. The dark basalt sand that covered the bottom of the lake was a double-edged sword. It would conceal the form of the diver on the bottom quite nicely, offering no contrast to his black diving suit. Unfortunately, pictures of the sphere were required, and for that, the SEAL would have to turn on his spotlight. Anyone on the deck of a nearby boat would have easily seen the light against the lake floor. Fortunately, luck was working in their favor. The closest boat to them was probably a half-mile away.

The deep blare of a horn made Tim jump, and he spun to see a black Lincoln Town Car pulling into the parking space next to him. A banana-yellow Mazda immediately followed. He cringed. Not the most inconspicuous vehicle, but he couldn't afford to be picky.

"Tim!" a silver haired man called, as he emerged from the Lincoln. "You've gone and grown up on us, my boy!" He strode across the sand and gave Tim an exuberant hug.

"Emil, it's so good to see you!" Tim said, patting the man on the back.

"Oooohhh! Look at you!" a woman squealed, as she glided toward the two from the Mazda. She was dressed to the nines. Her hair was done up perfectly, and a fresh coat of gloss had been applied to her lips. She embraced Tim and then held him at arm's length. "What a gorgeous young man!"

"And you look as ravishing as ever, Talia!" Tim said. "I see you're still going to the gym twice a day."

She waved off the compliment with a flip of her hand. "Oh, stop, Tim. This one keeps me too busy to go to the gym!" She slapped her husband on the shoulder playfully.

"How is retirement, Emil?" Tim asked the physicist.

"You can only see the Dead Sea and Haifa so many times," Emil said.

"If you were willing to leave the country, we wouldn't have that problem!" Talia slapped her husband on the shoulder again, this time a little less playfully.

"So, what have you been up to, my friend?" Emil asked. "Still running around Africa?"

"Yes. For the most part," Tim said.

"You need a good wife!" Talia gushed. "Running around Africa is fun for a while, I'm sure, but you need a family of your own. I just spoke with Tamar last night, and she's going to be joining us for dinner on Saturday."

Emil shrugged and rolled his eyes at Tim apologetically. Talia slapped him across the shoulder again. "Don't give me that look. Don't you think she's a good catch?"

"She's a wonderful catch, darling! But you have to stop playing matchmaker. These kids have lives of their own!"

The objection rolled off the woman like water off the back of a duck. She grabbed Tim's arm and boxed her husband out. "Tamar is in her second year at Sackler in Tel Aviv. Top of her class, you know. She's torn between obstetrics and pediatrics. Could there be a better match for a man who loves children as much as you do? And she is drop dead gorgeous. You probably hear that all the time, but as God as my witness, it's true of Tamar."

"You can give him her résumé on Saturday," Emil said. "The man has work to do."

Tim put his arm around Talia. "She sounds amazing. I can't wait to meet her. Are you sure she won't mind if I use her car for a few days?"

"Of course not," Talia said. "Tel Aviv is too crowded for a car anyway. It sits on our driveway collecting dust most of the time."

"Well, I can't tell you how much I appreciate it," Tim said.

Talia handed him the keys to the Mazda and loaded into the Lincoln with her husband.

Tim waved goodbye and tracked the vehicle all the way down Local 92, until it was out of sight. He then turned toward the lake to see the boat in the same location. The sphere must have been buried deeper than they suspected. The two SEALs had been at it for over three hours.

Tim gazed down the length of the beach and spotted David immediately. The grad student was over six feet tall and dark-featured. The girls on the beach were ogling him from their towels, pretending to be watching the kayaks in the water beyond him. He saw that David was giving instructions to a few of the undergrads who had been selected for the project. Although Naomi—Tim's primary contact at Ben Gurion University—would analyze the samples, her time was far too valuable to engage in fieldwork. All the better, Tim thought. David would follow any instructions they gave him, short of ludicrous. Tim stepped over the railroad tie that divided the sand from the gravel parking lot and made his way down the beach to where David stood, shaking a plastic container of water. "Hey, David," Tim said. "I just got paged, but my cell phone isn't working very well out here."

"Doesn't surprise me. Not a lot of towers around here."

"Well, it might be important, so I've got to go find a land line. Do you know where the nearest pay phone is?"

The grad student thought for a moment and then pointed south. "There's a little restaurant called Sid's about a mile down the road. They've got a pay phone."

"Thanks!" Tim said. He headed back toward the parking lot, but stopped suddenly. "If it turns out to be important, and I've got to get somewhere immediately," he said, "could you tell Bill and Jeff to head back without me?"

"Sure. No problem," David said, already engrossed in his sample.

As he strode toward the parking lot, Tim hoped that David wasn't a pragmatist with an eye for detail. *How are they going to get back, if you're driving the minivan?* Thankfully, David didn't ask the question. Tim was also hoping he wouldn't notice the banana-yellow Mazda he pulled away in. Even if he saw it, Tim doubted the CIA would have the resources to track him, at least without the help of the Israelis. And given the nature of what they were doing at the lake, Tim knew they wouldn't ask for help.

# # #

The hundred-mile drive down the Ghawr Valley to the Dead Sea was a pleasant one. In only ninety minutes, Tim passed through three distinct temporal zones: Mediterranean, Irano-Turanian, and Tropical Sudanese. The landscape changed from the barren rocky hills in the north, to the patchy green foliage common in the area that surrounded the Dead Sea. Then, as he neared his final destination, the vegetation became more sparse, finally giving way to the dry, sandy rock that distinguished the arid land of Qumran. Towers and buttes rose up from the flat plains, exposing eroded cliffs carved by rain and ancient floods. It reminded him of Sedona in Arizona, but instead of the red clay, the stones were a cream-colored marl.

As he drove by the sign announcing the entrance to Qumran National Park, he noted that it closed at five o'clock. He looked at his watch. It was three o'clock, giving him plenty of time to scope the place out, before returning after dark for his real purpose. He took a right turn off Highway 90 and rolled onto the national park's access road. He was disappointed to see a heavy steel gate standing sentry. The steel pipes were propped open, but they were probably locked after closing. No matter, he couldn't risk parking in the lot after dark anyway. Some security officer would notice the car and wonder who was out on the cliffs, and what they were doing there.

Tim greeted the cashier at the guard station and handed her some shekels. After collecting his change, he proceeded down the access road to the parking lot, where he was surprised to see so many other cars. Evidently, April was a busy month. He parked the Mazda and headed toward the visitor's center, an oasis of palm trees surrounding a marble courtyard and open air building. A strong breeze kicked up and sprayed him with droplets of water from the fountain. He hoped the wind wouldn't continue into the evening. He hadn't been able to pack much gear for his expedition, and goggles were not among the items in his duffel bag.

Tim spent an hour-and-a-half in the visitor's center, using a rented headset and tape to learn about the history of Qumran and the Dead Sea Scrolls. According to the narrator, Qumran had been home to many different cultures over time, dating back to the eighth century B.C. The most interesting to Tim were the

Essenes—also known as the Dead Sea Sect—who resided in the area between 130 B.C. and 70 A.D. They were an extremist offshoot of the Jewish Apocalyptic Movement, and believed that God decreed the division of mankind into two groups, the Sons of Light and the Sons of Darkness, each with a superhuman leader, the Prince of Light and the Prince of Darkness, respectively. According to their faith, at the time of the apocalypse, the Prince of Light would defeat his nemesis, and the Essenes—the true believers—would be rewarded. Members of the sect spent their entire lives preparing for Armageddon. They numbered no more than two hundred at the height of their occupation—an isolated group, to be sure.

The narrator went on to explain that in addition to the archeological ruins at Qumran, over eight hundred ancient scrolls were found in the caves surrounding the area. Local shepherds discovered them in 1947. Subsequent scrolls were found throughout the many caves in the area over the next nine years. Almost all of the scrolls were made from animal skins. Most were written in Hebrew, but some in Aramaic and even Greek. The age of the scrolls coincided with the occupation of the area by the Essenes, and, therefore, it was believed that members of the sect also authored them. Among other teachings, the scrolls contained the books of the Old Testament. They also contained prophesies by Ezekiel, Jeremiah, and Daniel that were not found in the Bible, and previously unknown stories about biblical figures, such as Enoch, Abraham, and Noah. One of the most amazing finds, Tim thought, was the Isaiah scroll, which predates any other book of Isaiah by a thousand years.

Tim had known about the scrolls, or at least had a general knowledge of their existence. He'd never delved deeply into their content, however, and much of what he heard on the tape had amazed him. He returned the headset to the visitor's desk and noted that he had a little over an hour to walk among the ruins, before the park closed. He stepped out of the visitor's center, and headed west toward the nearest plateau. All he wanted now was a visual reference, to help him navigate in the dark.

CHAPTER 36

Tim bolted across Highway 90 and dove headfirst into the roadside ditch. He kept his face glued to the rocky ground, and looked up only after he was sure the vehicle was well past him. He cursed his luck. Had he chosen to cross at any other span of the road, he could have seen the headlights coming from miles away. As it was, the stretch he had chosen was the only one obscured by hills. It was closest to the plateau he had ascended earlier in the day, however, so it seemed like a logical choice.

Groping on his hands and knees, he searched for the rope that must have flown off his shoulder. When he found it, he poked his head and right arm through the loop and adjusted it to fit snugly over his backpack. He peered down the road again to ensure no other cars were coming, and then headed toward the rise that marked his destination. He'd gone maybe ten feet, when he felt something warm trickling down his fingers. He raised his hand to survey the cut. It was hard to tell how severe the gash was in the dark, but it didn't hurt too badly. He wondered how much his adrenaline was masking the pain. He couldn't believe that he, of all people, was sneaking through Israel in the middle of the night. If spotted, Tim knew he could be shot as a Palestinian terrorist quicker than he could yell, "Stop, I'm American!" And even if he were fast enough to make that case, he could only imagine what they'd do to him upon uncovering the truth about his little research project in the Sea of Galilee.

Tim pushed all thoughts of capture out of his mind and continued east toward the plateau. When he arrived at its base, he climbed it carefully, not wanting to turn an ankle in the dark.

At the top, he pulled the GPS device from his backpack and took a bearing.

The moon was full and the sky was clear, a decided advantage. From his vantage point atop the hill, he could see the outline of the butte he'd picked out ten hours earlier. There was no way for him to know for sure that it was the right one, but he had to start somewhere.

To his left, he saw the outline of the palm trees by the visitor's center. Their sharp, narrow leaves whipped in the wind. Beyond them, the moonlight shimmered off the surface of the Dead Sea, a scant two miles to the southeast. To his right, he saw the lights of Jerusalem, only thirteen miles to his west. They stood out clearly against the dark, uninhabited land in the foreground. Tim was just beginning to turn away when his head snapped back. He froze. Along the precipice of the plateau stood a tall black figure, silhouetted against the city lights. It stood motionless, staring right back at him. Not a feature was visible, its body far too dark. Long arms hung down by its sides, meeting with equally long legs just above the knees. It wasn't human, of that he was sure. Suddenly, it was gone.

He scanned the ridge frantically, but the wraith was nowhere to be seen. He followed the slope of the mountain downward, but he detected no movement there, either. *Was it coming after him?* Without warning, he felt himself leap off the ridge. He plunged ten feet through the air before landing precariously on the severe slope. The thin layer of rocks gave way beneath him, and he fell flat on his back. He rocketed down the mountainside like a skier on the crest of an avalanche. He peered down the length of his body and between his feet, and saw a boulder dead ahead of him. He rolled onto his stomach and swam across the top of the rocks with arms flaying. He dug into the debris, powering his body laterally. He avoided smashing into the boulder by a few inches.

He only had a moment to celebrate his narrow escape, before he was catapulted off the lip of the mountain into the dark night. He felt like he was airborne for an eternity, before he crashed onto the ground. His lungs compressed and he crumpled up into a ball, rolling on the ground in pain. He wasn't down for more than a few seconds before he forced himself back up and began sprinting. The chime in the back of his mind was screaming— run, run, *Run!* Chemicals surged through his system, driving foreign responses he wondered if any human had ever experienced. His body was on fire, and adrenaline rushed like mercury through his veins. His synapses fired at lightning speed, pulling up data from his brain like it was a combat control center: *attacker approaching level from 40 degrees north by northwest, travelling at 30 m.p.h. Intercept time 40 seconds. Two possible escape routes: rocks at 20 degrees southeast, arrival time at current speed, 25 seconds; a fissure in the cliff wall at 10 degrees southwest, arrival time at current speed, 30 seconds.*

Instantly, he selected the second option. As he dashed for the cliff, he felt a cool wind buffet his face, but he knew the wind wasn't blowing. The sensation was driven by his own speed! How fast was he going? The answer came to him: *24 m.p.h.* He was halfway to the fissure, when his command center blared: *attacker's speed increasing—42 m.p.h…51 m.p.h…* His mind re-calculated the solution, and he realized he wasn't going to make the fissure before being overrun. Amazingly, he accelerated too: *29 m.p.h…35 m.p.h…* He shot through the gap in the cliff and wound his way through the head-high boulders. About a quarter of a mile into the canyon, he finally stopped and ducked behind an outcropping of rocks, completely winded. He gasped for oxygen and waited, straining to hear the creature that had been pursuing him. A full minute passed, but no dark figure emerged. He didn't waste time pondering his good fortune. He broke out his GPS and took another reading.

Tim ran south, mouth wide open, emitting a bizarre, unearthly scream. The fire still raged in his veins and sweat poured down his face. He sensed the ultrasonic pinging from his east. It was eerie. Like a bat, the creature was using echolocation sonar to find him. Tim knew he shouldn't have been able to detect the ultrasonic frequency, but he could—short bursts travelling through the air, sweeping past him like radar. He could even sense the overtones the creature was using to extend the signal's range.

Tim was in survival mode. He didn't question anything. He just let it happen. Almost immediately after detecting the echolocation radar, he had begun to scream a response. It was like an out-of-body experience: he had turned his head toward the source of the radar, and formulated a response. It had come out like a falsetto scream, the opening in his throat becoming so narrow it nearly choked off all sound. A high pitched sound had escaped, however, one above the audible range. It was a countermeasure, he was sure. Somehow, he had determined the exact frequency of the being's sonar, and sent back a signal that was exactly 180 degrees out of phase, effectively devouring the original search waves. Tim had discovered that he couldn't maintain the signal between breaths, however, which had forced him to leapfrog from stone outcropping to stone outcropping in order to take shelter between breaths.

He dipped behind a grouping of large boulders and took several deep breaths. After his body was re-supplied with oxygen, he headed south again. He barely made it to the next outcropping of stones before gasping for air. He pulled the GPS device from his backpack and took another reading. There it was. Two hundred yards directly in front of him loomed the butte he had been searching for. He could barely make out the dark openings of four distinct caves, staring down at him like the eye sockets of a giant skull. He focused on them, hoping his inner voice would tell him which one to enter. No such guidance came.

Pocketing the GPS device, he slung his arms through the straps of the backpack and took a final deep breath. He stepped out from behind the cover, countermeasure booming silently from his constricted throat. He had only traveled twenty feet into the clearing, when he came to an abrupt stop. The falsetto scream died in his throat. A slight breeze swept across his face. The creature's active sonar had stopped. All was quiet. The hairs on the back of his neck stood on end. *He's watching me!* Tim turned his head slowly and peered up at the peak of another butte several hundred yards to his left. There, on the precipice of the ridge, the black being stood sentry. One long arm rose from its side and a finger pointed down at him. Suddenly, the figure leaped from the edge of the cliff. It's sleek body stood out against the sky like a hole burned into a blanket.

Run! the voice in Tim's subconscious commanded. He bolted in the direction of the second butte. His mind sprung back into action: *Attacker descending from 100 feet at a speed of 64 feet per second, closing range from ground level will be 240 yards. Previously known maximum speed: 60 m.p.h. Remaining distance to cave 1: 120 yards...90 yards flat plus 30 yards ascent with average angle of incline 27 degrees. Cave 2: 132 yards...90 yards flat plus 42 yards ascent with average angle of incline 41 degrees. Cave 3—* He shut off the calculation. The second cave was the one. He felt it.

The voice in his mind urged him on: *You must reach the cave, Tim! If you reach it, you live. If you don't, you die.*

The second he reached the base of the butte, he threw the rope to the ground and started his ascent. His heart pounded and he struggled to breathe. Hand over hand, he grabbed rocks and imbedded bushes, propelling himself upward. At any moment, he expected long black fingers to close around his ankles. He listened for the creature behind him, but there was no sound. All he could hear was the thumping in his chest. His command center had gone silent, too. Finally, he hoisted himself over the cave's lip and turned to peer down the slope from which he had just ascended. Nothing. No sound. No movement. The being had vanished. *He's there, Tim. Don't be fooled.*

He unzipped his backpack and rifled through it. He pulled out a flashlight and a magnetometer, before scanning the slope for the creature one last time. He could feel its presence, but there was no visual evidence of it. Tim jumped to his feet and ran into the cave.

Knowing the area had already been explored extensively, Tim forged his way deep into the cave. Whatever he was looking for wouldn't be out in the open. He followed the tunnel for two hundred feet before it narrowed. He pressed himself into a fissure and moved sideways one step at a time. He squeezed his head through, scraping the sides of his face. His chest compressed between the tight walls and he thought he might get stuck. Suddenly, the space widened, and with his next step, he emerged into a massive cavern. Stalagmites rose up from the chalky ground in its middle and stalactites reigned down from above. Tim waved the flashlight around and saw two black openings at the rear of the cavern. He wove his way through the stalagmites and hurried through the first opening. He advanced a mere twenty feet when it dead-ended into a solid rock wall. He began to make his way back to the main chamber, when he stopped in his tracks. A thunderous snarl echoed through the cave. Tim looked around frantically, and noticed a ledge in the wall above him. Without a second thought, he jumped up and grabbed it, swinging his right leg up and over. He then shimmied into the little enclave and held his breath. The opening was no more than two feet wide, and it sloped down away from the tunnel, causing him to slide further into the fissure.

"Gruiieee!"

The shriek nearly pierced Tim's eardrum. The creature had entered the tunnel and was lurking within twenty feet of him! This was it. He was going to die here in this tiny tomb. Sharp nails dragged along the wall, coming closer. He closed his eyes and began to hyperventilate. Why did he have to go like this, in some godforsaken catacomb? Suddenly, it hit him. That's exactly what it was, a crypt! He opened his eyes and studied the side of the wall. It was made of the same rock as the rest of the tunnel, but it had several peculiar grooves. It looked like it had been smoothed over like clay, with some kind of instrument with sharp edges. By a *claw* with sharp nails? By a creature like the one chasing him?

Tim kicked the wall violently. He heard the black being shuffle toward him quickly. On the third blow, the wall gave way. Crawling frantically over the pile of rubble, he found himself among bones—the skeleton of a being, he was sure, that belonged to the same race as the creature below him now. Its skull was long and narrow, its brain casing extremely thick. Three flat bones on either side of its face came down from its ears, converging at its nose, like lines of paint on the cheeks of an Indian brave. Its mouth extended almost the entire width of its head. Long, razor-sharp teeth grinned at him from a mouth cavity that spread from ear to ear. Its bones, if they could be classified as such, were black and smooth. Sticking out from the chest of the being, lodged between pierced ribs, was a handle with a shiny round pommel. Without thinking, he grabbed hold of it and pulled. A dagger with four blades sung out from the fossilized remains. Between the blades was a ball that seemed to absorb, rather than reflect, the beams from his flashlight.

Tim could practically feel the breath of the creature behind him. In his mind, he could see it peering down at him from the ledge of the tiny enclave, waiting for him to turn around before slicing him open with sharp claws. Tim took a breath, gritted his teeth, turned, and lunged at the opening with the blade. Nothing. No red eyes stared at him and no claws struck. *It's toying with me.*

Tim poked his head out from the enclave cautiously and scanned the tunnel. He jumped down from the shelf and headed for the tunnel's entrance. He proceeded through the field of stalagmites until he reached the tight fissure that led to the front cave. As he stepped through it, he noticed a host of rocks scattered beneath his feet, evidence of the black creature's forced entry. When he finally emerged from the darkness of the cave, the light of dawn was a welcome sight. He scanned the horizon in all directions, looking for any sign of his attacker. The creature was nowhere to be seen.

As he gazed over the dry plain, he wondered where the skeleton in the cave had met its end. Had the battle raged on the field directly below him? Had it been night or day? How long had it lasted? Of two things Tim was sure. In all likelihood, the creature had died just over two thousand years ago. And, more importantly, whoever had killed it was extremely powerful. Tim took a deep, satisfied breath. The pieces were finally beginning to fall into place. A picture was forming.

CHAPTER 37

"That's a little tight," Kathy said, grimacing at Trainer.

"Sorry." He loosened the harness across her chest. "If the wind starts kicking up, it could get a little bumpy out there."

"We're on the same page, believe me."

Trainer placed his hands on Kathy's shoulders. "Are you sure you don't want me to go instead?"

Kathy nodded. "Positive. I'm the one who dragged you out here. I should be the one to go."

"Don't overestimate your powers of persuasion, Kathy. I'm out here of my own accord. I'm not some dumb jug head, you know."

"Could have fooled me! You already fell for the old it's-my-idea-so-I-should-go ploy." Kathy laughed. "Trust me, I'm not excited about going either. I'm just less excited about staying. I don't want to be on the other end of the com-link when Moyeur calls!"

"Oh yeah? Well, if he does call, I'm going to sell you out faster than you can say *pension protection!*"

"I bet you would!"

Trainer clipped the karabiner onto the harness at Kathy's waist.

"All right, over-communication is the phrase of the day," he said. "If you want me to speed up, slow down, stop, or pull you back up, just tell me. I'll be hanging on your every word. Got it?"

Kathy nodded and watched him return to the R4. Its nose was facing away from the Chasma, with its winch-laden trailer backed up toward it.

As always, she'd planned it all out ahead of time. Had they proceeded to their original destination as planned, they would have needed the winch. No one suspected anything out of the ordinary, except when she had insisted they replace the one-hundred foot coil with the five-hundred foot variety. After a suspicious look from Moyeur, she'd explained it away with a simple "I'd rather be safe than sorry." Now, they stood at the precipice of the Ius Chasma, over a hundred miles from their prescribed destination.

"Okay, I'm going to start her up," Trainer said, with a hand on the control panel. "I'll unwind it slowly, to let you get a feel for it. Tell me when it reaches a good rappelling speed."

"Roger," Kathy said.

She heard the motor catch and saw the line begin to roll out from the winch. With both hands clutched around the wire, she backed up slowly toward the edge of the cliff. Her head was turned away from the R4, looking down at the ground as she shuffled. The coil picked up speed. "Okay, that feels about right," she said.

"Roger. I'll lock the speed into memory."

The line continued to unravel, opening up several feet of slack. "Stop," Kathy said. She saw Trainer pull the knob backward and the winch came to a stop. As she backed up toward the cliff, the slack in the coil tightened. She stopped a few feet shy of the edge and turned to gaze out across the Ius Chasma. It was the most breathtaking vista she had ever seen. As if she were perched on the wing of an airplane, she surveyed the land four miles below her. What looked like tiny pebbles, dark against the pinkish clay of the bottom, were probably massive rock formations jutting up from the ground. She couldn't even see the other side of the Chasma, which was two hundred miles wide at their current location. The Grand Canyon, which she had visited when she was ten years old, was an awesome spectacle that had left her awestruck. Now, even making concessions for the sensationalized memories of a child, she could safely say that it was a mere ditch compared to this.

Refocusing on the business at hand, she took a few more steps toward the edge and turned to ready herself for her descent. Taking a deep breath and tightening her grip on the wire, she leaned backwards over the canyon wall, keeping her feet anchored to the ledge. Her stomach lurched as the last bit of slack ran out of the coil and it stiffened with her back teetering over the precipice. "Okay, start it up again, Warren. Take it slowly at first, until we get to the speed in memory."

The coil rolled out slowly and she leaned back even further. She took methodical steps, watching her large boots carefully as they made contact with the cliff. Her rate of descent continued to increase, until it steadied to a constant. She focused on the cliff itself and put the idea that she was four miles above the surface out of her mind. After rappelling for what seemed like hours, she finally turned her head and peered downward. Involuntarily, her diaphragm surged, causing her stomach to roil. Her head began to swim. Quickly, she turned to face the cliff. Just as she had done while in the drill-hole, she called upon her powers of intense focus. She studied the cliff. She picked out the smallest details—variations in color, texture, tiny holes, cracks. She maintained this focus and continued to rappel. Before she knew it, her right foot failed to make contact with the wall. "Stop!" she yelled.

The coil came to an abrupt halt and she bounced up and down. She gritted her teeth and waited for it to end. Finally, she yanked on the line until her body was flush with the cliff. "Okay, start it up again, but very slowly." Within seconds, she had cleared the mouth of the cave and swung herself inside of it. "Stop! I'm in the cave."

"What do you see?"

"Give me a second." She shuffled several feet inside the dark cave and activated her helmet spotlight.

"Oh, my God!"

"What's going on? What do you see?"

"Flowers, Warren! Living flowers, in full bloom!"

"That's not funny, Kathy."

"I'm not joking. The place is full of purple flowers!" Kathy walked among the blooms. The cave wasn't very deep, maybe twenty feet. The flowers grew thick all the way from its back, to a few feet shy of its lip. How could they be alive? Where was the water coming from? Where were the nutrients?

"They're actually…alive?" Trainer asked flabbergasted.

"As alive as you and I. As healthy as flowers in a greenhouse!" Kathy laughed giddily.

"Take some samples, Kathy. Moyeur isn't going to believe this."

"Nobody's going to believe this." Kathy leaned over and wrapped a gloved hand around the base of one of the flowers. With a tug, the stem snapped off. After picking about a dozen, she unzipped a pocket along the outside of her left arm. Pulling out a plastic bag, she stuffed the flowers inside.

"Jesus Christ!"

Trainer's scream startled her. "Warren? *Warren?*" She felt a rising sense of panic. "Warren, answer me! What's going on?"

"Something's up here! It just ran behind the R4!"

"What…" Kathy was cut off mid-sentence.

"I've got to pull you up. NOW!"

Suddenly, the slack from the coil whipped off the cave floor and out the opening. "Holy shit!" Kathy screamed. The line snapped tight, and yanked her forward, sending her tumbling to the ground. The coil dragged her across the floor of the cave like an enraged father dragging his child by its waistband. Before she reached the mouth of the cave, the wire tightened on its upper lip and launched her out over the Chasma. Arms and legs flailing, she swung back toward the cliff's face and her helmet collided with the upper ledge of the cave. The coil continued to drag her upward and then stopped. Her upper body rested against the cliff wall, while her lower body dangled below the cave's lip, making it difficult to breathe. "Warren, talk to me!" She bobbed on the end of the wire like a worm on a hook. "Warren, are you there? *Please* say something." She peered up the face of the cliff. A few stones tumbled off the precipice and sailed down at her. She threw her arms over her head and prayed the rocks weren't too heavy. Several seconds passed before they bounced off her thick suit. She peered up the face of the cliff again.

As if in slow motion, an object flew over the edge. *A giant seagull? What's a seagull doing on Mars?* Instead of flying out across the Chasma, however, it dove right down toward her. As it sailed by her visor, the horror of it finally registered. It was Trainer.

"Warren!" She followed his descent as he plunged into the depths of the Chasma. Several more small rocks flew past her head. Instinctively, she peered upward and saw something that made her blood run cold. Over the edge of the cliff, a long black head peered down at her curiously, red eyes beaming.

"*No*," Kathy whispered.

Just as quickly as it appeared, the head vanished.

Suddenly, the coil tightened on her waist and began to pull her upward. Quickly, she reached down and grappled for the karabiner. Her thick gloves and shaking hands made it nearly impossible to manipulate. "Come on. *Come on!*" She fumbled with the clip, all the while being dragged up the side of the cliff.

Finally, the karabiner sprung open and she dropped like a brick. Her boots hit the lower lip of the cave with tremendous force and her legs shot out from underneath her. Her chest crashed onto the lip with a thud, and she began to slide backward toward the Chasma. She thrashed her arms, trying to pull herself further into the cave, but she continued to slide toward the opening. As a last ditch effort, she swung her right leg up over the side. Fueled by adrenaline, she muscled herself over the lip and into the cave. She jumped to her feet and paced among the flowers, trying to think of a way to get word to the Santa Maria. She grabbed the PDA from her belt and punched in a message, praying that Moyeur was sitting in front of the electronic board, watching for transmissions in real-time.

The anode crystal display registered the words: NO SIGNAL. "Come on!" Kathy yelled. The thick walls of the cave must have been blocking the transmission. Kathy forced herself to concentrate, to think of an alternate solution. There was none. The longer she thought, the clearer her predicament became. Her only hope for survival was the winch. Even if she managed to get a message to the Santa Maria, though, how was someone going to get by the black being to activate it?

Why had the creature killed Trainer? Had they stumbled onto something that was supposed to remain a secret? Were the flowers the secret? Were they a link to the Martian civilization's destruction?

As her despair grew, she suddenly realized what she had to do. She sat on the ground of the cave and typed another message into the PDA. It took her several minutes. When the message was complete, she unbuckled her belt and placed it on the ground in front of her. She disengaged the PDA from the wire and programmed it for perpetual transmission. Kathy hoped the signal would be strong enough to clear the peak of the cliff, once out of the cave. She then stood up and carried it to the front of the cave. As she stared across the gorge, memories poured over her: Sunday mornings with her mother and father before they died; the last time she hugged them; the tears in her grandfather's eyes as he walked into her classroom on that horrible day; his unflagging devotion to her afterward. She recalled her first love, her first day of college, the first time she flew an airplane. All so bitter at times, but also so sweet, so intense…so short. Kathy's eyes narrowed, her jaw flexed. She wanted more. So much more. It wasn't to be though. This is where her journey would end, in a desolate cave along the face of the Ius Chasma, Mars. Kathy tightened her grip on the PDA. She then brought her arm back and hurled the communication device into the abyss. The unit spun in the air, arcing up to an apex before falling rapidly.

CHAPTER 38

Tim emerged from the plane expecting to see uniformed personnel waiting for him. To his surprise, only a few pilots waited to board the aircraft. He continued down the ramp with the rest of the passengers. Airport security personnel directed them down a stairwell and out a doorway labeled U.S. Customs. Five rows of twenty people each lined up in front of Plexiglas booths. He proceeded to the back of one of the blue lines, reserved for U.S. citizens. Trying not to look conspicuous, he glanced furtively around the marble-floored waiting area. What were they waiting for? Tim would have bet any amount of money that some of Bauer's cronies would be waiting to take him into custody. Maybe they wanted him to clear Customs, before nabbing him.

Suddenly, out of the corner of his eye, he detected a door open. As he turned, he saw a customs agent heading directly for him. Here we go.

"Sir," he said, grabbing Tim by the arm. "Would you please follow me."

Of course he would. What else was he going to do? Tim stepped out of line and followed the man. Rubber-neckers gawked.

The customs agent turned and pointed to the man who was behind Tim in line. "Sir, could you follow, too, please?" The agent unlocked the door to his booth and stepped inside. "Passport, please," he said.

Tim slipped his passport under the slot of the window separating them. The customs agent picked it up and slid the bar code through a reader. With bored detachment, the agent stamped the passport and slid it back under the Plexiglas. "Welcome back, Mr. Redmond."

# # #

Tim stood in line for a taxi, wondering why he was still walking free. Bauer must have been incensed, after learning he had slipped away from Dugit Beach. And that had been three days ago. Now, he was back in the lion's den. Surely, Bauer, with all of his assets, would have known the instant he checked in for his flight at Ben Gurion International. Why not have armed personnel waiting for him at the gate upon his arrival? At the very least, why not leave a directive with U.S. Customs to detain him?

A gray Grand Marquis pulled up to the curb and Tim jumped in.

"Where to, sir?" the driver asked.

"Eleventh and G Northwest, please."

As they proceeded down the Dulles airport access road, Tim noticed a light blue Volvo following them. It was soon replaced by a beige Chevy Suburban on Route 66, and then by a white van as they passed over the Roosevelt Bridge. As they neared their destination, Tim eyed the meter and got his money ready. The second the cab came to a stop, he handed the driver fifty dollars and jumped out of the vehicle, dashing toward the Metro Center subway station. Just before heading down the escalator, he glanced up G Street. Two men in jeans jumped out of the white van and ran down the sidewalk after him. He bolted down the escalator two steps at a time, ran past the Metro card vending machines, and launched himself over the turnstile. He continued down two more escalators to the platform for the Blue and Orange Lines and jumped onto a waiting train. Hiding himself behind a tour group, he peered out the window. The doors finally closed and the train pulled away just as his pursuers leaped off the escalator. One of them brought a hand-held radio to his mouth.

"Orange Line train to New Carrolton," the voice declared over the speaker above Tim's head. "Next station stop, Federal

Triangle." Forty seconds later, the train slowed to a stop. "Federal Triangle," the voice announced again. "Doors opening on your left."

Tim stepped onto the platform and proceeded to the other side. He waited eagerly for the next train, while watching the escalators. *Come on, come on!* Fifteen seconds later, two headlights beamed through the tunnel.

"Here comes the dragon!"

Tim heard a man's voice to his right and turned to see a little boy scrambling back from the tracks. His mother retrieved him and scowled at her husband.

"It's okay buddy, I was just kidding!" The father tried to make amends, but the boy's face was buried deep in his mother's bosom.

The dragon rolled to a stop and Tim hopped aboard. It glided down the tracks in the direction from which he had just come. Thirty seconds later, it rolled into the Metro Center station again. He peered out the window to see if his pursuers were still lurking. He knew it was risky, but he figured they would never expect him to return to the same station.

When the doors slid open, he made his way up an escalator and onto a Red Line train heading north. Four minutes later, he exited the Farragut North station onto Connecticut Avenue. After a few blocks, he took a right on M Street and slipped into a UPS store. He stood in the back for several minutes, eyeing the sidewalk from behind a stand of greeting cards. Satisfied he hadn't been followed, he pulled the string with the key on it from around his neck. With a shaking hand, he inserted the key into box 124. He was about to fit one of the final puzzle pieces into place—a piece he hadn't wanted to acknowledge until pushed by recent events.

Tim twisted the key, opened the door, and reached inside. There was nothing in the mailbox. How could that be? The people at the diagnostics lab had guaranteed him the results would be delivered by the 18th of the month, the day he left for Israel. That was four days ago. Tim was furious. He was ready to slam the door shut when he peered down the chute one more time. Lying flat on the bottom of the box was a thin slip of paper. Tim reached in and pulled it out. The text was handwritten.

Tim,

Not smart. Mail is never as secure as you think. Luckily, I got to the package first. I'm holding it for safekeeping. You can't return to the hotel. Don't go to the Pentagon, either. And don't contact anyone. Things have changed.

MLK Library, 901 G Street.

There's a workstation reserved under the name Kirk Flowers.

P

#   #   #

Tim thanked the librarian and sat down at one of the computers, the last one of the row against the wall. An intense looking woman banged away at the keyboard next to him. After logging on, he scanned the desktop icons for Instant Messenger. He found it and double clicked. A message was already waiting.

Peter: How was your trip?

Tim turned to survey the faces of those at the tables around him. Everyone sat heads down, engaged in their own work, so he looked back at the computer screen.

Tim: Enlightening.
Peter: Did you find what you were looking for?
Tim: Yes, and more.
Peter: More?
Tim: Some kind of creature was tracking me.
Peter: Creature?
Tim: It was black, very tall, and lethal.

Peter: Zaileen.

Tim: It was toying with me.

Peter: Why do you say that?

Tim: It could have killed me at any time. Which tells me that it's not after me.

Peter: Oh? Who is it after, then?

Tim shook his head. He was tired of the game.

Tim: It's after *you!*

Peter: Why would it be after me?

Tim: Because you killed the original judge.

Peter: Judge?

Tim: The one who planted the embryo in Mary. The same one who was tasked with observing mankind, following the lessons of Christ. The one who would have judged us, and destroyed us if we didn't embrace them. That was the one thing about Mars I couldn't figure out. Why would a sphere still be there? How did the Zaileen return home, after judging and destroying the Martians? The fact is, there's a skeleton somewhere on Mars, too, just like the one I found in Israel—the skeleton of the first Zaileen judge that never got around to destroying the Martians. Am I right?

Peter: You continue to impress.

Tim: Then who ended up destroying the Martians, if the Zaileen who was tasked with doing so was already dead?

Peter: Another Zaileen was sent.

Tim: And another one has been sent to Earth, hasn't it? And since it seems to be personal, I'm going to call "it" a "he." *He's* here to finish the job that the skeleton in the cave never got around to.

Peter: Yes.

Tim: Then what is he waiting for?

Peter: You already know what he's waiting for.

Tim took a moment to consider it further. So much was happening at once that he barely had enough time to evaluate current discoveries, let alone think ahead. Suddenly, the obvious occurred to him.

Tim: He knows who you are. He knows you're here. He's trying to find you.

Peter: No. Yes. Yes.

Tim: How can't he know who you are?

Peter: In the history of the Zaileen, since the epic struggle with the Turgoy seven billion years go, only four Zaileen have ever been killed. I'm responsible for two of those deaths, Tim. The Zaileen tracking you in Israel knows that. Consequently, he'd like very much to kill me. And, although he knows that an enemy of the Zaileen is afoot here, he'd be very surprised to find out exactly who I am. So you see, until he finds me and kills me, he's not going to destroy mankind.

Tim tried to see through Peter's riddles. The situation was becoming so complex, however, that it was almost impossible. The more he learned, the more he realized there was to learn.

Peter: I've already told you I've been awaiting your return for a long time, Tim. Implicit, therefore, is the notion of reincarnation. Do you believe in reincarnation?

Reincarnation? Why was he changing the subject? Was there an important discovery waiting in this line of questioning, or was Peter redirecting him? Was he getting too close to discovering something that he shouldn't? Either way, Tim had no choice but to follow Peter's lead.

Tim: Yes, I believe in reincarnation.

Peter: What purpose would reincarnation serve?

Tim: I believe souls are reborn to grow…to learn new lessons and evolve spiritually, if you will.

Peter: Sounds like a master plan.

Tim: It would have to be. How could souls be born into new circumstances that would require them to learn completely new lessons, if there were no plan behind it?

Peter: Who, then, supports the master plan? Who controls the recasting of souls into new bodies, when old bodies die?

Tim: Five days ago, I would have said the Zaileen. Now, I'm not so sure.

Peter: The master plan is controlled by something called the Guf, Tim. It's where all the souls in the universe matriculate. When someone dies—or more accurately, when their physical vessel withers or is destroyed—their soul returns to the Guf, and awaits rebirth. Only within the Guf does a being ever experience its collective consciousness—the knowledge and wisdom of all one's former lives. When a soul leaves the Guf and is reborn to another vessel, its collective consciousness stays behind…suspended, if you will.

Butterflies fluttered inside Tim's stomach. So many of Peter's insights, the ones he delivered with such calm, had rocked him. Did Peter even realize what a shock it was for him? What a shock to hear these revelations as fact, and not conjecture?

Peter: Upon discovering the Guf six billion years ago, the Zaileen seized control of its physical structure. They know it's ancient and they know it must have served a very important purpose at one time, but they don't know what.

Tim: Who created the Guf then, if not the Zaileen?

Peter: Those who came before the Zaileen.

Tim: Who are they?

Peter: No one knows.

Tim: I find it very hard to believe that the Zaileen have no idea what the purpose of the Guf is.

Peter: How could they? The only way to enter the Guf is to die. Only souls can enter the Guf, Tim, not physical beings. Once a soul is inside the Guf, it's all very clear—how souls are recast, the master plan, everything. All that knowledge is part of one's collective consciousness. When a soul leaves the Guf, however, when it is recast to another vessel, all that knowledge must stay behind. No collective consciousness has ever left the Guf. Therefore, no physical being living outside of the Guf knows anything about the master plan and the collective consciousness.

Tim: Then how do you know about it?

Tim waited for a response, but none came. Finally, he turned around and scanned the library. He wondered if Peter was in the building with him now, watching him, maybe even typing his responses on a laptop somewhere. Had someone entered his space, forcing him to stop the dialogue? When Tim gazed back at his monitor, Peter's response rolled onto the screen.

Peter: Some things must remain secret, Tim.

Tim took a moment to consider the Guf and the possibility of a universal master plan. He added this prospect to what he already knew about the Zaileen and their extermination policy. Suddenly, it hit him. He saw the ultimate dilemma.

Tim: The Guf is overflowing, isn't it?

Peter: You finally understand.

Tim: The Zaileen aren't allowing civilizations to advance. Without higher level civilizations, how can older souls be born into more demanding situations? How can they continue to grow?

Peter: The master plan is broken, Tim. The Zaileen aren't only wantonly exterminating civilizations, they are also preventing souls from evolving.

Tim: What can I possibly do about it?

Peter: A plan is in place. But in order to see it through, we must survive.

Goosebumps rippled down Tim's arms. *We* must survive? What was Peter worried about? What did he have to fear?

Tim: You're concerned about the second Zaileen on earth?

Peter: Yes.

Tim: I thought you already killed two of them. Why can't you destroy this one, too?

Peter: Not all Zaileen have been created equally, Tim. I killed two judges, mere foot soldiers, responsible for carrying out the most basic of Zaileen functions. The one lurking on earth is anything but a foot soldier.

Tim cringed.

Peter: You finally get your wish, Tim. We meet tonight at ten o'clock—Roosevelt Island. Don't forget your trinket from Qumran!

CHAPTER 39

Tim reached into a white bag, removed some popcorn and popped it into his mouth. As he chewed, he observed a pickup soccer game on the Mall lawn. It had been a pleasant diversion, but his backside was getting numb from sitting on the park bench for so long. He checked his watch again—six o'clock. The sun had just dipped below the spire of the Washington Monument, casting a long narrow shadow across the tall fence that encircled it. He prayed that Bonnie hadn't adjusted her routine, or that Stentz hadn't asked the think-tank to stay late. He'd thought about calling her cell phone, but quickly shot down the idea. It would most likely be tapped. He would have to play the odds and hope she came to the museum this evening like she'd done almost every other day following her work at the Pentagon. If she didn't, he'd have to invoke plan B—a plan he desperately wanted to avoid.

A green Saab convertible rolled down Madison Drive. He caught a glimpse of the driver, but it wasn't Bonnie. The car continued to 12th Street, where it took a right turn. He scanned the traffic moving down 9th Street, hoping her car would turn onto the museum's access road soon. The fact that Madison Drive was a one-way street made it a little easier for him, but her affinity for the Metro introduced another possibility. He turned and gazed down the sidewalk toward the Smithsonian Metro station. There were a few pedestrians, but none were Bonnie. When he returned his attention to the museum, he saw a woman about Bonnie's height heading down the sidewalk away from him. Was it Bonnie, just now *leaving* the museum? Had she skipped going to the Pentagon today?

Tim jumped to his feet and scurried across the street after her. Halfway to 12th Street he caught up to the woman, and confirmed that it was, indeed, Bonnie. He walked parallel to her, maintaining enough distance between them that she wouldn't look directly at him.

"Bonnie, it's Tim. Don't look at me. You're probably being watched." To his amazement, she didn't give any indication of surprise. She did as he asked and continued to walk at a steady pace, looking straight ahead.

"In a few seconds, after I've passed by you, stop and look into your purse like you've forgotten something. Then head back to the museum and let me in the side entrance at 9th Street." He continued walking past her and took a right on 12th Street.

Minutes later, Tim slipped through the open door and Bonnie locked it behind him. "I'm sorry about the cloak and dagger business, Bonnie," he said.

Unexpectedly, she embraced him. "Thank God you're alright!"

A man mopping the floor at the end of the hallway stared at them.

"Let's go somewhere quiet," Tim said. "Other than your office."

Bonnie nodded, guided him to a stairwell, and down a level. They emerged into a hallway lined with glass cases. Hundreds of exotic birds stood frozen in time, a marvel of taxidermy and man's need to physically possess beauty. Just as Bonnie was about to speak, Tim cut her off.

"What are you doing here, Bonnie? I was waiting for you to *arrive* from the Pentagon. Did Stentz let you go early today?"

"Stentz is gone, Tim," she said, reaching out and clasping Tim's elbow gently. "The day after you left, Bauer announced that Victor had been killed in a car accident on the George Washington Parkway."

Tim reeled and grabbed the corner of one of the glass cases for support. *I should have warned him! I knew something was going to happen!*

"I'm sorry, Tim. I know you were very fond of him. We all were."

Tim pulled himself together. "Did Bauer take his place? Did *he* start leading the discussions?" he asked.

Bonnie shook her head. "As soon as he gave us the news about Victor, he dismissed us."

"*What?*"

"Without a word of explanation or a 'thank you,' we were ushered from the building," Bonnie said. She then went on the offensive. "Where have *you* been, Tim? You were supposed to be back days ago. I was worried that something may have happened to you, too!"

Tim thought about sharing his information, but he didn't want to endanger her. "It's probably best that you don't know," he said.

Bonnie peered into his eyes and studied him. "I understand," she said. "But there's something else you should know. The Santa Maria is gone. I think it exploded."

Tim reeled again.

"As we were being escorted out, we passed the Mission Control area. It was a madhouse, Tim! People were running around like chickens with their heads cut off! Phones were ringing off the hook. I glanced at one of the display screens and saw a mushroom cloud over the landing area."

Tim was speechless. He felt the blood drain from his face. His failure to warn Stentz had cost the man his life. Now, it appeared that by sending the crew of the Santa Maria to the caves, he'd also cost them theirs.

"I just want to know one thing, Tim. Was the sphere there? Was it in the lake?" Bonnie asked.

He didn't even hear the question. He was still reeling from the news about Stentz and the crew of the Santa Maria.

"Did you find the sphere in Israel, Tim?" she repeated, grabbing him by the arm.

Tim looked up from the ground. "Yes, it was there, Bonnie…in the Sea of Galilee," he said. "But I don't want you to say anything to anyone about it. Do you understand?"

She nodded.

"Have you received a package? An official antiquities transfer from Israel?"

"No, I haven't received anything, Tim. If it's an official transfer on loan from Israel, it might still be in our receiving bay, though. Whenever we get something on loan, we have to document its condition very carefully, as soon as it arrives. It takes some time."

"Do you have access to that area?"

"Of course."

"Let's go!"

Chapter 40

The evening air hung thick and Tim labored to inhale the water-packed vapor known by Washingtonians as the wet death. A low growl rumbled across the horizon from the north and Tim looked up to see streaks of lighting dance across the dark sky. His shirt clung to his chest and the straps from his backpack dug into his armpits. A trickle of sweat inched down the side of his sunburned face, scorched from his time in Israel. He heard carefree laughter and turned to peer over the side of the Key Bridge. Young revelers packed the Georgetown waterfront area that abutted the Potomac River. The water was as black as the Zaileen who had chased him only days earlier. A deep chill rifled through his bones.

When he reached the end of the Key Bridge, he took a left onto Mount Vernon Trail and continued down the narrow running path along the water's edge. He finally reached a footbridge that spanned the Little River section of the Potomac and stared across it at Roosevelt Island. All was still and quiet. It was eerie. No more than fifty feet behind him, a steady stream of cars sped down the George Washington Parkway, while on the island, there was no sign of life. At least, no human life. It was like an invisible line had been drawn across the middle of the footbridge. Everything west of it—the GW Parkway and the city of Rosslyn—was reassuringly familiar, life as normal in the twenty-first century. Everything east of it—the Potomac River and Roosevelt Island—had been transformed into some eerie hallowed ground.

He reached deep inside himself and called upon the voice in the back of his mind. *Is this a mistake? Am I walking into a trap?*

Why would Peter choose a location like this, a single entry point surrounded by water? He received no discernable reply and reluctantly jumped over the gate and onto the bridge. The further he advanced, the cooler it seemed to get. He reached the far side, where a metal sign on a barricade stated that the park was closed after dark. He climbed up onto the gate, hopped down to the gravel walking path, and continued toward a thicket of trees thirty feet ahead of him. Suddenly, the command center in his mind kicked in: *High energy contact ahead; unable to pinpoint location!* The hairs on the back of his neck stood on end. Part of him wanted to run, but he continued down the walking path, passing marshland on either side of him. The park was teeming with wildlife. The noise from the crickets and frogs was almost deafening. Redwing blackbirds, robins and mockingbirds screamed from the trees around him. A beaver munched on a log in the distance, its tail occasionally slapping the shallow water. There was movement in all directions and he struggled to filter the data pouring into his command center. *That's why he picked this place. In addition to being isolated—with no other point of entry or exit—the noise and movement from the wildlife is acting as a jamming mechanism.*

Suddenly, the tree-lined path opened to a courtyard, the main traffic hub for the park. Around its outer ring, four other gravel walking paths converged. Tim's eye was immediately drawn to a bronze statue of Teddy Roosevelt, and he went over to read the inscription plate. Another warning fired from his command center: *Target approaching from 10 degrees northeast!* Tim swung left. Under the glow of the moon, a tall dark figure approached him. As he walked, the stones seemed to crumble beneath his feet, a sound far too substantial to be generated by a man. And yet, a man it was. Butterflies swirled in Tim's stomach.

The figure finally emerged from the shadows of the trees. As he stepped out into the open, the moonlight caught his face.

Oh, my God! Tim stood in place, completely paralyzed.

As the man walked up to him, a broad smile spread across his dark attractive features. "If I've told you once, I've told you a thousand times, Tim, if you don't start wearing sunscreen you're going to be mistaken for a crustacean and boiled!"

Tim couldn't respond. He couldn't breathe.

The man before him laughed. "If you don't say something soon, Tim, you're going to hurt my feelings."

The crisp English accent was the same one Tim remembered from Africa. "How?" Tim uttered. It was all he could manage.

"Some vessels are more malleable than others, Tim. My original form is almost pure energy. It takes tremendous skill, but I can mold it into nearly any living creature."

The history of his online discussions with Peter—or Simon as it was now apparent—swarmed through Tim's head. *Why wasn't he able to guess his identity?* "Have you been…anyone else?" he asked, wondering if Simon had not only managed to fool him in the written word, but also in the spoken word, in person as someone else.

Simon laughed again. "It doesn't work like that, Tim. We can't achieve any form within seconds. It's extremely complex. Every little detail must be mimicked. It takes years to perfect a life form. Once it's been perfected, however, we can change back and forth between our chosen form and our high energy vessel almost instantly."

"Then you really are one of them? A Zaileen?"

Simon nodded. "Yes. But I'm on your side, Tim. Of that you can be sure. I've been on your side since we first met. Since long before we met, actually."

"And when was it that we first met?"

Simon grinned and scratched his chin. "Hmmm…when *did* we first meet?"

Before he could finish, Tim blurted the answer. "Three-hundred million years ago!" The words tumbled out at the same time the knowledge registered in his brain. It hit him like a wave. The visions he'd had of Mars weren't visions after all. They were latent *memories*!

"Impressive!" Simon said. "It's all beginning to come back to you, isn't it?"

Tim wobbled and nearly fell. Simon quickly grabbed him by the arm and steadied him. "Why don't we have a seat," he said, guiding Tim toward a bench. "Your knees are going to be tested more than once tonight."

Tim slid onto the bench and took a deep breath. "Was I *him*? Was I the Martian prophet?" he asked.

Immediately, Simon howled. "What is it with you, Tim?" He held his stomach as he laughed. "Do you have a prophet-envy complex?" Finally, he pulled himself together. "I'll tell you what, Tim. If we are successful in our goal—if we manage to rectify the Guf—I'll do everything in my power to grant your wish. A prophet you shall be!"

Tim didn't appreciate the razzing, however friendly it might be. Even in Africa, Simon had always known exactly what buttons to push. "So, I'm not a Zaileen?" he asked.

"No, Tim. You are not a Zaileen."

"Then who am I?"

Simon turned to look Tim directly in the eyes. Humor was now replaced by somber resolve. "Remember when I told you that I was responsible for killing two Zaileen?"

Tim nodded.

"*You* killed the other two," Simon said.

Tim felt his head swim.

Simon's eyes narrowed. "Over four billion years ago, a civilization called the Coumlon thrived near the Albinoni supernova, some eighteen-billion light years from Earth. A very interesting civilization, the Coumlon," Simon said, eyes glazed as if transporting himself back in time. "Not that much different from Humans, actually. The best of the best, and the worst of the worst, you might say. The Coumlon were broken into four main factions, three despicable and one pure. As these factions evolved, they became increasingly different. Eventually, what began as a mild conflict between them escalated into an all-out war. It was during a particularly hostile period between these factions that the Zaileen prophet arrived. And, as you might expect during a period of intense fighting, the prophet's teachings fell on deaf ears. Predictably, the Zaileen judge—the one that implanted the prophet's embryo and walked among the Coumlon to adjudicate them—reached his verdict: total extermination. Just before the Zaileen judge was able to carry out this sentence, however, something amazing happened, something that had never happened before. The Zaileen judge was killed!"

Tim's head began to spin faster. He felt like a patient emerging from a bout of amnesia, grappling with facts once known, but long forgotten. Images came to him in blinding flashes—images of foreign places, languages, cultures, histories.

"Someone had sniffed out the danger, Tim!" Simon said excitedly. "The *someone* was the young leader of the pure faction. His name was Staphf. Somehow Staphf identified the judge, uncovered his plans to exterminate the Coumlon, and killed him before he could take action."

"How did he know?" Tim heard himself ask the question. It was a familiar voice, but weak and distant. Another, stronger voice was emerging from his subconscious.

"I have no idea," Simon said. "That's one of the questions I've been dying to ask you." He leaned toward Tim to take a closer look into his eyes, like a doctor assessing a patient. "To ask Staphf...when he finally emerges."

Tim's head felt like it was going to roll off, like it was resting precariously on top of his shoulders, balanced only by the girth of a Pixie Stick.

Apparently satisfied with Tim's progress, Simon continued. "You...rather Staphf...constructed the dagger—the one I used much later to kill the being in Israel. The one you have in your backpack." Simon patted the bag still hanging from Tim's shoulder. "It's made of the same material as the sphere, nearly indestructible. Yet another question that I've been eager to ask you—Staphf. How did you manage to extract the alloy from the sphere? And how, with such limited technology, were you able to construct the core...the black ball nestled between the blades? You may have already figured this out, Tim, but the ball is anti-matter. Once the point of the dagger penetrates the very tough exoskeleton of a Zaileen, the anti-matter devours the energy within. Staphf was brilliant! Not unlike another young man we both know." Simon winked.

"Help," Tim muttered. His plea was weak, barely audible. He struggled to keep his eyes open, teetering on the edge of unconsciousness. Yet Simon's words still registered.

"Tim, you have to let it happen. You have to give in," Simon said. "Your soul is Staphf's soul. You are one and the same. Your collective consciousness is simply trying to break through. Don't be afraid of losing yourself. Tim Redmond and everything you know about yourself will still be there. As you accept your collective consciousness, however, you will simply become a more comprehensive YOU. You'll have the collective wisdom of all your past lives."

Tim thought he was going to explode. "Help me," he muttered again. The fire was raging through his body like never before. It was excruciating.

Simon gazed into his eyes. "Just listen to my voice, Tim. It will help you to hear what I have to say. As I've already told you, I'm a Zaileen. One who, long ago, became disgusted with the mass genocide propagated by the Council of Five—the Zaileen's governing body. For centuries, I lobbied the Council to end its senseless exterminations. Unfortunately, the harder I pushed, the more ostracized I became. Finally, I was forced to conclude that the only way to set the Master Plan straight was to eliminate the Council by force. But how could one entity—as powerful as I was—destroy five others who were even more powerful? I was stuck. I had no solution. Then you came along, Tim. Or rather, Staphf came along and killed the Zaileen judge. As you can imagine, when the Council of Five learned that someone had killed one of their judges, they were none too pleased. They dispatched a second Zaileen—a warrior type—much more powerful than a judge. I figured there was no way you could defeat a warrior, especially one that had the drop on you. But I was intrigued nonetheless. So, I watched the brewing conflict unfold with great interest."

Simon stopped talking. He leaned back and slowly surveyed their surroundings. Then he slid Tim's backpack from his shoulders, unzipped it, carefully removed the dagger, and placed it on the bench between them.

Tim remained completely immobilized.

Simon continued his discourse. "Guess what, Tim? You defeated the warrior. You managed to do what had never been done before. You actually killed a Zaileen warrior! That's when I knew there was something very different about you. That's when I decided you might be the solution to my problem. Therefore, I left the Zaileen and set out to find you. I wanted to convince you to join forces with me in a bid to overthrow the Council. Unfortunately, the Council responded much more quickly and dramatically than I ever imagined they would. They released a force that I didn't think actually existed, a force I thought was nothing more than legend. A being called the Sept, Tim, more powerful than any Zaileen. Before I could get to you, it was too late. The Sept had already killed you."

Simon paused for a moment, to let Tim assimilate the knowledge and absorb the shock. He then began again. "Knowing you had already been killed, I searched for your body. When I finally found it—or what was left of it—I extracted DNA samples from your remains. Unfortunately, I didn't have time to devise much of a plan. Your executioner was now hot on my heels. It pursued me relentlessly; I didn't have a single moment of peace. It wouldn't stop until I was dead. Therefore, I had no choice but to do its bidding. I had to die. Or at least lead the Zaileen to believe I was dead. So, much like I did for your benefit in Africa—but on a much grander scale mind you—I successfully staged my own death. A brilliant bit of subterfuge, if I do say so myself. Thankfully, it worked, and Council of Five recalled the Sept. With the threat of my pursuer finally gone, I was free to plan. I headed straight to the Guf, to learn its secrets. Not an easy task, I assure you, with the Zaileen still in control of its physical structure, but I found ways. I explored it. I obsessed over it. I learned about its inner workings. I devised a master plan of my own. Eventually, I figured out how to unleash a being's collective consciousness, in conjunction with its soul as it is recast. My plan was in place. And when *your* soul was finally recast on Mars, three-hundred million years ago, I was there…waiting."

Simon picked his head up again and listened intently. Then he continued. "Unfortunately, things on Mars didn't proceed as planned. A collective consciousness had never been released into a physical body before. Despite all of my research and planning, there were still so many unknowns. Like, how would your body react to the sudden introduction of your collective consciousness? How would memories experienced in prior bodies, with entirely different neural processes, be interpreted by your Martian mind? How would your Martian-based consciousness deal with potentially conflicting knowledge or opinions established in previous lives? It was an utter disaster, Tim. Your Martian-based consciousness and body crumbled under the pressure. Whenever your collective consciousness attempted to engage, it was rejected, like a transplanted organ being rejected by a poorly matched host. Your Martian body and consciousness simply could not accept your collective consciousness all at once. It was too much of a shock. You went mad, Tim. And from that experiment, I learned a great deal. I had to figure out a way to make the transition smoother. I decided to retrieve your Coumlon DNA. What better way to precipitate a smooth transition than to have your collective consciousness—or at least part of it—be born into a body that it had already occupied at one time? So, after retrieving your Coumlon DNA, I returned to the Guf to determine when and where your soul was to be recast again. My wait this time was only three-hundred million years. And although that may sound like a long time to you, Tim, it almost wasn't long enough. You were slated to be born of a species on Earth—that was a long stretch from the Coumlon species. I couldn't very well have your soul be recast into a cloned version of Staphf, while the rest of the species on Earth—a species that you were supposedly a part of— looked completely different. How could you effectively grow and interact with the Earth-based species if you looked so completely different? And more importantly, how could you blend in with the rest of the Earth-based species and not stick out like a sore thumb, if the Zaileen came looking for you? I had to modify the entire species, Tim. I had to modify it to look like the Coumlon.

Not to be *exactly* like the Coumlon, mind you, but to look close enough to conceal you, when you eventually arrived. And I had to do it slowly enough to keep from tipping off the Zaileen. I tweaked the genetic makeup of the Earth-based species—what eventually became Homo Sapiens—hundreds of times over millions of years, tiny corrections here and there. In the end, modern man emerged very close to their Coumlon predecessors, at least in appearance. Of course, *you* are still quite different, at least at the base genetic level. You are pure Coumlon, Tim, an exact clone of Staphf, while mankind is merely a close approximation."

Simon paused again to peer into Tim's eyes. Suddenly, he jerked his head up and scanned the surrounding forest. After a few moments, he continued. "As complex as it sounds, Tim, preparing your Earth-based body was the easy part. Preparing your mind was the real challenge. Remember, it wasn't only your physical body that collapsed on Mars when your collective consciousness attempted to emerge. Your Martian-based consciousness folded, too. The shock of learning so much in such a short period of time was simply too much for you to handle. For lack of a better term, Tim, it literally blew your mind. Therefore, I had to make the transition smoother. In order to mitigate the shock to your Earth-based consciousness, you had to learn everything on your own. That's why I refused to spoon-feed you during our online dialogues. Only by discovering everything on your own—the truth about the Zaileen, the Guf, the role of the collective consciousness and your history as Staphf—could you believe it all. And only by truly believing it all could you reduce the shock to your Earth-based consciousness when your collective one finally emerged."

Tim struggled to concentrate through the pain that was raging in his mind and body. His collective consciousness was fighting to take over. Tim fought just as hard, however, to keep it out. He forced himself to focus on the final pieces of the puzzle, pieces that had moved into place with Simon's recent admissions. It was now obvious why Peter—Simon—had been so coy during their online discussions—why he had insisted that Tim uncover everything, and why he had refused to volunteer information himself. It was also now clear why Simon had killed the Zaileen judge, the skeleton Tim had found in Israel. Simon couldn't allow the judge to destroy mankind before Tim was born. It was probably this same reason that had prompted Simon to kill the judge on Mars. But there was still something that confused Tim. The Council had dispatched another Zaileen warrior to Earth shortly after the judge was killed, hadn't they? Simon confirmed as much during their last online dialogue. In the same discussion, Simon also made it clear that even he was no match for a Zaileen warrior. If this was true, then how, after two thousand years, had the warrior failed to locate and kill Simon? Tim tried to pose the question, but it was nearly impossible for him to verbalize anything with the painful storm raging in his body.

"Warrior...not kill you...how?" The half-baked question stumbled from Tim's lips.

"Where has the Zaileen warrior been all this time? How can I still be alive?" Simon intuited Tim's question. "I already told you. I'm very elusive. I would have thought you'd realized that by now. Of course, the warrior has been relentless in his hunt for me. I've always managed to stay one step ahead of him. Recently, however, it's been more difficult. Shepherding you through your discovery process has put me at risk. The Zaileen warrior has been using you as a means to get to me. That's why I've had to speak with you electronically. I had to postpone our face-to-face meeting until you were finally ready to accept your collective consciousness...and the powers that come with it." Simon peered into the woods beyond the courtyard. His eyes narrowed and he lowered his voice. "The Zaileen warrior has just set foot on the island, Tim. I led him here." He picked up the dagger from the bench and held it in front of Tim's face. "I'm sorry to have to do this to you, but you've left me no choice. You refuse to swim on your own, Tim. You refuse to fully embrace your collective consciousness. You've forced me to throw you into the deep end. If you don't allow Staphf to emerge before the Zaileen warrior reaches us, we will both be killed. It's that simple. Close your eyes and let go," he instructed. "Let Staphf take over." Simon continued to hold the dagger out, waiting for Tim to embrace it.

"I'm putting my life in your hands, Tim! *Let Staphf in!*" Simon placed his right hand on Tim's shoulder and shook it. "We're out of time!"

The soft wisp of an evergreen branch caused Simon to wheel around toward the woods beyond the courtyard. Suddenly, a guttural scream rang out into the night.

Gruiieee!

Tim's body was paralyzed with pain, but he could still see. He caught the blur that was the Zaileen warrior storming into the clearing. He also saw Simon instantly transform into a massive black shape and spring to meet his challenger. When the two Zaileen collided in the center of the courtyard, it sounded to Tim like a head-on train collision, metal impacting metal at a combined speed of over a hundred miles per hour.

Tim tried to follow the tussle, but it was too fast for his eyes to track. He only heard the primal screams, and the snapping of tree trunks, as the conflict moved into the woods. It was a blood feud. Trees continued to snap and violent screams continued to echo out into the night.

After two minutes, the noise finally subsided. All was quiet, except for the chirping of crickets, and the gurgling of the Potomac. Finally, a single voice rang out from somewhere in the darkness—sharp guttural bursts, in a language Tim could only assume was Zaileen.

"Who is the boy?" the Zaileen warrior said, standing over Simon's prone body with the dagger he had wrestled from his hand.

Simon stared at his captor, exhausted and beaten. He didn't say a word.

"It makes no difference," the warrior continued. "I am going to destroy him anyway."

A smile slowly replaced Simon's grimace. "You're too late," he said. His chest heaved and he whispered a parting word, *"From forgotten ashes long grown cold...I've resurrected the host of old."*

The warrior slammed the dagger into Simon's chest, instantly penetrating his exoskeleton. The ball at its center devoured the life force within him.

CHAPTER 41

*W*e are one, Tim. A unified force. We must work together as such. I have been an ethereal entity for billions of years now. Over that time, I have become unaccustomed to a corporal existence. Although part of me has occupied this body before, concessions must be made for my longtime inactivity. You will have greater control of your body than I, Tim. When I issue a command, you must execute it without hesitation, as you did in Israel. Things will be moving extremely fast. Faster than you ever dreamed. Any delays will result in our immediate destruction, of that you can be sure. Certain commands may be hard to accept as possible, but rest assured this vessel is capable of actions unfathomable by your Earth-based consciousness. Eliminate all doubts now.

When we resurface, Simon will be dead. Destroyed by the Zaileen warrior, who will have a singular focus…you…me…us. He may or may not intend to kill us. That will be the first thing I must ascertain upon emerging. I will know it instantly. You must react accordingly. Are you ready?

Yes.

Tim's eyes flickered open.

Gruiieee!

He intends to kill us! Two seconds to impact!

The Zaileen's dark body was already airborne, vaulting the final few feet to impact, dagger extended toward Tim's chest. While still seated, Tim spun his body sideways and grabbed the being's black wrist. An immense surge of energy pulsed through his arm and he tightened his grip and twisted. The warrior's body sailed right past him, and as it did, Tim yanked firmly.

The being's massive frame snapped back like a rag doll and he screamed out in pain. He dropped the dagger to the ground, and his body quickly followed with a thud. A split-second after impacting the dirt, the Zaileen was up on his feet again. He swung a sharp claw at the spot he expected Tim to be, but all he caught was air. He scanned the ground quickly for the dagger, but it was gone too. He was stunned. It had all happened so quickly. Even he, a Zaileen warrior, with neural processes fast as lightning, struggled to assimilate it. Had he just been manhandled? How could a Human possibly be that strong? How could he be that quick? It wasn't the warrior's job, however, to contemplate such things. He was a being of action, with a clear objective. When he detected Tim streaking through the trees toward the river, he bolted after him.

He took a direct line, smashing through branches and underbrush. The boy in front of him was remarkably fast, but he had to avoid the larger branches, costing him precious seconds. As the Zaileen closed to within a hundred feet, he saw Tim fling himself off the bank and into the river. The warrior smiled. He knew he could close the distance even faster through the air, while Tim battled against the current. He accelerated and vaulted off the bank. With any luck, he would sail past Tim, and enter the water beyond him. All he would then need to do is turn and finish him off.

As he sailed through the air, he peered into the water. Several feet under the surface, gliding swiftly back toward the beachhead, he saw the unmistakable outline of Tim's body. *Clever boy!*

The warrior dipped his head and thrust himself into the river, propelling his body forward with a strong kick. He then banked sharply like a seal, using his long arms and massive hands like flippers. He rocketed back toward the shore, still submersed. In just two powerful strokes, he propelled himself into the shallows and stood up quickly in the chest-high water. Steam rose into night air from his slick head. Suddenly, he froze. Not ten feet in front of him, standing on the shore with dagger at the ready, was Tim.

As much as he hated to admit it, it was a brilliant maneuver by the young man. By taking an offensive position on dry ground, and confronting him before he emerged from the water, the boy had leveled the playing field in terms of quickness. Was the young man slower, though? Hadn't the boy snatched his wrist while sitting on the bench with lightning quickness? Once again, he wondered how a Human could be so fast.

"My conflict is not with you, Bauer!" Tim yelled. "All you need do is turn around and swim upriver."

Bauer. The boy had even guessed his identity! Rage swelled inside of him. He was at once furious and unsure of himself, the latter giving even greater rise to the former. Who was this boy? He was a Zaileen warrior! He was one of the most awesome forces in the entire universe! How could a mere man be offering him quarter? And do it so confidently, like he was granting a reprieve? Something was terribly amiss. Bauer tried to rationalize the incongruity. The boy had been committed to a mental institution for a span of five years, a fact Bauer's contacts at the CIA couldn't even uncover, but one that he himself had managed to learn. Was it mental illness that gave Tim the confidence? Did Tim not recognize the fact that he was woefully outmatched? Mentally ill or not, what could possibly explain the boy's lightning quick reactions, his strength or the speed with which he had retreated into the woods? Bauer wondered if there were more to the boy than he had initially thought. Could the boy's brilliance be genuine? Could it be that Tim had come by all the information he'd shared with the think-tank on his own, rather than through his accomplice? The accomplice that Bauer had just dispatched with predictable efficiency? He now found himself even more unsure. It was a completely foreign sensation. He loathed it.

Was it not enough that he'd already been shocked once, shocked to finally uncover the identity of Tim's accomplice? Granted, it hadn't prevented him from killing him. But, Bauer had to admit he'd been surprised. He never suspected the Fallen One, the one who had turned against the Zaileen so long ago. He was supposed to be dead, killed billions of years ago by the one force that was perhaps more deadly than Bauer himself. Did this boy factor into that history somehow? How could he? He was just a Human! Before the questions could persist any longer, Bauer shut them down. None of it mattered now. The time for analysis was over. It was time for action. In a flash, Bauer dove underwater and shot his long body forward. The sand rose up to meet him quickly. The Zaileen warrior sprung out of the water with claws raised. As the blade penetrated his forehead, his last thought was a simple one. The boy cannot be Human.

# # #

Tim strode down the gravel path admiring the beautiful foliage around him from an entirely new perspective. He had been reborn into a world vaguely familiar to him, yet fresh and uncharted. Everything around him had intensified: his clarity of sight, sound, smell, and touch had all been amplified to the power of ten. Reeds in the marshlands stood out like blades of grass under a microscope. Even in the dark, he could make out every detail—rough edges gnawed by grasshoppers; near-microscopic veins of the xylem branching out like capillaries; tiny parachute-like seedlings blowing off cattails in the breeze. He smelled the rich soil and the tulips in the garden beds, the algae in the shallow ponds. He heard droplets of water sail from his soaking body, and the near-deafening boom as they impacted the gravel.

As he walked, memories of foreign lands, foods, cultures and ethics poured down on him as though from a spigot. The memories rushed straight through him, water cutting through the dry soil of a plant too quickly to be absorbed all at once, collecting in the overflow basin at the bottom of the pot. Tim wasn't concerned. He knew they would persist. When he was ready, his thirsty roots would reach down and absorb them—paradoxically experiencing each memory for the first time.

The fire still raged within his mind and body, but the pain had dissipated. Whether the result of some physiological change—his new consciousness moderating the dispersion of chemicals in his system more effectively—or the fact that he was simply tolerating it better, Tim was glad for it. A flurry of activity buzzed within his mind. His collective consciousness was assimilating new facts, formulating plans, re-drawing entire battle strategies. He knew that eventually he would become an integral part of it all, but for now, he was happy to lay back and observe.

He emerged from the tree-lined path into the courtyard where the evening's action had begun. He was bone tired and every muscle in his body ached. Lacerations covered his face, arms, and chest from the thick underbrush and tree branches. His eyes burned from the acrid water of the Potomac, and his wrist throbbed from thrusting the dagger into Bauer's skull. Assimilating one's collective consciousness was a taxing experience. Add to that a confrontation with a Zaileen warrior, and it was no wonder he felt like he'd been run over by a truck.

The moon cast a pale glow onto the splintered remains of the park bench. Iron and wood contorted in a grotesque swan song. The vision of Bauer's own contorted body flashed in Tim's mind— arms bending backward, chest heaving, chin stretching toward the stars. A chill shot down his spine. Somewhere among the trees behind him was another figure, splayed out like Bauer. Simon had been killed. He felt it. As much as Tim didn't want to see his remains, it had to be confirmed.

He picked the backpack up from the ground, and felt the strain in his hamstrings. Much work lay ahead to prepare this vessel for such awesome physical strain. He unzipped the bag, reinserted the dagger, and eased the straps over his sore shoulders. Following the visible evidence of Simon's retreat into the woods, he picked his way through the bushes to a small clearing. There, crumpled into an almost unrecognizable heap, were the remains of a long black figure. Its exoskeleton was completely shriveled and its mouth was agape.

CHAPTER 42

Tim strode across the Key Bridge as Staphf, pondering the irony of it all. Regardless of his selfish motives, Simon had resurrected him. Without Simon's help, Staphf would still be relegated to the Guf, unable to complete his mission—a mission that he had embarked upon four billion years ago. And by way of Simon's plan to use him, Staphf had somehow emerged with all the skills he had originally possessed. Four billion years ago, Staphf had thought that such an array of capabilities would be ample for his purposes, but he'd been proved wrong. He hadn't anticipated the Sept. Where had it come from? How could it have been powerful enough to kill him? Although that question still haunted him, there were more immediate questions that needed to be answered. How had Simon released Staphf's collective consciousness? How had he been able to learn so much about the Guf? Not just learn about it, but act upon the knowledge? He couldn't have actually entered the Guf, could he? Even with his own extensive knowledge of the Guf, Staphf had no clue how Simon could have entered it…not while still maintaining his physical existence. All the laws upon which the Guf had been constructed supposedly made that impossible.

Fortunately, there were still a few things that Simon could not have known. He hadn't figured out how to control the recasting process. He'd been forced to wait billions of years for Staphf's soul to be recast on Mars, and then another 300 million for it to be recast on Earth. If Simon had been able to control the recasting of souls himself, he would have accelerated the timetable for Staphf's next birth, rather than wait so long for the Guf to do it. Simon could not have known how Staphf had entered the Guf four billion years ago, either. Not by dying—the window through which everyone else had to enter—but through a back door of sorts, sent by an entity more powerful than even the Zaileen. And Simon could not have known about Staphf's original mission. Had he known that, he never would have resurrected him in the first place, certainly not with his collective consciousness intact. Simon and Staphf's goals were diametrically opposed. Simon's motivation for overthrowing the Zaileen Council of Five was strictly for power. Of course the Zaileen were exterminating dangerous civilizations throughout the universe, but it was a minute fraction of the one hundred percent that Simon had suggested. Fundamentally, the Zaileen were a very righteous species. No, Staphf didn't want to destroy the Council of Five...but he would if necessary. He would, if it served his greater mission, if they'd already been turned by the Sept. Yes, the Sept was at the heart of it all. The being was real. How had Staphf and the others failed to recognize that? He chided himself for the oversight, although he knew how it was possible. His origins were a long way from this universe. Only so much could be intuited over such an expanse, so he had to come in person.

When Tim reached the end of the Key Bridge, he took a right onto M Street. It was one o'clock in the morning, but Georgetown was still buzzing with activity. A group of college students, both men and women, walked by him on the sidewalk, gawking. Judging from their stares, he knew something had to be wrong. Maybe it was the bloody lacerations on his body. He glanced down to assess the wounds on his arms, and stared at them in utter disbelief. His arms were unblemished...completely healed. He reached up to touch his face. Where several cuts had once been, his cheeks were now perfectly smooth. They couldn't be staring at his lacerations, then. He glanced to his left self-consciously. Several young women in a convertible drove by and turned to stare at him. A taxi followed closely behind and the driver and both passengers peered through the windows at him.

What's going on?

CHAPTER 43

I t was a spectacular spring day in the nation's capitol. Bonnie felt the warmth of the sun on her face as she stepped out from the shadows of the Natural History museum. The Metro section of the *Post* had predicted a high of eighty-two degrees, but it felt more like the mid-seventies. For her money, May was the best month of the year in Washington. Nice and warm, but not yet sweltering. She glanced at her watch and frowned. If she were going to make her two o'clock meeting, she'd have to cut the run short—two laps between the Lincoln Memorial and the Capitol building. She skipped down the marble steps of the museum and headed across the pebble-covered walkway that ran the length of the mall.

The day was more than spectacular, it was invigorating. With relatively low humidity, she could actually feel each breath enter her lungs. It was a wonderful sensation, refreshing. She inhaled deeply through her nose and was rewarded with the scent of honeysuckle from flowering bushes lining the pathway.

It had been almost a month since the think-tank had disbanded, and it was all she'd been able to think about. The same unanswered questions haunted her day and night. Did God send a prophet to both Mars and Earth? Why would He need a sphere in which to send them? Was God actually the entity everyone on earth believed him to be? Or was some other force involved? Where was Tim? Was he still alive? Finally, accepting that she had no answers—and no control over it, even if she did— Bonnie had been able to push the thoughts from her mind. Almost immediately, she started sleeping better. Her daily headaches had disappeared and her overall zest for life had returned.

Consequences be damned, she wanted nothing more to do with Mars. She didn't even want to know the truth, and for a scientist, searching for truth was supposed to be one's raison d'être.

Bonnie stopped and jogged in place at the 14th Street intersection, while she waited for the light to change. When it did, she continued to 15th Street and then past the Washington Monument and the World War II Memorial. As she approached the reflecting pool, her mind drifted to thoughts of Mars and the think-tank. She tried to push them out, but to no avail. Her conversation with Tim at the restaurant came rushing to the forefront. Why had he been so eager to discuss evolution? At the time, the topic seemed to come up naturally, but now she wasn't so sure. What was he driving at? Had he known something that she hadn't? Given his brilliance, that wouldn't have been peculiar in itself, except for the fact that paleontology was her life's work, not his. She didn't care how brilliant Tim was, he shouldn't have known more than she about matters within her own field.

And then to have him show up at the museum a month ago, out of the blue, and head off with that mysterious package. Why hadn't she insisted upon seeing it? After all, it had been addressed to her. And perhaps the most perplexing question of all…where was Tim now? *Wait a minute, what the hell am I doing? Stop thinking about it! It doesn't matter anymore.*

Bonnie exorcised the memory and returned her attention to the beautiful scenery. As she neared the Lincoln Memorial, she glanced up at the white marble stairs. They were nearly overflowing with tourists who, like her, were enjoying the perfect weather of mid-spring. Out of the blue, her eyes were drawn to a man standing at the top of the second flight of stairs. He stood out from everyone else, noble like a statue. His hair was short, thick, and completely white, the whitest she'd ever seen. She tried to look away, but found it impossible to take her eyes off him. As she reached the end of the reflecting pool, she turned left and jogged directly in front of the stairs, in order to get a better look. A child ran in front of her and she had to dodge him. When she looked up, the man was gone. She stopped and caught her breath, scanning the crowd. *Where did he go?* She took a step toward the monument and was almost bowled over by another runner.

"Watch where you're going!" he yelled.

She didn't bother to acknowledge him. With an inexplicable urgency, she bolted up the stairs as fast as she could climb. When she reached the top of the first flight, she caught site of the white-haired man again, standing in the shadows of a marble pillar. He was staring right at her. Was it Tim? How could it be? What happened to his hair? She bolted up the second flight of stairs and when she reached the top, she knew. *It's him. It's Tim! But, what in the world has happened to him? It's not only his hair…it's his posture, so filled with confidence. And his face, it is positively glowing.* As she approached him, she noticed that everyone else was staring at him, too.

"Hello, Bonnie," he said with a smile.

Even his voice has changed! He sounds older…much older.

"Hello, Tim," she said. "Where have you been?"

"I've been…around," he said.

As she waited for more explanation, she stared openly at him. Finally, she put manners aside. "What's happened to you, Tim? Your hair…your voice…" Bonnie trailed off. She stared into Tim's eyes. They seemed fathomless, a million questions posed and answered in their depths at once.

"You might say I had a near-death experience," Tim said. "That's not important, though. I'm not here to catch up on old times, Bonnie, although it is good to see you again. I'm here with a message."

Suddenly, Bonnie's legs felt weak, and a sense of dread overcame her. *Run away now, before you hear it!* "A message? From whom?" Bonnie asked wearily.

"I'm sorry it has to be you, Bonnie, but you're the only one I can trust to see it through," he said. "You have to find out what happened to the Martians. The crew uncovered the mystery before they were killed."

Bonnie opened her mouth to voice a protest, but Tim cut her off.

"I know. It's not fair, is it? But, sadly, many things in this universe aren't fair. You're going to have to sift through the pieces in order to learn what they learned. And after you do, you're going to have to take action. I have no idea if it will ever be necessary, but you should be prepared all the same."

She felt a torrent of emotion sweep through her. She was surprised, confused, and angry all at once. "What's that supposed to mean, Tim? If you know something important, then tell me!"

"Don't misinterpret my vagueness for ambivalence, Bonnie. There are rules. I can only tell you so much. But make no mistake. This is a very serious task, and you should treat it as such."

She suddenly found it difficult to breathe, like the weight of the world had just been placed on her chest.

"It's okay, Bonnie." Tim offered her another warm smile. "Important doesn't always mean difficult. You're a smart woman. That's why I chose you. If you look hard enough, you'll figure it out."

Bonnie's entire body began to tingle. Tim's praise warmed her from the inside. It was emotional, intellectual, spiritual and physical all at once. She knew she would never again experience anything like it.

"Good luck, Bonnie." Tim turned and headed into the crowd.

"*Tim!*" Bonnie was shocked to hear the desperation in her voice. It wasn't concern over the task that lay ahead of her; she simply couldn't bear the thought of never seeing him again. "Where are you going?" she yelled, but he was already gone.

CHAPTER 44

Tim calibrated his respirator in the dark and listened to the water lapping onto the shore of Dugit Beach. Suddenly, he heard the droning of an engine in the distance—a Volkswagen GTI heading up Junction 92. He marveled at how well his Earth-based consciousness was working with his collective one. Obscure facts like the unique auditory signature of a car engine—something Tim would have never guessed was stored in his memory—were called up instantly and processed. As the car approached, he ducked into the thick cluster of vitex bushes and waited. After the car passed, Tim returned his attention to the respirator. Once he was sure it was working properly, he emerged from the bushes and headed toward the beach. He gazed at the highway to ensure no more cars were coming. It was just past two o'clock in the morning and Tim didn't expect anyone to be out at this hour, especially since the Jewish holiday Shavuot had begun at sundown.

As his feet hit the sand, he recalled his earlier visit. It seemed like a lifetime ago, and in some respects it was. In truth, however, it had only been six weeks ago that he stood on this very spot speaking with David, Naomi's grad student. Suddenly, his rumination was cut short. *Contact due south!* his command center blared. He spun to his left instantly. A dark figure advanced toward him along the beach. Instructions fired inside of his head in rapid succession. The urgency of the commands, however, stood in stark contrast to the image before him. The man walked casually up the beach, the picture of calm reserve. Was it a tourist? He carried himself like someone out for a midnight stroll. He was even smiling, a smile that Tim recognized immediately.

Tim had half expected him, although he was surprised it had taken so long. For the past week, he'd glanced over his shoulder at every turn, expecting to see the man behind him. Now, finally, the time had come. It was inevitable that they meet again.

"I was afraid I wasn't going to get to say goodbye," Tim said, letting the heavy oxygen tank fall from his shoulders to the sand.

The man beamed. "I wouldn't let that happen, my boy," Stentz said. His eyebrows raised as he pointed to the dagger in Tim's right hand. "That's a nasty looking corkscrew. You might want to put it away before you hurt someone."

"I think I'll hold onto it, if it's all the same to you." Tim tightened his grip around the dagger's hilt.

"Suit yourself," Stentz replied. He gazed out across the Sea of Galilee, and inhaled deeply. "Beautiful isn't it?"

"Yes, it is."

"On a dark night like tonight you can almost imagine what it looked like two thousand years ago, when the observer emerged."

A heated debate ignited inside of Tim's mind. *How much should I share? What information do I want from Victor in return? Is a conflict unavoidable? Does the chance for an alliance exist? No.* Tim shut down the possibility immediately. He'd already promised himself he wouldn't make the same mistake twice. He had to go it alone. He had to be a one-man show. It was the only way to ensure the secrecy of his mission.

"You killed one of my finest warriors, Tim," Stentz said evenly. There was neither anger nor admiration in his voice.

"He didn't give me a choice, Victor."

"He didn't *have* much choice. That's what warriors do—they battle enemies. Is that what *you* are, Tim…a warrior?"

"There's a little warrior in all of us, isn't there, Victor?"

"Some more than others."

"Is that why you brought Bauer with you? Because he was a more capable warrior?"

"He served his purpose, Tim. We've been looking for the dissident since he killed our observer on Mars, although I must admit I was shocked to find out who the rebel was. We thought the Fallen One had been killed billions of years ago. The fact he wasn't gives me a very important data point."

There was a long pause, during which neither man said anything. Stentz inhaled slowly. He shrugged his shoulders.

"You've been used, Tim, by the one you called 'friend'…the one we call the Fallen One. Or shall we use the name you humans have given him? Satan. Satan has never been the least bit interested in the welfare of civilizations throughout the universe. His singular interest has always been power. His pursuit of power is what motivated his coup attempt on the Zaileen eons ago. He caused quite an uprising, before the Council of Five put it down. After learning he was the instigator, the Council banished him forever. He's been out to destroy us ever since." Stentz stopped talking and gazed into Tim's eyes.

Tim detected the slightest bit of concern on Victor's face. He could tell that Victor saw something in him that he hadn't before during their close interaction on the think-tank.

Victor continued. "Apart from the process of sending out prophets and observers, which you already intuited yourself, Tim, everything Satan led you to believe is a bold-faced lie. His lies were concocted to curry your favor…to convince you to join in his struggle against us. We aren't responsible for a fraction of the exterminations he lied about. Of course, there are civilizations that don't respond, and after multiple attempts to turn them around, we must eventually take action. But we're driven to such drastic action less than *two percent* of the time, not the one-hundred percent Satan led you to believe. And we don't exterminate civilizations for our own self-preservation; we do it for the welfare of the entire universe. Corrupt civilizations are a far greater threat to others than to us."

Victor's words told Tim that his online conversations with Simon had been compromised after all. "Yes, I already know that," he said.

Stentz was taken aback, genuinely surprised. "Is that right? Since when?"

"I've known it for a long time, although part of me was in the dark, until recently."

"I'm afraid I don't understand, Tim. What do you mean *part* of you?" Stentz's eyes narrowed.

"You know what I mean, Victor. You just don't want to admit it to yourself. My Earth-based consciousness was in the dark about many things."

Stentz shifted uneasily. His calm exterior seemed to fade, even as he scoffed. "Your *Earth-based* consciousness? Are you suggesting you've achieved *collective consciousness?*"

Tim smiled but didn't reply.

"You can't possibly begin to understand collective consciousness," Stentz said, "let alone possess it! The fact that you've even heard of it, however, tells me I missed an important online dialogue session. What did Satan tell you about the Guf?"

"Everything…and all of it true, except for one fabrication: he said that the Zaileen didn't know what the Guf was for, which is obviously not the case."

"Obviously. But I don't understand how you could know that."

"Stop kidding yourself, Victor. You already know how."

"Collective consciousness, Tim?" Victor shook his head. "If you truly understood the Guf, you would know that one's collective consciousness can never leave it."

"That was true, Victor. Until now."

Stentz grunted. His confidence seemed to be returning.

"Whether you believe me or not is inconsequential, Victor," Tim said.

"Tell me about one of your former lives then, Tim. If you've truly achieved collective consciousness, you'll be able to describe a foreign world. I think you'll find my knowledge of the universe quite complete. I'm bound to recognize the planet, given sufficient details."

It was a good question, Tim thought. Multi-faceted. Not only would his answer help Stentz determine whether or not he was telling the truth about his collective consciousness, but, if true, it would also provide Victor with clues about his real identity. "Let's just say that long ago I was part of the *two percent*," he said. "On the planet where I lived, there were four distinct factions—three contemptible and one noble. You might say you threw the baby out with the bath water."

Stentz eyed Tim curiously, still unconvinced. "Your details are a little sketchy, Tim. Let's cut to the chase. How did we destroy the civilization? If you were truly a member of a culled civilization, you would likely know the answer to that question."

"I'll answer that question, after you answer one for me, Victor."

"Fire away, my boy."

"What are you doing here? I'm clear on Bauer's purpose—to identify and kill the dissident. But I don't understand why *you're* here. What could possibly motivate a member of the Council of Five to spend a lifetime—albeit a short one in universal terms—on Earth?"

"I'm here because of you, Tim. I'm here to find out who *you* are. The dissident was trying to use you, trying to use you in his bid to overthrow the Zaileen. He must have thought you could assist him in some significant way. He must have thought you could help him defeat us. How is that possible, Tim? How could he pin his hopes on a mere Human? No offense mind you, but what threat could a human possibly pose to the Zaileen? I've been watching you for a long time, and it pains me to say that I'm as confused about your identity now as I was twenty years ago when I arrived on Earth. For the most part, you are all too Human. An absolutely brilliant one, by all standards, but just a Human nonetheless. Satan was able to deceive you so easily. In all your transmissions, your questions, your uncertainty…half the time you were reaching for straws. Once in a while, however, you'd surprise me, Tim. You'd intuit something that a human couldn't possibly know—the fact that I'm a member of the Council of Five is a prime example. How could you possibly know that? Who are you?"

Tim peered at Victor, deep in thought. It all made perfect sense now—why Stentz and not Bauer had maintained such close contact with him; why Stentz had been so determined to add him to the think-tank, when everyone else was against it; why Stentz had kept tabs on Tim as a young prodigy; why he had even offered him a research position to work with him at the Jet Propulsion Laboratory, when he was only sixteen. To quell his own curiosity, however, Tim had to confirm one final point. "Is that why you allowed me to uncover so many secrets? Why you supported my efforts on the think-tank? You wanted to find out what I already knew and what I didn't?"

"Sometimes the best way to find out what someone knows is to figure out what they don't know first," Victor said. "In the interest of trying to find out who you are, Tim, I was more than happy to let you uncover nearly everything."

"Everything except how the Zaileen destroy civilizations that don't comply with your teachings," Tim said. "That's why you posted another Zaileen warrior on Mars...to protect that all-important secret."

Victor's eyebrows raised again. "Very good, Tim."

"Unfortunately for the crew of the Santa Maria, they uncovered that secret, and you had to eliminate them too, because of it."

Victor's confidence was visibly waning again. "You're dancing around it, Tim. Do you know how we destroy non-compliant civilizations or don't you?"

Tim studied him closely, trying to figure out which side of the fence Victor was on. He was almost certain they stood shoulder-to-shoulder, staring across at the Sept, and whatever evil minions the being had managed to assemble. There was no way to be absolutely positive, though. He had to continue the dance a little longer, in the hopes he could discover Victor's true intentions. "You kill them with kindness, Victor, with flowers. Shortly after injecting the prophet's embryo into a host, the observer goes on a world tour of sorts. The objective of the tour is to monitor the civilization...to establish a baseline of conduct from which comparisons can be made 1,500 years later. In addition to observing, however, the Zaileen spreads seeds—that, much like the prophet's embryo, conform to the indigenous environment. They conform to become flowers common to the region in which they are dropped. As these flowers grow, they release a toxin into the atmosphere, effectively blanketing the planet. It's undetectable and completely harmless, until combined with a potent catalyst. Only one drop of the catalyst activates the toxin around the globe in a matter of seconds, like igniting a fire in a warehouse full of propane by striking a single match."

Stentz's eyes burned red. "You're...the *Coumlon*!" He spat the words as a wave of heat rose over his body.

Tim knew instantly that Victor was gearing up to transform. "Relax, Victor!" he yelled. "I want no part in any conflict with you! Despite what you may think, I'm not here to exact revenge for the Coumlon's extermination!"

"What is your mission then?" Stentz demanded.

"I'm afraid I can't tell you that, Victor. I can't compromise its secrecy."

Stentz's eyes narrowed and the corners of his mouth drew downward into a frown. "You don't understand, Tim. I've spent a lifetime trying to figure out who you are and why you're here. I'm a member of the Council of Five. I'm obligated to know what's going on. I can't afford to have you gallivanting about the universe, unchecked. I *must* understand your mission!"

"We are of the same mind, Victor. We have very similar objectives."

"What is your mission, Tim?" Stentz pressed.

"It doesn't have to come to this, Victor."

"Come to what, Tim?"

"You know what—a confrontation. I would like to avoid killing you."

Stentz reeled back, stunned by Tim's bold statement. Then he burst into laughter. "Tim, I must admit, this conversation has been shocking—learning that you're the Coumlon, that you've somehow assimilated your collective consciousness." The smile slipped from his face and his eyes narrowed. "You may have defeated a judge and a few warriors, but their power is a far cry from mine. Lest you forget, I've already scouted you, not too far from here. You've got some interesting tricks in your bag, my boy, but I think we can both agree, you're no match for me."

Tim held Victor's gaze. "I appreciate the warning, Victor, I really do. And let me return the favor. I'm not the same being you tracked at Qumran. I've elevated my game significantly since your last scouting report." Tim could sense the energy spike and feel the heat radiating off Stentz's body.

"It's a pity that it has to come to this," Victor said, shifting his weight imperceptibly.

"It doesn't have to. We can both turn around and walk away winners."

Stentz smiled wanly. "It's nothing personal, Tim, but I can't do that. I'm sorry."

"I'm sorry, too," Tim adjusted his grip on the dagger ever so slightly.

"Perhaps we'll meet again one of these days," Victor said. "In the Guf."

"I'd like that." Tim smiled. "I'd like that a lot."

Gruiieee!

Epilogue

Yigal Rosenthal brought the Styrofoam cup to his mouth and took a sip of the scalding coffee as his eyes remained focused on the large console in front of him. Since it was Shavuot, most Israelis wouldn't be traveling, and the airlines had cut flights accordingly. Ben Gurion International Airport was at about half capacity, and that suited him just fine. Small triangles inched across his monitor in tiny clicks, each covering an eighth of an inch. "Air France Flight 1600, you may begin your descent. Follow heading one-eight-zero to runway two-niner left," he said in crisp English.

"Roger," the pilot of the plane responded. "Following heading one-eight-zero to runway two-niner left."

Israel was only seventy-five miles across at its widest point and roughly two-hundred fifty miles in length. Therefore, the Ben Gurion air traffic controllers didn't have a tremendous amount of airspace to manage. Although they began tracking aircraft well beyond their own borders, they didn't actually "take the ball" until the planes reached their airspace. Rosenthal placed the coffee cup on his console. Suddenly, an unidentified contact materialized on the screen in front of him. A shot of adrenaline cut through his caffeine buzz as he realized it was well inside the Israeli Air Defense Identification Zone. The contact was very faint, but it still registered. He immediately thought the worst: a missile? A stealth plane? After a moment of contemplation, he settled down a little. Probably some idiot in an ultra-light, he reasoned.

He glanced at the lower left-hand corner of his monitor and noted the time—5:12 A.M. It was still dark outside. Even an idiot wouldn't fly an ultra-light in the dark. Wait a minute…the contact was rising straight up! It had to be a helicopter. He adjusted a knob to the GUARD frequency—the emergency channel continually monitored by all pilots—and tried to hail the unidentified aircraft. "Unknown rider, unknown rider, position 32 12 02 N 35 34 50 W, this is Ben Gurion air traffic control on GUARD. Contact me at once on frequency 122.7. I repeat. Unknown rider, unknown rider, position 32 12 02N 35 34 50W, this is Ben Gurion air traffic control on GUARD. Contact me at once on frequency 122.7."

Rosenthal's voice was steady, but his stomach had tightened considerably. He waited several seconds for a response, but none came. The contact was still climbing straight up, and accelerating. He grabbed a pad from the corner of the console and scribbled a few notes. He took another bearing. The contact had originated from directly above the Sea of Galilee. "Unknown rider, unknown rider, position 32 12 02N 35 34 50W, this is Ben Gurion air traffic control on GUARD. Contact me at once on frequency 122.7!"

No response.

He pressed the button that alerted his supervisor and turned to face the controller next to him. "I have an unidentified contact," he said. "Can you to take my load? I have three birds, Air France 1600, Swiss Air 542 and El Al 120."

His colleague typed a command on his keyboard and the image on his monitor zoomed out to include the adjacent grid. "No problem. I have them," he confirmed.

Rosenthal turned quickly back to his console to take another bearing. His stomach rolled. The contact was travelling at over 3,000 miles per hour and accelerating. In the time it had taken him to transfer his workload, the thing had climbed to an altitude of over 100,000 feet! He reached for the telephone receiver, pressed a single button, and listened to the numbers being speed-dialed. Surely, they would have already picked it up themselves, but he had to report it anyway. Suddenly, a voice boomed on the other end of the line.

"Israeli Air Defense. This is Colonel Shabim."

# # #

Captain Ron Moore stared at his computer terminal, confused. He glanced over to his right and waved his hand to catch his supervisor's attention.

"What's up?" Major Tom Cummins asked.

"I think I've got a bogey coming out of Israeli airspace!"

Cummins' fingers rattled across the keys in front of him. After the image came up on his own monitor, he sat mute for several seconds while staring at it. "Where's the fucking heat signature!"

"Exactly! That's why I didn't pick it up sooner. It's already at 200,000 feet, and climbing fast!" Moore's voice rose an octave.

Cummins yanked the red phone from its cradle. "Sir, this is Major Cummins. We've got something bizarre coming out of Israel. There was no plume and no heat signature, so we didn't pick it up on BMEWS. It's already at an altitude of 45 miles and climbing. Airspeed is—" Cummins paused to make sure he had it right. "Airspeed is 8,500 miles per hour and *accelerating*!" He listened to the voice in the receiver. "Affirmative, sir. That's eight-five-zero-zero miles per hour." He paused again to listen. "Yes, sir." He hung up the receiver and turned to Moore. "We just made the big-board." He pointed across the expanse of the control center.

Both men peered over their consoles at the massive screen that dominated the far wall of the Cheyenne Mountain Operations Center—headquarters of North American Aerospace Defense Command and Air Force Space Command. The same image that had been on their twenty-seven inch monitors was now on the forty-foot screen.

Cummins typed another set of commands into the keyboard to call up a list of scheduled satellite launches from around the world. A quick scan of the list showed that Israel didn't have a scheduled launch. "Damn it!" he swore under his breath. He picked up his desktop phone and pressed the extension for USSPACECOM. "This is Major Cummins in the Missile Warning Center. I've just picked up a bird on my board. It originated in Israel. Current altitude is...110 miles! I don't show any scheduled satellite launches from Israel. Can you confirm?" Cummins shook his head as he listened to the response. "Thank you," he said.

Just as he hung up the phone, Howard Smythe, the general in command of the operations center approached his the console.

"Where is it?" Smythe asked.

"Altitude's 130 miles, sir," Cummins responded. "The good news is it hasn't wavered from its flight path. It's still going straight up."

"Speed?"

Cummins kept his eyes on the monitor.

"16,000 miles per hour and still accelerating, sir!"

"I just got off the phone with USSTATCOM," Smythe said. "They were contacted by the Israelis minutes before you notified me. The Israelis picked it up on ground radar. They have no idea what it is."

Moore and Cummins exchanged a look of disbelief. Both turned back to their respective monitors and watched the object continue to accelerate.

"What the hell can it be?" Moore said, shaking his head.

"It's no satellite delivery system, I'll tell you that much." Cummins said.

Suddenly, the object disappeared. Both men jumped from their seats simultaneously and stared at the huge screen at the front of the operations center. It had vanished there, too.

Smythe wiped the sweat from his brow. "I'm going to call the boys at Johnson. Maybe they can pick it up on their Tracking and Data Relay Satellites."

As he hurried off, the two Missile Warning Detection Officers continued to stare at the large blank screen.

"That train's pulling out of the station awfully fast," Moore said.

A long silence followed. Finally, Cummins spoke up. "Yeah. And it definitely ain't the local."

NOTE TO THE READER

Although this is a work of fiction, whose characters and events have been conjured from my imagination, there is a real-life individual who, in many ways, resembles the story's chief protagonist. His name is Gregory Smith, a young man of startling genius who is trying to make a positive impact on the world. Through his foundation, International Youth Advocates, Greg Smith is promoting peace by enlisting the participation of the world's future—its youth. Those interested in learning more about Greg Smith or his foundation can visit

www.gregoryrsmith.com